Two Brides

for

Ewan de Buchan

Highland Crusaders

Edited by Margaret Bates
Cover design by Cheeky Covers

Manufactured in the United States of America

First Edition originally published on Radish Fiction in April, 2018
Second Edition, August, 2018

ISBN: 978-0-9986751-1-4

Two Brides
for
Ewan de Buchan

Highland Crusaders

E. Elizabeth Watson

Titles by E. Elizabeth Watson

Historical Romance

Ladies of Scotland Series:

An Earl for the Archeress – July 2017
The Maiden's Defender – November 2017

Perthshire in Plaid Novellas:

One Scottish Knight: A Medieval Novella – April 2017
Christmas Wore Plaid: A Victorian Christmas Novella – Forthcoming
(Releasing Nov. 2018 as part of the Love Rekindled at Christmas anthology).

Historical Fantasy Fiction

Prince of Lions Series:

Prince of Lions – January 2016
Son of Ballymead – February 201

ACKNOWLEGEMENTS

A special thanks to my husband who is always supportive and encouraging, and to my children who inspire and motivate me on a daily basis. I'm grateful to Margaret Bates, for editing this story, and to Cheeky Covers for the stunning book cover. A final thank you to my agent, Barbara Collins Rosenberg, for her expertise and advice as I travel this writing journey.

CHAPTER 1

August, 1192, Somewhere between Jaffa and Jerusalem
Ewan remained sideways on the ground, limp, blood rolling down his temple from the unexpected blows he had received at the hands of his own commander. What a jest, he thought, for he had believed his commander to be honorable, a man who served King William "The Rough" of Scotland. True, they had not always been on the best of terms when he left Scotland, for Ewan had won many a cartography commission from the king over his commander who was another skilled mapmaker, but he did not think the rivalry had gone very deep. Clearly Ewan had misjudged him.

The heat danced and wavered before him in the blazing sun of the Holy Land while his vision blurred. This was it. He had come all this way, a crusade to be fought for Christendom to save the Holy Land from warring infidels, instead finding himself to be relieved of his body without the ceremony deserved by a Scottish earl, without any ceremony at all.

Somewhere in the distance, the wailing call to prayer from a minaret summoned the faithful to supplicate themselves for *Asr*. Even in this hellhole, this filth and bloodshed, the followers of this foreign religion stopped to prostrate themselves to God. It was admirable, he thought, as he blinked his eyes at the boiling mass of the sun blinding him, their commitment to faith. He had never had such commitment. Life had dealt him a generous hand, but it had never given him much else. And all his father's money was meaningless if it meant he should be tucked away in a separate estate as a child to grow up alone.

A tribesman was approaching. Perhaps he was a mirage, Ewan thought, surprised that he was still somewhat lucid and able to feel the throbbing pain surging through his head. Or perhaps it was an actual man coming to relish in finishing his life by slicing his neck with his gleaming scimitar while King Richard's flag continued to retreat from a battle that he, Ewan, had thwarted.

Thwarted. That's the reason I find myself in this state. It had to be. But why? Most men would have listened to their scouts before devising their attack.

The tribesman was standing over him now, casting his shadow upon him and offering a welcome relief from the sun baking his face. He muttered something in his foreign tongue to the other men who had accompanied him, and who were clearly under his command.

"Just kill me now," Ewan croaked to his executioners, his voice raw and his throat parched.

How long had he been lying there? It could not have been more than twenty minutes and yet it felt like an eternity. His whole body ached from the impressive blow to his head and the shove to the ground from his mount with a kick of the commander's boot.

"*La afham,*" the man muttered, shaking his head, before pulling forth a small yet equally deadly knife that caught the sunlight.

Ewan closed his eyes and anticipated the slice. To his neck? Or to his gut? How would the infidel carve him apart? Instead, he felt his sword belt slacken as the knife sliced the leather. He could feel it being dragged free from him.

Ah, so they're freeing me of my worldly goods before they cast me into the afterlife, Ewan sighed, unable to retain his waning consciousness.

Yet the next thing he felt was his body being hoisted upright. The bearded tribesman, he noted, as he willed his eyes to open again, was dressed in a dark *thawb* and *sirwal*, the typical robe and pants worn by most men in this land, studded leather armor strapped around his chest, and a *shemagh* draped upon his head and rolled up on the sides. His men then grabbed Ewan's bruised body under his arms and began to walk, letting his feet drag behind him, and soon the exhaustion, the heat, the need for water, and probably the nasty head injury he had sustained, overwhelmed him. His world went black.

CHAPTER 2

Nasim stood in her father's reception. It was rare that he would request an audience with his twenty-first, and youngest, daughter. In fact, she had never remembered once being alone with the important emir and military commander, the First in Command to Saladin the Sultan, and knew little of him except that he was kindly and doted on his daughters by lavishing them with gold. She had been given gold. Though she had rarely met him personally. Mostly, he would identify who his children were by asking them to name their mother, one of his twelve wives, so he could place their birth in a sort of chronology and from that, figure out who they were.

Yet he had asked for Nasim, by name, and her mother had fretted to make sure her veil of indigo and beige covered her face and head appropriately and her mantle was draped in such a way to hide her feminine curvatures. Her mother—her father's first wife and the bearer of seven of his sons—moved swiftly, hustling her out the door of their apartments in the escort of her half-brother, one of the sons of the emir's second wife.

Her father, Abu Abdullah Habib Abd-Al-Rachid, more commonly referred to as Habib, sat in a cushioned chair draped in fine maroon silk embroidered with camels. She stood before him, the only bare skin on her body being that of her toes protruding from the leather straps of her sandals and the soft skin around her eyes, and yet, she still felt nervous.

"*Salam*," he greeted her, and she replied appropriately, averting her eyes downward. "Come closer, daughter," he stated, and she complied. He turned to his son. "I must speak to my daughter privately. Make certain no one enters."

Habib turned back to her, resplendent in his white *thawb*, mantle, and *shemagh* draped over his head and held with a braided band. His beard was hearty and kempt. Grey flecks peppered what had once been thick, black hair.

"Please sit," he motioned her to a cushion upon an imported Persian rug.

She obeyed once again.

"You may unveil now," he continued.

Now she hesitated. Yes, this man was her father, and yes, this man was in command, but she still felt as if she hardly knew him. Common people and slaves might not be beholden to wearing a veil, but as a noblewoman, she was forbidden from unveiling before men who were strangers or merely family friends. Even cousins who she did not know well were unworthy of seeing her or any of his other daughters without the barrier of a veil in place.

"I am your father, and we will not be interrupted. I wish to look upon your face as I talk to you and see what sort of treasure you have become."

Slowly, she freed her hands from her folds of fabric and reached to her veil, unfastening it. The fabric drooped around her neck, revealing her face. The commander looked at her wistfully. Her heart was hammering and her fingers trembled, still holding the garment, waiting for the moment she could cover herself again. His gaze was unnerving. No man had ever looked at her so openly.

"You look just like Ghaniyah did when I married her," he said, before looking away and steadying his voice. Nasim swallowed. Ghaniyah was her mother. His first wife. And for a time, his only one. "Tell me about your studies."

My studies? Did he know she had a penchant for the arts of medicine? Did he know she read the tragic tale of *Majnun Layla* as if savoring fine tea, relishing the love Qays had for Layla, and crying each time Layla died? Her soul was hopelessly romantic.

"I have studied mathematics and the arts of medicine," she replied mechanically.

"What else, Nasim *azeezy*?" he asked with genuine interest, sitting back, crossing a leg regally.

She blushed at his use of "azeezy," an affectionate term, and looked up at him.

"I enjoy reading," she replied.

"Have your tutors treated you well?" he continued. "Has Solomon been kindly?"

She nodded, averting her eyes again, knowing her cheeks were reddening further. Solomon, the Jewish physician, treated her especially well. Her father valued education, and he had ensured both his sons and his daughters were well-schooled. Besides, her father could fetch a substantially better suit for his daughters when they were educated, knowing that only men of high standing would request marriage and not expect to be cast out by way of the rod.

"Nasim," he said, after some thought. "Have I not done everything to ensure the comfort of your mother and yourself?"

She bowed her head in deference. Such a phrase sounded an awfully lot like scolding.

"Father, you have always made certain that we are content. I'm thankful for your generosity."

He nodded, but continued to frown. "Then why has your mother continued to tell me of your displeasure in the suits I have found for your marriage?"

She felt heat capture her face again. Her father was an imposing man. She didn't know him well enough to know what came next if she pursued an argument. But God above, how could she marry any of those horrid men?

"I expect an answer," he stated.

"Dearest Father, I, I am truly grateful for the suits you have found but…" She bit her lip. And no sooner did she try to stop herself, her words flooded out without her permission. "But I fear Kalim is very ugly, and Abu Raj is nearly as ancient as Mecca itself, and…and Da'ud already has four wives and is fat and I had hopes to be a—"

She curbed her tongue and cast her eyes into her lap. Her face, flushed at the mention of Solomon before, had now paled. Would he punish her for speaking out of turn? It was vain to hope to be a first wife, or an only wife. Yet she couldn't help it, and kept her eyes riveted to her lap. She thought of Solomon. It wasn't always common that a Jew be welcome in their stronghold, but common enough, and he was a friend of her father's and a kindly man, too, much younger than her father, with arching eyebrows, a sharp jaw, and handsome features. Her father believed in sharing knowledge and knew the physician had much to offer. With one of her brothers as an escort, Nasim had learned much from the man who had tutored her. And she was fond of him. Which caused her heart to clench, because a match between them would never be allowed. Would it? A silly notion, for Solomon had made no indication that he was interested.

"Father, I wonder if you might consider another man…"

Her voice trailed away. She kept her eyes downcast. How bold she was being! Her face flushed once more as uncertainty coursed through her. There was no telling how her father would react. So far, he was being stoically silent.

"What man?" he finally asked, and in those two single words, the question of her propriety was laced.

She swallowed, certain he could hear her gulp. She didn't dare look at him.

"Is there someone who holds your favor?" he asked.

Her face burned. She had never noticed the crinkles in her knuckles as much as she did now, her inspection of them fierce. "Only from afar, and I'm certain he has never noticed me."

"Who is he?" her father repeated, and the creaking of the chair frame told her he had leaned forward.

"He is a man you hold in high esteem. He is accomplished and educated and—"

"What man, Nasim?"

She swallowed at his abrupt tone, and yet, she chose now to glance up at him. "I…I have learned much from Solomon. Might you consider him?"

Habib remained silent, his expression unreadable, then he reclined back again and began stroking his beard. Finally, he shook his head. "It is most unconventional that a woman would request her own suit. And as much as I value Solomon's skills and friendship, I could not allow you to marry him. Is there a reason I should be concerned by your interest?"

"No," she replied hastily, shaking her head. "I don't even know if he's interested, for I only see him during lessons. He most certainly has never expressed such a thing to me. Please, Father. He has never indicated such."

Habib nodded once in satisfaction. "It makes sense that you would want to marry a man whose intellect you respect. But I cannot allow it to be him."

"But...but should I not have input in the man I will be forced to wed?" she argued, before she could advise her tongue differently. "After all, I must live with him forever."

Habib's brow furrowed, giving his face a scowl, and Nasim fought the urge to cringe at her folly. She was always questioning things. Solomon welcomed questions. Perhaps her father did not.

"It is not your place. A father knows best in these matters. No more arguments," he replied.

She bit her tongue and nodded, but she felt a stab to her heart. And she knew her eyes welled with tears, though she blinked madly to push them away. Solomon would be her *Majnun,* the man she would never have. While the physician hadn't indicated any interest beyond friendship in her, on occasion, she had noticed his gaze lingering a little longer than normal in her direction. He only did so when she was preoccupied, and whenever she noticed, she kept her eyes busy on her work so that he wouldn't think she was paying attention. For without fail, the moment she returned his gaze, his eyes darted away. The sensation it evoked always sent butterflies fluttering through her belly. But he probably wasn't smitten with her like she was with him. Would he go mad if she were married to another like *Majnun* did for *Layla*? He probably wouldn't even care.

Yet the hesitation in her father's initial reaction hinted at a mind that was not fully decided. If she pressed him, just a little, would he eventually reconsider? Habib seemed to note her shame by the hand he placed upon hers as he leaned down to her. He softened.

"Nasim, none of your older sisters voiced a complaint when I asked them to marry the first man I chose. I would like to consider your wishes on the matter, but you need to be married and it cannot be to Solomon. You are too valuable and must marry for a strong political alliance. You are eighteen years now. It is time. I've picked Kalim. You will marry him in the spring."

"Kalim?" she choked, her voice lodging in her throat and wisely preventing her from speaking more damaging words.

Kalim looked like a sickly goat. Bony, knobby. And he was short. Shorter than her and she wasn't very tall. He was nothing like the Jewish healer who was kindly and patient not to mention tall and slender. Was she not worth more to him that that?

"Please, will you reconsider?" she whispered.

Her father patted her hand once, then sat upright again. "Kalim is a good man. A wealthy man who will keep you in gold," her father replied more firmly.

Gold? I care not for gold! She burned with anger, but kept her face down in shame of her loose tongue. "Is that why you summoned me? To tell me I must marry?"

"Only partly," he replied, then stood and walked to a tea tray holding gold-rimmed cups and a pot.

He poured two cups, the steam curling upward in swirls. This was most unconventional. She had never eaten in her father's company before, or men in general. Only her brothers' company. She watched him return her way with both cups in hand, his *thawb* swaying. Normally a servant would perform such a task, but they were meeting privately, and he was treating her as an important dignitary, not a daughter who ranked much lower than himself.

What kind of man was her father truly?

He handed a cup down to her. Her hands trembled as she took it, threatening to spill the hot liquid. She steadied them, resting them in her lap again. Thankfully, her eyes were no longer watering. As his hand pulled away, her eyes met his dark brown ones. Humor had turned his lips up. He shook his head and chuckled.

"Kalim is indeed lacking when it comes to appearances. I can see your point. But know, daughter, he is honorable, *mild* with his mother and sisters"—the way he said "mild" gave her pause. He had considered her well-being beneath the authority of the man she would marry—"and you'll be his first wife, a position of rank."

He resumed his seat on a sigh, then took a delicate sip from his tea cup. She waited for him to explain the rest of his reason for wishing to meet.

"We have a man in the infirmary who has suffered some injuries during the Christian attack two days ago. Of most concern is a contusion to his head. Because Solomon has traveled to the Mediterranean to collect more medicinal supplies from the port, I am left with no one to help make certain the man recovers. Your mother tells me that you have become accomplished thanks to Solomon's tutoring and have taken to treating the women's maladies." He sipped his tea again, a gentle slurp ensuing, and eyed her as she digested the information.

Had he been paying attention to her? He wouldn't know this, unless he had taken an interest in her work. And he had chuckled. Chuckled! She had only ever seen him straight-faced and serious.

"What man is this, Father?" she finally asked, sensing that his nature was an easy one. "One of our warriors?"

"He is a Christian. An enemy," he replied. Her eyes widened. "But an infidel who saved the lives of many hundreds of our soldiers, including your brothers. I would see to it he recovers to the point that I can reward him."

"And you wish me to share his presence?" she nearly gasped. "Father, would it not be shameful for me to even look upon him let alone touch him? For touch him, I must, if I am to treat him. I wish not to tarnish the family honor. I…" Again she wrangled in her tongue before her father saw fit to cut it out for overuse.

But he merely nodded, digesting her response, as if he discussed important issues with his peers. Except she wasn't his peer. She wouldn't be forced to wed Kalim if she were.

"I will be with you, or your brother, Abdullah, who is back

from the field. I will escort you to your mother's to gather any supplies you need and then we will go to him."

He enjoyed another sip of his tea and eyed her full cup. This was all part of business as usual when dealing with men, she realized.

"Does this tea not suit your tastes?" he asked, quirking a brow.

She quickly fumbled with the cup and took a sip. Silence ensued as they shared another cup. At that point, he rose and escorted her home to allow her to collect her things. He walked her through the gardens, past several wings of the palace, until they finally reached a sick ward. Her presence caught the attention of every man in the room, both patient as well as worker. Her skin tingled with every set of eyes that fell upon her. Yet one look at her father, and they immediately dropped their gaze.

She fidgeted her fingers, a basket slung over a forearm, having no idea what to do. Never had she shared so many words with her father. Was he displeased that she had refused marriage for such trivial things, such as a man being old? But Kalim? Her stomach clenched at the abhorred thought. He was horrid to look upon, let alone allow intimacies. And the idea of intimacies was already a terrifying topic. That her father found humor in it was heartening. That he had even paused when she suggested Solomon, was promising.

She had to find a way to influence her father's decision. She had studied the healing arts for too long to simply be married off to a man as his broodmare. She had studied with Solomon long enough to know that he was a much better marital option, even if he wasn't an important political man. And she couldn't even begin to think about touching this injured infidel they went to now. He was probably grotesque, and gangrenous, with no teeth and red, flaming eyes, all the terrible things she had learned about the infidels. Too much was happening, much too fast.

He guided her to a private chamber with no windows down a long corridor, walls plastered roughly, separated from the others by an earth-colored curtain. Inside was a man stretched out upon a table in the darkness, illuminated only by the light of a clay oil lamp. He was covered in white linen from the chest down, his broad shoulders exposed, as well as a chiseled face still caked in blood. She averted her eyes and watched the floor instead. Even wrapped within her veil, she felt exposed beside his nudity. And yet, there was no mistaking it. The man wasn't grotesque at all. He was well-endowed with pleasant looks, at least, what she could determine with his eyes closed and his face filthy and dangerously sun-burnt.

She resisted the urge to shake her head. She had heard her brothers' tales that the Christians from Europe were poorly equipped for the sunny heat of Jerusalem. It would seem they had been correct. No man from their corner of the earth with a whit of good sense traveled outside without a head-covering to use as a shield against the sun.

Finally, she approached him, arriving beside him, watching the rising and falling of his chest. She stared at his closed eyes. He looked peaceful. His hair was dark and thick, and ill-shaven stubble had claimed his entire jaw. She gulped. She could already tell that he was an attractive man, and lying down as he was, she determined that he was tall, lean, and well-muscled. *Like Solomon...* She shouldn't be noticing such things. This was why men and women dressed modestly, to prevent such perusals of each other.

And yet, as she made her mental assessment of his looks, she still noted that no matter how pleasant he was to the eyes, no matter how full his lips were or how proud his nose was, he still had the paler skin of Europe. But was he really so different from the men of her culture? After all, he was flesh and blood, like anyone else—

Stop your treacherous thoughts. She was thinking on this strange man too much already. She should simply treat him and leave and after that, give him no more care at all. He was an enemy. She didn't *want* to know him.

"Father, I..." she turned to the Emir who was watching her intently from the corner. "I wish not to do this... *min fadlak*," she pleaded. "I'm afraid that if anyone sees me, they won't understand that I do your bidding. I worry that—"

"You will do as I ask, Nasim." Habib folded his arms. "He

must be treated, and you are the only other capable person here. I will deal with any man who wishes to challenge your presence."

"And Commander Faraj? He is strict with his women and makes no qualms about telling on others to the tribunals"—or so her brothers had said. Commander Faraj was notorious among the men and women of Jerusalem for his hard-lined position on the war, on how to treat the infidels they took prisoner, and on issues of justice. Many a good man, it seemed, had been ruined by Commander Faraj's "good" intentions. Tattling, is what he really did. And even she and her half-sisters had heard the rumors that the man vied for her father's own roll as advisor to Saladin himself. If word should circulate that she had not only been in the presence of an injured man in such a grotesque state, but an infidel at that—and that her father had approved of it—Faraj would exploit it. "He'll find fault with me caring for such a war prisoner, and because of it, he will find fault with you."

Goodness, she needed to bite her tongue. She couldn't continue to talk so openly with her father. And yet, the man didn't seem to be put off by her forthrightness. He came forward and placed a paternal hand on her shoulder, chuckling.

"You have a spirited tongue for a woman, a trait I was not aware of before. It will be a curse for Kalim."

She gaped up at him. He said such, as if he wasn't worried in the least about how Faraj would gossip about him. As if it didn't matter how a daughter talked to her ranking father. And as if he wasn't concerned at all about how Kalim would treat her because of it.

"Faraj holds no power over me. He is a strict man of God, and strict indeed with his interpretations of faith. But he has no say in my business. I trust your ability. And I trust you to keep your interaction with this Christian decent. Nothing else matters. This ailing man, whoever he is, is to be awarded, and I need him alive to bestow such an honor. As soon as Solomon returns, he will take over the infidel's care. Proceed, Nasim."

He gestured to her to get back to work. She took a deep breath, gathered her wits, nodded to him, and turned back to the injured man. She was a healer, and this man was a patient. No different from when she treated the womenfolk—except for the obvious male attributes, which she would have nothing to do with and certainly wouldn't lay eyes on anyway. She would do what she could for the contusion was on his head, not his... She slapped her hand over her mouth at the mere thought, quickly dropping it again when her father cast a curious look at her. Lord, she blushed, her skin tingling as if her father could see right through her hijab.

This was what she had trained for. Treating people with ailments. *Get your mind focused, Nasim!* Imagine, if she were the first woman here to offer care to both men and women. Such would be an accomplishment indeed. She needed to act controlled.

Picking up the lamp and hovering over his face, she reached a hesitant hand to his eyes, pushed back a lid, and looked at him, ignoring the tingle that shot up through her fingertip at the contact with such a strange man. His eyes were still rolled back, unconscious. Then she trailed her fingers along his hairline to the side of his head where she saw the ugly contusion, the skin having split over the bone and dried blood sealing the breakage. She resisted the urge to shoot her father a pleading, terrified look, and then peeled back the linen from his chest and settled it gently at his waist, noting ugly swelling where a rib appeared to be broken and jutting forward under the skin. A light touch to the spot sent the man into an unconscious groan.

She flinched back.

"Relax, Daughter," Habib said more gently. "I know you do meaningful work. Continue."

She crept forth to the man again, and then turned to her father. "This man has a terrible injury to the head. Solomon has told me these injuries can be fatal. A man simply goes to sleep and sometimes can never be awakened. It's a game of chance if he will survive, or slip into death. I'll need fresh, boiled water free of festering particles and laundered cloths, as well as some clean dressings. He must be awakened immediately, for sleep is dangerous to a man with this ailment."

Habib nodded. "I will ask the assistants to bring your requests and return in a moment."

He bowed out of the room and she felt vulnerability sweep over her. She was alone. With a strange man, an *infidel*, without the protection of her brothers. Was her father growing senile to allow her to be alone with him, fully unclothed? It mattered not that the man was still sleeping. Her father seemed unconcerned with how Faraj might react, but Nasim's skin prickled with unease. Faraj would eat up a detail such as this like a starving mongrel frothing at the mouth for a juicy cut of meat, should he ever gain wind of Commander Rachid leaving his daughter alone with a potentially violent Christian.

Such tattling to the tribunals wouldn't do her father's family any favors and could cast doubt on his leadership. She was beginning to realize that her father was unconventional, what with his Jewish physician and his educated daughters—and his apparent affability. But others might not be so open-minded.

The man before her shifted, then groaned, but did not regain consciousness. She stepped back, taking a deep, shaking breath and swallowed a hard lump. What if he woke up on his own before her father could return? Still, from a healing perspective, it was a promising sign, one she shouldn't ignore if she wished to help him, as was her duty as a physician. She took another deep breath and attempted to shake him. It was met with a groan, but he still did not wake. Soon, the curtain swayed as two assistants came in, heads averted, and left an abundance of requested materials. None of them looked at her. It would seem her father had threatened them to keep their noses down.

She took a washing rag, saturated it, and pushed her mantle up her arms enough that it would not get wet. Wiping the man's brow, she cleansed the dirt and blood from him until his visage was clean. She would need to stitch up his head wound, for it still oozed blood, and it had been two days already since his…capture? Rescue? Was the man a guest or a prisoner?

Her father slipped in through the curtain again and in the back of her mind, as she became absorbed in her ministrations, she was aware that he observed her work. Solomon had told her once that her gentle hands moved with certainty and compassion, and she felt a sudden pang of longing for Solomon's approving smiles, and sadness for her skills. Such skills would go to waste when she was married, unless Kalim allowed her to continue her work. And if he did, it would be sheer torture to work alongside Solomon while her husband, the goat, Kalim, tried to get children on her at night when she was pining for her mentor. Her *Majnun*.

"Can you not wake him?" Habib asked from the corner, startling her.

She swallowed yet again and began to prod the lifeless man once more. "Wake up," she said, though he did not move.

She prodded more forcefully until he shifted and groaned again, and then, like rusting hinges that barely worked, his eyes blinked open. She froze, caught in the moment. Staring up at her were bright blue eyes, the likes of which she had never seen. The people of her family had dark brown eyes. Her friends and their families had dark brown eyes. Some visitors from the Persian lands had mixes of hazels, blues, and browns. But blue like this? It was like staring into two sapphires.

He lifted one of his arms, groaning in pain, and felt the head-injury, then looked at his fingers, now touched with his blood.

"Wa—water," he croaked, his eyes roving around his environs, then back to her, disoriented.

She shook her head, not understanding.

"He asked for '*maa*,' daughter," the commander translated.

She withheld her surprise. But her father knew this man's language? Of course he did. He valued education, and when the war broke out, no doubt had studied how to interpret their words. She gathered up a clay cup and dunked it into the water. Carefully, she slid her hand beneath his head and placed the cup to his parched lips. He reached up and clenched her hand with the cup, drinking wildly, groaning in pain as he shifted his torso, his thirst beyond his control. Water dribbled out the sides of the cup and around his mouth, and as she tried to pull back, he grasped her fingers and the cup, chasing the drops on the rim.

Even in his state of anguish, his grip was strong. She finally withdrew, tingling from the warmth and desperation of his touch.

"More," he gasped, his voice low and gruff.

Again, with a translation from her father, she refilled the cup and placed it back to his lips until his thirst was finally sated.

He fell back to lying, sweating from the exertion, exhaling through the pain in his ribs with a loud whoosh, and looked directly at her. He tried to shift again and his brow contorted on a moan. "Be damned…but my ribs are broken."

He hissed an inhale, slowly exhaling.

In the intensity of the moment, she hadn't noticed that her father had come forth. She noticed him now, his hand upon a blade at his waist, ready to draw on the man should his desperate clenching of her turn into something more. Habib seemed to be contemplating the man's strange accent.

"I am Abu Abdullah Habib Abd-al-Rachid, commander and advisor to Saladin," he finally addressed the man.

Nasim looked down, trying to decipher the strange language she heard her father saying.

"You may call me Commander Rachid," her father continued. "My daughter is tending to your health. She says you have an injury to your head and must be awakened. She will need to help bind your ribs as well. I warn you, it's most unconventional that one of our ranking women would be allowed near an unknown man, especially an infidel, and I ask you to honor her by averting your eyes."

The Christian looked at him, then Nasim felt the heat of his eyes upon her, before he shifted them to the opposite wall. Nerves, like a swarm of butterflies, exploded across her skin. That she was completely covered didn't matter a single bit. How could eyes, as cool blue as his, cause such burning intensity in her?

"Why have you helped me?" the stranger with the blue eyes asked.

Nasim shivered at the deep brogue of his voice despite not understanding. His voice rolled off his tongue in ways that her language couldn't. It was rough. Guttural. Curious.

Habib seemed to contemplate whatever the man's remark was, and finally replied. "Two days ago, your leader struck you from your horse and left you for dead in the desert. You saved my men's lives that day, as well as the lives of twelve of my sons. Why did you do it?"

Still looking away from her, the infidel spoke more gibberish. "I don't see the honor in such a battle. I had just returned from scouting you, but had not been afforded time to check our flanks, and knew not fully the odds we faced. My commander was bent on attacking anyway and I saw it as foolish, so I argued with him, which I presume you witnessed if you saw him smite me…" He groaned again and searched for more words through the haze of his pain. "I came to fight, because the priests told us that the Holy Land was threatened. But now I see it isn't true. This is the Holy Land for many people, and I do nay understand why our, our *prophet,* would preach words of love whilst our priests urge us to shed blood in his name. The charge on you that my commander wished to stage seemed ill-fated. In honesty, I wish to go home, return to my business, and leave everyone in peace."

Habib nodded thoughtfully. Irritation itched at Nasim. Curse her curious mind, but she wanted to know what was transpiring.

"Father," she said carefully. Interrupting a commander in the midst of a discussion wasn't normally done. "Who is this man? Of what do you both speak?"

Habib held up a hand for silence, though the gesture, while curt, wasn't menacing. She closed her mouth, much to her chagrin, and listened as her father continued speaking his foreign words.

"The war has made you a wise man. I am indebted to you. As it turns out, you did indeed have a greater abundance of men as well as an uphill advantage despite our reinforcements. We could have been wiped out."

"And I am indebted to you and your healing daughter." His eyes shifted back to Nasim. Their gazes locked, though he quickly looked away. She shivered, feeling the urge to pull her mantle more tightly around her. "Thank you—" His comment was interrupted by another groan of pain as he accidentally shifted his rib under the skin.

"Father, his rib must be pushed into place and he must be bound," she interjected again. If her father wouldn't impart the substance of their conversation, he would at least listen to her medical advice. "I understand this from Solomon's teachings, but I have never done such a thing before. I apologize for interrupting, but this must be done as soon as possible, for such a broken rib risks injuring other vital parts of his internal workings."

"I trust your ability," her father replied.

He finally sheathed his blade and helped lift the infidel to sitting.

"Ah, God!" wailed the foreigner with an excruciating pitch.

Once upright, his linen fell to his lap, exposing his private hair and barely covering his parts as he panted with the aftershocks of pain. Nasim whirled around.

"Father, I beg you, I cannot look upon him until he is decent!"

Habib readjusted the man's linen. "I'm sorry this is distressing, daughter. The injuries of war always require a stomach for the grotesque and vulgar. He is covered now. Bind his ribs."

She closed her eyes, summoning courage to turn around again, and pulled free the clean bandages from the recently-delivered supplies. Turning around, she was faced with the image of his naked torso, broad shoulders, and arms bunched with tense muscle as he braced himself on the bed. If it weren't for the obvious broken rib turning his face a sickening shade of gray, she would have paused to take in the entire image. How would she know what made a man handsome? She had never seen a naked one aside from her young nephews as her sisters bathed and dressed them, or the slaves and servants who toiled outside and sometimes removed their tunics. And most of them were thin and wiry from their daily work. But she knew instantly, on a primal level, that this was a man women considered handsome.

Her father finally glanced at her, his eyes furrowing in question, and she jumped into action. It would seem her pleading to her father moments ago, that she couldn't look upon the infidel, was a lie. More heat, this time shame, darkened her brow. Had her father seen her attraction to the stranger in her eyes? A calligraphic script written in blazing gold for the entire world to read? She breathed erratically, her heart thumped, and in the moment, she was thankful for the protection her veil afforded her as it hid the flush to her cheeks. But even with his dangerous sun burn, the man was beautiful, and no amount of scolding herself for her sinful attraction would make him any less so.

She took to washing his upper body, wiping away the grime and blood, wincing as she put pressure on his unfortunate rib. He stifled another groan, his eyes rolling back, his throat bobbing as he swallowed the torment she knew she was inflicting. Nasim fastened her gaze to her work so that she wouldn't seek out the blue depths of his foreign eyes again, and placed a stick between his teeth. Her fingers brushed his dry but full lips, and she made a mental note to apply oil to his fragile skin.

Finally, she looked at him. "I'm sorry for what I am about to do," she said, knowing he couldn't understand her, then positioned her hands upon his warm skin.

With a swift, firm, thrust, his rib popped back into place.

***

"*Iesus*...God...*fok*..." Ewan felt his head swim in agony.

He clenched the stick so hard it snapped. He spit out the remnants and groaned, panting, as anguish surged through him. Sweat beaded on his upper lip. Soon, it was just a throbbing reminder rocking him as he regained his power of speech.

"I...I might rather just die, sir."

The man who had introduced himself as Abu Abdullah Habib Abd-al-Rachid chuckled but said nothing. The woman, smelling of spices he had never smelled in his life, wrapped him tightly in loops of bindings, her fingers and the silks of her mantle brushing over his skin as if feathers dusting upon him, until his torso was rigid and tight. God, what a vision it had been, opening his eyes to the sight of her dark ones and feeling her gentle handling in the dim light of the lamp. In truth, he had heard her speaking before he regained the power of opening his eyes. Instantly, the energy in the chamber had shifted when she had entered, and roused his fading mind. And it was that voice—the higher-pitched, gentle, feminine voice trilling over consonants that had eventually given him the strength to pull his eyelids up.

She was speaking to him now. He furrowed his brows, his eyes darting up to hers again before remembering her father's request that he keep them averted. Damn, but he couldn't *not* look at her. He couldn't see a single inch of her, and yet, her eyes were the most stunning portals to the soul he had laid his gaze upon. Black, they were so dark brown. Shining with light and intelligence, wide and oval-shaped, and fringed in thick lashes. Her body moved like a willow branch, lithe, slender, with the occasional hint at curving hips as the silken fabric of her robes swayed and twisted about her.

"Where do you come from?" Commander Rachid asked him, his eyes firm, as if the man had seen his wandering gaze.

Ewan snapped to attention again. "My name is Ewan de Buchan. I am the Earl of Dunwiddie, from Scotland."

"*Scotland?*" Habib replied.

"It's north of England, a small country."

Habib nodded, though looked curious. "I know of England. King Richard hails from there. And I have heard of Scotland, though I've never met someone from this land before." Ewan nodded and allowed Habib to continue. "I know not what it looks like or where it is in relationship to the Turkish Empire. The maps I've seen appear distorted and poorly made."

Ewan thought. How dangerous was this man? How much did he dare tell him? Or dare *not* tell him? And yet, the man had saved his life. He, an enemy. If learning about foreign places had been at the heart of Ewan's decision to travel to this God-forsaken land in the first place—for if he were honest, fighting infidels in the Holy Land hadn't much appealed to him, but seeing an unseen corner of the earth had—then the best way to learn of these people and their world was to get them to the table, talking. Clearly Commander Rachid wanted to talk about maps.

"I could make a map for you," Ewan said, hoping he wasn't

29

offering too much.

The commander seemed to think it over and smoothed his dark, regal beard. Ewan glanced down at the woman's slender hands. He had been so focused on not looking her in the eye, he had been remiss to notice her delicate hands. They were decorated in such art as he had never seen. Suddenly, every place she made contact with trailed with heat. Suddenly, he was overly aware of each place her hands, decorated in dots and spirals, touched.

"Can you draw such a thing?" the man asked him. "For making maps with accuracy is a skill."

Ewan resisted the urge to harrumph. In part because it would hurt his ribs like hell to jolt them and even with the woman's expert binding, he didn't want to risk another bout of anguish. But little did this commander know, cartography was Ewan's profession and a trade that had increased the wealth his father had bequeathed him.

"Aye. I'm an expert cartographer. It was one of my roles in the army—to scout the terrain and make maps for us to follow."

The young woman began to smear ointment onto his burnt cheeks, those fetching eyes now roving over his cheekbones, his nose, his lips... But they never once glanced back to his. The paste was soothing to his burns, cooling, and he felt a twinge of relief. He inspected the patterns painted upon her hands as they flashed before his face. Her simple, yet elegant, mantle rested above what looked like delicate wrists. And the spices. Ah, they filled his nose and left him heady. Mayhap it was his head injury making him so sensitive. *Aye, it must be that.* There was absolutely no reason to feel so intoxicated over a woman he couldn't even see.

"And an *earl* is a position of wealth?" Habib continued, while Ewan began to take in his surroundings.

He was in an enclosed, plastered chamber. Clearly isolated from all others. *So the man saved me.* But he was still being treated with precaution.

"Aye, if a man is smart with his money," Ewan replied.

He thought of the sorry state of his betrothed's father's affairs. Landlocked, ailing finances, and in need of alliances with strong neighbors who could grant him favors. Fortunately for his betrothed and her father, Ewan was a wealthy man who controlled access to the sea, and his daughter, Margaret, was beautiful to look at in spite of her forked tongue. She was outspoken, and never put much credence in minding her place.

But she was fetching indeed, that much was true, and he only needed her, if truth be told, to give him bairns. He would suffer none taking his husbandly rights if he ever returned home to marry her. And just like that, as the word marriage snaked through his mind, his eyes strayed back to the strange woman before him now, covered from head to toe in blue and beige, her hands working meticulously and swiftly, with expertise and grace, to finish her ministrations. Odd that he would look at her now. Though it *had* been over two years since he had last slept with a woman, since he joined the Crusade. He was probably desperate for the relief only a woman could give, 'twas all.

"An earl is a position of title, rather, though I have the title and the wealth."

The commander seemed to consider him now, then his mouth turned up in a humored smile as he addressed his daughter in his foreign tongue, keeping his eyes trained on him. "No doubt, Nasim, this man is a sight better looking than Kalim."

Whatever the older man had just said in his foreign tongue, it caused the woman to freeze. Her eyes widened on her father, stunned, and then she looked straight at him with unabashed horror.

A messenger pushed into the cell, distracting the commander who turned away from him. In hushed tones, the messenger explained a matter of business in more foreign words that Ewan couldn't understand. The woman's father seemed to argue with the messenger, gesturing to his daughter and to him. The messenger gave a bow, his tone ringing with deference, and the commander relented and nodded abruptly.

He turned to his daughter, speaking in their Arabic tongue. "Unfortunately I must leave to attend to a pressing matter at the request of Commander Faraj. The matter will not wait for me to ensure your brother, Abdullah, arrives as your chaperone.

However, Abdullah has been summoned and should be here soon."

The woman was gaping at her father again, Ewan noticed. Then she began to argue, speaking in that soft voice that had woken him up. Sakes, but it was a balmy, soothing sound, even if her manner right now seemed agitated. The commander quelled her protests, and turned to Ewan, switching to Ewan's English with his halted pronunciation.

"I must attend a particular matter. My daughter is to keep you awake until her chaperone arrives. Her *oldest brother*. Your eyes, keep them averted."

He pointed knowingly at Ewan, and Ewan felt the urge to squirm under his glare, as if he were a wayward lad. Making a point of saying her "oldest brother" was meant to intimidate him, for it mattered not what part of the world people came from, a brother would beat any man senseless if his sister was wronged, and "oldest" implied there were more.

He swept from the room.

The woman appeared to be numb, rooted to the spot in surprise. She looked to and fro as if waiting for someone to materialize out of thin air. Then she turned her gaze directly at him again. Alone, Ewan looked up unabashed at her. Tears were brimming on her eyelids.

"'Tis all right, my lady. I won't bite," he said, feeling the need to assuage her fear of him.

She shook her head, unable to understand. *Of course she doesn't know what I said.* Instead he placed his hands outward, palms forward, as if conceding to a greater power, and bowed his head down, biting back the discomfort such an action caused his ribs. In all honesty, now that he was awake, he was feeling more like himself. He glanced at her and then motioned to the water basin again.

"Water?" he asked.

She hastened to fill the cup and this time, handed it to him so he could drink for himself. He took it from her, his fingers grazing hers. It was only a dusting of fingertips, lasting but a fraction of a moment, but it caused a wash of warmth to rush over him. *Don't be a fool, man.* It might have been quite a while since he'd lain with a woman, but he knew a woman's touch quite well, on every inch of his body. There was no need to lose his head over a brief touch of fingers from a strange, foreign woman he couldn't even see. She could look like anything, from a beauty, to a horse, for all he knew.

And yet, his interest was growing more piqued. He wanted to peel away the veil and see for himself what she looked like, even if she looked like a horse. He chuckled inwardly. Such a barrier between them seemed unnatural. Though he supposed it *would* seem that way. He hadn't been reared in this culture, where such a practice was probably the norm. Clearly she wore such a garment to thwart a man's interest. Humorous, he thought, that on him, it was having the opposite effect.

Stunned, she began to withdraw her fingers. He suddenly didn't want to be without them. He captured her decorated hand in his, his grip gentle, and examined it, turning it slowly so as to see the entire design. She froze. Her tear-brimmed eyes were wide, her gaze locked upon him. He should let go. If he wasn't supposed to look at her, he ought to assume that he shouldn't touch, either.

He glanced up into her dark, watery eyes. "'Tis beautiful," he said. "I've never seen anything like it."

She ripped her hand away as if he were a cobra about to sink his fangs into her. And after a moment, she tossed the cup aside and hastened from the chamber, leaving him alone. Ewan sat still, stunned. Then cursed himself.

"Be damned, man."

He had offended her. Which meant he would offend her brother and certainly her father, if they should find out. *If?* More like, *when*. The way she had fled told him he would be found out soon enough. And then, what would be his fate?

CHAPTER 3

Nasim waited in the darkened corridor, taking comfort in the veil such darkness offered. Her chest rose and fell in quick heaves, remembering the Christian's touch, his piercing gaze, his words. She watched the infirmary workers mill about from afar, men, their heads topped with skullcaps and their plain *thawbs* swaying as they walked from patient to patient stretched out on simple, clean cots.

Though she didn't really see them at all.

Her hand was burning. She braced herself against the wall with it, resisting the urge to clutch it to her chest and cry. She closed her eyes, trying to stave off the water threatening to launch over her lashes. What that man had done was forbidden. And yet, there was nothing unkind in his actions. She even sensed he was admiring the art upon her hands. Why would he be so fascinated by it? Hadn't he seen a woman's painted hands before? Surely the women from his homeland decorated themselves. Didn't they?

Maybe they didn't.

The thought struck her. Maybe women were nothing like her in his homeland. But what were they like if they didn't adorn themselves in art? She had only ever known her old home of Damascus and these palace walls in Jerusalem, the gardens within, and the women within. Her one *hajj* to Mecca, a journey that had excited her to the point that she had poured over books and drawings of Arabia for months before hand, had been thwarted by this horrid war brought against them. She still remembered that sinking feeling, like a stone dropping from her heart to her feet, when her mother informed her that her father had canceled her journey.

Who knew what women looked like, dressed like, or behaved like, in other parts of the world? Just like the man's words were frustratingly foreign, so was everything else about his home. His eyes…so bright blue, and yet cool, intense… Did women have eyes like his where he came from?

I should tell Abdullah what he did to me when he arrives.

Her brother was a fierce fighter, and fiercely protective of her, too. He would lop the foreigner's head straight off without question. There would be no prison, or tribunals, or beatings. No. Abdullah would draw his scimitar and behead him, right there, on the infirmary floor, and then wipe his blade on the blue-eyed man's linen—

"Why are you out here unattended?" Abdullah questioned, shocking her eyes back open.

Her oldest full brother, so proud and tall, was watching her with concern crinkling his thick brows and crow's feet from so much time spent in the sun. He looked much like their mother, but with the robustness of their father's features and stature. The family all agreed that Nasim—who also favored her mother in looks—and Abdullah, looked much alike, like twins separated by more than a decade of time. He was already an accomplished warrior with four wives of his own and a handful of children that Nasim adored.

Relief poured over her, though disappointment, too. Being alone with the infidel shouldn't appeal to her, and it didn't…did it? No, most certainly not. What if he was a rapist? Clearly, if he was part of the brutal foreign military that had descended upon them and sent all those ailing men down the corridor in the infirmary to their sickbeds, he was a murderer. And yet, his eyes, and those words, whatever they meant, as he inspected the designs on her hands that one of her half-sisters had created…

They were eyes that she would remember forever.

"Father had to leave," she replied. Now, this was the moment she should tell on the forward infidel who had dared to touch her and look at her with his beautiful, azure eyes. "I…I wished not to be alone with the man."

Abdullah stiffened. "What did he do to you?"

"Nothing," she said. Her mind was swirling again. "He is different, that's all. I've never been alone with an unrelated man. I thought to await you out here."

Abdullah's stiffness didn't receded, but he nodded once. "You shouldn't be out here in the corridors alone. Commander Faraj knew Father was with you and that you treated the cretin. And yet, he acted as if his summons was pressing." He scoffed and shook his head, but didn't elaborate. "You're certain nothing happened?"

"Nothing did. Truly."

Abdullah frowned. "Only Allah knows why Father would want to save this maggot's life. So what if he saved our lives? He didn't do so for the right reason. He only saved our lives by accident and ought to be put to death with the rest of our prisoners."

Nasim stood silently, waiting for him to finish grumbling. It was no secret that Abdullah hated the Christians and their bloody war.

"None of them are worth the air they breathe," he added.

"Remember, dearest brother, what the Quran says about compassion," she said.

She furrowed her brow. How was it, that she was set on telling her brother about the infidel taking her hand just a moment ago, and was now defending him instead?

Abdullah sighed. "I know it. But it's hard to take heed when we must continue to fight and die to protect our homes and lives. Come. Father is clearly more compassionate than I. If he wishes us to help this bastard, then let us do his bidding."

He turned to push through the curtain, and Nasim followed. The man was still sitting rigidly on the cot, exactly as Nasim had left him. He looked up, his eyes darting between her brother and her, then back to her brother, as if he had only just remembered he wasn't supposed to look at her. And clearly assessing the threat the other man posed. His eyes, sparkling with interest earlier, now sparkled with wariness, and his face fell to impassivity.

"Get back to work, Nasim," Abdullah directed, going to take a seat on a stool.

Nasim looked to her brother, decked in his proud, dark turban, tunic, and loose pants, a jerkin of stiff leather binding his chest, his scimitar hanging upon his belts, and his daggers strategically protruding from his sleeves at his wrists. He was an imposing man, intense, and his eyes were locked on the infidel's blue ones. He took out a sharpening blade at his waist, then pulled out his scimitar, the arching edge of silver skillfully designed, the hilt inscribed with swirling designs, and gold inlaid in the handle.

Never once did Abdullah's gaze sever from the Christian's as he took to making long, slow, scrapes, metal against metal ringing out into the chamber, sharpening his weapon. The repetitive scraping caused shivers to run up and down Nasim's arms, and yet, she couldn't stifle her smile at Abdullah's antics. He might be fiercely protective now, but he would jest and laugh at the foreigner's expense around supper with his brothers.

But that night, as Nasim lay alone in her bedchamber, resting her head upon her pillows, she stared across the space to the imported rug from Persia draped across her floor. Only her lamp burned, next to an open copy of *Layla and Majnun*. When she had finally returned home, she had felt a compulsion to read it again. She thought of Solomon, thought of Kalim— Goodness! But *Kalim?* And she saw a pair of the bluest eyes in her mind, confusing her. It was because the Christian was so different, that had to be the reason she continued to think on him and his strange words, spoken so deeply. It couldn't be because he was intriguing, or handsome, or admiring of her henna, or a man like any other.

For the remainder of the afternoon, until her father's return, the infidel man had kept his eyes averted and his hands to himself. It would seem Abdullah's presence had indeed dissuaded him from attempting any further contact with her. And now that Nasim was alone, having left her vulnerability in that sick room, she wished he would have cast his brilliant blue gaze upon her one last time.

Likely she would never see him again. And yet, she had never longed to leave these palace walls more so than she did right now as she lay curled on her side with her hands propped under her cheek, staring at her manuscript of *Layla and Majnun's* virgin love, wondering what it was like in the infidel's distant corner of the world...

***

"Nasim," Ghaniyah, her mother, said, jostling her awake.

Nasim drew up her eyelids at her mother's words, warbling with age. The woman stood over her, wrapped in a mantle. Nasim looked around. Her mother held a candle. The chamber was dark. She rubbed the sleep from her eyes.

"Nasim, daughter. You must make haste and dress."

"What's the matter?" Nasim asked.

Ghaniyah shook her head, looking unsettled. "Your father has come for you."

Nasim bolted upright, her blanket pooling down to her waist. She wore nothing but a sleeping gown and her hair was braided to keep it from tangling about her while she slept.

"What's wrong?"

"That infidel. It seems he has taking a turn for the worst and Solomon isn't yet returned and won't be for many days."

Nasim shivered at the prospect of seeing the infidel again. Ghaniyah stepped back and searched Nasim's chests for her garments. A black robe, deep red-wine mantle and veil. Nasim jumped from bed and allowed her mother to help her in the dimness. A few swirls of fabric, and she was covered as her mother straightened her veil and shook out the folds. She slid her feet into her sandals and hastened into the antechamber before her room, where she often met with her sisters, and grabbed a basket of ointments.

"I'm sorry to wake you, Nasim," Habib said, standing in the family's reception. Even in the dead of the night, he managed to look proud and regal.

"What is the hour?" she asked.

"Morning prayers are still some time away. Come. Ewan de Buchan is feverous, and his belly grows discolored. I know not what to do for him other than drain the bile. He moans in anguish."

Discolored belly? Fever? And had her father just used the man's name? His name was *Ewan de Buchan*? What a strange fusion of sounds. "What color is his belly?"

"It appears bluish or purple, though his binding obstructs some of the view."

She darted out the door and left her father to follow.

He did so, jogging to catch up. "Slowly, Nasim. You act frivolous, running through the corridor."

"There's no time to wait, my dearest father," she argued, ignoring his chastening as her deep red mantle billowed behind her like a banner in the night. "He must be drained and his injury found, staunched, and repaired. His life is imperiled. Every moment counts."

Habib didn't stop her, but simply walked briskly behind the gentle pattering of her sandals. She blazed into the sleeping infirmary, startling the night caregivers and ignoring their shock. Turning down the corridor, moaning echoed out to her ears. A fist clenched in her chest. Granted, she had never treated a serious injury before, but she had still never faced a patient's death, either.

The moaning grew louder. She breezed through the curtain. The Christian lay on his back, groaning, his head lolling on his pillow with the linen pulled up to his shoulders. The pillow was saturated with sweat. She yanked back the covers, grateful that he had since been dressed in a simple *sirwal* tied below his waist. Though in the moment of haste, she didn't care what she saw. Discoloring, spreading like a bruise under his skin, had purpled him. His breathing was rattling as if fluid were in his lungs.

"His lung could be punctured," she exclaimed. "Allah, I beg your guidance." She closed her eyes. "Father, I need my healer manuscripts, specifically a text by the great surgeon, Al-Zahrawi. I must have them immediately. They are in Solomon's study. I also need opium and four, solid infirmary workers to help restrain this man."

Habib turned to a couple workers who had followed Nasim's distressing jaunt down the corridor. "You heard my daughter. Get her books and opium, and go find four broad men to assist."

"And Father, I must have a complete set of surgical tools from Solomon's armamentarium: clamps and vises, knives for incisions, clean catgut for sewing, a small needle, and a fire in the hearth filled with a pot of clean, boiling water. You must get these now!"

She swirled away from her father, stripping her mantle to free her arms of the billowing fabric and tossing it aside, keeping her veil neatly in place, but taking a strip of bandaging and wrapping it around her neck to keep the silk from falling across her view when she bent. The running of feet, swishing of the curtain, and clinking of supplies all told Nasim that her requests were being met as she grabbed a cloth and drenched it in the nearby basin, washing away the sweat on his face.

She lined up a knife, a series of picks and tools already present in the room should the moment become dire and her surgical bundle was not yet prepared. The man continued to moan. She continued to pat his brow. "Rest easily," she whispered, knowing he couldn't understand her words. He might not even realize she was speaking to him in his feverous delirium. And yet, they were the first words she had directed at the infidel *Ewan* with the hope that he would understand, and some of the first words she had offered any man with whom she was unfamiliar. And at her words, he stilled, relaxing.

Her bundle arrived from the armamentarium, as did her manuscripts and the four infirmary workers she had requested.

"Please set the water to boiling," she said.

The men did as she directed. She dragged free the surgical book describing the great Al-Zahrawi's techniques. Solomon referenced it regularly and called the surgeon who had lived almost two hundred years before them a master and genius. She had studied his descriptions of the human body and the way in which it operated countless times.

She laid it out on her work table and began flipping through the parchment. The color slowly draining from Ewan's face and the rasping of his breathing told her she might already be too late. One thing was certain. She didn't have time to explore his insides to find the source of the bleeding. She would have to make her best guess quickly, and pray to Allah above that she made the right decision. She took a pair of shears and cut the bindings over his dusting of chest hair trailing up his abdomen, to his pectorals.

The bindings fell away and she saw the full extent of the discoloration. His rib was protruding again, and the darkest spot of bruising was forming under his arm on his side. She pressed her fingers into it, agitating it.

"Ahhh!" screamed the man

His eyes flew open. His pupils were wild, his face sweating and pasty white. She jumped back, yelping. He panted, his ensuing groan guttural, and he groped around until he gripped her. He dragged her close, his grasp ferocious, which caused her to wince. She gasped.

Her father lunged forth, a knife drawn and about to slice away the man's offending grip, when the Christian sputtered, "Help me. I beg you, lass, God above…"

His grip fell. His eyes rolled back. He was still conscious, for he swallowed and his breathing was controlled as he attempted to master his pain. But grabbing her had taken all his strength. She looked to her father, her eyelids brimming. Whatever the man had said, he was desperate. Her father's brow was furrowed, his face a raging red, and yet, he nodded once to her, sheathing his blade.

"He begs you help him. He pleads for his life and puts it in your hands."

She nodded again, her nerves pulsing through her body, setting her into motion. She turned to the workers and released a slew of words on one breath. "Put these medical tools in the boiling water. Set the time keeper over, and when the sand has run through, remove them with washed hands. Do exactly this."

They dashed into action again. She warred between cutting a drain for the pooling blood with the knife at her disposal, simply to offer some relief, and yet, she knew the risk of festering would increase after using a blade that hadn't been boiled.

Instead, she waited, and waited, and soon realized she was petting back the man's feverous hair with the washcloth. His eyes opened and gazed up at her. She returned the gaze. Neither of them looked away.

"Thank you…" he mumbled. "Thank you…"

She finally turned to reference her book. Such contact was inappropriate, even if it was only intended to offer comfort, though she hadn't wanted to stop. Her touch had soothed him, and he had been grateful. Just that brought her satisfaction.

She looked over at her father, suddenly remembering his presence. He was watching her every move, scrutinizing her, his face impassive. Would he punish her later for being so forward? In the moment, she didn't have time to worry. She found the opium in a small glass vial and began preparing an infusion to help take the edge off the anguish she was about to inflict. Carefully, she dropped in the strong pain reliever, the pearly liquid pooling and dispersing into the cup of water she had sprinkled with herbs. She stirred it, just as the time keeper ran out of sand and the workers scrubbed their hands and removed the tools with a pair of tongs.

"Lay them here, on the table," Nasim directed, motioning to a clean linen she had draped over the wood. The workers followed her instructions. She rested a gentle hand on the man's shoulder. "*En—an,*" she said softly. His eyes opened once more, and took her in as if searching for a miracle. "You must drink this."

He didn't understand, kept staring at her and laboring to breathe.

"My daughter says you must drink her infusion, to help with the pain," Habib spoke up from the corner. "She must cut you open and find from where you bleed."

Nasim had never seen a terrified man before, but right now, after her father's explanation, his eyes widened. And then, he did the most quizzical gesture. He closed his eyes, mumbled something in a language different from the one he had spoken in moments before, swallowed, and lifted his hand. He touched his head, then the center of his chest, then each shoulder, before bring his fist to his mouth as if kissing it, as if kissing an object even though he held nothing in his hand. He looked up at her again, the terror still alive in his eyes, yet his brow resolute. He nodded once. He was giving her his blessing to proceed. Whatever he had just done, it must mean something important, perhaps something meant to comfort him? Perhaps meant to bring him peace on the matter?

"I trust you," he said.

She had no idea what he had just said, but she touched his forehead anyway.

"I will do my best," she replied.

He nodded, as if understanding her sentiment if not her words, and took up her hand again, bringing it to his lips where he placed a kiss on the knuckles. She should wrench her hand away—her father was staring—and yet, she couldn't. He finally let go. She slid her hand beneath his head, tilting his face forward, and tipped the cup into his mouth so that the infusion trickled in.

He imbibed slow swallows, uncertain of the taste at first. It didn't take long for the opium to take effect, for she had concocted the drink strongly. His eyelids drooped, his breathing relaxed, and he appeared to almost fall asleep. She shuddered. This wouldn't be painless, even with the opium drink coursing through his body. Far from it. She washed her hands in the basin, scrubbing with soap, and returned to him, taking up the thin knife now boiled clean.

She placed a rod of wood between his teeth. There was nothing to which to bind his wrists and ankles. "Each one of you take an arm and a leg. He is a strong man, so you must hold him down with all your might, for he is likely to flail."

They each nodded and mumbled acquiescence. Once the infidel was secured, she slid her fingers down his side, finding where the rib appeared to be jutting into him, took a deep breath, and sent up a quiet prayer. Then she cut a thin, long, incision.

"God, ah!" Ewan bellowed, the rod blocking his tongue and muddling his sounds.

He thrashed, as she thought he might. Each man pinned his appendages down strongly. His chest arched, causing him to scream in more anguish. Surely he jostled his injury.

And then, blood flooded the seam of flesh. She took

another deep breath, exhaled, and felt sweat causing her silken veil to stick to her forehead and cheeks. She dabbed the blood away with a clean linen and referenced the book, the knife in hand.

"Move the light closer, please, my father."

Habib did so, holding the lamp next to her as Ewan passed out. She began to work, ever so often reverting back to the text, finding her place, and continuing. After how much time, she didn't know, she found the spot on the lung where the broken rib had made a tear.

"I've found it," she said aloud, if only to reaffirm to herself that she could do this.

Her father rested a strong palm upon her back. "Well done, Nasim *azeezy*."

She ignored the praise and packed Ewan's opened insides with wads of cloth to keep the blood from soaking through the tear. Her father's praise might validate that she had good instincts, but if she didn't successfully sew the tear shut and keep her patient alive, then it would be for naught. She washed her hands once more to clean them of Ewan's blood growing sticky and invading her fingernails. Then she began threading the catgut off the spool, the thin, sinuous thread of goat intestine, and pulled it through the needle eye. Carefully, she sutured the tiny tear, so small, yet, such a massive culprit of pending death.

Ewan began to stir again, groaning.

"Begin dropping the infusion down his throat, Father."

Habib tipped the man's head back and pulled down his jaw. He did as she bade, pouring tiny droplets of the opium medicine into his throat. He swallowed, gulping at the sudden intrusion. And after some time, he began to settle back down again. Nasim used her arm to wipe at her brow, knowing she had pushed her veil out of alignment and rebellious dark curls were pasted to her sweaty skin.

Hours had passed. The minarets began wailing the *Fajr* prayers.

"May Allah forgive your for missing your *Salat*, for you do good work right now," she said to the workers, implying they should refrain from their ritual prayers.

Still, she worked. Hours drifted by. Her father, unused to taking orders, did as she bade, handing her tools, threading the catgut, readjusting the lamp. People quietly swished in and out, replacing supplies, bringing fresh water. Never did she waver, even when Ewan groaned again. Finally, she began sewing closed her incision, and at long last, pulled the final needle and tied it, snipping it.

She took a step back. Then another. Staring at her handiwork. The chamber was silent and Ewan, recently dosed with another bout of infusion, was breathing easily. Only time would tell if the leak into his lung proved fatal or if he would recover, for she knew of no treatment for drying out the lungs.

She exhaled. Her breath came in a long tremble, and she closed her eyes, releasing the crippling tension from her chest that she didn't realize she had been containing. No. She had been so focused that she didn't even realize she had been afraid. She threw her face in the crook of her arm to hide her tears, but a sob managed to dislodge from her throat. What had she just done? Oh, if only Solomon had been here to guide her, and yet, if Solomon had been here, she never would have been summoned, never would have been put in such a position.

"Please dress his wound," she asked the nearest worker through the fabric on her arm, who did as she bade.

Nasim dabbed her eyes dry and glanced around. Various candles had been lit and were mostly spent, wax having collected around the bases in puddles. Bloody rags were littered on the tile where she had discarded them. Her hands needed washing again and the needle was still clenched between her fingers, causing the skin beneath her nails to whiten. By all accounts, she looked like a murderess and the small chamber was the crime scene. She set aside the needle with the other bloodied instruments, and turned to wash her hands.

"You please me, daughter," Habib said beside her ear, having stepped close without her noticing. "You work with such certainty, such a calm, steady hand. I never would have suspected you a novice in the surgery."

"My thanks for your praise," she replied.

Calm and steady? No, she had been a nervous wreck. Her eyes were still moist. She had felt nothing but an hours-long surge of energy, demanding that she try to save the man her father wanted saved, unsure the entire time if she could actually do it.

Her hands duly scrubbed, she patted them dry, and removed the tie holding her veil tight to her neck. The fabric, creased from being cinched so long, relaxed, and she took a breath of relief at having the saturated silk fall away from her lips and nose. She adjusted her head covering, tucking in the wisps of dark curls that had fallen loose, and collected her mantle to swirl it back around her.

She stifled a yawn. She needed sleep. But her patient, the infidel, shouldn't be left unattended, and she turned to her father, knowing what she needed to ask him next. She needed to remain in Ewan de Buchan's cell.

CHAPTER 4

Words, soft and foreign, lulled Ewan in his slumber. Whatever infusion he had been given was wearing off, and continuous pain was growing in his chest. At first, it had been a dull ache, though it slowly worsened now. The words continued. They weren't spoken in conversation. No, they were ritual words...maybe not, but they sounded subdued and recited... They belonged to the woman who had...*Christ, what did she do to me?* His mind was foggy.

He blinked his eyes open, but lay still. He knew better than to move, for the pain in his chest was burgeoning. The room was dim, as always, for no natural light could shine in. His stomach felt sunken and empty—he hadn't eaten in some time. And for some reason, he wanted more of that medicinal drink the woman had created. He could vaguely remember droplets trickling down his throat from time to time to help dull his pain. It hadn't tasted particularly good, but it had made his mind float and his limbs feel like liquid warmth. He listened, her words continuing, soothing his mind growing more and more aware of the intense pain in his chest.

Finally, he summoned the strength to roll his head to the side. The woman was sitting on a cushion against the wall, her legs folded, draped in dark red encasing her head, face, and body. She sat next to the clay lamp, the only source of light. Her left side was illuminated and her right sat in shadows. A book lay open in the crook of her lap, the front and back covers resting on each knee. And interestingly enough, the book flipped the opposite way from manuscripts in Europe, as if she were reading backward. Was that how they read in this land? He hadn't seen a book in ages. Since he had left home.

Each turn of the page as she read aloud caused the flame on the lamp to flicker in the gentle breeze it created. He closed his eyes again, basking in the sound of her. For some reason, he was growing attached to her presence and her beautiful voice. Aside from the other day when her brother—a man he now recognized as the one who had rescued him from his sunbaked death—had come in to sit watch and purposefully attempt to intimidate him, he felt at ease around her. He wished he could thank her. There was no telling if he would survive this trial, but if he did, it would be because of her and her expertise. And he suspected the midwife at Dunwiddie could learn a thing or two from a woman like this one.

What was her name? He only knew her to be Commander Rachid's daughter, and the commander hadn't offered him any information about her. Her voice was humming onward, like a song. He wanted to know her name. He opened his eyes again and gazed at her.

"What's your name?" he asked, knowing she wouldn't understand.

His voice came out gravelly and softer than he had intended. Her words ceased and she looked up at him. Her face was still covered, but the way in which her eyes crinkled told him she smiled. He smiled, too, and she looked down, as if embarrassed. She set aside the book, closing it, and pushed up to her feet. He saw a flash of gold—an anklet—bedecked in bangles as her long tunic fell around her sandals to cover it. And had she been wearing those loose pants? Interesting that women here wore many of the same things as the men.

She came to his side, tentatively, and for a rebellious moment, she looked directly into his eyes, as he did the same with her, before blinking away reluctantly. She placed her hand to his brow, his temples, patting him to determine if he were feverous.

She said something. He didn't know what it meant, but the way she nodded to herself, told him she must be satisfied with his recovery. He tried to shift, for his rear and back were growing sore from lying in the same position. Pain rippled over him. She gripped each of his shoulders and shook her head firmly. "*La.*"

He paused and looked back at her. Their eyes connected once more. Her hands on his bare skin were surprisingly firm, considering her wrists were thin and her fingers, so slender.

She said something else to him. He furrowed his brow, but the woman gestured, and it seemed to make sense: whatever was wrong with him, he wasn't supposed to move. She turned, and washed her hands in a basin that sat beside him on a roughly hewn table, patted them dry on a rag, and carefully pulled back his linen, revealing his chest. She folded it down to his waist, where she settled it across his hips. Then, she began to unbandage a dressing upon the side of his chest. He lay still, looking down his front to watch what she was doing. She peeled the bandaging spotted with his blood back, and revealed a new incision, now sewn shut.

Ah yes, the agony. It was coming back to him now. His pain had grown unbearable. He was moaning, delirious, feverish, and then hands were subduing him—and she was there, and hands were bracing him, and that foul infusion which made him feel so good was running down his throat, and then...the burning of the knife...

He thought of the butchering he had seen during this war, the violent, shredded limbs from flail maces and axes and the hacking apart of warriors that both sides had inflicted upon each other. This one incision was the source of his anguish that had caused him such hallucinations the day before. He couldn't fathom what those grotesque war injuries felt like if this little one had nearly killed him.

She inspected the incision, then covered the wound again with a clean bandage, just as the curtain to his room rippled. In came a serving boy, dressed in a plain, coarse tunic and the ubiquitous *sirwal* pants that tapered at the ankle, his feet dusty from running errands in nothing but sandals. He carried a tray of steaming food. Ewan's mouth watered, taking in the shining silver lids of several dishes. The boy set them down on a low table, next to…Ewan craned his neck. A cot? Was this woman staying by his side through night and day?

The boy removed the lids of each dish, laying them out, and wafts of savory smells, rich with spices Ewan had never smelled before, lifted onto the air. His stomach rumbled so loudly, the woman looked back down at him. He had been careful, ever since her brother's threatening knife-sharpening, never to look at her when others were present, but he heard her giggle now. It was so soft a sound, yet, he heard it, and it made his mind sober from whatever concoction she had fed him to ease his pain. And damn, but it was hard to resist looking at her.

But as the boy left, he glanced at her again. She had her back turned now as she prepared the food. God, he hoped some of it was for him. He was famished. She turned back to him and once more, he could tell she smiled by the crinkling of her eyes. Beautiful, soulful eyes, he realized. So dark. His betrothed's eyes were so far the opposite. Light blue, pale, and what most considered to be a sign of immense beauty where he came from. Ah, Margaret. Odd that he only just now thought of her, when he couldn't stop thinking about this mystery daughter of Commander Rachid.

The woman then turned to him and retrieved a couple pillows, covered in sun-bleached fabric. She leaned in closely, sliding an arm beneath his shoulders, and eased him upward. He groaned, an exhale blasting out of his mouth as he then swallowed the pain. She quickly propped the pillows beneath him and withdrew again. Her touch was so business-like, so efficient, yet he hadn't been touched by a woman so closely in over two years. He wanted there to be…affection, in her touch. He wanted the pain in his chest to dissipate. The ache made him visibly wince, and he dared not move for fear of jostling whatever the source of pain was.

Even with two pillows beneath him, he was still very much reclined.

The woman returned to the small table and collected a wooden bowl of broth. Coming back to him, she then placed it to his lips as she held a rag beneath the bowl. Slowly, she tipped it up, and the contents trickled into his mouth. He had no name for the flavors, but they were satisfying and bold, and warmed his stomach beyond simply the temperature of the liquid. He swallowed hungrily, dismayed when she removed the bowl, though rationally, he understood he couldn't gulp it, lest his stomach rebel and cause him to lurch it up. Such heaving might tear whatever fragile repair had been done to him. He took more grateful sips as she allowed it, and resigned himself to await more when she decided it appropriate.

Thankfully, she left him propped upon the pillows, which were soothing to his back that had now spent days laid out on the hard cot. As she checked him once more for fever, her hands soft on his brow, he felt her pet back his hair. Was it to move the unruly waves from his forehead? Or had it meant more?

You're still delirious. Of course it didn't mean more. In a world where one couldn't even look a noblewoman in the eyes, surely public affection was frowned upon, too.

"What are you called?" he asked again, wishing she could comprehend him.

She paused and furrowed her brow, saying something.

"Your name?" he persisted. He placed his right hand to his chest, for when he even twitched his left shoulder, he felt sudden pain. "I'm Ewan. *Ewan,*" he repeated, patting himself for emphasis, then gestured to her with a questioning lift of the brow.

"Ew-an," she replied, glancing shyly away. It sounded like a breeze on his face, the way she pronounced it.

He nodded, his movement catching her attention again. "Aye. Ewan."

Again, he gestured to her. Hesitantly, she placed a hand to her own chest.

"Nasim." She ducked her head as she said it, glancing around, then back at him, as if she were committing a crime. "Nasim," she said more confidently, her eyes flitting to his once more, then flitting away again.

"Nasim," he murmured to himself, watching her busy herself with her supplies, then go to the low table and sit upon a cushion, removing a piece of flat bread and using it to scoop up a mouthful of some sort of meat in a bright, orange sauce.

What meat, he didn't know. Lamb? Chicken? He could almost taste how delicious it was as she took nibbles, rinsing her fingers afterward, and replacing the lids to the shining silver dishes to then pour herself a cup of some hot liquid. She sipped it slowly, contemplatively, never once looking back at him though he could tell from the tenseness of her posture, she was well aware of him watching her.

He felt his consciousness waning again. She seemed to innately know he was drifting, because she suddenly set down the tea and came back to him. She pulled his linen up again, draping it across his chest. She said something reassuring and touched his forehead fondly.

"Your book," he said, wishing to be lulled to sleep by her soft, steady voice again, just like the way he had awoken. He wanted more of that infusion, too, but the woman wasn't offering it, and he had no way to ask for it.

She furrowed her dark brows at his remark.

He pulled his right arm up, pointing across the chamber. She turned to look around, then back at him. He thought about how to motion what he wanted. He gestured his hand as if he opened a book, then traced his finger through the air, repeating the motion a couple times to indicate reading. Her brow still furrowed, she glanced back at the book, then at him. He nodded, pointing at it once more, then at her.

"Will you read aloud?"

She studied him a moment longer, then returned to her cushion and picked it up. She held it up questioningly, and he smiled wearily. "Aye, Nasim." He pointed at her, then motioned to his mouth as if speaking.

She looked down, sitting still as if embarrassed, even nervous, then opened the manuscript to where she had left off. She began to read, glancing surreptitiously at him again. He closed his eyes and relaxed as her peaceful words enveloped him, feeling his weariness sink, his body lift, and his mind slowly shut down as sleep claimed him and blessedly dulled the pain in his chest.

***

"'Majnun lay down his head on the earth and embraced the gravestone with both arms,'" Nasim continued, glancing up to see that the man, Ewan, was now sound asleep, feeling the inevitable tears that always plagued her during this part of *Layla and Majnun* well in her eyes, making her voice wobble, "'pressing his body against it with all the force he could muster. His lips moved once more—" Her breath caught. "Then, with the words, 'You, my love…' the soul left his body…'"

She clapped a hand over her mouth, feeling the tear break her lashes and dampen her veil. Majnun had just died, mourning his Layla. Again. For the thousandth time—for the pages were worn to the point that the lettering was coming off. True, Majnun was reunited with her in heaven, and all knew heaven to be much more of a promised land than this war-plagued one, but still. The injustice, that neither should feel their love realized in life, always gouged her right in the chest.

She closed the book and gazed at Ewan. For some reason, her heart swelled that he had wanted to hear her read, that he found it satisfying. She inhaled deeply, then exhaled. It was wrong to feel affection for him. He was an enemy. But she did. She was a traitor, just for admiring his crystal blue eyes and fine physique. And yet, his admiration of her reading, of all things, and his trust in her healing abilities pointed to respect. Respect for the things that brought her simple pleasure and purpose. It was one of the reasons she liked Solomon so much. He appreciated her skills and would never think to suppress them like a typical husband might—

"I didn't know your love of literature ran so deep."

She jumped, her father's voice startling her. "I, eh…" She stood up, bowing her head down.

He had paused in the doorway, but entered now. "Your patient seems to be fond of his healer."

She dared not look up. Was he admonishing her? Had she led the infidel on in some way? How long had her sire been standing there, listening? She had been so conscious of the man lying on the sick bed that she hadn't paid an ounce of attention to the door.

"I'm sorry," she said. "He asked me to read."

"How could he ask such? Does he speak our tongue?"

She kept her eyes locked on her toes and shook her head. For some reason, the way he spoke sounded as if he already knew the answer. Which meant he had been standing there long enough to see the Christian man talking to her, and her, him.

"I gathered what he meant."

Her father said nothing else, just stood there, and finally she dared to glance at him. He was scrutinizing Ewan. Then he looked to her.

"How is his wound?"

"So far, there appears to be no festering. His wound is not irritated, and he kept down some broth."

"And so you fed him? I thought he wasn't supposed to eat yet?"

Why did she feel as if she faced a tribunal?

"The servant arrived with my meal tray. Ewan's stomach growled so loudly, I thought to give him some liquid, rich with salts." Such exertion had tired him, his body was so weak. How could a man as formidable as Ewan be weak? War, truly was a vile human creation, one that robbed people of their lives and of their strength.

"You would have had to touch him to do so."

Why was she feeling so guilty? She had done nothing wrong. Of course, she had touched him. It didn't make sense, being a physician, and not being allowed to touch a patient who needed her care. She lifted her head and looked at her father.

"Indeed, any man would have had to do the same. Ewan needed help and is in no condition to prop himself up without tearing his stitching and doing irreparable damage to his insides. It has only been a couple of days since his surgery. And I won't leave him to seek another's assistance. If something should happen whilst I am away, I would feel guilty beyond measure. He must be observed by someone with the expertise to do so, and I am the only one here available until Solomon returns."

Her father seemed surprised by her bold shift but finally nodded once and looked back at the man. The wheels in his mind were spinning, she could see it. What he was thinking on remained a mystery.

"Has he honored you?"

"Ewan has been most courteous. I feel perfectly safe with him."

Her father glanced back at her, his face stern. Only after her words had gained his attention, did she realize how they sounded. Thankfully, her veil shielded her blushing. She swallowed.

Without removing his gaze, he folded his arms. "Abdullah will return soon to remain with you. I don't like you alone with him, now that he is gaining lucidity. He knows not our ways. I saw him looking at you. And I heard him say your name. *Familiarly.* Be mindful, daughter, how that could be perceived if others should find out."

She shivered and nodded once, her blush draining from her face. And yet, she lifted her eyes to his once more and took a deep breath. "I am a healer, Father, and the patient put in my charge is a man through no fault of my own. My duty to him is to do what I must to see him well again. Have I not proven that I know how best to care for him? It is what I would do for any woman, too."

He scrutinized her. He could, of course, punish her for insolence, but she sensed he wouldn't. Somehow, through this whole, bizarre experience, she sensed he was a fair man who saw the merit in her skills—even if he was still willing to marry her off and kill any dream she had of becoming a physician.

"Would you?" he asked cryptically, then turned with his hands behind his back, and left.

***

"Nasim. It is good to see you again."

Solomon, trailed by her father, her brother, and his servant boy as well as a couple infirmary workers, pushed through the curtain to the infidel's chamber a sennight later.

Startled, Nasim whirled around at the familiar voice, dropping her hand from the infidel' forehead, and smiled. It mattered not that her veil obstructed it. She knew he could tell that she smiled.

"Solomon. It is good to see you safely returned."

Solomon was tanner. And smiling genuinely as he gazed

openly at her. It must have been a sunny voyage to the Mediterranean. Normally, Solomon spent so much time in his study, or in the infirmary, that his skin was paler. The added color suited him. And his hair was a bit longer than normal from lack of cropping while on his trek. Dark and curling in unruly locks over his forehead. *Like Ewan's hair.* She glanced back at Ewan, whose dark, waving hair had grown unruly from his journey through the Holy Land and his confinement in the infirmary.

Solomon came to her, stopped short, and bowed his head politely in greeting, though there was no mistaking the genuine happiness on his face. Then, he looked down at the Christian man, too, following her gaze.

His smile disappeared and was replaced with tension.

Nasim noticed no anger, but she watched both men assessing each other, taking in each other's full form, each other's fine faces. Solomon dressed differently than the other men. He wore a long, dark coat over his pants. She knew Ewan was noticing that Solomon was different, and a quick glance at Solomon told her he wasn't assessing Ewan for medical injuries with his sharp gaze. Their behavior made her uncertain. Nasim stepped back at the awkwardness it induced.

"Can you explain what procedure you completed, Nasim?" he asked.

"Certainly. As you know, I've never done such an invasive repair, but he seemed to have a perforation on his lower left lung. His fourth and fifth ribs were broken, and the fifth one had created a small puncture, allowing blood into the lung..."

She outlined what she had done, what steps she had followed out of Al-Zahrawi's text, at what points she had washed, who had helped her hold him, and how long it had taken.

Solomon nodded approvingly, smiling. Then he laid a hand on her shoulder. "You did a fine job. Truly a fine job. I am very impressed, for we have never done anything so extensive together. I am grateful you were able to succeed at such a challenging procedure in my absence."

Nasim's shoulder tingled. Burned. Emotions swirled

through her, making her feel confused. Solomon praised her good work regularly, but he had never once touched her apart from placing her hands properly when he wished her to learn a new technique while helping some of the women. She glanced to her father. He watched Solomon, then his eyes shifted to her. She turned away from both men so that her tutor's hand dropped. It had only lasted for a moment, but that moment had felt like an eternity. Uncertainty muddled her thoughts. Her father's face was unreadable, but with Ewan recently touching her, not to mention her confession to her father that she was interested in Solomon, she was beginning to feel painted in a suspicious light. Why would Solomon touch her so? In front of her father? *In front of the infidel?*

She glanced to Ewan, lying fully awake and propped upon a couple pillows. His eyes were riveted to Solomon. His face was also unreadable, but his bright blue eyes shimmered with intensity. Then he looked at her with no regard for her father, before glancing back to Solomon. Did he think there was something between her and the physician? Did it bother him to consider that there might be? She had wished for so long, that Solomon might feel attraction to her, but now, having cared for the stranger who liked to listen to her read, she wasn't so sure what to think.

"Well, well. What have we here?"

All heads turned to the dour voice in the doorway. A man, regal in his presentation in a flowing *thawb* and colorful *shemagh* held onto his head by a band that encircled his crown, stood just inside of the chamber. Nasim dropped her head, her hands held stoically together.

"Commander Faraj," her father said, the distaste in his voice detectable even if he summoned a polite tone. "*Salam.*"

Her father couldn't stand the man, from what she knew. She had only seen this man formally and only from afar. But the man wanted her father's position beneath Sultan Saladin, and the smile spreading on Faraj's lips made Nasim uncomfortable.

"Your daughter is quite *familiar* with your physician."

"He has been a loyal tutor and has taught her much," Habib replied, his tone sharp as he turned to give the other officer his full front. "Indeed, thanks to his tutelage, my daughter was able to successfully preform a surgery on this man."

Nasim's face reddened. Solomon hadn't intended to cause her trouble by touching her, but a sinking feeling weighted down her gut. Faraj's disconcerting smile made her mistrustful.

"Why save him? Saladin is equally confused about your decision to do so," Faraj said. "So this sick man interrupted a charge on your men. He saved your sons' lives by accident, not because of any valor. Let the bastard rot."

Nasim glanced at Abdullah who had remained relatively quiet this whole time. She knew he felt the same way. He saw nothing heroic in what Ewan had done. And it was becoming clearer to her now, that her father was much more a peacemaker than a war monger. Her father probably saw saving Ewan's life as an opportunity to bridge a divide. Reward the "Scotsman," as she had heard him talked about, whatever that meant, and thus, begin a process of understanding one another. It made her admire her father in ways she never had before.

"There is much more to this man. This 'earl.' He is a peaceful one, who sees the error of this war."

Faraj smirked. "Indeed, I'm sure he is ever the repentant prisoner, considering he is in the custody of enemies who control whether he lives or dies."

"I do not think he lies."

"You're an idealist. And your judgment is clouded."

Now Habib smirked. "My intuition is what has helped hold Jerusalem from being captured. My judgment is capable of detecting threats, and determining the absence of them. I believe you were in charge of protecting Acre."

Nasim withheld her gasp. But her father had just insulted the other man, and no matter how much the two disliked each other, being impolite in public wasn't done. Acre had fallen to "Crusaders" in hot, dusty battles. Jerusalem had not.

Nasim, her mother, and all others who lived in this bustling city had been well-protected because of her father's efforts, combined with other leaders who were all able to work together. They were ruthless when they needed to be. But Saladin was a benevolent leader, with many charities established to help the poor. And her father's philosophy, she realized, mirrored Saladin's.

"Perhaps, Good Commander," Habib continued, "our sultan realizes what I do and why I do it, which is why he has given me his blessing to see this man saved. Our sultan is not confused, as you say. He has given me counsel on this matter."

"Has he also given your daughter his blessing to be touched and eyed so openly by infidels? Your prisoner, lying there, continues to look her up and down. If you're not careful, she'll become a wanton and a harlot, seeking the attention of men. First, your Christian Scotsman eyes her so openly, talking to her directly, and now, your Jewish physician…"

Nasim felt her stomach, dropping moments ago, hit the floor. She backed up a step, then another, panic welling inside of her. Both Abdullah and her father stiffened. Even Solomon stiffened, and glanced at her, if only briefly. She bumped into the sickbed, clenching the edge of the mattress with whitened knuckles behind her back to steady herself in the face of the horrible things her father's competitor said.

"Imagine, Commander Rachid, the proud protector of Jerusalem, having such a disgrace for a daughter—"

Metal sliding on metal rang out. Scimitars were drawn from their metal scabbards. And then, she heard a growling voice rumble from her father's throat, a frightening sound she had never heard from him before, as all of the men surrounding her postured in front of her to meet Faraj's confrontation.

"You had best—*never*—make mention of my daughter again," Habib threatened.

Nasim felt fingers touch hers, gently, reassuring in their grip. The blue-eyed infidel was squeezing her hand, as if hoping to pass her confidence or support—what, she didn't know. All she knew was that in the moment, it felt good. And instead of ripping away, for surely such touching, if discovered, would paint her even more guiltily in Faraj's eyes than before, she gripped him back, finding a moment of solace in the joining of fingers. There was no way this man, only days out from a life-threatening surgery, could protect her, and yet, his touch was comforting. It steadied her nerves, even if she grew more nervous than before.

"Solomon is a close family friend, and my daughter is an expert healer," her father continued, stepping forward, so that he came toe to toe with the other commander. "She is well on her way to being designated a physician. It is her job to take care of the sick and injured, and she does her duty to me and to Allah by using her skills for the good of others. She is pure, and you dishonor me, *friend*, by such a suggestion."

Habib turned to her brother. "Abdullah. Take your sister home. Solomon is just returned and can take over care of the infidel"—she ripped her fingers from Ewan's grip, clasping her hands in front of her instead.

Abdullah nodded once to his father, and Nasim hastened out of the chamber with him, without looking back. Her time being an equal with Solomon was over. And now, she truly wouldn't see Ewan's beautiful blue eyes again. As she entered her mother's atrium, she ventured out into the garden and plopped down beneath the shade of a cherry tree, breathing deeply the fragrance of their garden blossoming around her.

She closed her eyes.

Her heart ached restlessly. Why? Because she would now marry Kalim and her career would end? Because Solomon was back and making her confused? Because of Faraj's ridiculous claims that she invited men's attentions? Because the blue-eyed stranger would disappear back into a world she had never seen and never would?

She tipped her head back, resting it against the tree trunk as her mother came outside to join her, followed by a servant bringing tea. She dragged away her infernal veil, letting it slump around her neck so that her dark, curling hair could blow free. So often, she sought refuge behind her coverings. But right now, they felt entrapping. Her mother didn't speak. She simply sat beside her and wrapped an arm around her, and Nasim leaned over and laid her cheek on her mother's aging shoulder, swallowing at the thoughts warring through her mind and the upset churning in her gut.

***

The days seemed to pass in a blur. It had been a fortnight in this palace, and finally, blessedly, Ewan was being taken outside to enjoy the evening sun. He stood with the help of two men, who held him around his waist to keep him upright and steady. The male physician, Solomon, a match for him in height, assessed his movement, making notes on a long sheet of vellum. It had been more than a full sennight since he had seen Nasim. And blast it, but he missed her.

He shouldn't. They had never shared a conversation or gotten to know each other. And he was betrothed to Margaret Fyvie, while Nasim, as Solomon had been certain to tell him—for he, too, spoke the English tongue—was also betrothed. Odd, Solomon's face had pursed up in distaste as he imparted the news of her recent marriage contract. No, it wasn't odd. Ewan was every bit a man as this physician, Solomon, was. He knew the look on Solomon's face. Solomon was in love with his pupil, Nasim, and would never have her, just as he, Ewan, would never have her, either. He and Nasim had only crossed paths for a short moment in time, and now diverged on their own ways. He shouldn't be thinking on a strange, foreign noblewoman who he couldn't even see, as if longing for a lover he had never even bedded. And yet her voice, so soothing, her touch, both certain and gentle, her clothing, so flowing and colorful, and her smell, so fragrant. It was as if everywhere she walked, the scent of fruit and spices and fresh breeze lingered in her wake. And those designs drawn all over her wrists and fingers...they were beautiful. Artistic.

Nasim. He said her name over and over in his mind. It was such an interesting sound. One of the few times she had spoken to him, and the only time they had communicated with words, rather than charades, had been when she had told him her name and returned his bold gaze.

The sun blinded him. He dropped his head, moaning, and shielded his face from the stabbing of the light on his sensitive eyes. It mattered not that it was the warm glow of evening. His sunburn had faded, leaving him with a peeling tan, and the heat felt good and refreshing. He smelled Nasim so suddenly, his head whipped back up again before his mind could decide what to do. He looked around, his eyes watering while spots made his vision blurry, seeking a peek of her fluttering silks. But it was a trick. She wasn't anywhere around. There was an abundance of fruit trees and flowers in this garden, small insects and birds flitting to and fro. It smelled like her, he realized, and disappointment dampened his otherwise decent mood.

The men guided him across the earth, covered in grass, with flat stones used to pave a pathway. They moved slowly, careful not to upset his injury – *a tear in your lung*, Solomon had explained. Even now as he thought about it, he shook his head in disbelief. Nasim had successfully cut into him, found the injury, stitched it, and sealed him back up, all while preventing festering. For hours, he had been fileted open like a fish, his breathing organ exposed to the air. For hours, she had stood on her feet, meticulously finding the source of his injury, never once wavering in her concentration or determination to save his life. It was a miracle. When Solomon described what she had done, all he could do was furrow his brow and contemplate how such a surgery was possible.

They came to a tent, underneath which sat a table atop a rug bordered in ornate designs, and it was then he noticed Commander Rachid sitting there, sipping more of this drink they all consumed here. Tea. A boy stood nearby, and upon the two men from the infirmary helping him sit, the boy came forth and poured him a serving.

"You are healing well," the commander noted.

"I'm feeling better by the day," he replied, "thanks to your daughter. I am forever indebted to her. Such a wound where I come from would have been fatal. My thanks to you for calling her into service. It's my hope that I'll have an opportunity to thank her directly."

The commander nodded, his face impassive, and lifted his cup to take a sip.

"That is not possible. But I will gladly tell her of your gratitude. As I said, it is most uncommon for a woman of her rank to consort with men outside her family."

So no. You won't be granted one more chance to see her again, he told himself. Asking the commander was worth the chance, even if he knew his odds were slim.

"Your care up to now, I trust has been just as fine, too?" The commander changed the subject.

"Indeed," Ewan said, glancing to Solomon who stood beside him. "You have skilled healers in your land."

In honesty, he liked Solomon. The man was wise, intelligent, bookish, and had fine taste in women from what he could determine. He sensed that if they were in Scotland, the two of them would have been friends, for they had much in common. And since neither of them would be blessed with Nasim, the man posed no threat of competition to him. The way Solomon had touched her so freely, in front of her father, told him Solomon and Nasim shared a friendship. The way in which Solomon had entered the chamber the sennight before, with such exuberance, spoke of a man who would have swept Nasim into his arms had his common sense not stayed him at the last minute.

"I've called you here to discuss two things. As soon as you are deemed healed, you will be returned your weapons and given your horse to leave, along with a coin reward for your valor, granted you do me a favor in return."

Ewan looked askance, then back at the man. "In truth, Commander Rachid, though I am glad to know that none of your men or your sons met an end that day, I had no knowledge of what I had done. I'm more perplexed at my commander's violence toward me. I considered our relationship to be a good one, so his turn against me and the beating he administered has made me concerned. He left me for dead, when I had done nothing but try to do my job. I'll be grateful to leave with a horse, but no coin is necessary."

If all his possessions were returned from his saddle packs, then he would have coin within them. The commander considered him.

"I request that you make this map of Scotland for me. When all of this fighting has ceased, I would be pleased to learn more about it. You make this map and tell me about your land, and I shall grant your freedom."

Ewan thought about what the commander's intentions

might truly be. A siege on Scotland was ridiculous to think about. But why did he want to know about Scotland so badly? What was the harm in telling him?

"What is your interest in Scotland, sir?"

The commander smiled, knowing what he was getting at. "Trade." He sipped his tea. "Nothing nefarious. I seek to open a spice trade farther inland to Europe."

Ewan smiled too. "Indeed, you can nay get father inland than Scotland. My country is nearly the farthest reach, all the way on the opposite side of the continent and on a wide expanse of ocean that has no end. All right." He took a drink of his own tea. "I'll need parchment and ink. I haven't my cartography tools, so it will depict my best rendering of what I know to be true about the size and shape of our landmasses, and the way in which I've traveled here. Anything beyond that would be conjecture."

"Fair enough," the commander replied.

"I have some maps that I've created on this voyage in my saddle packs. I'd be obliged if someone would fetch those for me."

He took another sip. *Cardamom.* He was starting to recognize these strange spices and herbs, and to like them.

Nasim's father nodded once and summoned a servant to go and see about the maps, considering all of his effects, including items as benign as parchment, were under lock and key. He looked about the garden—an expanse of fruit-bearing trees and colorful blossoms. Birds tweeted and chirped, as if there was no war taking place. Servant boys ran on errands, delivering steaming pots of food. Important-looking men walked in dignified groups. A cluster of women walked together, clearly wives or daughters of someone ranking, for they, too, were covered across their faces, though they giggled and chatted among themselves. Instinctively, Ewan looked for Nasim's flashing gold anklet or decorated fingers, hoping to see a glance of her in the bunch. He didn't.

Odd, that never having seen her without her obstructive veil, he could still instantly recognize that she wasn't among them.

He sat peaceably and finished his tea, something the commander seemed inclined to do in silence, though his energy began to wane. The physician delivered him back to the sick room and ensured he was guarded, now that he could move about, before leaving to see other people with ailments and injuries. He reclined on his pillows, absorbing the solitude, and could hear Nasim reading aloud from her book as he drifted off to sleep. The call to prayer floated over the air and wound through the corridors, distant and muffled in his ears. His lack of strength was disheartening, however, he had made great strides, thanks to that woman. No doubt his strength would continue to grow. And then, he would be on his way back to Scotland from Jerusalem. The trek would take months, and he had no choice but to travel overland, through Anatolia, through Greece and Italy, through France... *To Margaret.* He was no longer sure how much appeal that held.

CHAPTER 5

One month later

Nasim glanced up at her half-sister, Fatima, the daughter of her father and his third wife, and Fatima's young son who was barely old enough to stand.

"Look at you smile!" She cooed, holding her nephew's hands and shimmying him gently, mimicking dancing.

The babe giggled, and both women laughed. It was good to see Fatima laughing again, for when she had first arrived, she had been on the verge of tears. She and her husband had argued that day.

"A message for you," a household servant said to Nasim, coming through the door and interrupting them.

Nasim looked up, then passed the child back to his mother and took the letter offered her. The servant left. She opened it. Disappointment infiltrated her thoughts and upset her stomach. Why wasn't her father giving her any information on the sick Christian? She had written to him thrice requesting to know how the infidel was healing, to determine if her work had been a success, but this was the first, formal reply in a month. *A whole month!* And it was vague.

"The infidel, Ewan de Buchan, leaves tomorrow morn. Your surgery was successful. Please do not ask after him again."

That was it. Did her father think she liked him? Did he see her requests for information as unseemly? For days upon days, she had envisioned his blue eyes. Had he fully healed? Had he thought about her? She needed to stop obsessing. Clearly, the

66

man had made a full recovery. She should be satisfied. Knowing such should indicate her expertise… Didn't it? She shook her head. A good physician would at least wish to know how the recovery had gone, to improve their learning in the future should they face a similar circumstance. *What future?* She thought wryly. *You know not if Kalim will even allow you to keep working.*

"What is it, sister?" Fatima asked as she lifted her mantle for the boy who crawled onto her lap and grabbed her breast to suckle it.

Nasim shook her head again. "It's nothing. The man I operated on is leaving. He is recovered."

Fatima's cheerful face brightened. "That's great news, Nasim. Your first surgery, under so much duress, I might add, was a success. Why do you look so forlorn?"

"What does it matter, if it was a success or not? I must still marry Kalim, and it's doubtful I will be allowed to continue my work. It is known that Kalim wants many children."

Heaven help her, but she and Kalim had been formally introduced a fortnight earlier, and he was even scrawnier, *and shorter,* than she had remembered. As he had looked at her, she had felt revulsion at the lust she saw in his eyes. To him, it mattered not that he couldn't see her face. He knew her to be young and virginal, and had practically unwrapped her clothing with his gaze. It made her think of Solomon's beautiful brown eyes and his gentle gaze in contrast.

And then of Ewan's blue gaze.

Fatima frowned, too, but was always optimistic, which was why she had chosen to call on Nasim after her marital discord. They always had cheerful conversations, and Fatima had wanted to be happy, not upset.

"Well, I'm certain the success mattered to the infidel. Just think, you've given him another chance at life that he certainly doesn't deserve, considering what side of the war he is on."

True, Nasim thought.

"Still, I had hoped to see him again."

Fatima's eyebrows raised. "Why? Didn't you say that Solomon told you that he was betrothed to a woman in his home country? Such wantonness is unseemly, Nasim."

"I don't mean it like that," Nasim replied, her eyes downcast at the letter, then glancing at her nephew nursing. That would be her in the near future, saddled with Kalim's babes, and while the idea of children wasn't a bad idea, the idea of Kalim with his knobby fingers groping her most certainly was, no matter how kindly he supposedly was with the women in his life.

"How do you mean it, then?"

"I only mean that he was my patient, and it was an important moment in my profession. I wished I could have remained caring for him, to see him recovered, and ensure I knew all the right steps to promote healing." She held up the letter. "But Father has told me I'm not to ask about him again."

Fatima smirked at her. "Because Father sees you growing attached to the stranger, and though he might have wanted to save the man's life, he most certainly doesn't want his only daughter with Ghaniyah to pine after such a villain. The man is a *Christian*, sister!"

"Pine after him? Truly, you misunderstand me!" Nasim gasped.

But Fatima was right. Because all of these things should appall her, and yet, she still wanted to see him. It made no sense. She knew nothing about him. She knew he came from Scotland, but didn't know what that really meant. Didn't know what he did for his livelihood. Didn't know of his family or friends. They'd never communicated, other than to exchange names.

"Not to mention, he is a warmonger."

"He isn't a warmonger," Nasim defended, even though she had just admitted to herself that she knew nothing about him.

Fatima smirked at her. "He came here with an army under the enemy banner. Warmongers. Infidel men bent on beastly murder and rape."

Nasim shook her head, but didn't argue it further. But she had touched Ewan, and felt his hand touch hers, take hers, hold hers in that moment of Commander Faraj's confrontation. Such a man couldn't be a warmonger, no matter the cause that had brought him to the threshold of the Holy Land.

And he had admired her. For days, she had slept on that

tiny cot in the back of the chamber, never once feeling unsafe, slowly weaning him off of her opium infusion—for such poppy juice caused many a man to lose their mind if imbibed continuously. Though his inspections of her were bold, they were almost reverent. And he had enjoyed her book, without understanding a single word.

Such a man just can't be a warmonger.

"I suppose what it really boils down to is that I'm curious. He's so…*different* from us. His language is so…*strange*, rough sounding, and yet, he doesn't strike me as rough at all. He was polite, when all we have heard of those Christians is like you say, that they are barbarians, bent on rape and murder. He seemed nothing like that. I suppose I wish I could see the places he has been. I wish to know of his world, as he knows of ours."

She sighed.

"His world is horrid. They are barbarians. And you should dismiss these thoughts, Nasim. Father would be most displeased to hear this from you. You ought to know by now that Father favors you. Because you are ambitious. He never gave us a choice other than to marry when he commanded it. But he has allowed you to refuse several proposals."

"Not really," Nasim shrugged, serving herself some tea from the ornamental tray beside them on the floor. She leaned back against the wall, her mantle slouching to her elbows. "He planned on marrying me to Kalim all along. The choice was an illusion. The only favor he did me was postpone the inevitable a couple of years, and I suspect it was to allow me to study a little longer."

Fatima clicked her tongue. But for the remainder of the day, Nasim brooded over the letter. As she sat with her mother that eve at supper, along with a couple of her older brothers who were not yet married with families of their own, all she could think was that this stranger was going to be leaving in the morn, and she wanted to say so much and ask him so much about the outside world and the far-off place he had come from, and she would never get the chance… *Unless I go to him.*

She clamped her hand over her mouth, just as the thought entered her brain. Her meat and vegetables fell from the flatbread in her hand, splattering her mantle.

Her mother and brothers looked up.

"What ails you, Nasim?" her mother fretted.

She swallowed. Had she done that? In front of them all?

"Noth-nothing." Nasim shook her head, wiping her fingers off and taking a linen to the sauce speckling her clothing.

"You look pale," Ghaniyah said, feeling her brow with her hand.

"I'm fine, really. I just remembered a gruesome image from one of Solomon's texts," she lied. "A torn muscle."

Her mother screwed up her face in distaste. Such wasn't always a welcome topic when they gathered around the silver trays and dishes on their mats.

"Nasim. Some of us don't like descriptions of human flesh whilst we eat," her brother, Malik, teased.

She stuck her tongue out at him. But as supper resumed, the idea spun in her mind. She could get into much trouble for sneaking about. She made trips by herself to visit her half-sisters and girlfriends living nearby unescorted, but that was it. But visit the infirmary alone? Madness. Her father would be angered at her.

Except the infidel was leaving in the morn, and she felt a sense of urgency that she couldn't explain, as if it were her last chance for something. Meeting Ewan had been so memorable, such a strange occurrence in her life. She had to try to see him. She could wear a coarse, beige mantle. She could attempt to look of lower birth than she was, remove her gold. Would that make her vulnerable to men who milled out and about, hoping to discover a girl for the night? She had heard of this happening, even if those guilty men were generally punished if caught.

But it was only to the infirmary and back, hardly a part of the city complex where such men lingered. *I'll go to Fatima's to ensure she and her husband have resolved their differences, for I've promised her I would check on her, and from there I'll go to the infirmary. If Ewan isn't there, I'll come straight home.* Who knew if Ewan even still remained in the infirmary? Perhaps he had been given quarters elsewhere. This was all such a foolish idea.

So why did it sound more appealing the more she thought

about it?

***

Guilt sliced through Nasim for the dishonesty she was committing as she pulled closed her mother's front door. She had never committed such a defiant act, never gone against the edicts of her parents. What if her ruse was discovered? Her plan was already in place. If her whereabouts were questioned, then Fatima would be able to honestly say that yes, Nasim had been there.

Upon leaving her half-sister's home, she peered around the corner, looking up and down the pathway, and saw no one close by. The sky was darkening, though wasn't yet dark, and the western horizon glowed orange as the bright orb of the sun sank low on the horizon over the city walls, still pock marked with injuries inflicted during Saladin's takeover of the city. She hurried along the path, weaving past buildings daubed and smoothed on the outsides, and turned toward the infirmary. She passed through the doorways and skirted along the walls, in the shadows, through the massive room lined with cots. Clutching her mantle to hide all clues to her identity, only a couple infirmary workers lingered. Many beds were empty and not a lot of extra help was needed. She ducked into the corridor and traveled along the tiles to Ewan's isolated chamber.

It was black, as if the corridor was abandoned. The farther she went from the infirmary, the darker it grew, whereas a couple well-placed lamps had lit the way when she had first been summoned to care for Ewan. Nerves flared in her gut.

She should turn back. This was nonsense! No light shone from beneath the curtain, and it was so dark in this forgotten hallway, she wasn't entirely certain where his doorway was. Clearly, he had been moved elsewhere. She wanted to slap herself for being so foolish. Why on earth would he remain here if he was healed? Ewan, no doubt, was being supervised under lock and key, now that he was mobile. She pulled back the curtain. Already, she could tell the chamber was empty, based on the sound. It was also cleaned and smelled fresh, ready for the next leper or contagious person who needed care and couldn't be allowed in the main infirmary to infect everyone

71

else.

She backed up, letting the curtain fall, and hastened down the corridor from whence she had come. *You are foolish, Nasim. Foolish! To attempt something so dishonest, so dangerous, simply because the Christian has pretty eyes.* That wasn't all of it. She wanted to see him living, breathing. See his body working and take pride in knowing she had put him back together again. *Your pride is another horrible thing! You simply helped, and should move on, and forget he ever existed!*

But in the future, when she was lying in bed, and Kalim was rutting upon her to make her pregnant, she knew she would have regretted not at least trying to see the infidel one last time. She might be confined to this tiny section of the vast world, but her mind was a free spirit. She wanted something different, as many experiences as she could get before she was nothing but a wife and a mother…and then only one of several wives…

And none of this made sense! The Christian had nothing to do with Kalim, nor had Kalim anything to do with her curiosity over the Christian. Except that Kalim represented her future, a boring, miserable place where a woman's intellect was buried and laid to rest, whereas this foreigner was all questions, intrigue, and different. Her mind was an eddy. She pushed back out through the infirmary doors, into the dusk that had claimed the gardens in front of the guest houses, and pattered through the trees to take the short cuts home.

She ducked her head, hurrying onto a narrow path paved with sunbaked bricks that wove between the guest houses, descending sharply toward a lower street, when she rounded a curve and slammed into someone. She jumped back, huddling against the wall, and looked up.

"Please forgive me. I wasn't being careful," she said to whoever the person was—a man, by the sensation of his tall, sheltering presence and his large, booted feet.

"Na…Nasim?"

Oh Allah above, forgive me! Her heart stopped. No, it galloped. No. It plummeted to her feet!

She knew the voice before she even saw the face. It couldn't be *him* in this darkening passageway. But it was. It was him. *Ewan.* The infidel. He was dressed in a plain, dark tunic over his *sirwal,* like the men in her land, though his feet were booted in leather from elsewhere, in a style from someplace foreign, probably his homeland of Scotland. His face was cleaned and shaved, and his waist was belted. The western horizon was purple and grey, taking with it the vibrancy of his blue eyes, but not the beauty of them, nor the intensity in them. She looked away again, every nerve on end.

Her father would be angered if he knew she was alone with this unmarried enemy in this surreptitious place. As would her mother. And her brothers. And her half-brothers and sisters. And should Faraj catch wind of this, he would drag her father's name through the mud at first opportunity, to see her father demoted and himself elevated, or, at least, to see her father humiliated. She felt sick and gripped her stomach. Yes, that was more likely. Her father had been instrumental in taking back the city of Jerusalem from the Crusaders and instrumental in keeping it under Saladin's control. He probably wouldn't be demoted, but he would likely be made to look a fool, something that would still tarnish his entire family's reputation. That Ewan, an infidel from the enemy camp, was walking around unattended, made no difference. There would be no escaping punishment now, no matter how mild her father seemed. What on earth had she been thinking?

"Are you all right?" he asked.

He said such strange words! What was he saying? Her mind spun.

She was going to be in so much trouble. And then, he took her arms. He did it gently, as if steadying her. She looked up, and for a moment, felt frozen. She clutched at her veil, trying desperately to think of how to escape this situation without being discovered. Heavens, but even in the twilight, his eyes were heart-stopping. And he was so tall. Like Solomon. Her forehead only reached the center of his chest. And his shoulders were broadly set, his belted waist tapering down to his heavy boots. He wasn't bulky like a warrior. No. Whatever he had done for the military, he didn't have the physique of a warrior whose robustness was a result of carrying so much heavy mail and armor.

And did she see something eager in his eyes? Was he pleased to see her? She felt herself nodding. She didn't know what he had said after her name, but the least she could do was acknowledge that he had addressed the proper person.

"Ew-an."

His mouth turned up into a handsome grin, revealing teeth that were kept clean and fairly straight. She had heard so much ill about the marauding Crusaders and their disgusting hygiene, that she was surprised to see such a kempt mouth. His sun burn seemed to be completely healed and he was out walking alone, meaning if he was a prisoner, he wasn't considered a threat... unless he was being watched.

Of course, he is being watched. Which meant, so was she.

"I have to leave," she whispered, extricating herself from his hands on her upper arms and darting away.

"Nasim, wait," he said, grabbing her hand before she was out of reach. She turned to look at him. "I want to thank you. You gave me back my health. Your hands, they worked a miracle..."

What was he saying? She was so confused, frozen, wanting so badly to speak to him and be in his presence, yet knowing she needed to run and run fast. And then he lifted her hand. She sensed nothing untoward, for he was so different. Everything he did was different. But he brought her knuckles to his mouth, leaning over them, and placed his lips to them.

The kiss was quick—he didn't linger with his mouth pressed to her skin, but his thumb caressed over her the knuckles he had just kissed so tenderly as he inspected the copper patterns. She gazed at him, dumbfounded—

"What is this?" Abdullah bellowed.

Nasim ripped her hand away and whirled around to see her brother running toward them, his scimitar drawn. Fury boiled in Abdullah's eyes. In a flow of dark clothing, he lunged at Ewan. Ewan grabbed her and dragged her behind him with an authoritative yank. To protect her?

"No, Abdullah!" Nasim cried as her brother lifted his blade. She jumped in front of Ewan. "Stop! Abdullah! Stop!"

"Get out of the way, Nasim!" Abdullah shouted. "This man dishonors you! And he'll pay for it!"

Ewan wrenched her aside again, shielding her with his body.

"You would risk injuring your sister?" Ewan shouted in reply, as more men began to fill the passageway, confused mutters, and unsheathing of blades filling Nasim's ears with commotion.

No one understood Ewan, but Abdullah dragged him apart from her, careful to avoid slicing her, and shoved Ewan's chest to flatten him against the wall. Ewan's face went grey with shock. Still, he shoved Abdullah back, wrestling with his wrist to keep the scimitar from his face, then jabbed his knee into Abdullah's gut. Abdullah grunted, winded, then sliced his blade with fury through the air, nicking Ewan's shoulder through his tunic before Ewan could deflect the blade.

"Abdullah, no!" Nasim screamed, grabbing her brother's sword arm. "You'll re-injure his chest wound!"

Abdullah whirled around on her, seething. She took a step back at the image of fury he created, towering over her. "He deserves to die for what he's done. Why are you defending him?"

"I'm not," she pleaded, crying. "I repaired this man's body. Don't murder him!"

"So we should keep him alive because he represents your pride? Medicine? That's all that is important to you." Her brother growled.

"No! What he did was forward, but he didn't mean anything by it! He doesn't understand—"

"He most certainly does!" Abdullah retorted. "He kissed your hand! Somehow, he lured you out here, hid away with you on this pathway without knowledge that I was put on patrol to watch him! He shames our entire family, Nasim, as do you!"

She froze, her eyes widening. Abdullah had never spoken to her so cruelly. He was her oldest brother, a man who had played childish games with her when she was small, simply to make her smile. Regret bloomed instantly on Abdullah's face. He swallowed, pain and anger swirling in his deep, black eyes.

"I'm sorry, Naz," he shook his head. "But don't you see what has just happened? You... you'll be found guilty..."

Abdullah trailed away, then turned back to Ewan who stood in a feral, wide stance, as if a lion ready to pounce on a challenger. His initial burst of anger was tempered by the same realization hitting Nasim now: if she were found guilty of any lewd behavior, there was no telling the punishment due her. It would be much more than her father meting out discipline. If a tribunal was involved—and there most certainly would be one considering the angry mob of witnesses surrounding them and jeering at Ewan now—she would be at the mercy of their dictates, as would Ewan. Did the foreigner even know his life hung in the balance? He seemed so tall, so strong in his will to heal, and yet, so naïve when it came to the way of things in her world.

Abdullah tossed aside his scimitar and whipped loose a knife. "I'll carve his heart out. You two, restrain him."

Two men emerged from the funnel of bodies closing in on them and filling the tight passageway. Nasim shook her head, tears wavering on her eyelids. "Abdullah, I beg you. Please spare him."

But Abdullah wasn't listening.

Ewan was watching the two men coming forth and studied Abdullah's knife. His eyes darted back and forth between the threats. "I can explain."

Again, no one understood his strange words. The two men grabbed his arms. Ewan ripped free, striking one, kicking the other, sending them both off balance. But they soon overpowered him, shoving his back against the wall in spite of his twisting.

"I can explain!" he bellowed.

Nasim covered her eyes to the obvious injury they were causing his chest. "Allah intervene, stop them..." She prayed.

Abdullah placed his blade to Ewan's throat. Both men's eyes bored into each other.

Nasim panicked and grabbed his arm once more. "Brother, I beg you!" He shook her off.

"Stop!" came a deep shout. Her father's voice rang along

the enclosing walls.

A hush fell over the gathering. Nasim saw her father's headdress pushing through the crowd. And then she saw Commander Faraj, along with several other military leaders in a string behind him, as if they had just been in a meeting. Her stomach flipped over, and all her color drained away. Faraj was gazing at Abu Abdullah Habib Abd-al Rachid's children and the Christian infidel, putting the clues together. His face rose in a slow, devious grin.

Abdullah showed no sign of backing down, though refrained from slicing Ewan's neck, as Ewan still strained against the burly grip of Abdullah's two men.

"This infidel deserves to die for daring to touch Nasim, Father."

"No, dearest Father!" Nasim fell to her knees in earnest supplication as Habib arrived beside them. "Please don't let him kill the infidel! It wasn't his fault. None of it was."

"Then why were you alone with him, here, in this dark alley?" Abdullah retorted. "How did he seduce you out of doors?"

"He didn't," she pleaded. "He didn't know I was here!"

Habib turned toward Ewan, all kindness he had seemed to feel for the man vanishing. He pushed Abdullah's knife away and gripped Ewan's throat, squeezing.

"Is this true?" he shouted in English this time, and Nasim wanted to scream that she couldn't understand. "You seduced my daughter out of doors?"

Ewan winced as Habib's crushing grip squeezed, though Nasim noted his posture had relaxed a degree. He wasn't fighting back against her father. He gulped madly, trying to expand his throat, take a breath, speak.

"Father, please," Nasim pleaded once more, her energy drained, and placed a hand on his arm. Habib looked down at the gentle touch and her soft words, then into her tearful eyes. She dropped her gaze to her feet. "This is all my fault."

The anger on her father's face turned to anguish, and he dropped his hand. Ewan gasped, doubling over as the two men on either side of him also dropped their holds, and braced his hands to his knees. He coughed, then palmed his chest where his surgery had taken place.

"Did he touch you?"

She nodded, her eyes still downcast. "But he didn't know I was here. I ran into him."

"How is that possible, for him to not know? What, he lured you out here by *accident?*"

Her father's words were incredulous. His disappointment in her made her chest ache. She took a deep breath, knowing so many eyes and ears were witnessing this, and knowing now that her life was over. What would happen to her for such a dishonor to herself and her family?

"I came looking for him in the infirmary, after I got your message that he was leaving in the morn. But I didn't see him and was hastening home after visiting Fatima, your daughter with Um Hakeem. We visited together tonight. I don't know what came over me."

Ewan was watching them, unable to understand by the confusion on his brow as he regained control of his breathing.

"This was my fault, sir," Ewan was saying. More foreign words she couldn't understand. "Whatever is happening, don't be angered at her."

"You stay out of this," Habib replied, jabbing a finger at him, then returned the full image of his scowl to Nasim and switched languages again. "Why did you disobey me? I wrote in my missive to you that you were not to ask after him again. What is going on between you two?"

"Nothing," she said, wiping her eyes. "I don't know him. I just...I...he was leaving...he was...I wanted to see him one more time! To know he truly was well."

She dropped down to her knees at her father's feet, placing her face in her hands.

Abdullah shook his head, staring at his sister. "Why, Naz?"

She shook her head, keeping her eyes buried in her hands. "I don't know... He was my patient. I was intrigued. I wanted to know about his world, places I've never seen, just—"

"He was kissing you. *I saw it.* He was holding your arms, and then he was kissing your hand—"

"What?" her father growled, his face raging with fury. "What?"

He turned back to Ewan, and spoke in Ewan's confusing tongue, his words low, soft, and menacing as he, now, withdrew a dagger from his belts and brought the point up to touch Ewan's throat. God above, Ewan was going to meet their maker. And it was all her fault!

"No..." She grabbed at her father's *thawb* and mantle, rambling. "Father, please, I sensed no ill-will from him. I beg you do not kill him on my account; he was kind, he didn't mean anything, I beg you—"

"Enough, Nasim!" her father barked. She froze at his anger. "Abdullah! Take your sister home and see her confined to her bedchamber. And meet me back in my council chambers immediately."

Nasim's lips quivered. "Father..." She burst into a sob. "I'm sorry I've disappointed you!"

"Rise, Nasim," Habib said. "Go to your chamber whilst I get to the bottom of this—"

"I'll accept your marriage suit without any further complaint, I promise this, and *inshallah*, I will be a dutiful wife you will be proud of!"

Habib paused, then squatted down and lifted her chin. And she saw pain on his brow when she finally returned his look. Though he was still stern, he was also afraid. For her. He whispered, "Go to your chamber, *azeezy*."

"Please don't kill him," she beseeched one last time.

Her father gazed into her eyes. "I might not have a choice." She took a deep, shaking breath, a sob about to wail from her throat, when he said put his fingers to her mouth to stay the sound, "*Go.*"

She nodded, water bubbling over her eyelids as her nose began to clog. She pushed to her feet and took Abdullah's hand, allowing him to lead her away. But if Ewan was killed because of her foolishness, she would never, ever forgive herself.

CHAPTER 6

"Sir, I *swear* that I had no idea this was a transgression," Ewan stated for the hundredth time, pacing in the corner of the commander's council chambers, adorned in mosaic tile and gold-engraved furniture. "I had no idea she would be out of doors. I went for a walk, as I've done for days now on Solomon's orders, to ensure I rebuild my stamina. I rounded a curve and she smacked right into me."

Commander Rachid's guardsmen eyed him, their hands at the ready on the hilts of their weapons should they need them. The commander himself, stood some feet away, his face grave. Ewan stopped pacing and faced him, gesturing for emphasis, for nothing seemed to be getting through to the man.

"When one greets a woman of high birth, when she shows a man simple kindness, it's customary where I come from to kiss her hand, in deference of her position." He swallowed again. "It's a sign of deep respect and honor, I swear it."

"Honor?" Habib said, rounding on him. "What honor is this that finds you hidden in a private passageway kissing her?"

"I swear it is true," Ewan repeated. "I know nothing of your customs. I had no idea it would cause her trouble. I didn't mean to dishonor you or her. But your son attacked me and I had to defend myself, and Nasim has been sent away, what, to be punished? The lass looked like an animal being sent to the butcher. What will you do to her? She did nothing wrong."

"Yes, she did," Nasim's father replied, and with resignation, he finally exhaled his anger. "She was out alone."

"And that's a crime?" Ewan argued.

He exchanged a glare with Nasim's father. The man, so formidable in stature, so proud in dress, and so commanding with his men, looked weary. Old. "It is, when she lied to her mother about her whereabouts, because the reason she snuck out, *alone...*" He hesitated, his glare deepening. "Was to find you."

Ewan paused. His brow furrowed. *Nasim wanted to see me?* The idea, in spite of the dire hour of his fate, pleased him, and his eyebrows shot up. "She wanted to find *me?*"

Habib sighed, then nodded. "She's been ever persistent to learn of your fate. If you *healed*, if your wound *festered*," he said as if reciting words he had heard over and over again. Ewan raked his hand through his hair. *Nasim was searching for me?* "I ignored her requests. Her interest in you concerned me. She's betrothed, and it's improper for her to talk so openly about another man, let alone talk *to* the man. I wrote to her today and told her you were healed, and you were leaving, and not to ask about you again."

Which meant Nasim, in spite of the confines of her existence, had a spark to her character. If she knew he was leaving, she knew she wouldn't have another chance to see him and took a risk to seek him out.

"But she repaired my lung. She saved my life. God worked a miracle when he guided her hands, for such an injury as mine would have been a death warrant otherwise. Why is she being punished for her concern?"

"Because I don't think it is only her concern as a novice physician that led her to sneak out to find you."

"Why do you think she did it, then?"

Habib shook his head. "She'll deny my words, but I believe you intrigue her. You're different, and she's fought me on her betrothal because that man is significantly less..." Habib looked away. "Less appealing to the eyes."

Ewan's heart skipped a beat. Nasim found him handsome? "*I* intrigue *her?*"

The idea swelled his pride. Why, he couldn't say. He had felt himself falling for her reading voice, for her healing ministrations, not her body or beauty, both of which he couldn't even see. How was that possible, to feel an attachment to someone he'd never once looked upon? It made no sense, but he still felt it. It didn't matter than he was betrothed. Margaret would satisfy him in the marriage bed and fulfill her obligations as the Lady of Dunwiddie. Just because he was due to marry her—if he ever returned, didn't mean he couldn't feel attraction to someone else. He simply needed to restrain his impulses, which shouldn't be hard, because Margaret was beautiful and lush and would do well to sate his masculine urges, no matter whose beauty inspired them.

"Don't you see?" Habib said, glancing at him. "You both are guilty. She is now impure. No one will know with certainty that you haven't had relations."

Ewan scoffed incredulously, his moment of happiness gone. "How on earth can you think that? It was a coincidence, nothing more, that caused us to meet there. *Fully clothed,* I might add, unless your men are blind in addition to daft."

Habib's brow turned angry at his words. "No one will know if that is the only time you've met! My family's reputation is now damaged."

"*Your* family?" Ewan spat. "*My* reputation, too, for I've *never* deflowered a lady. Ever. I was thanking Nasim. I was trying to be polite!"

He had lain with others but never virgins. Such was a big responsibility, and after the way he had been raised, he had never understood men who would do such a thing.

"You have much more to be worried about than your reputation, Ewan de Buchan," Habib said. "A tribunal is convening to determine that you should be killed."

"What?" Ewan practically roared. "Because I ran into a woman in a passageway and kissed her hand to thank her? I'd been denied the opportunity to do so, and when she suddenly appeared, I took advantage of the chance. I wished only to thank her, before I left in the morn to never see her again. What an absurd punishment."

"It doesn't matter, man! It looks bad. It looks planned. And it's not just your life that hangs in the balance. Nasim's does, too! She is my only daughter with my first wife. Do you realize how distraught this makes me? Makes her mother?"

"That makes no sense! Fine. If someone is going to be put to death over a kiss on the hand and a kind salutation, let it be me. I'll take the punishment if you'll spare her."

The commander sighed again, pacing away to a window to inhale a deep breath of nighttime air while the other guardsmen watched him, unaware of what their English words meant.

"I believe you," he said, his tone calmer, "that you knew not our rules and customs. It is improper to look upon, let alone touch a woman of status. And it is certainly forbidden to sneak off for a secret liaison."

"But sir—"

"Regardless, you have dishonored me and my daughter greatly. My people will not comprehend this misunderstanding between cultures, and she is worthless now as a bride for she will now be seen as unclean."

"How so?" Ewan argued. "That is the most preposterous thing I have heard. I would *never* dishonor any lady. I am the one who kissed her hand. It is my fault alone. I will gladly take any punishment meant for her if it will spare her such humiliation. My commander left me for dead anyway. What does it matter to my country, or to you, if I live or die? But don't allow them to sentence your daughter to something so brutal."

"You show honor…" The man was clearly thinking. When he wasn't glaring at him, the cogs in his mind were grinding. "Tell me, are you married?"

Ewan calculated him. "No," he finally replied. "Not yet. But I'm betrothed."

"Then you might be married soon enough if I can use my influence to sway the tribunal's minds."

Ewan shook his head, an anchor sinking in his gut. *What is he suggesting?* "What do you mean?"

"She faces death, exile, or a life secluded in the shadow of shame, and I cannot fathom any of those." The older man also shook his head, though Ewan could see the weight of the world resting on his shoulders. "And if she is allowed to live, knowing what dangers she might face alone if she is banished…" He turned back to Ewan. "She's never traveled, except with our household from Damascus to Jerusalem. She is young, and has no understanding of the ways of the world. I might not be able to get her out of a strict punishment, but if she is married off, her chances of survival would be best."

"To her betrothed, right? You would see her married to her betrothed?" Ewan asked, hedging.

"To you. Her transgressor. Some will demand I see her stoned. I cannot do it, and her betrothed will likely not want her anymore once he catches wind of this."

"What exactly are you saying?" Ewan replied, his eyes narrowing angrily.

He'd heard the words. But it didn't change the fact that he couldn't believe them. Forced to marry? It mattered not that he felt attracted to Nasim, even had looked forward to her company when she was treating him. He'd never seen her. She was of a different world. Different culture. Different religion. The churches would never approve. And he had never been forced to do a single thing in his life that he didn't want to do, except visit his father on rare occasion. And there was Margaret...

"If I can convince the tribunal to be lenient, will you marry her and take her back to your home country? It is the only solution, since you seem so *fond* of her, for if she remains and is allowed to live, her life will be over. She'll be shamed and shunned. She'll forever be seen as a scandal. Nasim will never practice healing arts again, and she'll whither and decay until her death."

"I won't marry her or anyone else I do nay choose. I'm betrothed to a woman in Scotland. Such a contract where I come from cannot be broken easily." Ewan fumed.

"Can you not have two wives?"

Ewan scowled. "It's *unchristian* to be married to more than one woman."

Habib's face hardened, a divide ripping open between them. "You will marry her, or you both could be executed for her moral dishonesty and your violation of her."

"I did not violate her!" Ewan exploded.

The guardsmen lunged forth at his angry outburst.

"Stop!" called Commander Rachid. The guardsmen surrounded Ewan, but didn't touch him.

"Like hell I'll be bent to this nonsensical dictate. I'm an earl, not some rich emir's puppet!"

"You may as well have violated her," the commander hurled back at him. "You are found alone, hidden, kissing her. She is now corrupted! Choose now. Marriage? Or take your chances with a death sentence? For I have pulled some strings to see you healed, and now I've been made to look like a fool! No doubt you will be used as an example."

"This is shite," Ewan muttered as he began to pace once more, running his hand through his hair, the pain from his injury when Abdullah had shoved him against the wall flaring again.

He put his hand upon the healed incision on his chest and took a deep breath. What would Lady Margaret think of him if he showed up back in Scotland saddled with an infidel woman veiled from head to foot through a wedding in a foreign land? He was betrothed, and knew Margaret well. She was flirtatious and beautiful, nosy and opinionated, so much so it was a nuisance. She enjoyed drinking wine and kissing him. Margaret was fetching, young, blonde-haired and blue-eyed, and genuinely excited at his suit, as she had been chasing him the moment she had reached womanhood. Her body was perfectly curvy in all the right places, with hips meant for childbirth. And she would know anger the moment Ewan arrived with the infidel woman as his wife. Then again, he had little hope of even living beyond this moment if he didn't marry the infidel woman.

And who knew what Nasim looked like with her infernal veil obstructing his assessment of her appearance. They could not understand one another. She was from a world so different than his. Would she ever be able to cope or integrate to life in cold and rainy Scotland? After only ever knowing this fruit and flower-filled paradise?

"You do nay understand the nature of a betrothal in my land," Ewan growled. "It's nearly impossible to break this contract."

"Then you choose death?" Habib asked.

"Shite," Ewan repeated again, rubbing the bridge of his nose while Nasim's father refolded his arms, his presence unrelenting. Did he even have a choice in this matter? No, not if he wanted to live. No, not if he wanted Nasim to be safe and protected. Odd, that at this exact moment of life and death, he should be thinking about the young woman's well-being more than his own.

***

Nasim sat dumbly in her chamber, her hair stringy. She hadn't bothered combing it, or fixing it, or doing much to care for herself since the night before when she had been confined. Life was over. She had been so foolish. *So very foolish.* What would be her fate? Stoning? Beheading? She was surprisingly calm, though she knew when the moment of her punishment was upon her, she would still probably scream and beg.

Please, Allah, allow it to be swift. At the very least, I beg you be merciful.

"Nasim," called her mother, bustling so suddenly into her chamber, she jumped. "Your father has come to tell you of your punishment. He awaits with your brothers. Come."

Nasim froze, then her eyes strayed to her mother's distraught face. The woman seemed as if she had aged overnight. She was already old, but she looked grey, sallow-faced, bags of anguish sagging beneath her eyes. Nasim had cried to her mother about all that had happened, cried to her half-sisters and sisters-in-law, but her mother had not been able to do a thing. Her mother had followed her father's command, and locked her chamber upon Abdullah escorting her there, leaving her within. She still remembered Abdullah's face. He had deposited her in her chamber, turned to leave, then whirled back to her and embraced her. He hadn't hugged her so fondly since she had been a small child riding on his back around their home while he pretended to be a horse. Such an embrace spoke of a dire fate. Whatever it was. She would know now soon enough.

"Hurry, Nasim," her mother fussed, prodding her. "Do not delay your father. He is a busy man and holds your punishment in his hands."

Together, they straightened her mantle and brushed away the creases in the fabric from sitting bent for so long. When she was decent, she was escorted to her father. She didn't bother with a veil. It was only family, and her modesty didn't seem to matter anymore.

"Daughter," he said, concern for the bedraggled image she portrayed flitting across his brow.

She stopped before him, dropping her dead eyes to the floor. She couldn't look at his disappointment in her. He didn't speak at first, but still, she stood silently, looking at her bare feet, feeling her mother clenching her arm so fearfully, her fingers were going numb from lack of blood flowing.

"I've gone before the tribunal, as has Abdullah, and pled for you," he began, his voice rattling from fatigue. No doubt, he had not slept much. "Commander Faraj demanded my demotion, and my morals investigated, but Saladin has been ever-deliberate and knows this doesn't reflect on my whole family, only upon you. I've assured him, and the remaining council, that I can handle this problem within my family, and that there is no need for their intervention…as long as I follow through on my suggested punishment. Therefore, I've decided: you are sentenced to marry Ewan de Buchan, the Christian, and Earl of Dunwiddie, for your transgression of indecent and lewd behavior, and come tomorrow morn, will be exiled."

At first, Nasim was not sure she heard him correctly. Then slowly, her head began to shake. It couldn't be real. Her mother started wailing beside her, clenching her, but she barely heard it. Married to one of the European barbarians? An infidel? Why not see her beheaded instead? There would at least be more dignity in it.

"I must act on this, Nasim"—she couldn't stop shaking her head, feeling her body lurch as her mother clutched her, cried out. There was no worse insult than being forced upon the infidel and exiled. It didn't matter that he was much better looking than Kalim. Blue eyes weren't a good reason for marriage. She might have felt attraction to Ewan, but she didn't know a thing about him. Sickness roiled her stomach at being handed off to an unbeliever. "I am Saladin's First in Command

and it's expected that my family will be perfect. This is the best option."

"But I am betrothed to Kalim," she whispered.

Her father frowned, his eyes filling with what? Sympathy? She wanted to laugh. "Kalim has heard of the incident."

She didn't need to hear more. Kalim did not want her now.

The panic hit her so suddenly, she hardly knew what was happening. She threw herself face down into the floor and held his feet. "Oh merciful father, please reconsider! Please reconsider!"

She fell to keening. Her mother collapsed beside her, holding her, crying supplications of her own. Her father squatted down to her level and took her arms. "Nasim—"

"I have tried to be obedient!" she persisted.

"Nasim—"

"I will do as you bid! I'd rather die! I'd rather never step into a surgery again. I'll do anything you ask!"

"Nasim!" he shouted.

She froze, her eyes red-rimmed and wet as she buried them in her hands.

"Nasim," he now croaked, his eyes closing in anguish as her mother beside her continued to cry and plead for her husband to spare their only daughter together.

He grabbed her, pulling her against his chest.

"I do this for you. Daughter, hear me," he stated, holding her to him as she cried. "It is the only way to restore honor, and more importantly, *save your life.* The tribunal called for you to be stoned, and Saladin assures me the decision will fall to them if I do not act. I cannot bear the thought of it." He caressed her cheek. She lifted her head and saw the full picture of his sadness. "You will be married this afternoon, and you will go with Ewan immediately into exile tomorrow. And that will be it. I'm sorry it has come to this, Nasim."

***

Her wedding was surreal. She sat still for hours, unable to crack a single expression. Her long hair, plaited behind her, was beginning to make her head sore the way it pulled on the roots. Fatima had done the styling and cried the entire time. As had her mother, as the women helped her into a white robe and mantle bearing her mother's delicate embroidery—her mother's wedding clothing, she realized, for there was no time to prepare clothing of her own.

Nasim felt a tear trickle over her eyelid but was unable to stop it as she stared at the somber gathering. No one was joyous. The men sent Ewan glares, hurled insults at him. He, too, sat grey-faced, his brow furrowed angrily and his eyes leveled directly at her, though she knew he didn't really look at her. He looked at nothing at all. He was simply trying to survive the moment, as was she. Her tears further saturated her veil. This was the ultimate dishonor. She would rather be stoned.

She would never see her mother or her half-sisters ever again. She would travel to a world so foreign she could not comprehend what the differences might be. Of course, she had wanted to see the world, and know what lay beyond these walls. But not like this. And tonight, they would have to consummate their union. What would happen? Fatima had been unable to speak of it, as had her mother. Fatima was convinced Ewan de Buchan was a rapist. Her mother was convinced he would be violent and ruthless, and that she would eventually either die from Ewan's heavy hand, or die of misery. What would she face in the bed chamber?

She avoided Solomon's face, seeing him among the onlookers. She sensed his eyes resting upon her and had made the mistake of looking at him when the ceremony started. He was grey-faced too. Eyes dead. Solemn and somber. It had hurt so much to see it. He was upset, if the wrinkles on his forehead were any indication, which only upset her more.

The ceremony finally came to an end. They sat beside each other now, yet, she felt miles away, as everyone filed past them. Her brothers passed by, making certain Ewan was aware of their hatred for him with their glares. Abdullah's eyes were narrowed, as if he would still slice Ewan's neck if given another chance to face each other in that passageway. But what hurt the most, was that none of them looked at her.

She was banished.

"Whore," came the insult, so suddenly, she flinched.

Kalim walked by her and spat at their feet. She felt Ewan stiffen beside her. He might not understand their language, but he understood the universal insult of someone spitting at his feet. She remained straight-faced and kept her gaze forward as though looking past him at the wall. To cower, or snivel, would only give the diminutive man satisfaction. Instead, she waited for him to pass, then felt Ewan's fingers snake into hers and squeeze.

And there it was again. His assurance. He had offered it when he lay practically paralyzed by his surgery, and he did it now, even though she had seen the anger brewing on his brow. In this tragic moment, it gave her one tiny shred of hope that her life wasn't completely over.

CHAPTER 7

Ewan unclenched his jaw, standing in the doorway to their private chamber for the night. It had been clenched so hard throughout the ceremony, he was surprised he hadn't cracked his teeth. "What's expected of me now?"

He looked over his shoulder at Nasim, standing apart from them with her head bowed as if she had just attended her own funeral.

"You take her to bed and have your way. Nasim's mother is here to watch for proof of her virginity."

"And if she fails the test?" Ewan asked.

Habib scowled at him as if he had just suggested a grave insult. "Are the women of your land not required to be pure when they marry?"

Ewan pried his lips apart barely enough to reply. "You, man, do nay get to be offended by such a question. For if you feel so certain her virginity is intact, you would have had no reason to force this sham of a marriage upon us."

Habib scowled further. "If she fails, I will have less say on the matter than the council. But if they allow her to live in the face of your rejection, her life will be one of shame, and she might just wish she were dead."

The weight of that hit Ewan like a boulder. Who would do such a thing? He might not want this marriage, but he could not allow such a horror to sit on his conscience.

"Then, sir, I shall be keeping her, regardless of her virginity. There's no need for her mother's vigil. If she's exiled, then consider this union binding now and go on your way."

The commander considered him, then finally nodded. Ewan knew he was proposing the best thing for Nasim, and was grateful that even in this strange culture, the commander was wise enough to see it, too.

"Two horses, a purse of coin, and a cart with provisions will be delivered to you before the first call to prayers, at which point, and by sun up, you need to be gone. Say nothing about the coin, for the tribunal did not want Nasim to have any means upon her banishment. Consider it a payment for the fine map you drafted for me instead."

Ewan nodded and shoved shut the door. It stopped on the commander's foot. He looked back at the man, seeing pain on his face.

"See to it that Nasim is cared for. Please."

"That *was* your concern, but is no longer, for as far as you know, you have thrown her fate into the wind. And it seems you have done so entirely without care for her at all. Leave us. You've done enough."

The commander conceded. Considering Ewan's mounting anger, it was wise of the man to finally leave. He shut and locked the door.

The two of them were finally alone. Nasim was still facing the other way, her head down. Some of Ewan's anger subsided as he watched her. His wife was just as unwilling, and she had done nothing wrong. In a matter of a day, her life was forever ruined.

He finally approached her, the tiled chamber silent, and the bed mattress draped in fine linen, partially concealed behind an ivory screen—a luxurious piece of furniture.

"Nasim," he said. It was the only thing he knew to say that she would understand.

She cringed at his voice.

His frown deepened, if such a thing was possible. He was certain his frown had been fixed on his face ever since Abdullah had assaulted him the night before. He turned her to face him and slowly unwrapped her veil, which fell and slackened around her hair.

His breath caught in his throat. And if he was still frowning, he was suddenly unaware. She was…lovely, in spite of her eyes looking sore from crying. Her skin was as smooth as cream. Her lips were full, her nose, slender but even. And God, but those eyes, such dark, brown pools they were more like obsidian, surrounded by an abundance of long eyelashes that created the image of kohl even though she wore no makeup.

And I had thought she might look like a horse, he thought, fool that he was.

He had just been saddled with a veritable beauty who would surely make the women of Dunwiddie jealous beyond reason, assuming they ever made it back and his estates hadn't already been parsed apart by the crown. Especially Margaret Fyvie. Damnation. What on earth was he going to do about everything? Margaret was going to be furious. And he didn't necessarily blame her. He had made a promise to her when he signed those betrothal papers so long ago. He supposed he could always set Nasim up with a household in the country, and marry Margaret. The churches wouldn't see this situation as valid, and so, he would get away with such an arrangement. He had the money to furnish Nasim nicely for the remainder of her days.

But for some reason, the thought seemed insincere, dishonest. None of this was Nasim's fault. Why punish her with yet another exile in a hidden, country estate in a foreign land when she had already been shunned by her family? And it mattered not the religion. He had just taken vows, forced or no. He had still had a choice. He could have chosen the chopping block. No. Nasim was his wife. Whether either of them liked it or not.

He began to unwrap her mantle from her figure, realizing that she had a fine one. Slender, yet lush in all the right places. But the fear in her eyes told him she knew what was coming. He guided her to the bed behind the screen and saw her seated. She was shaking, her face having gone ashen. There was no way he could bed a scared, unwilling lass. She would need to give herself to him in time, when she was ready, and he did his best to ignore the heaviness burgeoning in his trousers. Shame upon him, but he didn't even know how old she was, and he quickly looked away. What if she, by Scottish norms, wasn't ready for marriage yet? Clearly, she was young. *Nay, she's old enough*, he reasoned, *for how can someone too young for marriage gain so much experience as a physician? Or possess such womanly curves?* She had the figure of a woman, and the expertise of a physician who had trained for a long time. She was young, but she wasn't a child anymore.

He dragged a pillow and linen free from the bed and went to a hearth where a fire blazed, and laid them out. Nasim was sitting across the chamber from him, watching him, he could feel it. He sat, pulled free his boots, and removed the belt, mantle, and tunic he had been given to wear until he sat shirtless, in nothing but the long pants afforded him, the scar from his surgery still bright and blazing like a beacon on his chest and the nick in his shoulder from Abdullah's blade, gotten only the night before, still crusted with blood.

"Please," she said in her own tongue. He had no idea what she was telling him, but as he glanced over at her, he saw fear upon her face. "You mustn't sleep apart. You must do this."

He gazed at her, his blue eyes sizzling her with intensity as he tried to decipher her words. She began to pull free the veil that had slackened around her shoulders. Her hands shook and tears renewed in her eyes, she reached down to the hem of her robe and began to drag it free.

He moved swiftly to his feet and closed the gap between them as she revealed the skin on her belly, and grasped both hands so that the robe dropped back into place.

"No," he shook his head.

"But they will see me stoned!" she cried, falling to her knees before him to beg. "Please do this. Only tonight. I don't want to die!"

He furrowed his brow, unable to understand. She began to motion frantically, as if stones were being thrown at her. The charades were confusing at first until he finally put the act with the words the commander had said. *She thinks she might be punished if she doesn't appear to be chaste…she doesn't know I'm keeping her.*

He shook his head with complete understanding and held his palm up to her to stop. He sliced his hands through the air as if to say "cease." "You are now with me. Forever," he continued, squatting down. He touched her, and then placing his hand to his own chest to suggest ownership.

She didn't seem to understand, and sakes, but he couldn't think of another way to convey his point. He stood back up. She grasped at his pants. Confused, he paused again, until an idea struck him. He shook her free and looked around. He went to the hearth and found a metal prong for poking the fire, the only sharp object he had since his weapons hadn't yet been returned to him, and proceeded to use it to gouge the inside of his lip. Nasim watched in mute concern.

He then took a sip of water from a decanter, swished it in his mouth, and came back to the bed where he gently spit the bloody water onto the center of the sheet, creating her 'proof' of virginity. Realization dawned on her brow and she simply stared at him.

"Go to sleep," he said, looking at her impassively. "'Twill be an early rise for us."

With that, he motioned her to lie down. Then he went to the oil lamp and extinguished the flame. He returned to his make-shift bedding in the dimness that had settled around them and stretched out on his back, not once looking back at her for fear of making her more nervous. He didn't need to look, anyway. The striking beauty of her face and the supple curves of her body remained branded beneath his eyelids. Lady Margaret might have been deemed a beautiful woman, but his unwilling wife was breathtaking.

He felt himself growing aroused again, yet made no move to find a more comfortable position, hoping it would soon abate. If he were honest, it wasn't the first time he had felt the urges of attraction toward her. Somewhere deep down, he had known she was beautiful, by the gentleness of her hands, the learnedness in her voice, and the beauty in her dark eyes. Somehow, it wouldn't have mattered if he had unveiled her and found her to indeed look like a horse. He already liked her, for her talents, nay her body. Yet lust for a woman he did not know and could not understand made no sense. And she hated him. He could see it in the way she cringed from him, felt her sadness surround him like a dark blanket as he watched her cry throughout their wedding. Mayhap, with time, they would warm to one another. Only time would tell.

***

It was early morn when Nasim roused to knocking on the door. She had hardly slept, and for a moment, thought the ordeal of the past day was only a nightmare. No. Ewan, shirtless still, was already rising from his bed on the floor to answer the caller. She pulled her mantle around her head and face, but no one came inside the chamber.

She studied Ewan from the safety of the bed. Confused. Why had Ewan rejected her last night? Not that she was complaining. And of all things to be worried about right now, when the moment of their exile was upon them, it was ridiculous that she should feel disheartened by his lack of interest. Had she cried too much and made her eyes too red? Was there some imperfection that he saw? Was he simply not interested in a woman so different from the ones in his homeland?

His expression of anger hadn't cracked since she met him at their ceremony the day before. She supposed some of that might be due to his military experience as well as the fact he was surrounded by her father's men who wished only to murder him. No doubt, his guard was alert. That, and it was clear he hated this marriage, too. Would he ever smile at her again, as he had in that passageway when they had run into each other? As he had when he had watched her from his sick bed, listening to her read?

Ewan closed the door and turned, a purse in hand, as well as a thick bundle of cloth and a straight and massive sword. She had never seen one like it before.

He turned to her, studied her, and spoke in his foreign tongue as he tossed down the bundle and lit the oil lamp. "It's time to leave."

His face looked ill-shaven in the light of the lamp, and yet there was a handsome quality to the set of his stubbly jaw. He turned his attention back to the bundle and unrolled it to find what she could only assume were his old clothing, his daggers, and a rolled piece of parchment. She watched him unfurl it, his face furrowing with a dark chuckle. It was a broad, detailed map. Of what, she couldn't determine from her vantage.

He shook his head, muttering, "Rachid returns everything in exchange for me taking his daughter away over a meaningless kiss on the hand. Should I be honored or insulted?" He scoured his hands over his face, as if he hoped to scrub away a bad dream. "For fok sake…"

She didn't need to understand his words. He was still angry. And had absolutely no recourse. He finally began rummaging through everything again, and pulled loose a wrapping of beige and blue fabric. Another outfit for her. Though the confounded look on his face told her he didn't know what it was or why it had been given to them.

But she knew. Her wedding was over. There was no sense in wearing her mother's beautiful wedding embroidery anymore. She had disgraced it enough. The way her mother had cried as she helped her don it, told her she was saddened and disappointed. Nasim got to her feet and took the clothing from him, glancing straight-faced at Ewan as she slid the fabric free of his fingers. She only noticed him glancing at the swirl of fabric encasing her after she was securing the veil across her face.

And for one, curious moment, the anger that had perpetually furrowed his brow since their wedding, was gone.

The sun had yet to rise, but two horses, one that looked to be a European breed, for it was thicker, stockier, than the ones Saladin kept in his stables, and a cart of provisions were at their door. Nasim followed Ewan from the earthen-plastered apartment and let him lift her onto the saddle of the other horse harnessed to the cart. She had never, in her whole life, been touched so intimately. He paused, his hands upon her, his face stoic, and his eyes staring at her stomach, as if staring right through it. And she realized, in her anguish, she hadn't thought much about him.

He was betrothed in his homeland. Perhaps he wasn't just angry. His world had been tipped on its head, too.

***

It wasn't the first time Ewan had felt lost in thought. Ever since Abdullah had attacked him, he had felt as if all of this was surreal. He tried to make sense of the past day as he stared at the beige tones of Nasim's clothing, staring at nothing at all, feeling the curve of her body beneath his palms. None of this was what he had bargained for when he had come naively to the Holy Land to fight in the Pope's Holy War. But this was his reality, and dwelling on how angry it made him to be forced into matrimony wouldn't keep either of them safe or see him returned to Scotland.

No doubt, news of his death would reach Dunwiddie long before he did. And he felt certain that the fact he was left for dead by his commander would be a fact officially omitted. Pray that his estates were still his upon his arrival. God in heaven, what was he going to do with this woman? He looked up at her. Her eyes were so sore, so tired, even though she no longer cried. In that moment, he made a vow. He would make the best of this for her sake. She needed someone to be strong for her, and he was the only soul she had.

Ewan finally dropped his hands and mounted, took her reins, and led her horse and the cart it pulled beside his mount through the labyrinth of paths, between the earthen walls rising like windowless cliffs on either side of them. Finally, at the gates to the city, just as the sun tried to crack over the horizon in the east, the guard who had led the way opened a tall, wooden gate, waited for them to pass through, then heaved it shut behind them, clanking the lock. The wailing from the minaret called the faithful to their *Fajr* prayer.

And when Ewan looked at Nasim, she doubled over her horse's neck and cried the most mournful, long, wail he had ever heard. His heart cracked. How could it not? This skilled woman had been thrown to the dogs as if her skills meant naught. How would he have felt, he thought, if his family had suddenly exiled him?

In a way, his father had, from the day he was born. He reached out, took her hand, and squeezed it in his. She looked at their hands, then up at him.

"I'm sorry," he said, and he tapped his horse into a walk.

***

Habib, escorting Ghaniyah, arrived at the wedding chamber of his daughter. They entered the room, finding the pillows and sheets neatly in place and folded. Ghaniyah clutched her wedding garments, also folded and left behind. In the center of the bed was a dried stain. Habib nodded sadly. The deed had been done. His daughter had been pure and was now gone forever. The burden of the action he was forced to take weighed down on him, but he had misjudged how much it would distress his wife. She collapsed beside the bed, saw the mark, and began to sob.

"Nasim!" she cried. "Nasim!"

She upturned her head toward the heavens and outstretched her hands, then doubled back over the bed again as her mournful cries filled the silent room.

"My daughter is gone!" she repeated, over and over again. "My only daughter!" and the commander reached down and collected her in his arms to lead her away.

Ghaniyah shoved his hands off her, refusing to look at him, and left, cradling her wedding garments. Slowly, he moved to the door behind her. Never before had Ghaniyah rejected him. Not once had she been cold to him. His heart already ached at the loss of their only daughter together. And now, it ripped apart.

CHAPTER 8

"Five coins? Too much," Ewan argued, shaking his head.

He withdrew his hand just before the merchant, his head wrapped in a turban and skin like wrinkled leather from living a life in the elements, took the five coins he had separated out. Ewan looked on at the flat breads, apples, and dried dates hanging from the man's camel longingly. It had been three sennights since he and Nasim had embarked on this journey, and he had opted to continue wearing the tunic, mantle, and *sirwal* Solomon had furnished him in Jerusalem. The clothing made more sense in this part of the world, and otherwise, he and Nasim would make a mismatched pair, rousing suspicion and questions. As it were, with his skin now bronzed and his hair naturally dark, few gave them much of a passing glance. But they needed food. Some of their provisions were already used up.

And blast it, but I can nay communicate a single damn word. This merchant was going to cheat them and overcharge for his food. And Ewan would have to pay it. He rubbed the blazing sun from his eyes, pulling his mantle over his forehead for a bit of respite.

The merchant rattled something off. He stared at him, watching his wild gestures. The man was irritated, obviously, the crow's feet at his eyes crinkling all the way to his temples. Why? Because Ewan wanted to protect the precious coins he had? They would have to charter a ship across the English Channel, assuming they ever made it to Northern France. He couldn't spend all his money in the first three sennights of travel.

"Too much," he tried again, interrupting the man. The man held up five fingers, gesturing. "Bloody hell," he muttered, succumbing to withdrawing the five coins, when Nasim stepped up beside him. She placed her hand over his, staying his payment, then turned to the man.

The words that rolled out of her mouth, he only wished he could understand. She gestured. Her tone was sharp, and her eye contact, direct. The old merchant's face dropped at her harsh rebuke. Then paled. Then he bowed his head profusely, over and over again. Nasim took the bundle of food stuffs the man now held out, twice the amount than he had originally offered, and Nasim then plucked three coins from Ewan's palm, depositing them into the merchant's outstretched fingers.

She gave him a curt nod, then averted her eyes from Ewan as she handed him the breads and fruits. The merchant climbed back up onto the camel's back, into a saddle decorated with colorful tassels, and urged the beast to move with a crop and some foreign words. Ewan stood still, stared at the man leaving, then turned to stare at Nasim now waiting dutifully beside her horse for help remounting. When he didn't come to her, she turned, her eyes shy. His face split into the first smile he'd brandished since that fateful night he and Nasim had smacked into each other.

He walked to her, held up the bundle, then lifted her hand and kissed it, still grinning. Whatever she had told the man, she had clearly evoked some sort of authority over him. He chuckled.

"My thanks, my lady. I must have seemed like a bumbling fool."

Nasim's veil obstructed her face, but she giggled, and the way in which her eyes rose told him her smile lingered. He felt his heart opening to her. He couldn't help it. She hadn't cried again since the morning they'd departed Jerusalem's gates. She had shown amazing resilience during a time when her heart had surely been breaking. And he wanted to kiss her. He wanted to dip his head to hers and kiss those lush lips she kept hidden behind her veil. Had she ever been kissed? Probably not.

Kissing might not even be something people did in this land.

His smile softened and he released her veil, pushing it aside and tucking it back so that her face and neck were exposed. She ducked and turned away from him, but he stopped her with a hand on her shoulder, turned her back, and let the full impact of seeing her hit him.

Beautiful.

He brushed his thumb across her chin, grazing her lower lip, watching blush rage red across her cheeks, watching her dark eyes dart to and fro before they finally settled back on him. He didn't kiss her. He dropped his hand and lifted her back into the saddle, his palms spanning her petite waist, leaving her face exposed, then offered her food. She hesitated at first, but he offered again, and finally she took some dried dates. Normally they would wait to sit before they ate, but he knew she was hungry. He certainly was.

They continued northward. Navigating this land was more of a challenge than he had anticipated, for he and his horse had originally arrived upon a ship. There were no taverns as there were in his homeland, where they might find shelter. He had taken to setting camp in secluded spots, to avoid the armies making occasional treks nearby. Twilight was setting in. Soon, it would be completely dark. The glow of the setting sun across the rocky hills and a scraggly copse edging a pond seemed like an oasis. He pulled back the reins on his mount, dropping Nasim's reins, and helped her down. She spread out a blanket while he unharnessed the horses and took their water bladders to the pond.

The water flowed with gentle bubbles in the middle, indicating it was fed by a spring and therefore probably clean. Water insects hovered here and there and the frame of the trees against the setting sun created a vision, so different from Scotland, and yet, it was the same sun here as the one at home.

He stood back, bladders dripping, and closed his eyes. He had not slept soundly since departing Jerusalem, for fear of someone of authority coming upon them. But he was already so tired.

A scream pierced the air. Ewan's eyes whipped open at the

sound of Nasim's fear. He bolted back through the trees. If some traveler was molesting her or harming her, visions of what he might do to them flashed through his mind like lightning bolts. He skidded to a halt, dropping the bladders with a splash, and saw her arm outstretched, a scorpion perched midway up her sleeve.

Despite her panic, she was holding her arm perfectly still.

"Nasim, hush," Ewan said. "Hush now." He held his finger to his lips.

He had seen a man die from a scorpion the year before outside of Istanbul when he'd failed to check his boots before dressing for the day. The critter had pierced his foot and the man, miles from any form of civilization, had died a slow death.

He pulled free his sword from his horse's packs, heart hammering his ribs, and extended it. Nasim withheld her cries, her eyes so wide he could see the whites brightly. He crossed himself out of habit, then slid the point of the sword beneath the scorpion, flinging it off of her. He followed it to its landing spot and whipped loose his dagger, chopping it in half.

Turning back to his shaking wife, he tossed down the blade, grabbed her arm, and shoved the layers of silk up past her elbow to examine her for a puncture wound. Rubbing his finger up and down her arm, his brows furrowed as he searched. He looked up at her.

"Did it sting you?" he asked, motioning his finger like a scorpion tail darting against her arm.

To his relieve, she understood his meaning if not the words, and shook her head.

"*Laa,*" she said, throwing a frightened look at the mangled scorpion.

Laa, he thought. *That must mean "no"…* and he drew her into his arms to hold her.

She didn't resist him and in fact, seemed relieved, wrapping her arms about his waist. He rested his chin upon her head and then placed a kiss upon it. Her willing embrace felt bloody good, the first time she had returned his affection with her own. She drew back enough to look up at him, resting her hand upon his chest, and he reached to her fingers and placed that damning kiss upon them again, never once letting his eyes stray from hers.

***

Nasim's breath caught in her throat. Ewan's eyes, still so serious and guarded, shimmered with energy. The feeling of his lips on the back of her fingers still lingered, making her skin tingle with a sensation that was surely a sin and an indulgence. If his kiss had not meant to damn her before, it was certainly damning her now, for she felt those shameful flutters in her stomach. When he finally ended the kiss, he reached to her face to brush a callused finger down her cheek. She shivered, but it had nothing to do with a chill. It had nothing to do with unease. She was growing to relish his touch. These occasional moments of affection had kept her grounded, when all she wanted to do every day was rock and cry and mourn the loss of her life, her medicine, her family, her mother, her sisters...

She searched Ewan's eyes for meaning, feeling his chest rising and falling as rapidly as hers. She could feel his heart thump beneath her palm. He had truly feared for her, and the revelation that he cared about her in spite of all that had happened, meant something.

"You don't need to be afraid of me, Nasim. I wish I could make you understand."

He said the words, and like always, she knew not what he had said. They hadn't communicated at all, except with frustrating charades. He guided her through the trees to the water, a sudden purpose seeming to pop into his mind. The sun was just barely hovering over the western horizon and quickly falling. The water looked dark, the ripples crested in silver from the sideways slats of light filtering through the scraggly trees. The sky above them turning from purple and orange to dark blue. He scanned his hand in a slow panorama, then looked at her and quirked the corner of his mouth into a smile. She stared up at him, then smiled too. She loved his smile, the way his chiseled jaw growing shaggy with stubble looked as his cheek dimpled. It was boyish, even though he was every bit a man much older than herself.

"Beautiful," he said, looking back out onto the water.

Whatever he had said, she wasn't sure if he was saying it about her, or about the scenery, but she looked out at the landscape, as he had. It was, indeed, a lovely spot. She had seen the sun set time and again, and yet, out here, unobstructed by buildings and with the sounds of insects around them, it was almost magical. And for one, tiny sliver of time, Nasim was thankful she was finally seeing the world. She just never imagined doing so would be under such circumstances. And she never imagined she might find a moment's pleasure ever again, until now.

Ewan knelt and splashed the water, lifting it in a scoopful and letting it trickle through his fingers.

"Water," he said, pointing at the substance on his skin. "Water." Then he pointed at her, lifting his brow in question.

Her face brightened. She remembered the word from when he had begged a drink while abed in the infirmary. She nodded, also kneeling. He was trying to communicate.

"*Maa,*" she said, then also dipped her fingers in it, holding up the wet tips to his eyes. "*Maa.*"

"*Maa...*" he repeated. "Water."

Her face broke out into a wide smile. He seemed to freeze, his eyes darting to her mouth. She brought her hand up to cover it. Surely such a big grin looked grotesque. But Ewan didn't seem put off.

"Wa...ter," she said, her tongue rolling on the R.

He nodded, and picked up a rock in the water. "Stone. Stone." He handed it to her.

She said it in her tongue.

He grinned and repeated it, the smile making him glow. The man was entirely too handsome. A far sight better than Kalim. An equal in both looks and kindness to Solomon. She thought on her tutor, a taste of sadness tainting this moment. She had spent so long pining for him. And now, she didn't know what to think. She looked back at Ewan's sparking eyes and tall physique. At least one request in a forced marriage had been granted.

Oblivious to her thoughts, Ewan walked her around the oasis, touching leaves, tree trunks, pointing out insects, clouds in the darkened sky, the emergence of stars, sharing the words in their own language and making easy sentences. And somehow through the walking and talking, they ended up back at the water's edge.

He smiled at her. She returned it. The sky was now black, though the land glowed from the expanse of stars and the bright moon. He reached to her face, brushed a strand of her dark hair back, his thumb brushing over her lips as he seemed wont to do whenever he grew pensive. He looked at her lips often, and when he did, he appeared to exude desire and regret. He spent a lot of time thinking, she realized. As did Solomon.

"Kiss," he said, his voice low and gruff. She knew he was going to kiss her this time, before his head dipped to hers and his lips pressed against hers.

She stood rigidly, unknowing of what to do. Her heart leapt and her stomach buzzed. She felt off balance and yet, felt planted like a pole. He guided her, patiently brushing his lips against hers and breathing deeply, as if drinking her scent. She had to smell horrid from three sennights without a proper bath, but he didn't seem to notice.

Slowly, she began to kiss him back. He exhaled, wrapping a long arm around her, pulling her flush with his firm chest so that her breasts were pressed to him. She sighed. There was an attraction between them. It hadn't just been her imagination. It hadn't just been a one-sided feeling. She had been attracted to him since the first moment she had seen him lying on the sick bed, ever since he asked her to read, ever since he examined her body designs and admired them. He was attractive, not just for his kindness, but for his interest, for his differences, for the freedom from the confines of her existence that he represented. And for the first time since leaving home, she felt possibilities, realizing fully that she embarked on a future unlike any other she could have imagined. Who knew what would become of his betrothal to the woman in his homeland? Likely, he would take two wives, perhaps more, but right now, in this moment, they had a future. And she looked forward to it, even if she still cast a sad glance behind her at the past.

He slid his other arm around her and deepened his kiss,

nudging her lips apart with his tongue.

"God, Nasim," he murmured against her lips.

Her breasts tingled, pressed into his hold as she was. He kept kissing her, deeper, his tongue laving over hers, encouraging hers to return the gesture. And when she finally did so, he groaned, bearing down, as if he couldn't get enough.

He finally separated, leaving a trail of pecks up her cheeks, onto her nose, then looked down at her. His lips were moist from the kiss, and both trust and confusion warred through her mind. She must look dazed. He lifted her fingers to his lips, then placed his mouth once again to her knuckles. Her eyes fluttered closed for only a moment, remembering all the feelings she had experienced when he had done such a thing before, and realizing now what the nervous feeling was that she had felt: pure, intimate attraction.

"Kiss," he croaked again. Then he dipped his head and brushed his lips once more across hers.

"Kiss," she whispered.

The corner of Ewan's mouth lifted again. "Aye. And bloody perfect at that," he whispered.

***

Ewan gazed at Nasim's gentle smile, and felt his heart open an inch further. He envisioned a future with her as the matriarch of Dunwiddie, not a future of damnation. He still didn't know what to do about Margaret, but he had plenty of time to figure that out. Obviously, he would have to beg out of the contract, and hope that her father agreed, for there was no way his marriage to Nasim would be seen as legal in his land. The legality of his forced marriage wouldn't matter if he weren't engaged. But he was. So it did.

And he was fully aroused. It had been over two bloody years since he had been given service apart from what his hand could give, for there weren't an abundance of tavern wenches in this land for taking care of men's needs. Each hitch of her breath had made him want to lay her down on their blanket and finally consummate their union. He should be embarrassed, for there was no way she could ignore his readiness to mate, pressed together as they were.

Yet he wouldn't ruin this special moment for any amount of rutting. He felt a connection forming, *and be damned, but it feels wondrous*. He'd certainly never expected to have a connection with Margaret, and he sensed Margaret didn't really want one, either. But there was something about Nasim, about her resilience and intelligence, that was sucking him in.

They turned back to the pond, listened to the insects, and watched the water ripple with dark reflections. He placed his hand around Nasim's shoulder and pulled her against him so that her head rested on his chest, protecting the scar she had made when she'd saved his life, and he wove his fingers into her hair. They stood together in companionable silence.

CHAPTER 9

Northwestern Scotland.

"Rider approaching! A messenger bearing the colors of St. George!"

The portcullis was cranked, metal grinding as the chains hoisted up the heavy gate, and the rider, decked in a St. George cross upon his white surcoat sullied by travel grime, rode into the outer ward of Dunwiddie Castle. His mount panted into the cold air, as waves from the Minch could be heard crashing in the distance.

"To whom should I deliver news in the absence of Lord Ewan de Buchan?" the rider asked as a guardsman strode to him from the barbican.

"To the castle steward, sir," said the guardsman, a burly man named Hamish sporting a rough, chestnut beard.

"And is he currently in residence?"

"Aye," Hamish said, "Colin Donald is the man ye want."

"And where might I find this man Donald? For I have an important missive needing delivery. News from the Holy Land."

"Up there," Hamish replied, pointing up the path leading to the inner battlements. "He resides in the castle and is typically found in his offices. Is Laird Buchan returning to us?"

The messenger shrugged. "I know not the contents of this missive, only that I was sent from Westminster to see it delivered. The journey has been long, but I am sworn not to open these correspondences."

Hamish nodded once. "Ride on through, man, and good

day to you."

The messenger nodded in reply and tapped his sweaty horse into a trot. The inner gatehouse also gave him entrance, and as he rode to a halt and a groom came out of the stables to see to the horse, the rider dismounted and climbed the steps.

"I seek Colin Donald, your trusted steward, with news from the Holy Land," he said to the guards manning the main doors to the keep.

"Indeed. Come in whilst he is summoned," the guard said, pulling back the door, while another sentry retreated within to locate Colin.

The messenger entered and walked to the hearth where a maidservant offered him a refreshment. Soon, Colin, a man of greying hair but still formidable poise, descended the main stairs leading down from the gallery above and strode across the rushes, weaving through the trestle tables being dressed for the supper meal.

"Good man. I am Colin Donald, the steward you seek," he said to the messenger.

The messenger bowed his head briefly, setting aside his tankard, and withdrew a missive bearing the royal seal of King Richard the Lionheart.

"News from the Holy Land, sir. Relayed to the King of England, who sent word to Westminster, from where I was dispatched to travel here."

"Is this news of Laird Buchan?"

At Colin's mention of this, several maids gathered round.

"Is the laird well? Does he return home finally?"

Colin held up a hand to calm their questioning, and returned his attention to tearing open the seal. He unfolded the parchment and read the script. He read it several times, then looked up, his eyes furrowed. "This can nay be true," he replied. "Surely, there has been an error?"

The messenger shook his head. "I know not the missive's contents. I was only ordered to deliver it, not read it."

Colin reread the missive, then dropped it and gazed at the expectant faces of the castle workers huddling close.

"I am disheartened to read this news. Laird Buchan has

sadly, met with a horrible fate." He shook his head, as if in disbelief. "I never thought such would be possible. But it seems he was killed in Jerusalem. The news relayed to King Richard of England from his commander describes his death at the hands of infidels. The missive states they were unable to retrieve his body, and rather it was picked off by the enemy's warriors."

Gasps ensued. The maids covered their mouths. Myrtle, the head servant and a woman of aging years, declared her disbelief.

"Nay possible," the old woman exclaimed, going ashen, her hand coming up to rest upon her heart.

Colin shook his head, placing his grip upon her shoulder. "I'm afraid, Myrtle, 'tis true." He looked back to the missive, then to the people of the castle who had now begun to gossip and whisper. "It's right here. In the missive."

More utterances of disbelief followed, and then a maid ran off, calling to the other castle workers going about their business.

"My thanks for this," Colin said to the messenger who stood solemnly. "Please, remain for the supper meal and fill your belly. It's the least we can do for you."

"Colin. What are we to do?" Myrtle said, tears brimming her eyes.

Colin shook his head further. "I know nay what to do. Write to the king, I suppose, to ask who might be put in charge of this estate until it is determined who will take over ownership, or determine if Ewan, by some slim chance, sired a bastard heir."

"You know as well as I do he has no descendants or relatives, aside from some half-sisters. And they are bastard born and of course, though their sire financed them all, he never recognized them. He only recognized Ewan. Not likely they will be declared heiresses," Myrtle snapped. "Oh, goodness, my heart." She clenched the fabric of her dress and began to cry as other sobs of disbelief echoed down from the gallery.

Gossip burgeoned through the hall and off-shooting corridors.

Colin patted her. "Go and sit, woman. I know he was like a son to you. I'll figure out what to do, and will try my best to preserve this estate and all its people."

Myrtle nodded, holding a rag to her nose, and scurried away.

***

A cloaked shape stood on the shoreline, within a rock shelter carved into the cliff side beneath Dunwiddie. The hour was late. The sky was dark, and the inland coastal waters of the Minch churned angrily as an impending storm pushed waves onto the rocks below. The messenger from Westminster, who had elected to remain the night in the village, made his way along the rocky coast on foot, no longer donning his noticeable St. George's cross, but rather, a plain, dark grey surcoat.

In fact, had the cloaked person not been looking for the messenger, they might not have seen him. The messenger began looking around, his hair and surcoat whipping in the burgeoning winds, and finally seemed to notice the rock shelter. He made his way up, climbing over the rocks and around the tumbling boulders, until he finally pulled himself up into the shelter and stood face to face with the concealed person.

"Was this the news you were hoping for?"

The cloaked shape nodded. "Indeed it was, good sir. What happened? In truth?"

"As you know, I didn't come from Westminster, mind, but I came from Anatolia at Commander Murray's orders, though I did stop in England to also relay the news of the current death toll. I saw it with my own eyes. Commander Murray beat him off his horse. Left him for dead. For nearly an hour, he didn't move, and the sun there will bake all forms of life to death. The infidels sent men out to drag his corpse away. They've likely torn him apart. There's been no sign of him, and no request for ransom, so we know—"

"That he is dead." The person beneath the cloak finished the statement, followed by a soft laugh. "Ever since I learned the news today, I haven't been able to believe it."

The messenger, slightly taller than the cloaked figure, ran a hand through his hair. "Our commander, as you know, when presented with your 'suggestion,' decided he was happy to oblige. Doing so has removed the stiff competition Ewan de

112

Buchan posed him for cartography commissions."

"Did anyone else see Buchan's termination transpire?"

"Indeed, much of the army did, for it happened near to Jerusalem's gates as they prepared to stage a charge, but they didn't hear the argument that led up to it. Your Lord Buchan argued with Commander Murray, stating that he, as a scout, hadn't finished mapping out the enemy's location. Commander Murray insisted he was ready to charge anyway. Ewan obstructed Murray as he turned his horse to deliver the commands to his troops, and urged him a final time to hold off on his offensive, or else the *Moslem* infidels might overtake them if they outnumbered St. George's army. It gave Murray the opportunity he wanted to rid himself of Buchan."

"But how did he explain his censure of Buchan to his men?" asked the anonymous person.

"He said Buchan threatened him, and that he was forced to defend his position."

The person donning the cloak nodded slowly, thinking, then bowed their head in thanks. "A shame, really, that he had to die, for Ewan de Buchan was a fine man. But so long as he lived, I was never going to get what I was owed. I suppose it was necessary if both Commander Murray and I were to gain the ends we wished. And you, messenger, where do your loyalties lie?"

The messenger bowed his head. "I serve Commander Murray and his household. Not King Richard and not King William." He moved to the opening of the rock shelter. "One of the village woman has agreed to warm my pallet tonight before I depart in the morn. I'd hate to miss out on a sound rutting."

He said no more, allowing the implication of his treachery to linger, and hopped back over the edge of the rock shelter, retreating down the cliff, and wrapping around the shore toward the village.

CHAPTER 10

"I've never seen anything like it," Nasim said, staring up at the Grecian ruins of the old Parthenon while Ewan's horse, tethered with the cart at the base of the ancient rubble, nickered lazily and shifted.

She walked among the columns, gazing at how the sunlight played with the shadows, and felt her husband's eyes on her as he lifted a sore foot to rub it. Her horse had broken its leg stumbling over a rock a fortnight before, and Ewan had put the beast down, walking, while his horse pulled the cart and carried her in the saddle. Their pace had slowed significantly, and more than once Ewan had muttered that they were *"only in Greece, for God's sake."*

"What was it used for?" she continued.

Ewan shrugged and stood up, replying in her native tongue. As it turned out, he knew several languages already, and had swiftly picked up on hers once they had learned how to communicate. "Ceremonial, I believe. The Greek civilization existed a long time ago. They created beautiful architecture and sculpture. Beware though, much of it is of nude men," he teased.

She blushed and shook her head, laughing. "You try to embarrass me."

Ewan laughed as well, a low rumble. "Ah, Nasim, I do. But you see the Greeks saw the beauty in the body's design. And the body *is* a beautiful creation. There's no need to be ashamed."

He gestured to the top steps, seeing her seated, then sat

beside her. It was secluded here, a relief from the bustling city filled with vendors, merchants, people on their routines, or on errands crowding the narrow streets. He handed her a cloth containing roasted lamb purchased off a vendor with a round of flatbread. "How do you know so much?"

Ewan shrugged. "I learned enough from tutors and university. Then of course, I've traveled. Learning about a place or thing from tutors or monks is one thing, but seeing it in all of its splendor is entirely different. The world is full of such splendor. It seems a shame to never leave home just once to see what it beholds."

"Is that why you came to our land?"

Ewan thought for a moment. "I suppose. I was disillusioned about the war; that's certain. They needed my skills in exchange for a handsome compensation. I agreed, and we had success securing Acre and Jaffa from your sultan, Saladin. But you're right. The idea of seeing a foreign land held the most appeal."

"I've never left my home. Aside from moving to Jerusalem, I've never traveled outside the city gates. My mother told me many tales of the places my father and brothers have seen. One place is the sea. It sounded beautiful. I would like to visit the sea someday."

"Your family never took you to the seaside?" Ewan asked. "It wasn't far from your home, you know."

She shook her head. "I've always wanted to travel. But the war has made it difficult. I was going to go on a pilgrimage once, but the war arrived and my party was canceled. I've never gone anywhere different until now."

"Why is that?" Ewan asked, pulling her close.

She rested her head upon his arm. "The daughters of the emir, Commander Rachid, are seen as important goods. We remained out of the public eye and apart from men so that we didn't become corrupted and could be married off to those with important standing. But it also meant that in many ways, I was ignorant. For that reason, I sometimes wished I had been born a peasant, for at least they don't have the same restrictions upon them."

"But as your father's daughter, you had the best of everything and are now well-educated. You repaired my body when in my own land, I would have died. Peasants die every day from illness or injury. In some ways you were lucky, if not well-traveled."

"I suppose you're right." She sighed.

She looked up at the crumbling monument looming over them, feeling the tingling she always felt when he enveloped her in his arms. Sometimes he even pulled her into his warmth while he slept. The feeling was nothing short of heavenly, resting her ear on his steady heartbeat. She had memorized its cadence, steady like his presence. It made her wish for his kisses.

"What will my life be like in your country?"

***

Ewan considered the question. On the surface, it was simply a curious question, but he couldn't help but think how helpless being a woman must sometimes be. She could not make any decisions for herself without permission, and he doubted it was often a woman in her world even requested permission. Women were seen as lesser. Less intelligent, less strong, less rational.

Less intelligent? They hadn't met his healer of a wife yet.

Memories of his father swirled to life again. He had only met the man on a handful of occasions. His father had thought little of women, boasted of his virginal lovers, was playful when he wanted attention, dismissive when tired of the women providing it. That had never appealed to Ewan. He had been given his first experience as a young teenager by an older village lass somewhere in Ireland, a face and a name that had escaped him long ago. Taking virginity was a big responsibility with serious repercussions, and he knew after the times he had been invited to his father's castle, watching his sire from afar—*always* from afar, for his father's wife hated Ewan—that he could never do it.

Those memories of his father came freshly to mind, the way he toyed with women for his own pleasure, simply because he was wealthy and he could. *My* faither *was a selfish man.*

Now, more than ever, he was glad he had spared Nasim on her wedding night. She had already been through enough. It was good that he hadn't made it worse by insisting on his rights, even though she had been willing to give in to him in her panic. She had begged him to bed her because she feared for her well-being, not because she was impassioned. Though if she continued to shy away from his advances now, he wasn't sure how much longer he could last. He had long since grown weary of his hand jerking himself. He wanted his women. A shame, that though friendship and affection had bloomed between them, love-making still had not.

"Your life will be different. Women in my country also have rules that you will have to learn, but know that it's the husband's job to enforce them, and I will give you much freedom, as do many men give their wives."

Her expression remained passive, but he noted a curious twinkle light her eye. "What sorts of freedom?"

"As my wife, you will lead a public life, and for that you will need the freedom to come and go from the castle. My men will respect you and escort you if you require it. You will be in charge of managing certain household affairs. On some matters, I will value your opinion to help me make decisions. Though ultimately you must obey me, I have come to enjoy the openness betwixt us and hope that you realize I will always treat you well. You have nothing to fear from me."

"I realized that a long time ago," she replied.

A curious smile tugged his lips up and his brows inward. "How so, when we had naught a way to communicate?"

She took his hand and squeezed it, before letting go again and picking a piece of meat out of her bread to eat. She swallowed. "When you bartered with that traveling merchant for food in Anatolia, I could tell he tried to swindle you. It's not often that I speak out of turn, but I do sometimes lose control of my tongue. And I'm afraid my tutor encouraged my bad habit, telling me to always ask questions. You weren't angered with me for interfering, and so I sensed you were kindly."

Ewan stiffened at mention of her tutor. He could see, plain as day, that the man had longed for her. And yet, his brow softened and his smile warmed his eyes. Nasim was too demure and kind to lose control of her tongue. Being inquisitive wasn't the same thing as being argumentative. "Ah, in truth, woman, I was relieved. I knew he took advantage of me, but we needed food and I couldn't argue with him. What did you say to him to make him change his mind?"

She smiled, nibbling another bite. "He was on his way to Jerusalem. I informed him that I was the daughter of the emir who is held in favor of the Sultan, and that if he cheated us it would be brought to his attention." She shrugged, glancing sidelong at Ewan. "He was careful then to offer us twice the amount for half the price, along with a grand apology."

Ewan tipped his head back and laughed, making Nasim giggle. "You're a smart woman, Nasim."

She looked at him, her eyes bright. He gazed at her, her lips upturned but not yet smiling, her dark gaze and thick lashes juxtaposed against her skin. She was so beautiful, especially with the sun seeping through the columns. He felt himself thickening and inwardly rolled his eyes. One look, one impure thought of her, was all it took these days to stand his cock at full attention.

And yet, she was gazing up at him so playfully, clearly pleased with herself. He leaned downward, his eyes drifting from her eyes to her lips, and offered another kiss. She returned it. It did nothing to ease his lust. Sakes, but two and a half years, he had rested celibate. The pain might actually kill him at this rate. He turned toward her, his other arm weaving around her waist.

He caressed up and down her sides, feeling her jump beneath his touch, feeling her hand come up to hold his shoulder, then squeeze. His whole body burned as her nails pressed into him. Was that an invitation? Did he dare take his seduction further? For he had been spurned each and every time he tried, and be damned, though he could hardly stand the pain and frustration, he still couldn't force a woman to his will. They were in a secluded yet still-public spot as Athens below them carried on with daily living. He had always wanted her first time to be special, but he'd take her right here, if she was finally offering.

Her cheeks were burning. He could feel her pulse racing through her blood as his hands slid across her jaw, into her hair.

She wasn't yet shying away. Did she want this? Sakes but couldn't she give him a sign yea or nay? He brought his hand down from her jaw, down her neck, over her shoulder, then down upon a breast to hold. She flinched backwards, yanking away from him, and scooted to put an inch of stone between them. He stared at her, the sudden severance a surprise as she hid her face and wiped her lips.

Hurt burned like acid in his gut and his expression shuttered. He let go of her, turned forward again, and ran his hand through his hair. He laughed. Though it was only a gruff exhale and a wry smile. It fell away, leaving his jaw set firmly and his eyes furrowed. He shook his head at his own stupidity, propping his elbows on his knees and squinted up at the sun.

"You are my wife, Nasim," he muttered, looking sidelong, but unable to give her his full face. "How long will you force me to wait?"

He shoved to his feet, his food toppling off his lap into the dust, and strode down the steps to the horse and cart to secure things that didn't need any assistance. He needed to busy his hands and steady his thoughts. Not once had they actually put the sentiment of intimacy into words until now. And if he wasn't careful, he might frighten her.

Unable to look up at her, he unpacked their cart, then repacked it again, sweating as the sun beat down on him. He wasn't inclined to brute aggression like some men were, but he wanted to take out his mounting frustration on anything that could bear the beating. What was it? Simple fear of losing her virginity? Or was it because he was a 'filthy infidel?' Did she harbor feelings for Solomon? Did she, on some deep level, resent him? Hell, but it hurt to be so repulsive, like a leper, and be unable to do anything to change it.

At long last, as his frustration waned, he looked up at her sitting on the ruinous steps lost in thought. The sun had moved in the sky. He had been stewing for longer than he thought. He forced a smile. It probably looked strained.

"The sea is just to the west and south," he called. "If you wish to see it, we should move onward."

She hesitated to rise, but finally did so, pattering down the steps. With cheeks red from embarrassment, she handed him his food, picked as clean as could be done from the soil in which it had landed. She wouldn't look at him, and stood silently with the offering held out, waiting for him to take it.

He shook his head, took the food, and put it in the cart. His appetite was gone but aye, he couldn't afford to waste it. He should apologize for his abruptness. Neither of them had asked for this marriage. It wasn't her fault that she didn't want him in the way he wanted her. But the bitterness of rejection lingered, and he couldn't put the sentiment into words. Every day, when he thought for sure they made headway together, she regressed a step.

He led the horse onward, sensing, rather than seeing Nasim walking a pace behind him. The streets were busy, markets thriving with a potter selling his wares, a vendor roasting lamb, and a man outside of a ruinous fresco selling wine in large, clay vessels. And despite the fact it was autumn, the air was sultry as they neared the waters.

They rounded a bend in the road lined with tiered apartments as the path dipped downward, and suddenly, between two tall, narrow walls connected by a plastered arch, the crystal sea came into view. Nasim stalled. Sensing her awe, he stopped the horse to allow her a moment to absorb the view. He still couldn't look at her, and instead, started walking again. They came to the cliff that overlooked the beach. He began winding down the stone-cut path, guiding the horse until they reached the shore below where he parked the cart and dropped onto his rear in the sand against a rock. He leaned back against the jagged surface, propping his feet up and resting his elbows across his knees.

Nasim walked closer to the water, jumping back as a shallow wave roll toward her feet. Ewan simply watched her as she clutched her mantle against the breeze. Finally she turned to him, her mantle fluttering free from her grip like a banner caught in the wind, and smiled. He looked away, swallowing, unable to watch the happiness returning to her face when he felt more and more miserable. She was so bloody beautiful, and rejection was still coursing through him.

"Can I put my feet in it?" she asked.

"Aye," he replied, looking up at the sun to gauge how much longer they had to walk.

"Will you come with me?"

His eyes finally connected with hers. "In truth, wife, I'm weary. I bid you enjoy whilst I rest."

He didn't want to stand next to her and feel what it was he was feeling. He didn't want to hold her hand, see her smile, and remember that his desire wasn't reciprocated, even when it felt like her pulse was humming as strongly as his. He propped his head back against the rock and closed his eyes.

Was he flawed somehow? He knew his beard grew scruffy, unlike the well-maintained beards of the men she knew. Was religion really to blame? He was beginning to doze off. It didn't take long these days to drift to sleep. A shadow covered his face and he opened his eyes. Nasim stood above him, her smile gone and her face solemn. Sad. She knelt and took his hand in her delicate one. She bowed her head down, her brow contorting, then spoke in the broken English she was still learning.

"I am sorry, Ewan. I am just scared. I do not know how to be a wife. But I am trying to learn."

His resolve softened on the spot. He studied her, her head down, her eyes brimming with redness he hadn't seen on her face since that fateful morn of their departure into exile, and brushed an errant hair from her face.

"I know," he replied, "but you haven't a reason to be scared of me."

Hesitantly, she leaned forward and pressed her lips to his. All of the strained thoughts of the afternoon washed off of him like receding water. He wove his fingers into her hair, bracing her neck to hold her close and drank hungrily from the kiss. He was always the one to offer intimacy. Not once had she offered any gesture of her own until now. It must have been difficult for her to do.

But she was trying. He couldn't ask for more than that.

She pulled back and smiled. God that beautiful smile. How could he say no to it? He hoisted himself up while she pulled his hand. Excitement to see the water and experience it with him exuded from her radiant expression and filled him with something. Was it love? How could he possibly love someone who he had never bedded? It didn't matter. He relented to her and the two of them jogged to the water's edge as a wave crashed over their feet.

CHAPTER 11

Lady Margaret Fyvie clenched the missive penned by Dunwiddie's steward to her father with disbelief, pacing the length of her chamber to the fireplace, pacing back to the bed again, and repeating the ritual. The news could not be real. Ewan de Buchan was dead? The handsome Buchan heir with whom she had flirted? The man who had brazenly kissed her at court so long ago, awakening her feminine longing for a man's touch? The man with the tall stature, dark hair, and piercing blue eyes? The man she and her father, Laird Fyvie, had signed betrothal papers with almost three years before?

She had waited and waited for him to return, to take her to wife, to give her the grand home and status she had always wanted. And now he was dead? *Those blasted, disgusting infidels. Heathens. The church declares them vile, and they must be to kill such a man as Ewan...* She had always been appalled by the occasional reports that trickled through the church to the congregation. And now, those wretched animals had killed her ascent to higher status. What was she supposed to do now? She was twenty years old, practically unmarriageable. Her mother had long ago told her the key to happiness was to marry well, like she had. Her mother had been the daughter of a baron, so marriage to her father, the Laird Fyvie, was certainly an improvement. And like her mother, Margaret wanted better, too: fine meals, fine gowns, fine jewels, and a fine looking man beside her in bed, whispering indecencies in her ear as he took his pleasure, indecencies he had hinted at whilst at court, attempting to make her blush. And succeeding at it.

That fantasy fizzled away now, leaving a dreary emptiness in its place. Surely there were other eligible men who had good finances and hadn't been murdered in the east, but not many with the resources and wealth Ewan owned, which if she were to be honest, had been just as attractive as the man's physical attributes. And her father had wanted the marriage because Ewan's castle sat on the closest access to the sea, a bonus that would reduce his shipping costs to Ireland for his wool by not having to pay Ewan's tariff once they were married.

Questions tumbled through her mind. Who would be granted Ewan's estate now that he had perished? He had never been married and had produced no bastard heirs to inherit his wealth. The king would be a fool to let the prized Dunwiddie falter with no laird instated there. There was no question about it. She would ask her father to escort her to Dunwiddie, to oversee a memorial in Ewan's honor. It would allow her an opportunity to listen to the gossip within the castle and perhaps glean who the new leadership might be. She would ask her father to tell her the courtly news and encourage the king to select an eligible man to replace Ewan, with whom she could enter into a new betrothal contract.

Her father had always provided for her, but he had neither the prestige nor wealth of her late betrothed. Despite her fine belongings and noble status, she could always sense a lingering tension beneath the surface, as if her father was always living month to month with his finances. The ale was watered, the mutton was tough, and on occasion, there was no meat at the board at all. Hallways that were in slim use had only a couple torches lit, sometimes none, and her father was forever pouring over his account ledgers. She sensed that one expensive repair or perhaps one thin winter would be enough to devastate them.

She was tired of feeling insecure, despite her father always ensuring her he would finance her needs, and now that her passage onto bigger and better things had been thwarted by an unlucky death in the east, she would simply have to determine a new strategy.

She moved to her toiletries and examined her face and hair

in her copper plate. She was beautiful, and men so loved a bonny face and figure such as hers. She had been told as much many a time. Perhaps already being twenty years of age wouldn't count so terribly against her. She took a deep breath and straightened her shoulders. It shouldn't be hard to snag a new suitor with an innocent bat of the eyes and a suggestive smile or two. She smiled at her reflection, practicing the smile that had caught Ewan's attention. A woman needed to use what valuable assets she had to her advantage, and as soon as Margaret knew who would be granted Dunwiddie, she would make the most of her assets to catch his attention, too. She turned sideways and smiled again, perfecting her flirtatious grin. The new laird of Dunwiddie might not be as handsome as Ewan, but she would make do.

She dropped the copper plate back to the table top and marched to her chamber door to exit. The corridor was a claustrophobic passageway, thick with the smell of smoke due to poor ventilation and torches lighting the path. She skipped down the spiral stairs, dashing along the lower corridor that passed the kitchens, and arrived at the hall, a dank room with one large, blackened hearth, covered in rushes, where her father stood conducting affairs with a guardsman. He drank from a tankard.

Pausing in the doorway, she pinched her cheeks to give them color, rubbed her eyes to redden them, and fixed the thought of losing her future with Ewan in the front of her mind. Her smile faded. As soon as she was ready, she thrust herself into the hall and ran to Malcolm, the Laird Fyvie.

"Oh *Faither*!" she exclaimed, the missive still in her hand.

The greying man, still broad and proud, turned to her as she launched herself into his arms.

"*Faither*! How can I go on now that he's dead?"

She forced the sobs until they became genuine, cried for Ewan's loss until real tears materialized. The man nodded to his guard to give them privacy and the guardsman bowed out, exiting the hall, as did some of the serving staff.

"There now, Margie love. I know how you loved him."

"I did! I truly did!" she cried, clenching him harder. "And

those murderers killed him, they killed him... Who will I marry now?"

"Hush, lass. We'll find someone. But you must grieve his loss first. It will take some time."

She shook her head against him. "I know how badly you were counting on this alliance to lessen your export expenses—"

"Do nay fret yourself with my matters." He silenced her. "Times change, and men die in war. I'll just have to recover from the loss and figure something else out."

The missive from Ewan de Buchan's estate this morn had shocked their household. His death left Fyvie in a tight financial lurch.

"In the meantime, you must grieve Ewan's death. We cannot enter another betrothal when your heart is with Ewan's memory."

She smiled a hidden smile, tucked against his chest. "Speaking of memories, *Faither.*" She added a sniffle. "I wish to go to Dunwiddie, to see how the people are faring and plan a memorial for him. I feel it's only fitting, considering how close Ewan and I had become. I did, after all, love him so. He deserves to be honored."

Malcolm Fyvie fell silent. She had seen him do so often, and knew he was tallying the expense of traveling to Dunwiddie. It would cost him, and God only knew things were getting thinner. But it would serve him well in the long run, to spend the coin now. If she could learn who the contenders were for inheriting Ewan's wealth, she could reveal whoever the bachelors were to her father while batting a flirtatious eye at her preferred man of the bunch.

"Please, sir," she beseeched, adding a well-placed sniffle again. "It would mean so much to me."

The Laird Fyvie patted her back. "All right, Margie. We'll travel to Dunwiddie at the sennight's end. I'll send a messenger to inform their steward."

"Thank you, my laird," she murmured, knowing the title of deference would appeal to him. "Thank you so much."

CHAPTER 12

Como, Lombardy

No. He mustn't think on the prostitutes they had passed in town, the women who had offered him so blatantly their services. He needed another distracting thought. Anything. Would it be better to wait out the coming winter and continue on through the hills after things thawed? It was growing cold, though the ground wasn't frozen yet. If they moved on diligently, without mishap, they might be able to make it through the more mountainous parts before the temperatures fell dangerously low.

Ewan rubbed his thick beard and settled his hand on the hilt of his sword, considering his options, and unhitched his poor horse from the cart, turning the beast out to graze on the hillside below the shallow cave he had discovered for the night. Nasim spread a blanket out on the ground for them to sit and sleep upon. He eyed her, hating that they were still sleeping on the ground, but so far, he had pinched his coin tightly, to ensure that he could purchase a new horse should his faithful mount go lame or cover their cost across the channel and up the coast. And Nasim—bless her fortitude—had not once complained.

There would be luxury awaiting them after this arduous trek, should, God willing, they make it home.

Home.

It had been so long, well over two and a half years, since he had seen his castle overlooking the sea and slept in his massive, four-posted bed draped in rich, red canopies. He envisioned his hearth and a decanter of stomach-warming whisky on the table beside it, the grate loaded with crackling wood or peat along with his plush, upholstered chair, his heavy woolen blankets, combed so finely they were soft to the touch. And his solar, lined with maps and rolls of fresh parchment waiting to be transformed, bottles of ink, measuring tools, manuscripts... Ah, but it was where his creations were made.

He missed it all so strongly, he felt wistfulness threaten to break his visage, and carried his saddle and blanket up the incline, dropping them into the dust at the entrance of their shelter. He took a deep breath, feeling a slight twinge in his chest where Nasim had made her life-saving incision. He was fully healed, but he was beginning to realize he would always bear such an unseen reminder.

The faint sound of bells from the Basilica of Sant'Abbondio tolling the vespers competed with those of San Fedele, muted in the distance. He turned to take in the sweeping lake that spread out below them, no doubt rich with life. He had splurged as they traversed the city, and took Nasim into an inn, filling their bellies with polenta and fish. It was the first time in over a month that they had been so satisfied. They couldn't splurge like that again until they reached northern France and their ship was chartered, but it had been so long since they had traversed a town center that bustled as much as Como, and he couldn't resist satisfying the look of longing on Nasim's face as they passed the savory smells permeating the air from the inns and vendors.

Nasim looked up at him, offering a distant smile, then returned her attention to spreading the wrinkles from the blanket. She had grown distant as they traveled through Como's town center. She had seen the deplorable way the prostitutes had behaved and had hardly spoken a word since. He had stopped trying for his marital rights. She was approaching nine and ten years, he had learned, was so experienced in some ways of life, and yet, with her chastity, she was so innocent, seemingly growing more and more nervous each time he kissed her. And so he had stopped kissing her, too. Ever since that day in Greece, he had slowly backed away. Their relationship was quickly becoming one only of friendship, with the benefit of someone warm to sleep against at night. He missed kissing her. Missed that excitement he had felt so often while he was still growing accustomed to her company.

He took comfort in the church bells ringing up from Como as darkness settled over the landscape, having missed the familiar predictability of churches when he was in the east. And he didn't return her smile. God be damned, but as they'd passed that brothel in the town and the whores had started heckling him, offering him their wares and flicking up their skirts, his cock had stirred with unquenched need. Need that hit him so suddenly, he'd looked at Nasim to see if she noticed the shame on his face. Aye, she had. So shocked by it all, she had stared at them, then stared at him, then looked away, burying her face to blind herself to their lewdness. She had refused to speak of it. Refused to speak at all, even though she had surely seen him stare at the women for more than just a glance.

"Are you hungry?" he asked her now.

She looked up at him, shook her head, then looked away and bit her lip. It was mostly dark now, and the lake shimmered with ribbons of ripples. He turned away from the view and sat down upon the blanket, assuming his normal sleeping spot. It was cold, and he shook out their extra blanket, lying down. He had long since donned his St. George cross again, his traditional surcoat, which added a layer of warmth, but it still wasn't enough. He needed to collect his horse still, but he was cold and with the sun down, a moment of respite wouldn't hurt.

Nasim lay down, too. He rolled away, feeling her heat at his back, and tried to vanquish the prostitutes from his mind. But he couldn't help thinking about them. None were exceptional. A few were attractive. Many were clearly well-traveled in the art of pleasing men, and well-tilled, too. A long time ago, a fetching wench at a tavern wouldn't have been an odd way for him to pass his time on his travels. He felt guilty now for wanting one. *No. You do nay want one*, he realized. He wanted his wife, but didn't feel invited. A forced marriage wasn't what he'd wanted, but now that he had Nasim, he had grown to relish the fact that she belonged to him. A shame she didn't desire him.

They remained like that for so long, staving off the chills, that he began to wonder if Nasim slept.

"Ewan?"

So she doesn't sleep.

"Aye?"

"Those women…"

He stiffened, waiting to see what she would say, and rolled to face her, staring beyond the dark outline of the back of her head at the emerging stars. She didn't say anything else at first.

"What about them?" he ground out. He didn't need to ask which ones she talked about. He sensed where her thoughts wandered, and had no idea how to broach an explanation.

"Why did they behave in such a way?"

He thought about his answer, and finally decided being straightforward was the best policy. "They offered me intercourse for a payment."

"Intercourse? As in…" Her words trailed off as her comprehension dawned.

"Aye, as in sexual relations." He looked over at her.

She lay in shocked silence, her back and rear to him. He closed his eyes to resist the urge to wrap her in his arms.

"They offered you their bodies without being married to you?"

"Aye."

"Why?"

Because they can spot a desperate man in need of a lay, he thought. "Because men enjoy a woman, and many men are willing to pay for intercourse when they cannot have it otherwise."

"Would you pay?" she asked timidly.

He didn't know how to answer. He had bedded his fair share of tavern whores when he was younger, before he had gone to war and experienced the darkest side of humanity. And the fact she was asking was curious. If she didn't desire him in that way, why did she care? She waited for his reply, and once again, he determined honesty was best.

"At one time, I did. Though, I was a younger man."

Just admitting his past behavior made him feel cheapened. He didn't like the feeling.

"Were you married then?"

He shook his head, even though she wasn't looking at him. "Nay. I've never been married before."

"But you're married now. And they would still offer in front of your wife?"

"They'd have no way of knowing you're my wife, Nasim, for you won't even touch me—" He curbed his tongue, realizing as the words flowed out that he was lashing out in frustration.

He rolled onto his back and stared up at the rock ceiling. For a moment, they lay silently, then she turned over toward him, tentatively resting a hand on his chest. He looked down at it, then at her, but didn't raise a hand to hold it.

"You haven't kissed me in some time," she whispered.

"You haven't seemed to want me to," he replied. "But Christ, woman, I—"

Just having her so close made his chest ache. Their exile was no longer new. They had long grown accustomed to each other, spoke each other's languages, even if they did so imperfectly. He had spent months doing nothing but prove he would look after her and not cast her out into an unknown world. Nothing had seemed to soften her to the idea of consummating their marriage.

She scooted closer to him. He could feel her breasts press against his arm and her feet mix with his legs. His whole body buzzed alert. She hadn't initiated any intimacy since that moment they sat on the beach in Greece. Did she sense competition for his attention with the whores? She wouldn't be wrong if she did, even if she were wrong to think him capable of acting on them. All evening, the temptation to steal back to the town to find a wench who would get on her knees, take him in her mouth, and suck him off had plagued him, followed swiftly by guilt slicing through him just for thinking of straying. But stray from what? Nasim and he certainly didn't have a true marriage.

He shoved to his feet, her hand falling off of him. He needed space between them, and paced to the entrance of the rock shelter.

"What is it about me?" he finally said, turning back around

to see her pushing up to sitting. He rested his hands on his hips, his tone deep and frustrated. "Why will you nay lie with me? Is it that I'm a Christian and you're a *Moslem*? You should know me well enough by now to know that I care for you. Did you know I've grown to love you?" He saw her smart at his admission. "Are you in love with another? *Solomon, perchance?*" Now he watched her flinch at his barb. "Would you have allowed him beneath your clothing? What? Am I flawed? You find me ugly? Just tell me. Because I can nay read your mind. Because from the moment I met you, before I had ever looked upon your face, I found you beautiful, and I've grown to care for you, in spite of this marriage put upon us. It wasn't just you foisted onto me against your will. Do nay forget that I, too, had a life, had plans. But I'm trying to make the best of it. Why in the hell can nay you do the same?"

She scrambled to her feet at his heated onslaught.

"Dammit," he cursed under his breath. He kicked himself. He didn't want her fearing him.

"I'm sorry," she whispered, shaking her head, and then she dropped her head in her hands and cried. "I'm sorry!"

"I do nay want you to be sorry," he fumed. "I want you to desire me, not flinch from me the moment I vie for more than a kiss. I want you to return the favor I show you. I want you to lie with me as a man and wife do! Or at the very least, tell me why you won't! For if you truly love another and wish me nay to kiss you anymore, or perchance, make love to you, I'll respect it. I'll put you up in your own household in Scotland, leave you be, and do what I must as a man and allow you to do what you must. But I do nay want half a marriage. I want all or none—"

"Ewan—"

"You owe me a simple explanation, so that I know what you're thinking. I won't force a woman. I never have, and I never will."

She was fretting. "Ewan, I'm sorry—"

"What do I need to do to win you over? Do I need to be a physician like Solomon—"

"I'm sorry!" she yelled, recoiling from him further. "I know not what to do. I know not what to expect. I'm scared! I did! I loved Solomon. But then I met you. And meeting you made me question everything. Being married to you was a punishment to me! It was meant to degrade me. I knew not the future when I was sentenced to this marriage. But I've come to see my father's wisdom in the decision. And I realize now that I *want* to be married to you. I want *you*! I just don't know how to show it. And the more you pull away from me, the more I wish I could just, I could just—acquiesce."

He paused at her outburst, the first bold argument a woman had ever lobbed against him. His chest heaved breaths in and out as his anger receded, leaving nothing but unsated frustration and an argument not yet finished. But he didn't want to argue.

"'Tis my duty as your husband to show you what to do, Nasim. If you'd only trust me. If you'd only give us a chance to experience the beauty of it. Making love knows not *Christian* and *Moslem*. It simply knows when it is right, and be damned, lass, but I thought that we were r…"

When she continued to hold her face, crying silently, and didn't speak to him further, he abandoned his train of thought, turned, and walked out, exhaling an exasperated sigh. "I go to collect the horse. Go to sleep. I'll be back later."

***

He left. He had been gone for some time, a lot longer than it took to round up a horse. Had an injury befallen him? Nasim still worried about him, even though the wound she had repaired was fully healed and his health long-since restored. Then, a worse thought paralyzed her. Had he gone back to the prostitutes to have intercourse? She suddenly couldn't sleep. She couldn't even stop crying after such an argument. What was he doing with the prostitutes? She felt ill at the thought of him fornicating with another. She was too restless to sit still and paced to the edge of the cave again, looking for some sign of movement in the moonlit countryside. No one was coming. Nerves threatened to toss the contents of her stomach around.

She hadn't been left alone at all on this journey, and being alone now, in such a foreign place, made her worried. Worried that she was losing Ewan when she'd never really allowed herself to have him, and worried about what might happen. And it hit her, how much she had come to depend on him. How much he had done for her this entire journey when he hadn't even known her, and how much she missed his steady presence.

That was it. He was always so calm, so steady, that his frustration with her tonight had left her disoriented. Had she grown complacent? Grown to expect that she could continue to take his generosity without meeting him halfway? They were married, and it had been months. And each day, she felt herself pushed another nudge toward a precipice. She would eventually fall over it. Whether or not she would land in his arms and experience his affection for her, or simply fall off into an abyss, alone, remained to be seen. Perhaps, she was the only one who could steer the direction of her fall.

And she wanted to land in his arms.

She missed the idea of Solomon, but she didn't really miss him, she realized, because just as with Ewan, she hadn't known him. She had only known an ideal of him. And now, as she shivered alone while Ewan could be anywhere, doing anything, she realized how much she truly…loved him? It really was love. *I love him. As he said he loves me. And I've pushed him away.* She felt a cry hiccup into her throat and brought her hand up to cover it. She loved him, and she was losing the one man to stand by her through the darkest trial of her life. It was true. Being married to an infidel was meant to be a punishment, but love knew not religion. It only knew when it was right. She and Ewan had grown to fit each other like a hand and gauntlet.

The moon had moved considerably when she heard horse hooves crunching closer and closer, heard the horse's heavy breathing from what could only have been caused by galloping, and then saw Ewan's tall silhouette draped in his surcoat, boots, and sword, ease quietly into the cave. He paused, noticing she was sitting up, her hands limp in her lap. Waiting up for him had caught him off guard. He turned away from her, unhooking his belt and sword sheath, and tossing them onto the ground beside the blanket with a clatter of buckles.

"I'm sorry for the manner in which I spoke to you," he said, his voice gravelly, refusing to look back at her. "It's my shame alone that I did nay control my tongue better. Trust it will never happen again, wife."

She bowed her head. "I'm sorry, too."

He shook his head. He plopped down beside her, stretched out, and pulled up the blanket. He exhaled. A fermented odor, a smell she had never smelled before, emanated from his breath. His words were resigned. "You have no reason for regrets. It's nay your fault you're stuck with me. It's mine. For kissing your hand, and thinking I would get away with it."

He rolled away, giving her his back, and lay still. Maybe he had gone to sleep? Nasim chewed her lip as the time passed and the moon continued to move, trying to decide what to do. She knew what to do. Even if she really didn't know exactly what needed to be done. As Ewan had said, it was his job to show her. She lay down and inched closer to him until her thighs touched the backs of his and her chest pressed to him. Did she hear him hiss an inhale? It had been soft, and he was lying so still.

"Ewan," she whispered.

No answer.

She placed her hand at his waist, and slowly snaked it around to his navel to offer him the affection he had always offered her, that he had stopped offering her over the passing sennights. Her pulse was racing with thoughts of what she was initiating, with thoughts of the unknown.

"Ewan," she whispered again. Still, he said nothing. "Ewan, please turn to me."

He finally rolled partway over, craning his head over his shoulder. "Go to sleep, woman. More traveling awaits us in the morn. You do nay have to pretend anymore."

He began to roll back, but she kept her hand firmly upon his waist, leaned up to his ear, and whispered, "I'm not pretending, husband. I love you, too. I just don't know the ways in which to show such love. Betwixt a man and woman."

He held perfectly still, his shoulders having tensed upon hearing her words. Then he rolled onto his back, up against her, and looked directly into her face.

"Nasim, I know you wish nay to lie with me. I should have

minded my tongue earlier for I fear I've made you feel guilty. You do nay have to do this."

"You are my husband…"

He clenched and unclenched his jaw, his voice going gruff, and searched her eyes. "What are you saying?"

She looked at his stern face, his glaring eyes burning with a new sort of silvery light in the nighttime, and heat crawled up her neck and claimed her face.

"I'm saying that…I'm… I'm willing to lie with you and…and allow you your rights…" Her voice trailed away.

"Do nay offer me something you wish no' to give." He shook his head and rolled away again, but this time, she sat up, dragging the blanket free from him as she did so.

He turned over his shoulder to determine why she wasn't allowing him his rest, when his eyes caught on her, and he froze. She sat on her knees, and slowly, with trembling hands, lifted the hem to her robe. She dragged it up her thighs, feeling a kiss of nighttime air to her navel as she exposed the skin on her stomach. She had never done such! She focused on breathing, trying to hold all the air she could into her lungs. But her breath was erratic and her belly, nervous.

She dropped her gaze away, feeling the fabric slide up and over her breasts, when Ewan shot up to sitting and took her hands in his. Her clothing dropped to her lap. She looked into his eyes, confusion contorting her brow. "But I thought you wanted…"

He was shaking his head. "Naz, sweeting," he said gruffly, caressing back her hair. "I don't want it to be like this. I do nay want you to submit to me because you feel badly or guilty. I—I won't have it on my conscience that you lie with me because I lost my temper on the matter—"

"You didn't listen to me at all, did you?" she said, staring at him.

His brow furrowed.

"I told you that I realized I *wanted* to be married to you, that I've wanted *you*. I just never knew how to show it." He watched her quietly, so she continued. "I've been so nervous, because I know not what is done, betwixt a man and woman. I was forbidden from learning the details. But I never expected to have a choice in this matter. I never expected you to yield to me just because I was nervous. I don't want to be nervous anymore. I don't want to feel reservations about something others do so freely. I want to know what it's like, but have never known how to ask without seeming wanton. All my life, I've been told to guard my purity, guard myself against lust. But you are my husband. How can it be wrong to feel lust with you?"

His hands had taken to stroking hers as his gaze burned into her and he listened to her.

"You've taken on the burden of me," she continued. "You claim it's your fault we've been thrust together. But whilst I couldn't understand it then, I understand what I'm feeling now. I was drawn to you, too, as you say you were to me. From the moment I laid my eyes upon yours. And this nervousness, it's, it's—"

He placed a finger across her lips. She silenced. Then he slid his hand upon her cheek and combed his fingers back into her hair. He leaned in, pressed his lips to hers, licked at the saltiness of tears upon them, and kissed her deeply. She inhaled. Exhaled. It had been a long time since he had kissed her, and his mouth tasted of the same substance that had caused its smell. It didn't taste poorly, but she had never tasted it on him before. A kind of drink, perchance? She kissed him in return, hungry for such affection she had felt starved of as they traveled from Greece. And he wasn't holding back. Such a kiss was rougher than usual, more insistent, and yet, she knew if she flinched away from him, he would still stop. But she couldn't flinch from him now. Her flinch was what caused him to halt each time. He took it as a sign that she was scared and respected her enough to stop.

He dragged his lips from hers, to her cheek, then her jaw, pecking a trail of kisses along her skin, and slid his other hand free of their grip to hold her waist. She inhaled. He slowed, then paused. "You mustn't shy away from me, wife. If you truly wish to do this, then do nay pull away."

She nodded. But then, he pulled away from her. Nasim opened her eyes, not realizing they had fallen shut. Ewan was scrambling away from her, stacking firewood into a pile a few feet from their blanket.

"What are you doing?"

He turned to her and grinned that grin. She could barely see it in only the moonlight seeping in. She hadn't seen it in so long, the boyish dimple, the youthful hope that had captured his face as they ran into each other in that narrow passageway. It was back now.

"The night air bears a chill and you'll be cold, and I do nay want to miss seeing a moment."

He seemed suddenly eager. The frustration they had felt earlier had vanished. He rummaged through his packs, found his flint, and cracked it until it ignited the kindling. At long last, he had a tiny flame. He leaned over on his palms and blew on the thread of smoke until fire crackled through the twigs. She had watched him do such a task time and again, sometime with his sleeves pushed up, his forearms rippling with toned, lean muscle. Supposedly, he was a man of wealth, intellect, and prestige in his land. And yet, here he was, bearded, travel worn, behaving like a lad in the woods.

Satisfied that the rest of the kindling would begin burning, Ewan sat back on his haunches, took a deep breath, and turned to her. Their rock shelter was dim. Light danced warmly around them, creating shadows. The blue in his eyes sparkled.

"And I want *you* to see every moment, too," he finally added.

She nodded. He simply stared at her. Finally, she pushed to her feet. He seemed intent to wait for her to disrobe, the way his eyes kept roving over her body, then back to her face. She unwrapped her mantle, the fabric swinging in a circle around her as she pulled it free, and discarded it on their blankets. She heard Ewan suck in as her hair tumbled free past her rear. Then she bent, her hair cascading over her shoulder in curling waves, and took the hem of her robe in hand. She dragged it upward, her fingers shaking, her stomach raging heat in need of satiation she couldn't explain, and she watched her husband watching her like a hawk.

His eyes seemed riveted to each movement. Her navel felt

the coolness of exposure, and his eyes seemed to stop moving, fastened to her bare stomach. She continued pulling the garment up over her head, then let it drop to the blanket. Her hair hung over her shoulders, draping down either shoulder to her waist and covering her naked breasts. Immediately, her arms encircled her waist to shield herself.

Frozen, Ewan seemed caught in a snag, his palms braced to his thighs as he remained on his splayed knees. His brow was serious and his eyes, glittering. He was so handsome. His thick, dark beard only added to his beauty and masculinity. The resignation that had been on his brow as they traveled from Greece was gone. His throat bobbed as he swallowed. Still dressed in her pants, she averted her eyes, when she felt his hands upon her waist.

He was in front of her, on his knees. He simply held her waist at first. Then, his hands roved over her. She felt the roughness of his callused palms as he began to caress her, prickling the skin of her lower back. She looked back down at him, but he was looking at her body, his mouth a hair's breadth from her navel… He pushed her heavy locks away, draping them over her shoulders so that they hung down her back, and inhaled as he gazed up to her breasts.

"Naz… You're so beautiful…"

A reverent hand slid up her stomach, up through the valley between her breasts, then over one, sliding over her nipple. Just the gentle grazing caused it to tighten. She shook, trembled so badly that Ewan finally looked into her eyes, awestruck.

"Relax, sweeting. You must, if we are to join as one."

She nodded, and before she could respond, he brought his lips to her navel and kissed her. He breathed in hard, as if inhaling her smell, his nose and lips trailing over her skin, and her eyes fell shut. True, she was nervous, but the heat in her belly was only intensifying. It wasn't something to be ashamed of, she realized, even if it had always made her flinch before. She was with her husband. Doing such was no longer deemed fornication but marital relations. No one, neither her mother nor her half-sisters, had ever prepared her for what to expect. They had certainly never said it might feel…*good*.

"Ewan," she whimpered, grabbing both his shoulders when she felt his lips trailing up her stomach toward her—

Heaven help her. His lips were pecking slow kisses on her breast…then the other… She jumped, unable to help it, but for once, he was undeterred by such an abrupt movement. Then his mouth encased her breast, pulling upon her and kneading her nipple with his tongue as his lips latched onto her. His beard tickled as it raked across her skin.

She sighed. A long, low groan escaped him, as if encouraged by her reaction. His hand upon her back braced her against him, and his other hand slid up her front to encase her other breast, teasing it until it, too, tightened. She dug her nails into his shoulders, never once having imagined such an explosive sensation. Her blood pumped like liquid fire. Dissatisfaction formed in her belly. She needed more. Wanted more. And yet, she was sure her legs would soon give out and she would collapse.

***

Ewan released his hold upon her breast, migrating over to the other one. His head was swimming, and not from the ale he had imbibed earlier. He had only nursed two tankards in Como, hardly enough to make him lose his senses, and felt even guiltier about leaving her alone and spending the money when they needed every coin they could get to make it back to Scotland. But he had been so miserable. He had needed time to work out his frustration and refocus his thoughts. He had been angered at himself for lacking self-control. Angered that he had said what he'd said. He wasn't the type to lose control. He wasn't a man who ran away with his anger and shouted at women. And blast it all, but he loved her.

The taste of her skin… Ah, but he could hardly think. He had wanted this, with her, for so long. Knowing how she really felt did nothing to temper his lust. But it made sense. Their worlds had been so different. She had been brought up to behave distantly around men. He doubted public shows of affection were common in her world, considering he had never seen men and women together there, except for the occasional man with his wife or sister moving about the gardens on their way somewhere. Of course she didn't know how to express her desire for intimacies. He thought of how courtiers flirted with a suggestive smile, a coy look over their shoulder, or a giggle. Maybe with a touch on the arm or with a bat of the eye. Typical ways in which women in his land flirted. How on earth would Nasim understand when she'd been brought up in a world where running into a man by accident would be cause for all to chant their disgrace?

He was daft. He should have tried to read the signs better. She hadn't shied from him all this time because she disliked his attention. She had shied from him, because she didn't understand seduction. And yet, with her full, beautiful lips, her enchanting eyes, her waterfall of dark, lush hair, and *good God, these breasts*, she was the most seductive creature he had ever known. Her bosom, so lush and womanly, so soft, with peaks of dark pink… Sakes, but was he truly feasting upon their bounty right now?

Nasim's fingernails bit his shoulders. She whimpered.

"Ewan…" she sighed again.

He could sense her legs trembling. Felt her fingers migrate from his shoulders to his head, weaving into his hair, grasping it at the roots. These slender fingers that had saved his life, were surprisingly strong, and he felt a twinge of discomfort from her grip.

He welcomed it, laving his tongue over her nipple, acquainting himself with her taste. God, he needed to join with her. Needed to feel her wrapped around him. He had wanted to know that she admired him as much as he admired her for so long. How he would dismiss his betrothal to Margaret, he still wasn't sure, but *this* with Nasim was what he wanted. This was a woman who would be his partner, not just the mother to his children. He had always known he liked her, from the moment he woke up in Jerusalem to realize he hadn't died but was being tended by a woman with soulful eyes and decorated hands. He had come to understand a woman like he never had before. Nasim hadn't once complained of the arduous trek, hadn't once succumbed to her tears of grief for the death of her former life. And he loved her all the more for her show of strength.

Nasim's knees were trembling so badly, he slid his hands free of her back and other breast, and trailed them down her legs to her knees, up her thighs, down to her knees again, repeating the caressing to soothe the nerves causing her to shake while he continued to nurse upon her. As she exhaled, as her trembling ebbed, he slid his hands back up to her waistline and slid a finger below the fabric. He skimmed around to the front where he found the ties securing the *sirwal*. Her breath caught.

"Ewan," she whimpered again. "Ewan, hold me up."

Her beseeching made him smile. Getting her to let go of her inhibitions had been a bloody challenge spanning months, but now that she was allowing herself a glimmer of how sweet it could be; she was melting. He trailed his lips back down to her navel, inhaling, kissing, and began to pull the ties apart. She jumped, but didn't pull away.

"That's it, Naz," he encouraged. "Have trust in me. I'll nay let you fall."

The waist slackened. He let go of the fabric. It slid down her legs, pooling at her feet. Ewan took each of her rounded hips in hand and held her, kissing her navel, then sank lower, lower, holding her steady, feeling her nearly rip at the hair on his scalp in her reaction. Her stomach was so flat, so smooth, her skin so creamy soft. His lips touched her nether hair. It made him heady, dizzy. He wanted to touch, to taste, to feel the part of her she had kept so secret. He had never felt such lust, never wanted anyone with such fervor. But by God, he wanted to lay her out on the blanket, caress her whole body, cherish every inch of her. For what she had been through, she deserved nothing less.

He pulled back an inch, looked up, seeing her perfectly lush breasts protruding overhead, and saw her eyes open slowly. She gazed down at him, the coolness of the air causing goose flesh to rise on her arms and stomach. Her lips were full and red, slightly parted, and her cheeks were flushed. Her eyes... A tress of hair had fallen in a curling cord upon one of them, lending her the look of a skilled seductress.

He was at full attention. He had hardened on command when she had first snaked her hand around him, his body reacting in the most primal of ways. Such was, sadly, the immediate reaction these days, when he simply imagined a conjugal joining with her. He needed more room in his trousers, needed to just take them off. But Nasim was new to this. He didn't want to rip away his clothes, toss her down, and thrust hard. He would frighten her, make her fears a reality, and put her off to ever bedding with him again. Not to mention, it had been so long that he had bedded with anyone, he was certain to disappoint her if he wasn't careful, for it would be over the moment he took the first eager plunge.

Nay, he needed to be gentle, slow, and by doing such, the burning of love making would make them pleasantly scorched by the time they both sought their pleasure. He leaned back on his knees, resting his rear on his heels, and simply took in the sight of her. Dark curls protected her virginity and smooth, slender thighs tapered from curving hips to delicate ankles. Her arms cinched around her middle now only served to press the soft pillows of her breasts together, accentuating their abundance.

"What's wrong," she whispered, fretting.

He shook his head, his lips curling up. "Not a thing, love. I just want to see you. God, Naz…" He reached to her hips and slowly turned her. She moved, shivering, and Ewan swept her hair over her shoulder so he could see the curvature of her back as is sloped out to her bonny rear. He stroked a hand up and down it, his fingers trailing down her rear, down the back of a thigh, then up the inside of it, grazing her juncture as he went. And to his surprise, she didn't jump this time. She inhaled, exhaled, and when he guided her hips again, she completed her revolution to face him once more.

He swallowed. How he had gone to the Holy Land and returned with this woman, he hadn't a clue, but indeed, this was her former betrothed's loss and his gain. He stood, so much taller than her, and felt his breathing coming deeply. He pulled up his surcoat, reaching behind his head and dragging the fabric over his shoulder blades, over his hair, then cast it aside. Then he pulled loose the lacing of his tunic and discarded it, too, so that his chest was bare.

Her eyes settled on the scar to the side of his chest, a long incision. A shiver of anticipation washed over him, leaving gooseflesh on him.

"Would you like to undress me?" he asked. *Discover me?*

She dropped her gaze to her feet. "Would you like me to?"

He lifted her chin on his fingertip. "I want you to know my body as I know yours now."

"I don't know what to do," she replied.

He let go of her chin. "Take it at your own pace. We have all the time in the world."

She nodded. Her cheeks were still burning. He loved the sweetness of it. He waited, watched, until she reached a hesitant hand to his bare chest. She placed her palms to his pectorals, sliding them along his flesh, over his nipples, down the plane of his lean stomach. He shivered. It felt so damn good. Then her finger caressed the length of his healed incision. And unexpectedly, she leaned in and placed her lips to it, pecking a kiss upon it.

"Naz…"

He closed his eyes, his head tipping back, feeling her hands touch his pants. She hesitated. He couldn't open his eyes, but nodded as his throat bobbed. She must have seen his affirmative, because her fingers began pulling his laces. He felt his pulse increase, feeling her hands grazing over his shaft, teasing it to a point of pain. He looked down again. He reached out and scooped her hair falling in her eyes back over her shoulder.

Finally, the laces were undone. She flashed him a shy smile, and he nodded his approval once again.

"You're doing well, sweeting," he said, and waited for her to drag down his trousers.

She did so slowly. Her hands shook as she opened his undergarments to bare him to her. He should be embarrassed, bedding his woman for the first time in a cave looking like a vagabond with a thick beard and unwashed feet. But he was desperate to finally have this moment with her. And in a way, such an occurrence, out of doors, alone in the wilderness, with shadows lapping over their skin from the fire, was one of the most sensual experiences of his life.

His undergarments came down now, too. His cock bobbed free, heavy, thickened, and pointing to his navel from between his thighs. She froze, staring at it, then up into his eyes. His smile had long since fallen away. He wanted her honest reaction and searched her eyes for it. She swallowed, her gaze roving over him, from his feet, over his clothing around his ankles, over the hair on his legs, lingering on the robustness of his shaft, up the path of dark hair trailing over his navel and to his pectorals, where once again she examined his healed wound. He pushed the heel down on one of his boots with his other toe, flicked it off, repeated it with the other foot, then stepped out of his clothing. He reached to her, took her hands, and reeled her close.

"That is how it looks when you wish to mate, yes?" Her voice was a mere whisper.

Her question was the inquisitive words of a physician, and yet, in that sentiment was the desire of a woman, and the nervousness of a maiden.

He nodded. "Aye. It has two purposes," he said, his fingers caressing her cheek, stroking over her ears as if clearing more hair from her face. "First, to bring you pleasure, always, and secondly, to seed you with my heirs." He dipped his lips to hers, pulling her flush with his stomach. "I hope to do both well enough that it leaves no doubt in your mind, the affection your man has come to hold for you."

He could feel the blush blooming on her cheeks. He kissed along her brow, along her jaw, along her neck, and as he planted kisses across her skin, he took her hand and moved it down between them so that she touched his manhood. Her breath was erratic as he did so.

"Wrap your hand around me," he whispered between pecks.

She did so. He resumed kissing her and encased her hand in his, stroking up the smooth skin of his shaft to his helm, then back down to his jewels, repeating it, a groan of pain and pleasure rumbling from his throat with no control to temper it. He hadn't been touched like this in so long. Over two and a half years. A lifetime by any healthy man's standards. And yet, it wasn't just a tavern wench coaxing out his seed. He was Nasim's first. This was special. He released her hand, feeling it work on its own, and gripped her head on either side. He slid his fingers into her hair and tilted his head to deepen the kiss. He pushed into her hand, his hips rocking in gentle thrusts. He couldn't help it.

"Ah, lass, that's the way of it."

And then he felt the pressure, the pent up release burgeoning within his bollocks. Abruptly, he pulled her hand away, resting his forehead to hers. He swallowed.

"Did I do something—"

"Wheesht," he admonished. "Nay. God, woman. It felt too good."

He'd nearly spilled his seed. That couldn't happen. He had to join with her, not lose his burden like a green lad anxious to cross his first finish line, even if that was how he felt. Nasim had never done this. She wasn't anxious to rut. He picked her up, cradling her against him, and laid her down on the blanket, shaking out their other one so he could pull it up and over them.

He paused, setting the blanket back down. There was no way he was covering up this body before he'd taken in the whole image of her. Her hair was splashed about her, curling tendrils that he could bury his face in and remain happily lost within. And her body...

At first he simply stared, as if choosing which part of a magnificent feast to sample first. He wanted to touch her, suckle her, ply her with his fingers and explore every inch of her soft skin, but he refrained. She didn't need him ravaging her like a starved wolf. Yet as the dim firelight wavered across the bountiful flesh of her breasts, his thoughts disobeyed him. Damnation, but he wanted her.

"Do nay shy away from me," he whispered, leaning over to kiss her. "This might feel strange at first, but I would never hurt you."

She nodded, her eyes full of trust for him, and it nearly broke his resolve. Fleeting thoughts of Margaret rolled through the back of his mind. He tried to vanquish them. But how was he going to break off his betrothal to Margaret? Betrothals were nearly as binding as marriages. Such things were not done. Yet he would do what he must, even if it was unconventional or caused hard feelings. His undocumented marriage to a foreign woman might not mean something in his world, but it meant everything to him.

He stretched out beside her, on his side, his cock pressed to her thigh, and snaked his arm beneath her head to cradle her face to his. He kissed her again, his tongue seeking entry as his other hand settled on the luxury of her breasts once more, rubbing and teasing a nipple, and toying with her. He basked in them, their softness his boon forever.

She inhaled sharply, but already seemed to understand the heat it evoked, for she arched her back ever so slightly, thrusting her breast into his palm.

"Mm, you like that, my love?"

Still locked at the lips, she inhaled sharply again, nodding. Encouraged, he drew circles around her nipple, trailing his finger down her chest, over her ribs, onto her stomach and then over her navel, brushing his nail into her nether hair. She froze. Jumped. Held her breath.

"Easy, love," he crooned, trailing to the juncture of her thighs, back up to her navel, down again, up again. "Have trust in me." Trust? He was losing trust in himself to take it slowly.

She remained still for him and slowly, she relaxed, tensed, then squirmed. He grinned, knowing she was warring between nervousness and the restlessness that could only be sated with sound loving.

"I'm going to touch you now betwixt your legs," he whispered against her lips, his finger still caressing her privy hair, feeling his own hips begin to rock gently against her leg to ease the frustration between his thighs, "and prepare your body for me. I wish to save you from as much discomfort as I can. Let your knees part."

She did as he asked, her own breathing ragged. His fingers caressed a few tender circles upon her hair, and then they descended further, between her parted knees, trailing gently along her seam already damp with anticipation. Her breath caught again. Her body froze. Her knees began to pull shut. He pulled his lips away from hers and looked down at his hand's progress.

"Nay, love. Open for me."

She nodded. Heat radiated from her cheeks.

"And breathe," he encouraged in her ear, taking to nibbling along her neck and then her collarbone, nuzzling his nose against her cheek, his lips dropping to one of her breasts and settling upon it.

She suddenly moaned. And he knew, in that moment, she wanted him. His middle finger slid through the soft hair shielding her womanhood, between her chaste folds, and within her. Nasim clamped her legs together and arched her back, pushing onto him.

"Ewan," she cried on a strangled exhale.

"Do you wish me to stop?" he asked, but she shook her head rapidly no.

He kept kissing her skin, basking in her cries, allowing her a moment to grow accustomed to the feeling within her. How incredible it felt, being the first man to satisfy her. He hoped he never failed her expectation. A woman's opinion of his performance had never mattered before, but anticipating her opinion left him feeling vulnerable.

Slowly, her legs fell open again. He kissed her again and her hand reach out to hold his forearm as her other hand grabbed his arm woven beneath her head and shoulders. His tongue pushed gently into her mouth and caressed hers, dancing with the kiss she returned more boldly than before.

"Naz, love…" he sighed, unable to stay away from her breasts.

He had to taste every inch. His suckling, though still gentle, grew insistent. He groaned, feeling himself throb. She would feel so good. He rubbed himself against her thigh as his tongue and lips continued to create magic on her breasts, his finger beginning to massage slow circles within her. She sighed, tensed, squirmed with what could only be deemed desire. Encouraged, he gave gentle thrusts, plying her.

She was so smooth. His need for her was nearly killing him.

And she was relaxing onto his finger, her hips lifting slightly with each thrust, pushing down to meet him. His mouth came back to her lips, his kiss urgent. He added another finger, his rhythm growing firmer. Bolder. Sakes, he had to join with her. He wasn't sure when he snapped, but he could bear it no longer. She was ready, relaxed, perfect for receiving him. He withdrew, relishing the whimper of disappointment that escaped her, and moved onto his hands and knees so that he was hovering over her, erect and ready to unite them.

"Nasim," Ewan said, staring into her eyes. "Hold onto me. Trust me to be as gentle as a man can be." He brushed her hair back, seeing that fear assert itself, but then her trust in him overshadow it. "I want this to be a memory that you cherish forever."

***

Nasim had never thought of marital relations as a cherished memory. She was confused, wishing she had been allowed to learn about this aspect of life. Solomon had been forbidden to teach her anything involving conception. The one time he had to approach the topic, his face had bloomed bright red as he looked at her. *He cared for me*, she realized. She knew the way Ewan looked at her now. She knew when he gazed a little longer than normal, smiled gently, searched her eyes with his, it was because he found her beautiful, inside and out, and wanted this final connection with her. In hindsight, when she thought back so long ago to her life in Jerusalem, she realized, Solomon had been looking at her in the same way. She swallowed. At one point, after her betrothal to Kalim was made known to her, she had considered Solomon to be her *Majnun* in the tragic tale of her life. Now, she realized, mayhap Ewan had been her *Majnun*, and she had been given to him.

"You have done this many times before, no?" she asked on a sigh.

He paused and continued to look at her. He didn't answer at first. Then he looked away and seemed to collect his thoughts.

"Naz, do nay concern yourself with the past. All that matters is you and me, wife and husband. I'm devoted to you."

From that she knew his answer had been yes, even if he didn't flaunt it. Of course he had done this before. He had even mentioned that at one point in his life, trysting with a tavern wench hadn't been an unusual happening when he traveled. He seemed to know everything to do, and he was doing it right, for she could hardly breathe.

"Ewan, I'm so nervous."

He settled down on top of her so that they were pressed together. His body heat blanketed her and provided comfort.

"I'll stop if you ask it of me," he whispered, the tip of him nudging at her entrance. "But give yourself a moment to try first, okay?"

He was holding back. She gathered now how this was going to work. He had been rubbing in gentle thrusts against her. His fingers had been thrusting in the same rhythm within her. When he had held her hand wrapped around his shaft, he had also encouraged her to stroke. His fingers within her had been so forbidden, and yet, so deliciously sweet. She had wanted more. He was going to use that part of him to stroke within her, too.

Marriage to Ewan was supposed to be a punishment. But she finally shook her head. Her world had cast her out into this man's arms, and he had never once failed her, even if they had been perfect strangers. She loved him.

"You are my husband. I'm your wife. I want to please you."

"I hope to please you, too," he whispered. With that, he took himself in his hand and began to slowly guide himself into her. She looked up into his blue eyes, so dark in the firelight and full of curiosity as he watched her. She couldn't look away. His gaze, so intense, made her feel beautiful. Made her realize that she had become special to him. Slowly, she felt stretching. Slowly, he nuzzled her nose with his, pushing firmly yet tenderly, finally arriving at her maiden's barrier and with a quick nudge, breached her completely.

She cried out and jerked her legs tightly around him, not because it hurt overmuch, but because it was different, new, and it would only happen once. Her eyes flew shut. Her body arched against him. Her hands whipped up to grip his shoulders. He stilled, not twitching a muscle and keeping her enveloped beneath him. Yet he didn't stifle his moan.

"Ah, love." He placed small pecks at her lips and cheeks. "Relax and you will grow accustomed to me."

She buried her face against his chest, feeling embarrassed and uncertain, yet an urgency she had not felt before began to warm her belly with insistence, a need for friction, for motion, to satisfy what she was feeling. She needed him to move as he had when it had only been his hand.

He remained still in spite of her nails digging into his bare shoulders and her knees clamped tightly about his hips.

"Do you wish me to stop?" he said gruffly, as if he could barely form the words, worry for her evident in his tone. Overwhelmed, she couldn't force out a reply. "Naz? Nasim, look at me. I need to know you're all right."

She finally uncurled her face from him. He noted the tear leaking from her eye, and withdrew from her so swiftly, she gasped.

"God, Naz, I'm sorry," he said, resting his elbows beside her head and petting her hair back. "I'll stop."

But all she felt was disappointment. Why was she being such an imbecile? He had been careful, gentle, and with him no longer inside of her, she felt empty. And now he was worried he'd hurt her.

"You need not," she blushed.

"I can nay do this if you cry," he muttered, pulling away and pushing up to his knees. He raked his fingers through his hair almost violently, as if he were in pain.

She caught him around the waist. His eyes shot down to hers. "Please. I was just beginning to enjoy it."

"You were crying," he replied.

But the longing for him to be back within her was unmistakable.

"I was overwhelmed. Ewan, I... I want you. I want this. Please listen to me."

He looked at her and paused, withdrawing his hand that had begun to grope for his clothing.

"Show me what to do," she encouraged, pulling on his waist, until he lowered himself back over her.

"I don't want to hurt you," he finally whispered. "You've been hurt enough."

"Then finish what you started," she beseeched, drawing him down by a hand upon his neck and another hand on his waist. Slowly, he succumbed to her. He took hold of his manhood and slid easily into her, then began gentle thrusts, retracting himself, sheathing himself. Her eyes fluttered shut, her lips parted, and she rubbed her hands up and down his back. When she looked back up at him, his eyes were closed and his jaw, clenched. The sensation was growing more and more urgent in her belly, his hands braced over her head beginning to tenderly pet her hair.

She closed her eyes again, basking in the sensations overwhelming her, when she felt his lips warm her cheeks and kiss their way to her ear.

"Do I still pain you, love?" he murmured against her.

Her flushed face broke into a shy smile. She shook her head and peered up to see him grin with relief.

"I'm glad," he replied, and steadied his stride to a more moderate pace.

She squirmed. Unable to speak.

"Do I feel good to you?" he whispered, nuzzling her neck.

She looked away. "*Na'am*," she nodded.

His breathing grew heavy, becoming more insistent in his pace.

She encircled his neck tightly and a moan, long and low, rumbled from his throat as he braced himself over her on one forearm, the other roving over her body to settle on a breast. His pace hardened, his thrusts gaining strength. She felt the pressure plunge into her, feeling the need to lift her hips to meet each joining. She roamed down his back and over his rear, holding his narrow buttocks now flexing and releasing in steady, firm undulations. His face was beautiful, his eyes closed tightly, his hand upon her hair gripping her, and his other hand sliding from her breast to her waist to brace her hips against him with each drive. The muscles of his arms bunched tightly.

She cinched her ankles over his rear, gripping it in her fingers, soft cries escaping her in synchrony with his rhythm growing louder in her ears. His groans of pleasure matched hers, intensifying as hers did. He suddenly pushed up, splayed his knees beneath her thighs, and lifted her hips. His chest was gloriously lean and toned. His muscles were chorded yet sleek and slender. His incision on his chest, a relic of a dark time in his life, was more like a beacon of rebirth, of lungs that were pumping air in and out as he pleasured her. He braced each of her hips in his hands, holding her steady, and lost control, sinking into her with hard, fast thrusts.

She cried out, tossing her head to the side, and grabbed his chest with her palms, attempting to grip the taut flesh, his pectorals, his abdomen flexing and undulating. Such touching only encouraged him to move faster.

"Ewan," she moaned. She grappled to anchor herself on his arms.

"Naz, ah…" He couldn't speak. Sweat glistened on his brow. "Naz, I'm going to… Love, come with me…"

She had no idea what it meant, and yet, as he commanded it, a wash of warmth flooded through her, surging within her womb. She tossed her head back, arching her neck, a strangled cry of release whooshing from her mouth as heat rushed between her legs, flowing over his hardened manhood. A deep, guttural cry escaped him. His head fell back. His pelvis slammed against her and he held himself tightly to her. His hands shook. His seed exploded inside her. His head was still fallen back as he wrung himself spent in steady surges, as lesser guttural expressions of ecstasy panted from his lips. She felt the pulsating sensation of him deep within, knowing on a primal level that he had brought her to a profound realization of the body that she would never have been able to study as a pupil of healing arts.

She bit her lip, tried to slow her ragged breath, and when he looked down at her, his naked skin bronze in the firelight, she reached up to capture his cheek in her palm, smiling. He remained joined, a grin breaking onto his face, and he slid his hands up her stomach to cup each of her breasts with such ease and confidence, it was a wonder she had never allowed him to touch her before tonight, for it felt so natural for him to do so.

He leaned over her, resting his stomach to hers again, and took her lips in his, sucking them seductively into his mouth as his hands captured hers and braced them possessively to the ground over her head.

"You were beautiful. Incredible," he murmured, biting at her skin playfully. "Superb. *Perfect.*"

She kissed him back with earnest, relishing the way his beard raked pleasantly on her skin, then whispered in his ear as he nuzzled her. "If this is how it is to be, then the shame is on me for denying you for so long."

He chuckled, nodded, and she giggled at his appreciation of her jest. "You surely tortured this man for much too long, yet if I had known such a gift awaited me, I would have gladly suffered patiently. Naz, sweeting," he said, swallowing. "I pleased you, aye?"

"I love you, husband," she replied. "I wanted this for so long, too, I just didn't know it was what I needed. Is it wanton of me to say I hope you'll do this often?"

He laughed, nipping at her. "Wife, I command you to be wanton for me. I'm starved for you. 'Often' might be more than you bargained for. Wait another moment or two, and I'll repeat the performance before the fire dies." My, how she was growing to relish his boyish smile. But then, he grew serious, looked down into her eyes, and held her head. She soaked in his doting expression, the typical firm lines of his face having softened. "I'm yours. You're mine. Our bodies now share a communion with one another. I shall never deny you for I love you, too."

***

The hour was so late it was early by the time they both felt sated. Ewan collected Nasim in his arms, her cheek tangled in her mess of dark curls against his heart, and pulled up their blanket. He was completely drained. Nasim would definitely be sore once the aftershocks of euphoria wore off and her body had rested through the night. He would need to be careful in the days to come. But in this moment, she was nestled in his arms, a contented smile on her face, her body completely languid in her nudity as she draped her arm across his waist to hold him.

Her fingers drew circles on his hip, and his own thumb

lazily stroked her upper arm as they both looked into the glowing cinders still rolling with orange light, even though the flame had burned down.

"How many wives do you have?"

Her question caught Ewan off guard. After all this time, the topic of wives had not once come up. This was the first time their words had taken a turn toward this aspect of marriage. His thumb paused its rubbing and he looked down at her, his brow furrowing. Aye, many of the ranking men in her country had been married to more than one woman. And for some reason, this was the first moment he had considered that mayhap it'd had something to do with Nasim's resistance to him.

"Here, in my world, a man is permitted one wife only," he clarified.

Her eyes widened, but she continued to gaze into the fire instead of return his look. "One wife forever?"

He nodded. "Unless one of us dies, marriage joins a man and a woman in a permanent bond."

"And if one of us should die?" she asked.

He looked at her, feeling that pull in his chest much like when the scorpion had nearly stung her. Before tonight, it had made no sense to love a woman who still, months after their wedding, clung to her maidenhead. But he had. Only making it hurt more when she hadn't seemed to love him back. And it made him remember Margaret waiting for him in Scotland. Unless word had come of his death already. Pray she was already exploring other suits by the time he returned home. It might make it easier to beg out of the betrothal, if she was already interested in another man. With her looks, she would have no problem snagging even the coldest blooded bachelor's interest.

Still, the issue of Margaret, receding farther into the recesses of his mind as his love for Nasim had grown so much he often passed a whole day or two without Margaret's name crossing his mind, loomed tall and menacingly in his thoughts now. Pray he could resolve any issue quietly when he arrived home, for, *blast it! I've just promised Nasim that I can only have one wife.* And he knew the law might not see the validity of this infidel marriage in an enemy land in a ceremony unverified by the churches. Pray the issue of Margaret could be easily taken care of.

For take care of it, he would. He just didn't want to leave a wake of hurt feelings and damaged relations with Margaret and her father, Malcolm of Fyvie.

"Then after we have mourned our loss for the proper amount of time, we are free to marry again. But church law only allows one marriage at a time," he explained, resuming his thumb rubbing.

"But you can lie with prostitutes if you wish it?"

He narrowed his eyes, trying to determine in what direction this was going. Was she still thinking on the day before in Como? When the whores had lifted their skirts for him to see their lack of undergarments?

"It's morally wrong, but some married men still do so."

He felt her chewing her lips against him. "I didn't like it when you went to the prostitutes tonight," she whispered.

"What?"

Her head tilted up to his now, her eyes sad. "You left to retrieve the horse and didn't return for so long."

He shook his head. Did she think he had gone to sleep with another? Damnation, the thought had been ripe on his mind, but he hadn't been unfaithful. "Nasim, I never did such. I bought drink, nothing more—"

"Do you regret having wasted your one marriage on me?" she asked, nervously awaiting his answer.

Baffled at the randomness of her thoughts, Ewan, paused, then shook his head. "No."

Nasim, however, sensed his hesitation. "You are unsure?"

He cleared his throat and thought about his reply, looking back to the cinders. "I know you were unhappy marrying me. I didn't need you to tell me that you felt punished. It was clear on your face from the moment you entered the ceremony. I could also tell Solomon liked you," he added. "And I could tell he asserted himself in front of me."

"How so?"

Ewan chuckled wryly. "I'm a man, Naz. I can tell when a man likes a woman, and he could tell that I liked you, too. He touched you in the infirmary, in front of me, in front of your *faither*, to send me a message that my interest in you was nay welcome."

She looked down, blushing, unable to give an answer.

"Look, the circumstances, my ignorance of your culture…it tipped both of our worlds over. If you harbored love for Solomon in return, I can understand. For it's not as if you chose me. And no matter what you say, it *is* my fault alone you're married to me now. If I hadn't kissed you, but kept walking, or ignored you, then you probably wouldn't be exiled with me. Mayhap, you'd be marrying your former betrothed. Hell, I don't know…"

Though the thought of her favoring Solomon in return irked, as her blushing suggested now, it did seem to clarify her continued rejection.

"You were also betrothed to another, were you not?" she asked.

God. Margaret. He was still betrothed. Good Christ, what was he going to do? Pray, pray, pray, his fair-haired betrothed accepted his rejection gracefully without causing a fuss. Pray she didn't bring objections to his desire for a severance after so many months of flirting and kissing her. Pray he could quietly resolve this whole matter without hurting Nasim in the process.

CHAPTER 13

Margaret arrived overland to Dunwiddie wearing proper mourning attire complete with a black over gown embellished with imported velvet from Lucca and before that, most likely imported from the very East that Ewan had gone to fight in and ultimately die. It had probably cost her father a pretty penny, but she was a noble daughter, and one who had just lost her betrothed. He would surely recoup his expense somehow.

She looked down at her lap to hide the smile creeping onto her lips from her two handmaidens who looked ill from the violent jostling of the cart. She appeared the grieving lover, her mien complete with a sheer back veil draped over her head. It was a pity, she thought for the thousandth time, that Ewan would not be her husband. The man who took his place might be hideous. But ultimately, the thrill of a new pursuit hummed through her bloodstream. She wasn't required to mourn for any length of time, seeing that she and Ewan had never married. But playing the dutiful fiancée served as a good excuse to reside at Dunwiddie where she might be privy to talks of who would replace Ewan at the head of his estate. It had been a sennight since she had learned of Ewan's death, and it was high time she got on with determining her future.

Her cart hit a particularly jolting rut and she grabbed the side, the smile wiped from her face. *Just as well. I can nay very well face the service at Dunwiddie grinning from ear to ear.*

"Ho there! Laird Fyvie!" came a call from the wall as they arrived at the portcullis after climbing through the village.

Margaret scrambled onto her knees and peered out of the front curtains. Their party, consisting of her father, three guardsmen, and a second cart loaded with their trunks, came to a halt. Sure enough. The sturdy, looming walls of what was supposed to be her future home stood before them.

"We have come to pay our respects to the people of Dunwiddie, I who would have been the Laird Buchan's father-in-law, and my daughter, Lady Margaret, who was promised to the laird as his bride!" Malcolm stated. "The news has hit us hard, and Lady Margaret mourns for his lairdship's death. May we partake of Dunwiddie's hospitality?"

The response was affirmative and the portcullis was lifted. The carts and horses lurched forward again. As they pulled into the outer ward, along the castle road to the main keep, and through the inner gate, the cart finally stopped. Soon after, the captain of the guard, a broad man, opened the flaps to help the ladies alight.

Margaret gained her footing and looked around. The castle still thrived. The outbuildings were busy, the blacksmith's shop contained a healthy fire where two apprentices hammered tools side by side as men unloaded bales of hay against an inner wall with pitch forks and people came and went on errands. The people were busy despite the somber mood of mourning for their laird. Dunwiddie had a prosperous population and it seemed that Ewan's death hadn't hindered its industry.

Colin Donald walked down the steps, the stately man she knew to be the castle's steward, and clasped Malcolm's offered wrist. "Good day, my laird. Welcome to Dunwiddie."

"I wish it was under better circumstances," the Laird Fyvie replied.

Colin bowed his head. "Shocking and tragic news. The castle is reeling. I tell you, no one here could have expected it. Our people loved Laird Buchan. He always tended to their needs, earned substantial money, and under his direction, I was able to ensure this home remained in fine repair. Earning Dunwiddie was, after all, his lairdship's first achievement as a man apart from what his father bequeathed to him. The king himself awarded him the castle due to their mutual report and his lairdship's reputation as a man of standing and exceptional cartography skill. His Majesty knew that Laird Buchan would make this remote place glorious."

"It is indeed still glorious. You have done a fine job in Ewan's stead," Margaret interjected, glancing around the upper walls. "You are to be commended."

The remark seemed to have a profound meaning to Colin, Margaret noted, as he bowed his head again. "My thanks, Lady Margaret. It is always heartening to know that one's efforts are recognized. I wish Laird Buchan could have returned to see that his home was so cared for in his absence. I think it is a fine thing you are doing, my lady, coming to honor your late betrothed with a memorial. Please, do come inside."

He extended his arm to her and she took it, leading her and the rest of the party up the steps into the main hall.

An old servant woman scurried by, a bundle of graying hair tied back in a sensible bun.

"It's Myrtle, is it nay?" Margaret asked, sighing with fatigue.

"Aye, milady," the woman bobbed a curtsy.

Margaret removed her traveling gloves and held them out, dropping them, assuming Myrtle was prepared to take them. "See that my luggage is brought up to the lady's chamber. I'm tired and wish to rest."

"The lady's chamber?" the old woman questioned, looking at Colin for guidance.

"Ah, well, we have suitable accommodations already prepared, Lady Margaret," Colin began. "In anticipation of your arrival"—

"I was to be Ewan's wife. I should be placed in the lady's chamber. Does this not make sense?" She summoned a tear, just one that reddened her eyes as she lifted a handkerchief to her nose. Then, she bowed her head."

Myrtle seemed unimpressed with her, which only made her dislike the old woman. The maid leveled a gaze at Colin.

"To where should I direct the lady's trunks be taken?"

Margaret added a sniffle. "Do nay mind me. I'm just distraught. Standing here in Dunwiddie's proud hall and seeing Ewan's heraldry above the dais only makes me think of how he will never return."

Her father reached to her and pulled her to his chest. She sensed Colin looking at her, unsure what to do.

"I suppose there's no harm in offering her the lady's chamber for the time being," Colin said.

"But Colin, it's nay prepared. It hasn't been in use since the former laird of the castle resided here, and that was many years ago. The chamber has become a storage vault."

Margaret cleared her throat, swallowing, and dabbed her eyes. "I am happy to wait whilst you tend to it. Thank you, Colin, for offering. And fetch me wine, Myrtle." She swayed away from the group to a plush chair positioned before the hearth, having noticed Colin cast an appraising glance at her before she turned. All men did. She was fetching.

***

Myrtle attempted to protest as Lady Margaret moved out of earshot, but Colin quelled her with a stern look, pulling her aside and lowering his voice. "Their visit here is only temporary. Do as she bids for now. No one else uses the chamber, so it matters not."

"It matters to the maids who must leave their current tasks to empty, sweep, dust, and dress a room for company entirely from scratch. 'Twill take them the whole of the afternoon."

"I will see them compensated," Colin replied.

"But it's improper. His lairdship and the lady might have been betrothed, but he never made her our mistress."

"I know, but look at her," Colin argued.

"Aye, a grand spectacle of playacting. If you believe those tears, then you're a fool, Colin Donald."

"I'm aware. But the laird has passed on and cannot object. Surely she's harmless. Go and see about it, Myrtle."

"Aye, sir," Myrtle finally conceded with a hearty roll of the eyes, and scuttled out of the hall to fulfill the lady's demands.

***

Nasim dipped her head over the side of the ship and retched. Ewan, conferring with the ship's captain, strode across the deck to the bowsprit where he rubbed her back.

"Naz, you should really go back to the cabin and rest," he

advised.

She cast him a bland look. "The idea of being shut in that wooden prison cell, rocking and tilting, makes my stomach roil more. This is a trip I hope never to make again," she croaked, clutching a rag and wiping her mouth. "I believe the sea has lost its mystery now."

Ewan chuckled, lifting her hand from the rail, and examining the ring he had purchased for her off a jewel vendor at the market in Lyon, France. In spite of her churning stomach, she smiled briefly, too. She loved the simple ring. And by the time they'd reached Saint Nazaire in Brittany, Ewan had saved so much of their coin that they had rented the largest private chamber available at an inn on the coast, chartered their voyage, and he had spoiled her with the rest while they awaited the vessel's return trip from its previous deployment. The weather had turned frigid. And yet, as Ewan went looking for a cordwainer in the village to construct him a new pair of boots—for his old pair had worn holes through the heels—she had marveled at the bustling market crammed with awnings displaying goods, trinkets, raw beans, seeds for next season's sowing. And she had eyed the jewelry cart.

Somehow, even though she never asked to inspect it, he knew she was interested. *"Aye, no matter what culture one comes from, women still have eyes for adornments."* He had said.

Her hand migrated to her neck, where hung a matching pendant he had gifted her simply because he loved the look of it upon her.

"This ring, in my world, means that you're married," he had explained. *"No other man may claim you now, so long as I live."*

The adornments were crafted differently than in her world, but she had been mesmerized by them all the same. And although she had never needed to be draped in luxurious gold, these simple sapphires were given to her with such a hopeful smile, she hadn't been able to resist kissing Ewan in public, which had only invited further attentions from him as they arrived back to their inn.

She blushed now, in spite of her seasickness, thinking of how he had whispered in her ear as he made love to her in Saint

Nazaire with her sapphire pendant draped between her breasts. And yet, here she was, vomiting so grotesquely, while Ewan rubbed her back like her mother had done when she was a child. Certainly she disgusted him, no matter his soothing words. Her veil was soiled. She had no choice but to allow the ship's crew to see her visage. In a way it was liberating, and in a way it was frightening, like she betrayed her roots, like God might strike her down on the spot.

"We will pull into port soon," Ewan said. She crinkled her brow at the term. "The ship will meet land. Have faith, your misery is almost at an end."

"Praise be," she whispered.

He chuckled again. "If you look there," he pointed to the passing shore at a rocky cliff lined with trees, "all of this land is mine. We're practically home."

Home, she thought wistfully. This was a strange, cold land. The sky was grey and the seawater whipped about in the wind slapping the boat and the rocky shore. It was nothing like those warm, blue waters in Greece. She had no home anymore. She missed her mother with intense longing and had to bite back her tears. Her mother's home had been the only one she had ever known. Those days were no more. She had done so well not to dwell on her former life and family this entire journey. Every time the feelings of loss tried to grip her, she had tamped them down, for she had Ewan, and Ewan continued to prove that he would never abandon her. Ewan loved her. He was devoted to her. She was his only wife. But now, as she stood retching over a rail into the choppy ocean, freezing air lapping at her face, the longing crept up and consumed her. Ewan might be rubbing her back now but things would never be the same.

"Nasim," Ewan began, running his hands up and down her arms. "Where did you just go?"

"I was just thinking that I have no home now."

He pulled her to him and rested his chin atop her head. "You belong to me. My home is your home."

"I'm out of place… People stare at me," she added.

Every time they had walked in the market in France, people had stared, turned to gossip, or made remarks in French she was glad she couldn't understand. And the gawking had persisted up to now. The ship's crew and oarsmen had all stared, shared a word or two under their breath when they thought they were far enough away.

"You're different. And though I have offered to clothe you in the way of our culture, you've chosen not to. It's admirable, do not misunderstand, but your garments are odd here and people are puzzled by them. 'Twill take them time to grow accustomed."

"Do I embarrass you?" she croaked. *Mercy, have I displeased him?*

She pulled her mantle across her face self-consciously.

"Naz, I care nay what gossips say. If I were embarrassed, I would have ordered you to change." He sighed. "People here haven't met foreigners like you. But my people will grow to love you and you will soon see you have a place here, different as it may be in Scotland. If you'll nay listen to me and go rest, then go pack your belongings. We're nearly there."

***

Ewan could see his runners on the shore carrying the message back to the castle that a vessel was approaching. By the time they made port, his trusted steward, Colin Donald, would be waiting at the dock with several of his guardsmen to assess the threat. The air was icy, and though the seas churned, Ewan finally breathed easily, the first time since his departure almost three years before.

They rounded a peninsula, keeping close to the coastline. Finally, Dunwiddie Castle came into view, perched proudly atop a cliff overlooking the sea, framed by mountains in the background. His heart swelled with pride, that he was finally seeing this sight again after so long. The village was not entirely visible, extending behind the castle on the hills that rolled out to the mountains, but the image of the castle's proud outer walls was more welcome an image than he could recall seeing.

Nasim returned from the cabin to stand at his side and gazed up at it. "It is so different from Jerusalem," she said.

"It's not like the lands of the east, but I assure you it's grand in its own right. Your father forced you upon a wealthy man."

He winked, his jest earning an appreciative smile. But he knew that it pleased her. After everything she had been through, knowing she had means surely helped her feel grounded. And thank goodness she was no longer evacuating her stomach. Perhaps the sight of the dock and hence, her freedom from the ship, improved her mood. Ewan tightened her fur cloak around her as the ship began to list gently, following the crank of the rudders to turn it toward the dock. The sails were adjusted to keep it on course. The crew was in motion, calling out commands and running to gather ropes for anchoring the ship. Swinging down from the main sail to the deck below in an organized routine, the crew pulled smoothly into port.

Ewan waited for the ship to settle and for the crew to jump onto the dock to tether the vessel. Then he leapt over the rail to land easily on the decking where Colin and his party of guards waited. Colin had aged more, Ewan thought, noting the grey that speckled his steward's temples. Nasim extended her arms to brace herself on his shoulders. He settled his hands about her waist, lifting her overboard.

"My laird!" Colin bowed, a look of grey shock on his face. "Wh…what a complete surprise! Praise God you are nay dead! However did you manage to survive? You look thin as a rail!"

His guards relaxed. Fergus, the head of his guard grinned as did Hamish, one of his trusted soldiers. Both men removed their nasal helms and came forth to clasp his wrist. Everyone looked to Ewan's side to regard the cloaked woman with her mantle drawn across her face.

"Colin, man. 'Tis indeed good to see you." Ewan strode forth and extended his wrist, then they wrapped each other in a one armed embrace. "Six months of walking whilst eating slim victuals will thin any man."

He moved on to the guards waiting in metal-plated brigandines. They beamed and bowed low.

"Rise up, men," Ewan said, clasping their wrists in turn and lifting a hand of greeting to the others.

He returned to Nasim's side and walked her forward. "Allow me to introduce you to my wife, Nasim bint Habib Abd-

Al-Rachid de Buchan."

The welcoming party fell silent. Colin recovered quickly and extended his hand to her. Nasim turned to Ewan with eyes that begged what she should do.

In her tongue, he said, "Extend your hand to him. He will kiss it. Like I said to your *faither* once, it's a custom in my land to kiss the hand of a ranking lady. And make no mistake, as the wife of an earl, you rank highly."

The men watched the foreign exchange, and Nasim extended a hesitant hand to the older man who took it in warm, creased fingers and placed a kiss upon it.

"Nasim comes from the Holy Land, Colin," Ewan offered, "and is still learning our customs. Nasim, Colin was the distinguished steward for King William and his father before him, King Henry of Scotland in the royal residence at Stirling. He moved to Dunwiddie nine years ago to serve me."

An unrecognized cousin to the king, Ewan knew that working as the steward chafed Colin. Such a cousin deserved a lairdship at least, a title at best. But the man had stood by Ewan and made himself invaluable and for that, Ewan paid him handsomely.

"Is Lady Nasim one of their Christians?" Colin inquired in the Scots' tongue, for it was well-known that a mix of people lived there due to the first and second Crusade as well as a smattering of other religious skirmishes.

"Nay. She is a *Moslem*. But that will have no bearing on how she's treated. She is my wife."

Colin nodded and bowed his head to her, reverting back to English. "And she will be treated with the utmost respect, my laird. My lady, you must be cold, hungry, and exhausted by now. Allow us to escort you to the main castle."

Colin snapped his fingers and Fergus offered his massive hand to her. He was intimidating, huge in his costume and jingling weaponry, his sword slapping his thigh with each step. Again, Nasim looked at Ewan with questions on her brow.

"What should I do?" she asked in her native tongue.

"Take his hand and walk with him. That's Fergus, one of my most loyal men and the captain of my guard. I'm right behind you, Naz. I need to speak with Colin. All is well."

Her eyes lifted with a trusting smile and she turned to take the burly Highlander's hand, still holding her mantle across her face. Ewan ordered their things removed and fell into step with Colin, watching Nasim move gracefully up the path to the rocky stairs cut into the cliff. A warm bath, a sound meal, and a restful sleep with his wife in a proper bed would do him well.

"My laird, by now it has been almost three years since you went to war, and we recently received word that you were dead. A missive arrived nearly two months ago stating that you had valiantly died in battle," the steward began.

"Valiant death my arse," Ewan retorted. "My commander beat me off my horse. 'Twas a cheap blow, for I wouldn't have been expecting it from a Scot loyal to the Crown."

Colin's eyes went wide. "What happened?"

"A local leader, an emir and one of Sultan Saladin's commanders, had his son collect me and brought me back to his palace where his daughter helped heal me. Nasim," he gestured to her.

"And he gave you his daughter why?"

Ewan turned a brief but steely glare upon him and chose to ignore the direct question. There had been no 'giving' involved. "I thwarted a doomed battle against him. 'Twas why I was struck down, though as my commander's scout, he should have awaited my counsel before preparing his attack. I still did nay know enough about the enemy's possible reinforcements or their locations. It was folly for our men to take such a risk. As it turned out, we did have the advantage and my thwarting the attack saved the life of Nasim's brothers."

Colin digested his terse reply. "Might I ask then, what you plan to do about Lady Margaret? She's currently in residence, after I sent her word of your death. She arrived a month ago."

"What?" Ewan froze, though quickly recovered and began walking again. "If word came of my death, then what business does she have here?" *Damn it!* He cursed. There was no reason for Margaret to be here and sakes, but he was exhausted. This wasn't an issue he needed thrown in his face the moment he returned to hearth and home. After so much work to earn

Nasim's trust, he had hoped to resolve things with Lady Margaret quietly. After he had slept for a day. Nothing about it would be quiet if she was here, face to face. Margaret would make certain of that.

Colin shook his head. "She wants to oversee your funeral."

"A funeral without a body?" Ewan scoffed.

"You know her reputation. She's insistent and has wanted to be Lady of Dunwiddie ever since she reached womanhood. This gives her a chance to look the part of a grieving widow."

Ewan's face fell grimly. "Nasim!" he called. She stopped and looked back at him. "Walk with me now."

His words were sterner than he had intended, and when she hastened back down to his side, he feared he had sounded authoritative. He took her hand and rested it in the crook of his arm, forcing a smile for her benefit.

"Colin," Ewan said in Scots. "Walk ahead and do your best to hold the lady off as we come in. I would hate to embarrass my wife. I'll speak with Margaret after Lady Buchan is settled in private."

Colin nodded once and strode ahead of the others. "I'll do my best, but you know her… A tempest might be brewing."

Ewan squeezed Nasim's hand and turned to her. "My command was sharp, but please know, wife, that all will be well," he reassured, as they reached the top of the stairs and approached the raised portcullis.

His blood pulsed and he felt nervous. And as they traveled beneath the gate and traversed the yard, the sight that met his eyes proved that not all would be well after all.

CHAPTER 14

"Ewan!" a woman exclaimed, leaving the charge of Ewan's steward partway up the main steps to the castle.

Nasim tensed. What was going on?

"Margaret!" the steward hollered, pursuing her back down the steps. "I told you the man would like to retire before seeing company!"

The beautiful woman, resplendent in a rose gown with silver embroidery that brought out a natural blush on her cheeks, ignored him. She dashed across the dirt, and threw herself and her ample cleavage at Ewan beside her. The woman planted her lips to his, throwing her arms around his neck.

A gasp left Nasim's lungs.

"Ewan! You've returned to me," the golden-haired, blue-eyed creature cried.

Ewan ripped his head back from hers, gripping her arm, and pushed the woman free, while cinching Nasim's fingers in his elbow to ensure she didn't pull away. She couldn't pull away. She was stunned, petrified in place, confusion and disbelief causing her stomach to turn flips.

Finally, she pulled the end of her mantle up across her face once again. The commotion of many bodies, both male and female, filled the yard around them with activity. Foreign faces, more foreign clothes, another foreign language, buildings, tools, and this utterly foreign woman attempting again to lean up and kiss her husband. She swallowed, knowing her own face had drained of color.

"Ewan, dear, Colin was actually trying to make me come inside and look at fabric samples for a new gown of all things, when I knew a ship had docked, and I could tell from the overlook on the curtain wall that it was you. You look so thin! And my, this beard! Pray you shave it immediately. What can I do, my love, to fatten you up?"

She held her hand out to him, smiling like a beautiful seductress, and waited for Ewan to kiss it. Ewan shot his steward a glare and Nasim watched Colin return the look with a defeated shrug, arms out, and something else. Dejection?

"What could I do?" the steward sighed.

"On whose coin was this gown to be made?" Ewan inquired of Colin. Though his tone indicated he might already know the answer to his question. He squeezed Nasim's fingers so hard, she winced, though sensed he wasn't trying to hurt her. She squirmed them loose. She wished he'd look at her, but ever since the fair woman had kissed him, he had refused to look down. Finally, he took the other woman's hand and placed a chaste kiss upon it.

"My heart is singing, Ewan. Colin sent us the most dreadful news that you were dead. It's as though you're a spirit, come back to finally take my hand in marriage after three long years of waiting."

***

Ewan's face actually flushed, though his beard masked it. He was speechless. And from the way Nasim's fingers had just stiffened further, he knew she had understood Margaret.

"Are you feeling well?" Margaret continued, placing a hand to his cheek. He pulled his face back. "You look angry, and pale. What did those heathen wretches do to you in the war?" she asked with concern as she placed her hands upon his forearm to pull him to her. He held his ground and replaced his hand to cover Nasim's again.

"Who is this?" Margaret asked, finally flitting her gaze to Nasim, and he saw Nasim clench the weather-worn blue and beige mantle across her face more tightly from his periphery. "Don't tell me you brought us a servant from the Holy Land. That *is* how they dress, is it nay?" There was an uncomfortable silence as the stars cleared from Margaret's eyes long enough to see the intimate way in which Ewan was escorting her.

Ewan didn't relent his hold on Nasim's hand, and placed his other at the small of her back.

"I should like to retire for the afternoon, Lady Margaret. It's been a long trek."

He tried to bypass her, guiding Nasim with him, but Margaret wouldn't be moved.

"Who is this, Ewan?"

Her demand was icy. There was no escaping a confrontation. He might as well spit out the news and get ready to clean up the carnage.

"Lady Margaret, this is my wife, Lady Nasim…de Buchan."

Silence.

Margaret blinked, her face transforming into an angry scowl.

"Your…*wife?*"

"Aye. If you will excuse us, we are tired. I haven't the time for a discussion just now, but we will talk later."

Ewan moved past her, guiding Nasim through the throngs of guards and castle workers now gathered around. Margaret spoke behind them.

"You married an *infidel?* Are they as hideous as we know them to be, that they must cover themselves to spare us the horror of looking at them?" Disgust saturated Margaret's voice. Ewan felt Nasim's fingers grip him tightly. "We have a contract. You must annul this farce, or I will get my father involved."

Ewan paused. Everyone hushed. The urge to throttle her for this embarrassment in front of his entire clan burgeoned in his thoughts. No one insulted Nasim, and no one threatened him or ordered him around. Especially in his own home, whether he had been gone for three years or not.

He unclenched his teeth, feeling anger surging though his veins, and took a breath to buy a moment of time for considering his words.

"A contract you considered null, up to now."

"Aye, I thought you dead. But you're nay dead. And therefore, the contract stands."

Ewan's glare deepened. "Much has passed, Lady Margaret, to change the course of my life over these years apart. But it seems to me some things have nay changed at all. Namely your manners." Margaret gasped at his public criticism. "Fergus, escort the sweet-tongued Lady Margaret to her guest chamber and *away* from me."

He began leading Nasim away again when he stopped one last time and pointed at Margaret. "And neither you, nor anyone else," he addressed the onlookers, "insult my wife again. Or there will be consequences for wagging tongues. 'Tis no fault of hers that she is shackled to me in marriage. She was given no choice in the matter."

The silence was deafening. Margaret stood muted.

"See to it that the lady's chambers are prepared for Lady Nasim," he directed to Colin over his shoulder.

"My laird." Colin hastened after him, speaking in Scots so Nasim wouldn't understand. "Such venom over a woman... what happened to you in the Holy Land? This is most unlike you."

"Fulfill my orders, Colin, if you please," Ewan said, ignoring the questions.

"Eh, there's one problem."

"What?" Ewan snapped, stopping to face him.

"Lady Margaret has, well, taken to, em, staying in the lady's chambers whilst visiting."

"You mean the chamber meant for the wife of the Earl of Dunwiddie?" Ewan asked through clenched teeth. Colin shrank back at his anger. "Who gave her permission? I did nay give her permission. Those are my wife's chambers."

Colin gave a placating nod and spoke sheepishly. "'Twas me, sir. It didn't seem extraordinary, if indeed a bit presumptuous. But she requested it, and the betrothal was signed by both you and her *faither*—"

Ewan held up a hand. He had heard enough for one day.

"See that Margaret's belongings are relegated to a guest chamber at once, and have it prepared for Lady Nasim."

Colin bowed his head and turned on his heel to see it done.

Ewan moved Nasim at a clipped pace. They climbed the

rest of the stairs leading away from the grand hall lined with his family coat of arms and the inherited familial banners sent to him after his father died. He would deal with Margaret after a burning swig or two of Highland whisky, the likes of which he had missed. He felt a headache setting in and finally chanced a glance down at Nasim. She didn't look at him. She wouldn't even look up, like the meek woman he had first met. He shook his head, irritated with this entire situation. And yet, if he had warned her, instead of hoping he could somehow manage Margaret quietly, it might not have been as bad.

They walked along the gallery overlooking the dais below, and arrived at the laird's chamber to await the preparation of Nasim's room.

The heavy oak door to the laird's quarters was open as a maid finished the final touches for his surprise arrival. She hauled up a bucket of dusting supplies and gave one more tug to the freshly laundered linens on the mattress. The thick posts of the bed and the plush canopy were polished. His hearth was blazing with a fresh fire. The private door to his solar was also open and beyond it, Ewan spotted his desk, manuscripts, ink, quills, measuring instruments, parchments, vellums, and maps lined in rows along the plastered wall beside the pointed window that overlooked the sea. The shutters were open. A breeze traveled through the space. In spite of his frustrating homecoming, he felt a wave of relief at the familiarity of his work, his belongings, and his freedom.

He released Nasim's hand and gestured with his arm that she should make herself comfortable. She drifted to the red cushions upon a window seat that also overlooked the sea. Pulling her knees up to embrace them, she said nothing, and gazed out at the churning waters of the Minch.

"Nasim," Ewan began, running his hand through his hair. "I did nay know Margaret would be here—"

"You need not say anything," Nasim replied.

She was hurt. He could hear it.

"I'm sorry. She is the woman I was betrothed to, and she had no way of knowing I would return home married. She's angry. I would never have expected her to be here, for this isn't her home. But she thought I had been killed."

Nasim didn't turn around.

"Her behavior was inexcusable, however, and it will be dealt with," he added. "I... Nasim, there's much I didn't tell you. I thought to handle this quietly. Make no mistake, I'm devoted to you, but it could take some time to revoke a betrothal contract."

"Shouldn't being married already sever it?" Nasim asked. Her words were soft, not spoken with malice. Her logic, of course, made sense.

"It should. The problem I attempted to explain to your father, was that our marriage wasn't conducted in the church. There's no documentation of it. No way to prove that a ceremony occurred to legally bind us. I'll get to the bottom of this, make no mistake. Nasim, will you look at me?"

She didn't.

Dejection sliced into him, but he finally backed away. "Get some rest. It's been a rough voyage. Personal chambers are being prepared for you," he muttered and strode to his solar, closing the door.

***

As soon as he was gone, Nasim threw her head into her knees. Tears leaked out onto her threadbare mantle. Of course, she knew he had been betrothed. But she had thought he said he could only be married to one woman. Why was this betrothal even a point of question? Why was the woman allowed to reside here, being unmarried as she still was? The woman named Margaret had been beautiful, bold, and that kiss she had given Ewan felt like a slap. True, Ewan had forced her off of him. He hadn't invited the public display. But it didn't change the fact that Margaret wanted Ewan, and hated her. A horrible feeling niggled its way into her thoughts: *Margaret is going to fight for Ewan.* She could see it in the fair woman's eyes as she lobbed insults and demanded that Ewan annul his marriage.

And here she was, crying in a window seat in an utterly foreign world, with a husband she never doubted was her own until now, dressed in a tent of ugly fabric that hid any type of curve she had. And modesty was what was proper, wasn't it?

174

But she was also an experienced woman now and she knew that a man's urges were related to how attractive he found a woman. And there was no mistaking the lust such a woman as Margaret would stir in a man.

She wiped at the tears. She missed her mother and family. Not once had she envisioned such a stinging welcome to his home. *It isn't his fault, you know this.* But her reasoning did nothing to assuage the hurt. She swiped at the tears rolling down her cheeks to replace the previous ones. But he could have warned her of this problem. *Our marriage might not be seen as valid?* It was several hours later when she woke up, realizing she had drifted to sleep. A blanket had been placed over her and a quick glance around told her Ewan had slept on his massive bed draped in deep, red curtains, for the linens were mussed. He wasn't there now.

The door to his chamber was closed, as was the door to what had looked like his offices. Suddenly the bedchamber door opened and an older woman came inside. She bobbed a curtsy to Nasim and scurried to the hearth to rouse a fire, adding more wood and throwing furtive glances at her. Then she scuttled to the bed, tightening the linens and fluffing the pillows. After wiping down the already gleaming surfaces of the chests and tables, she approached Nasim with a hesitant smile.

The woman spoke. Her words were foreign.

"I don't understand," Nasim said.

"Can I do anything for you, milady?" the woman repeated, this time in English.

Nasim shook her head and stood. She was starving, but was uncertain about the proper etiquette. The old woman busied herself picking up Nasim's blanket, folding it, then fluffing the cushions.

"This must all seem very strange to you. What is your homeland like, milady?"

Nasim smiled at her despite her upset. "'Tis hot. The sun is always shining."

"We celebrate when the sun shines here, because when it does, it's glorious. Though I must say, the middle of January is a brave time of year indeed to travel."

Just having a cheerful face to talk to eased Nasim's mind, and she continued to smile.

"Where is Ewan?" she asked.

The woman nodded toward the solar door as she put fresh coverlets on a stack of extra pillows, giving them a stiff jerk to slide them into the case. "He's in a meeting."

"What sort of meeting?"

The old woman cast her a sympathetic look, when her face sparked with an idea. "Let's put an ear to the door and find out."

She waddled to Nasim and took her hand, pulling her toward the solar door.

"No," Nasim said. "Is it not wrong to intrude on his private business dealings?"

"Oh shush, my dear. He claims to be your husband. You have a right to know what he's up to."

She tugged Nasim across the rugs to the door. Faintly, Nasim heard muffled voices on the other side. She pressed her ear to it the way the old woman was doing, biting back the nervous feeling such eavesdropping created in her stomach.

***

"…but you didn't marry the infidel in a church with a priest," said Malcolm of Fyvie. "Therefore, this marriage is void. Your betrothal to my daughter is still valid. You must fulfill your part of the deal."

"I choose to honor my marriage to Nasim," Ewan replied tersely. "I must break our contract."

"I will take this matter to the king if I must," Malcolm threatened. "My daughter wishes this, and we had an agreement."

"I had no choice but to marry this lass. What would you have had me do? It's nay my lady's fault that I'm a Christian, nor is it her fault that her father discarded her so easily. But I've come to know her over these months. I care deeply for her and consider her my wife. I refuse to dishonor her in such a way by casting her aside given all that's happened."

"So you dishonor my daughter instead?" Malcolm fumed. "Make a mockery of her in front of your clan? Is that the way to

176

treat not only a guest, but a lady of breeding that you are supposed to marry?"

Ewan raked back his chair and shot to his feet. "Insulting the laird of the castle is nay a way for a guest to behave either, sir. Your daughter was out of line."

The old man, groomed and donning his great kilt, pinched the bridge of his nose, sighed, and then spoke. "Fine. So you wish nay to hurt the young woman sleeping in your chamber—"

"My *wife*."

Malcolm waved his hand at the remark. "Call her what you will. Install her in one of your many estates with a household to look after her, go and sard her day and night if you must, but marry Margaret in the church. Many men keep mistresses on the side. Your own *faither* had several in his lifetime." The remark made Ewan's pulse rage. He knew his father's reputation well and didn't need it thrown in his face. "It's common enough. And Margaret will cope with it, as long as she does nay have to see her. Breed Margaret with legitimate heirs, and then go to your infidel mistress for comfort. Problem solved."

Ewan fell silent. Anger coursed through him. Guilt also snagged him. He remembered having a similar idea back in Jerusalem. But his conscience, growing up the way that he had, prevented him from considering it. And the war and his commander's unprovoked violence had changed him. When had he changed? When he had finally made love to Nasim and claimed her innocence? No, it had been well before that. That very first morn when they departed Jerusalem and she had mourned? That fateful evening when he had kissed her hand? No matter when it had happened, he knew he loved Nasim. He couldn't just discard her in an estate like one would discard a cow in a byre. She wasn't just a woman. She was his...*other half.*

Margaret had never been his love. He hadn't known what love was, until he had come to love Nasim. He had known manners, etiquette, cartography, and what it was like to grow up without a parent wanting him because it made his step-mother upset. He had always been a chivalrous man, but even he now realized his attitude toward Margaret had been based on presumptions of marriage and customs for men and women. He would need heirs. He wanted to bed someone pleasant looking. He'd known Margaret wanted a suit. She'd stirred his base impulses with her sensuous curves and wanton lips, seductive eyes and blonde hair. Her father was a peer and wanted a trade. Ewan had never seen his father love a woman. How would he have known what love felt like before going to the Holy Land and having Nasim's very survival thrust upon him, as his very survival had been thrust upon her?

"Well?" prompted Malcolm. "The idea does have merit, does it no'? This infidel is only a woman. What does it matter?"

It would be too hard for Laird Fyvie and his ambitious daughter to understand, Ewan realized. Malcolm, though he certainly loved his daughter, considered her a commodity just like a sheep or a cow. *Malcolm must never have loved a woman, either.* Many men would jump to have two beautiful women at their disposal. But Nasim wasn't "only a woman." He wanted her beside him. She was a skilled healer, educated, smart, strong, and someone he'd respected from the moment he'd been thrust into her care. And one did not betray someone they held in esteem.

Malcolm and his daughter had never fought in a bloody war like the Crusade, in a foreign land, nearly died, or endured what he had endured. It changed a man, put things in perspective, and made the simple pleasures like loving a woman and making a home together treasures of more worth than gold.

Ewan shook his head. "I can nay do it. I love my wife. Call it a code of honor, but I made her mine, in body and in name. I've always vowed to be a faithful husband. I'll nay do this to her."

"You said yourself you were forced to marry. Why should you care? Are you afraid of her reaction? Surely no, man." Fyvie was baiting him.

"I *respect* her," Ewan retorted.

"Then your belligerence leaves me no choice. I'll have to request an audience with King William."

"Why not see reason and talk to your daughter?" Ewan said, for it was clear the man hadn't listened to him while formulating his rebuttals. "Why marry her to a man who doesn't want her any longer? I understand the legalities here, but why condemn Margaret to someone who claims favor for another? After all, I'm willing to compensate you for the severance. I know this creates a hardship for you."

"We're owed this alliance. Margaret deserves to get what she is owed, and I need our business arrangement, not a severance pay—"

"You get nothing from this!" Ewan erupted. "I'm the one who gets the dowry and a woman. A dowry you can ill afford to part with if I am to understand your current financial state!"

"You know that I talk of my free passage to the sea and Margaret's rightful place of prestige in the Buchan line! You're right! My finances have always been thinner than yours! I did nay have a *faither* of rich means bequeath me a vault of assets when I was born, like you did, and I can ill afford to pay you taxes over the years. I will gladly pay a dowry now to avoid being destitute later."

"Be gone with you, man!" Ewan barked. Watching Commander Rachid toss out his daughter over a trivial matter had changed his perspective. No matter Margaret's disrespect upon his homecoming, he had little respect now for Fyvie's line of reasoning. "Any man willing to sell his daughter just to avoid taxes is a fool."

Malcolm kicked his chair aside and stomped to the door, slamming it shut.

"Dammit," Ewan grunted, and pounded his fist on the desk, then took a deep, calming breath, and shoved aside his chair to step away.

***

Nasim and the kindly servant woman retreated back to the window seat.

"I don't understand this man's words," she began. "What language is this?"

The servant woman took her hands.

'Tis 'Scots,' milady. Our local tongue."

"Of what did they speak?"

"It's an unfortunate position you are in, as well as his lairdship." The woman patted her hands. "But I can tell he loves you."

"Why must they argue? Do they argue about me?"

The woman remained silent, which told Nasim that they did.

"My father made us marry. And Ewan said he can only have one wife."

"Legally, yes. Why is that odd?" the maid asked.

Nasim shrugged. "My father has twelve wives."

"Twelve? At the same time?" the woman gasped. "But that's unchristian—" She cut herself off.

Of course it was unchristian, Nasim thought. And undoubtedly gossip would soon rage through the castle, for in this land, people seemed less disciplined about who they talked to and what they talked about. She had just eavesdropped on her husband's private dealings, for goodness sake.

"Please tell me why they must argue," Nasim insisted.

"Milady, I really think you should nay worry yourself." The woman rose to leave.

"I would like to know."

The woman paused as if weighing her options, then finally resigned herself on a sigh. "Since you did nay have a Christian wedding, nor are you of Christian heritage, your marriage might not be considered valid here. The other man wishes the laird to marry his daughter in the church and keep you as his mistress. But Laird Buchan is refusing and wishes to remain true to you."

Nasim froze. "I would be a whore?"

It took her a moment to realize she had spoken in her native language by the quizzical look on the maid servant's face. But if a noblewoman was not a wife and had intercourse, she was a whore, plain and simple. The idea of Commander Rachid's physician daughter as a lowly whore made her double over. But she was no longer the commander's daughter, either. He had exiled her to fend for herself. Her family was no doubt forbidden to speak her name. They had vanquished her from their hearts and minds.

Vomit roiled in her throat and no sooner had it started brewing, the old woman hurried to the empty chamber pot and thrust it under Nasim's mouth as the contents of her stomach came tumbling up. Considering her earlier seasickness, there wasn't much in the chamber pot.

"You poor dear," the woman crooned, brushing her hair back which had fallen loose in her sleep. "Come lie back down now. All will be well, you'll see. Laird Buchan is an honorable man. I know this to be true, because I raised him. He will look out for you, no matter what."

CHAPTER 15

Ewan stared out at the sea, resting his arm above him on the window frame as the cold January air reddened his face. His great kilt of red plaid woven onto a field of green, wavered in the breeze blowing in. He adjusted the tartan over his shoulder, pulling it around his arms to ease the chill. The candles lighting his solar had burned significantly since Malcolm had barged in on him while he reviewed the past three years' finances, and he had stormed off in equal anger, letting in a draft. Ewan felt like drinking and nothing more.

He indulged his want and poured himself a dram of Highland whisky, tossing back the contents and swallowing the burn as he eyed a dirk with Colin's colors sitting on his desk. Colin had maintained his affairs during the whole of his time in Jerusalem and had done a fine job of it, too. He picked up the dirk and tucked it into his waist to return it.

He closed his eyes. But the heartbreak on Nasim's face waited for him beneath his eyelids. What would possess Margaret and her father to reside here long after news of his death came? Mourning should be well underway. What would possess Margaret to thrust herself upon him so wantonly in front of the entire castle? He could understand her initial elation, but he couldn't understand her prejudicial words afterward. *Aye, you can. No one here has gotten to know people like Nasim the way you have. They haven't lived a month of their life in the confines of the Holy Land, nor have they lived for many more in that sweltering place of minarets and east-bound prayers. They can nay possibly comprehend how Nasim's world is both treacherous and beautiful, the way in which Europe is in its own right.* His people had misconceptions that they would need to learn were wrong. Like he had learned. But he'd never seen how ugly such ignorant sentiments appeared until now.

He had no idea what to do. If Fyvie brought his grievance before the king, it was more than reasonable that the king would agree with Laird Fyvie's idea. *Hell, even I had the same idea at one time.* Well, if Margaret and her father would play dirty, he would as well. He might be forced to marry her, but he would make every effort to thwart it first. If a wedding must still proceed, Margaret would be a wife in title only, and he would make it clear his disdain by refusing to legitimize their union by parting her legs, leaving her a virgin. Eventually, he might be able to secure an annulment if their marriage was never consummated. And if Margaret should suddenly no longer be a virgin in an underhanded attempt to tether him down, well… a cuckolded husband *did* have some rights to speak of.

Nay, Margaret might be underhanded enough to push this betrothal before the king to see it enforced, but she wouldn't stoop to that level. Would she? *Nay, such a scheme likely won't come to pass,* he reasoned. If he was forced to marry her in the church, he would send Malcolm's daughter home to their stronghold after their "nuptials." Her father could look after her. Margaret could sit in her father's great hall and be proud of her marital alliance. Alone. By herself. He would fight fire with fire of his own if that was what it took.

He swiped the whisky decanter up and took another swig, this time straight from the vessel. In the meantime, he would write to the king and explain that he still lived. And explain the nature of his supposed death. His commander had it in for him, seemingly out of the blue. It made no sense. Unless he had wanted to get rid of his competition for cartography commissions. It was no secret, Ewan was skilled and his business had once been booming, as had Commander Murray's.

He scraped back his chair and dropped into it, drawing forth a sheet of pounced parchment. He dipped his quill pen in the inkwell and wrote a meticulous letter to His Majesty King

William. Done with his task, he folded the dried letter, held his wax to his candle flame to drip a dark pool onto the seam, and stamped his seal into it. He exited to find a messenger. While he waited on his letter to reach the royal court, he would try to talk some reason into Laird Fyvie.

***

"Coming through!" called a page as he wove around the hall with a platter of roasted fish held over his head.

The great hall bustled as servants prepared for the feast Colin ordered to commemorate Ewan's safe homecoming. Serving girls and boys laid out platters of deer, mutton, roasted vegetables, meat pies, berry pies, and seasoned porridge. Ewan listened to the dampened commotion coming up the stairs to his chamber door. He could smell the food.

"Wife?" he asked as he turned back to Nasim who still sat silently on the window seat overlooking the sea. "Will you do me the honor of accompanying me to supper?"

She smiled amiably at him, seemingly having recomposed herself, but Ewan could see it was all the act of a dutiful wife.

"It would be an honor indeed, but I'm overly tired from the voyage," she replied. "May I remain here and dine in private?"

"Naz," he said, walking to her. "I wish to show off my lovely wife, have you by my side. 'Tis the way things are done here. You needn't hide away from everyone. No one will come to know you if you refuse their company."

He took a seat beside her and reached for her hand. She shifted uncomfortably, so he refrained and rested his hands on his knees instead.

"Ewan," she began, trying to paste a pleasing smile back on her mouth. "I'm not your wife in front of your people. Your betrothed wishes to be, and from what it sounds like, she aims to get her wish."

She ducked her head down. Ewan's teeth clenched. Myrtle must have been eavesdropping at his door and shared her findings with his young bride, for Myrtle had been the only one to visit Nasim. He took a deep breath and shook his head.

"*I* honor our marriage. That should be enough," he

insisted. "With time, everyone else will accept it, too."

"I'm sorry, Ewan. I knew you were betrothed. I just thought that what you said was the truth. That you could only be married once at a time. It shouldn't bother me that you might have to marry her. I've thought all my life that when I married, my husband might take more wives, too. I'm just surprised. I have no right to feel hurt."

"Aye, you do," Ewan said, defending her. "How Margaret behaved was unkind. It was intended to be hurtful."

"She didn't know you would return home married, if you even returned. It isn't her fault for being angry. But that kiss…"

Was Nasim jealous? "'Twill never happen again, love. I wasn't prepared to fend her off and it took me by surprise."

"I'm not angered. It just hurt to see." Nasim shrugged. "But what hurts right now, husb—Ewan—is that I realize I now belong to a man who isn't considered my husband at all, which makes me a whore. In my country, there's no greater shame."

"We're no' in your country any longer," Ewan argued. "And never call yourself such a vile name again."

"Tell me, are the rules different here?" Nasim snapped, surprising him. "Is there no shame in bedding a man each night who isn't your husband?"

He couldn't answer. Sometimes, mistresses were held in high esteem, but it was still, at best, frowned upon by the church. At worst, punishable, depending on how wealthy the man and how strict the priest.

"That's what I thought," Nasim whispered, looking away. "Please, enjoy your supper and your homecoming. But this isn't my home. With time, mayhap that will change."

His heart clenched. He reached for her. She was stiff.

"Nasim. Like it or nay, this *is* your home now. You have only ever given yourself to me. I consider us married."

"But no one else does—"

"Only Margaret and her *faither*," he interrupted. "Everyone else knows to respect you and with time, will come to love you, too."

"Because you told them to," she argued. "But I saw the way they stared at me, the way they whispered."

"As people stared at me in Jerusalem. As people gossiped about me. Hell, I was attacked for being different, for showing you my thanks for saving my life, for kissing your hand. And make no mistake, whilst you're here and this is different, I had the added boon of being in the enemy's lair, where every able-bodied man wished to see me drawn and quartered. And I suspect your brother, Abdullah, needed little provocation to see the deed done. But I didn't hide away in a chamber to avoid the curiosity. Is that what you will do? Hide in here day after day because people stare? If you make yourself part of them, they will eventually stop staring, and see your presence as part of the normal goings-on. When I married you, I made a vow. I wasn't going to abandon you the way your people did, no matter what. But nothing about this ordeal has been easy, for either of us. It'll nay get easier today, unfortunately, but it will with time. The journey is over. This is your home, whether you accept it or nay. And in your new home, you're expected to sit beside your laird and husband at board."

She shook her head, pleading. "How can you expect me to show my face?"

Ewan bit back his mounting frustration and stood, no longer attempting to ease her mind.

"The same way I showed mine as I sat at our wedding. The most uncomfortable day of my life." He strode to the door. Bitterness threatened to overtake his mood. "But I did it for you. I wish you could do the same for me. I had hoped to resolve things with Margaret quietly upon my homecoming so as not to embarrass anyone. I'm sorry I did nay succeed. But as much as this day has hurt us both, it was nay my fault she was here or that she behaved as she did."

Nasim looked up. Did he see regret in her eyes?

"Did you love her the way I loved Solomon?"

The way I love you? Impossible. He should simply say the sentiment in place of the biting words forming on his tongue. But he couldn't. He sighed and lifted the latch, ignoring how mention of Solomon's name drew his ire. He had given Nasim his all this entire journey, and dammit, but he was angry at her self-pity. The odds had been against them from the beginning, yet they had succeeded. They had overcome the weight of the world thrust upon them, and not only survived, but fallen in love, and while he hated that the problem of Margaret Fyvie might cast a shadow on his union's legitimacy, he'd be damned if he was going to give in to his sorrow now.

"I do nay love Margaret nor have I ever. But marriage isn't about love, is it?"

Her eyes reddened at his censuring words.

"I'll have Myrtle bring you a supper trencher. If you should change your mind about accompanying me…" His voice softened, but after a pause and no reaction from her, he shook his head and left it at that, heaving the door shut behind him.

He strode to the gallery and overlooked the hall, noting two chairs at the center of the dais for the laird and lady. If only they could be back in Lombardy, in their rock shelter, basking in the aftermath of their first joining while the stars twinkled over the lake. She had been so content. He hadn't wanted to move. He could have rested in front of that waning fire, tangled with Nasim forever. The soreness of their long journey had receded away, leaving two peoples' bodies sated and happy. The problems they had left behind and the ones awaiting them hadn't mattered in that sliver of time.

This is a big change for her. Imagine how you would feel if Solomon walked up to Nasim right now and planted his lips to hers… You would rage red, man, and you know it. But try as he might to reason with himself, her rejection sliced, just as it always had. Women were considered the lesser sex, yet did she realize the power she wielded over him?

He made his way down the stairs and entered the hall. Men and women at the trestle tables and those still searching for a seat were already imbibing their share of ale. He was the laird and would have to push what he was feeling aside. It had no place in leading his people. Perhaps dinner in the great hall would have been too much of a shock for Nasim, he resigned himself to think, trying to find any reason at all to justify her absence. Such abundant displays of women's cleavage and men pinching the serving girls' rears might leave her mortified after an afternoon already fraught with high emotions.

Stepping up on the dais, the hall around him let out a cheer, raising their tankards. He smiled, lifted a hand, and found his seat.

"I apologize," he announced, "that my wife is feeling unwell from many months of journeying and is in need of rest. But you shall meet her soon."

The people cheered harder, offering shouts of curiosity. Suddenly, Lady Margaret entered the hall on her father's arm and wove her way through the onlookers, arriving to the dais steps. Her gown was a soft blue with a violet kirtle and creamy embroidery accentuating the lift of her chest. She walked with habit to the lady's chair directly to Ewan's side where her father saw her seated.

"My laird," she smiled seductively at him, as if nothing had happened, as if she hadn't already been removed from the lady's chambers and placed elsewhere.

Ewan stiffened. The presumption and audacity made rage he had never felt toward a woman pulse to life in his blood. An uneasy silence settled over the hall as the clansmen and women watched the exchange. He took a slow, steadying breath. Reacting when he felt so enraged was a poor idea and would lead to regrets.

"Do nay embarrass my daughter again," came the whispered warning from the Laird Fyvie as he reached to clasp Ewan's wrist in mock greeting. "This is Margaret's rightful seat and you know it."

Ewan smoldered the explosion that nearly burst from his lips. Margaret wasn't his wife, and even if he should be forced to marry her, he was not married to her yet. And this was his home, dammit! What gave anyone the right to override his authority?

"If you know what is good for you, man, you'll remove your daughter from my presence immediately," Ewan murmured in reply.

"And if I do nay?" Malcolm said, eyes narrowing.

Nay, Ewan wasn't going to make a scene right now. True, he could order his guardsmen forth to physically remove them both, but he wouldn't. The punishment would be exacted later, when he had a chance to check his anger. But regaining control of Dunwiddie was a task he needed to assume immediately.

"Speech!" someone called into the uncomfortable silence. "Speech!"

His people began chanting the word, anything to ease the moment. Ewan caught Myrtle's attention and waved her over. The old woman hustled to the front of the dais and looked up. He leaned over, lowering his voice.

"See to it two trenchers are brought up for Lady Buchan and myself. We will be dining separately tonight."

The woman bobbed a curtsy and threw a quick glance at Lady Margaret beside him who was trying to reach out to take his hand. Ewan drew his hands together, out of her reach. Myrtle scurried away to the kitchens.

"You used to favor my touch," Margaret said, her tone sad but her eyes seductive.

His jaw muscles ticked as he pumped them.

"Speech!" the hall demanded.

Ewan held up a hand to silence them. The noise softened until the room was calm.

"I'm grateful to be home with my people after such an arduous journey." He cleared his throat and grew wistful. "The war...*wars* are never what they seem. I spent almost three years away from home, two of those years using my map-making skills to track armies and kill men whilst trying to nay be killed myself, all because we have a different faith in the same God."

The hall, with its tall, echoing ceiling, remained still, the joyous ruckus of a few moments before, gone now.

"I almost died. My ribs were broken and they tore my lung. Nasim, my wife, put me back together. She cut into my chest, stitched the tear, and did it all whilst staving off festering... Understand that there was no real point to the war. Any of it. At least, none that I can see, except the typical battle to control an important city." Tired, Ewan pushed his seat out of the way so he could step aside and leave as the words "incredible," "amazing," and "miracle" circulated the hall.

"Why did the English messenger say you were dead?" came a question.

Ewan paused in midstride and formed a response. "One of King William's commanders beat me off my horse and left me for the buzzards or the enemy. If it was nay for my wife's *faither* taking me in to heal me, I would have died, as my commander assumed when he sent the missive of my passing back to Scotland."

What little noise remained was sobered by complete silence now.

"Please. Enjoy the food and drink until your hearts are content," Ewan smiled, swinging his arm wide to encompass the bounty before them. "I hope you celebrate, but I shall be dining in private with my wife. I dare say she has been made to feel less than welcome. The Lady Margaret occupies my lady's seat tonight. I bid she enjoy it. For it does nay mean what she thinks it means. She'll nay have the privilege again," he added with a sidelong glance, watching Malcolm's fuming face.

He turned a cold face to Margaret who was no longer smiling and then at Malcolm. "I hope she isn't 'embarrassed.'" Then he strode away.

CHAPTER 16

A sennight was a long time to remain in seclusion, in a castle not designed for women to live separately from men. Nasim watched as a crew departed by sea, Ewan aboard a vessel, she in her lady's chambers looking out. The view was spectacular. She'd always wanted to visit the sea, and now she got to live by it. The distant rushing of waves breaking was soothing and peaceful. Her heart felt anything but peaceful, however.

The ship set out to sail. How long would he remain gone? What business had called him away? They had hardly shared two words since arriving and the few times he had asked to share her bed, she had stiffened. Like she used to when he made advances. And he had taken it as rejection, rolling away from her, just as he used to do as well. Heaven above, she wasn't rejecting him. She just couldn't come to terms with the uncertainty of her fate.

Malcolm and Margaret weren't relenting in their arguments. Ewan was constantly frustrated. And now, he was gone, having left her alone without even a word of good-bye. It's not as if she had made good company anyway.

She felt her eyes mist again, a symptom all too common over the past seven days, when she had shed hardly any tears at all the whole of their arduous trek. She dug her fingers into her palms to stave off the water once and for all. This was her life now. She should be grateful that she still had one, thanks to Ewan vowing to keep her after their forced wedding. No amount of missing her mother or wishing to be gone from within these strange walls and Margaret's presence would change a thing.

To where was he going? Too busy wallowing in her self-pity, she hadn't afforded him time to tell her. That wasn't true. She had just been hiding in her chamber and stayed unmoving. Her healing skills were growing dusty with no books to read, and she made for poor company. Ewan had tried to spend time with her, asked her to accompany him to board, to go out and meet his people and see his castle and village. He was certain she would be fascinated by Scotland's landscapes, cold as the winter weather was. But she had rejected his company.

A horrible thought seized her. What if he had given up? What if she had killed his desire to care for her?

A knock on the door brought her attention back to the moment. She turned, pulling her mantle across her face, more out of habit than anything else. Myrtle opened the door and came in with a nooning tray. Nasim dropped the fabric away and smiled weakly, returning her eyes to the ship growing small on the horizon as it sailed out to catch a current.

The old woman clicked her tongue and shook her head. "If you do nay mind my saying so, you're a fool, lass."

Nasim furrowed her brow.

"That man does naught but defend his marriage to you, and you can nay even bring yourself to appreciate it." Nasim opened her mouth to speak, but Myrtle continued. "It's caused him great pain, dealing with the legalities of the past sennight and you canna' even find it in yourself to trust in him."

Trust. He had wanted to win her trust from the beginning.

"I'm not considered his wife," Nasim defended.

"*Shush*," Myrtle waved, her tone scathing. "I changed the man's breeches when he was just a wee lad, taught him his manners, what was right and wrong, and I know that in his core, he is a wonderful man. A bit playful in his teenage years, but always respectful, and he has turned out nicely. I helped raise him to be so when his *faither* dumped him on me at the tender age of two."

Nasim stared at her. "I don't understand. Was he not raised by his mother?"

"Have you ever heard him talk of a *mither*?" Myrtle questioned.

No. Not once has he spoken of her.

Myrtle glared at her with a look of satisfied anger. "He's a bastard. Did you know? His *faither* kept many mistresses apart from his wife. Ewan was an illegitimate bairn but his *faither's* only son. So his sire recognized him as a Buchan and took him from his mother's arms as soon as he was weaned. He was installed in an estate in the country so that his wife would nay have to see the bounty of his seed sowing, and I was put in charge of rearing him."

"Goodness…" Not once had Ewan told her. Not once had he pitied his position in life and begged that she feel sorry for him, and here she was, crying because the nature of their forced marriage had caused them some tumult with his betrothed. *I'm acting like a babe. Ewan, a bastard?* "Does Ewan know his *faither*?"

"The arse of a nobleman never had much to do with Ewan, except to pay my wages and pay for his tutoring. He sent him to be fostered by another noble in Ireland when he reached adolescence, then sent him on to university, and left him his entire inheritance. But they only met a handful of times. His *faither's* wife hated him, and on the occasions he was summoned to their castle for a visit, his step-mother sabotaged him, locking his bedchamber door whilst he was in it, 'accidentally' of course, seeing his clothing tailored to the improper size, seeing his dinner portions cut in half…small unkindnesses intended to hurt his feelings. The man does nay even know who is *mither* is to this day."

"He has never even met her?"

Myrtle shook her head. "All he knows is what he was told. That she likely came from Glasgow. His *faither* had a taste for noblewomen instead of wenches, and therefore, her identity was probably kept secret to protect her reputation."

Nasim felt even worse for her behavior now. He had been so selfless, so giving to her, and this was how she had repaid his kindness. "I had no idea."

"You would have, if you would set aside your own pain for a moment and look good and hard at the man. He honors you.

He hated growing up as the bastard son, and told me once at the age of three and ten that when the day came to marry, he would honor his wife so that no woman or child of his would have to live with the humiliation of being illegitimate."

Shame washed over Nasim. If only Ewan were still here! She would run to him to apologize. In all of her pain after her loss of her own family, she had never realized the circumstances out of which Ewan had come.

"Every night when he dines with you, or alone in his chamber, he is honoring you by refusing to share his presence with Lady Margaret. Every time he argues with Margaret's *faither*, he honors you by demanding that they respect you as his wife. Have you no idea what sort of position he is in? Either die in the Holy Land, or take you to wife to save you both, knowing the legal battle that might await him at home? I can guarantee you that if the king orders him to marry Margaret, he will make certain Dunwiddie knows you hold his heart. It is clear to me he has come to love you."

Marriage has never been about love... Ewan's voice sounded in her head. No it was not about love, but somewhere along the way she had grown to love him, too. Ah, had she, *Layla* in this tragic tale of love, actually been given to the man she had always wanted? The parallels in her life to her once-favorite love story seemed as of now, so weak, that they didn't even compare at all. She had been holding onto the threads of a story to make sense of her predicament.

"I don't want to be seen as a whore," Nasim whispered.

"And you're nay thought of as one. That is something in your own mind you need to banish. Ewan's people know to accept his decision. Some are even ready to accept you publically, in a show of their unwavering fealty to him, even if they are curious about your differences. You *are* different and people are bound to be curious, but everyone is beginning to think you've taken to the sick bed since they have nay seen you since your arrival, and if I do say so myself, it is time you quit acting childish."

Nasim's eyes opened with shock.

"Your *faither* cast you out, and you can nay change that. But you can decide what kind of life you make with the laird. Do you love him?" the old woman demanded.

Nasim nodded. "I've grown to love him so deeply, and that's why this predicament hurts so much."

"Then you must act the part of his wife. You can nay change this circumstance. Margaret will not back down until she has what she wants, and she has the law on her side. The king might very well demand he marry her. But Ewan recognizes *you*, and a wife joins her husband at supper, assists him in the bedchamber with private ablutions, honors him in public, and runs his household. Now either you do that, or eventually, you could lose him. Which will it be?"

Nasim wrung her hands in her mantle. Stepping out without an escort terrified her... *No, it doesn't. The entire reason your life has changed this much, is because you stepped out without escort to sneak off and find the blue-eyed stranger.* Heaven above, she didn't want to lose Ewan on top of her family. She gulped, then looked at the old woman who despite her harsh reprimand had sympathy in her eyes.

"I know not the first thing to do. Will you help me?"

Myrtle's wrinkled face split into a smile. "I was hoping you would ask." She bustled to a trunk and heaved the lid open. "I had these brought in when the laird asked this chamber be prepared for you." She laid out several gowns, kirtles, chemises, and ribbons. "These belonged to one of Ewan's half-sisters who lived with him for a spell until she was married, and you are of a similar size. They should fit fell enough until the seamstress can take your measurements and create a wardrobe for you. The first thing to do is look the part of the chatelaine. You're no longer in Jerusalem and your clothing is nay customary. Let's get you cleaned and dressed. Sit and eat. And I'll nay have another argument about it. I will have a bath brought up for you."

The woman scurried out of the room and Nasim nodded to herself. Myrtle was right. There was no changing the past. But Ewan was offering her a good future here, no matter the outcome of his marriage debacle. And she loved him. With a renewed sense of purpose in this utterly foreign land, she lifted the lid off her tray and sat down to the contents of the steaming meal before her.

***

Dinner in the great hall was a loud affair. Nasim arrived early, allowing one of Ewan's guards sent by Myrtle, to escort her on his arm. Her stomach turned flips, cinched within the confines of her unusual dress. But she did it. And God did not strike her dead for having touched the man. He saw her seated in the chair next to Ewan's empty seat and as the room filled, the serving staff brought a veritable feast to the head table. People cast glances at her, gossiped in whispers. She held her head high, in spite of the discomfort.

But if she had hoped the discomfort would abate, she was mistaken. Margaret entered the hall with two of her handmaidens and walked upon the dais, halting in her steps. Her soft blue eyes settled upon her. Finally, Margaret found the strength, or anger, to march forward.

Nasim, sipping from her goblet. Looked up at Margaret coming. And smiled as amiably as she could.

"I demand you move," Margaret said, stopping beside her.

"It was my husband's wish I dine here with his people," Nasim said softly but firmly.

"He isn't your husband," Margaret retorted, her pale cheeks turning pink.

"He isn't your husband," Nasim replied. "But in my country, he *is* married to me. He was not given a choice, I admit. Our marriage was forced upon us both. But he does honor me regardless, and I have been too childish these past days to honor him in return. I have decided to change that. I bid you sit next to me and we will talk and get to know one another."

Margaret's face twisted with disgust. "I'll nay share my meal with an infidel fornicating with my betrothed like the whore she is—" Nasim knew the words would sting. She knew, at some point, she would be compared to a harlot. She steeled herself now. "If my *faither* were here, he would force Ewan to make you leave at once."

Malcolm had left shortly after Ewan, and the gossip was that he was seeking the king.

"Your sire is not here, and I only do as my husband bids.

Please reconsider and sit with me. I'm not your enemy nor are you, mine. All of this is a grand conundrum, and none of our faults."

Margaret glared at her, then at her goblet. "I would be careful if I were you. Should you sip from the wrong cup one of these days…"

"Do you threaten me?" Nasim asked, her back straightening a degree.

Margaret smiled a smile that didn't meet her eyes. "I'm simply warning you the king will force the laird to marry me, and when he does, I will then be the lady of the castle and you will have to obey me. And I plan to make your life a miserable hell that no dog would be able to withstand."

"I wish not to be your enemy," Nasim began, swallowing her anger. "I wish you no ill will. But as long as he claims to be my husband, I must honor his wishes."

Margaret's eyes narrowed and her voice became a hiss. "You'll be sorry." She whirled around and stalked away. "Myrtle, bring my dinner to my chamber."

Myrtle scowled at Margaret's unkind demand as she bustled away, but sent Nasim a discrete wink as she went. Despite her fears, when the hall had filled and the merrymaking was underway, a guardsman, burly with a chestnut beard, came forth.

"Stand, milady," Myrtle whispered, miraculously passing her by at that moment again. Was Myrtle hovering? Was she trying to help her? She stood to address the clansman's query.

"Milady," he reached to her.

She extended her hand and he kissed it. It was one of the men who had greeted her at the dock a sennight earlier. "What a radiant, dark-haired beauty you are. Laird Buchan has done well to bring you back from Jerusalem."

He backed away, but already more and more clansmen and women were coming forth.

"Elegant…"

"Voluptuous curls…"

"So dark, eyes…"

"Beautiful…"

In fact, Nasim did find the hair styling to be beautiful.

Myrtle had shown her the intricate weave in a bronze looking glass, and she had marveled at the glossy paste and shining bobbles the woman had painted upon her lips and clipped to her ears. The men kissed her hand, over and over again, the women, curtsied, declaring their fealty to protect and serve her as their lady. She stood stone still, barely remembering to smile and nod as she was rendered speechless. To think, a world that used a simple kiss to show respect…and Ewan had made that fatal mistake in a dusky passageway in Jerusalem. Look at the trouble in which it had landed him.

A glance around the hall took her eyes to the gallery above where Margaret was watching. The other woman turned away into the shadows with anger clouding her face. The hall filled with chatter, oblivious to Margaret pouting, and the drinking and eating commenced.

Colin came to the dais and stood before her. "My lady. I'm heartened to see that you have finally decided to join us this eve. May I speak with you?"

Nasim smiled and nodded.

"Laird Buchan is nay here, or else I would have sought him."

His face looked grave.

"What's the matter, sir?" Nasim asked.

Colin cleared his throat. "I received a missive earlier this eve. My younger brother has taken ill, and I request leave to go and see him."

Nasim smiled. "Of course you may go to him. Why would you need to ask?"

"He lives in Stirling, in one of King William's strongholds, which is where I'm from. 'Tis a few days' journey from here, and as the steward of the castle, my presence would be missed."

Myrtle came by with pitcher in hand and filled Nasim's goblet. She cast one more look at the gallery where Margaret had stood moments before. Colin followed her gaze, but turned back to Nasim.

"You're welcome to depart whenever you need, sir. I will let Ewan know you have gone as soon as he returns, should you not be back yet."

"Oh, I have no doubt I will be back well before his return. He plans to be gone for a month at the least and a ride to Stirling and back shouldn't take nearly so long. He knows my brother. He would worry overmuch if he knew of his illness."

"A month?" Nasim said, feeling daft for not knowing.

"Aye, and Laird Buchan has been kind to me over the years. I beg you nay burden him with something such as this. He has much on his mind already."

She nodded to him, smiling at his compliment of Ewan as he retreated back into the dining hall. Ewan really was a fine man. Everyone here could see it, for he had provided for them well. A shame it had taken her so long to come to her senses, but she would be ready to apologize to him upon his return.

"They seem to like you so far, milady," Myrtle murmured under her breath.

"They hardly know me," Nasim replied. "I wonder what ails Colin's brother. I might be able to help."

"How so?" Myrtle asked.

"I was trained as a physician in my land under one of Jerusalem's finest masters. Indeed, I have studied the treatment of many ailments."

"That is a superb skill. Tell me, would you like to make use of your trade for your peoples' benefit here? It might help the bonds of trust grow stronger betwixt you and them."

My people, Nasim thought, reminding herself that though the kisses were symbolic, they did not necessarily equate to fidelity. Still, being a healer could be valuable to Ewan's clan. "In truth, I've only treated women."

Myrtle's face lit up. "Except for his lairdship, eh?"

Nasim blushed.

"I knew it," the old woman grinned to herself. "We've all made wagers as to whether or nay you and the laird are *truly* in love, or if you merely say you are. You admitted such to me in your bedchamber today, but seeing you blush now proves I'll win a copper over this."

Nasim couldn't help the shock, then the smile that split her face.

"Healing is a most valuable skill. And the man's body isn't

199

so different from a woman's." Myrtle leaned down conspiratorially. "If you've seen beneath one man's kilt, you seen beneath them all."

Nasim's eyes widened, horrified at the lewdness. Myrtle chuckled.

"Nay true," said a kitchen maid in passing, grinning as she wiggled her fingers to wave at Hamish, the chestnut-bearded guardsman sitting across the hall. Hamish was watching her and returned the grin. "Some men are much more *endowed* than others."

The two servants giggled together, then laughed harder at Nasim's scandalized face.

"If there is a local healer, I would be honored to meet him," Nasim said, desperate to change the subject.

"You mean *her,*" Myrtle corrected, her hands laden with trenchers ready to be taken back to the kitchens.

"Her?"

"Aye. In the cities you might find the important physicians are men, but out here, in the countryside, midwives act as healers much of the time. We have but one midwife, and the poor woman is overworked. I'm certain she would welcome a woman physician gratefully."

"And I would have much to learn, I'm sure," Nasim replied, feeling purpose burgeon within her.

Myrtle waddled away again and Nasim smiled, returning her attention to her trencher burdened with a surplus of food she couldn't possibly eat. It would be a long while before Ewan's return, a long and lonely month at the least. But she would use that time to find a way to fit in and help. She would do as Ewan had suggested and come out of her shell. When Ewan returned, she hoped he would be pleased with her.

CHAPTER 17

Ewan resisted the urge to rub the bridge of his nose.

"My laird, I simply cannot perform a *Christian* wedding in good conscience betwixt you and your mistress from the Holy Land," the priest in Glasgow said. The candles burning along the wall, illuminating the banners above them, wavered as the man swept past Ewan in his cassock. "Care for more wine?"

Ewan accepted, if only to help dull the headache throbbing in his forehead, and handed him his goblet.

"Now, if she were to, say, convert to Christianity, and repent for her sins," the priest continued as he poured the wine, "she would then be eligible for a marriage in the church, but of course, that process can take some time."

Time was not something Ewan had if he was to get to the altar before Margaret caught wind of it. And asking Nasim to give up the very foundation she was raised upon was asking too much. She had already lost her family, her home, and her world because of him. He couldn't take her religion too. Could he?

"I must remind you, *Faither*, that I've already been married to her, and only wish to legitimize here what has been done elsewhere. It might be in the name of a different faith, but their intent to bind us was the same. Her family had no problem seeing the two of us married even though I was not of her religion."

"And it sounds as if they needed it to suit their convenience. Do you wish this to now suit your convenience? Our *true* God does not grant favors for the bad decisions of his flock," the man retorted. "He asks that you repent."

Ewan took his wine and gulped it down before the priest had reclaimed his seat behind his desk.

"This was not a poor decision on my part. I simply transgressed against her people without knowing I did so. How would I know that kissing a noblewoman's hand would be cause for marriage jesses or brutal death?"

The priest sighed thoughtfully and with exasperation at the same time. "I wish I had a better answer for you, but you should know that for a marriage to be legitimate, it must be conducted in the church. If there's a register you've signed somewhere, I will of course, make note of the legal measure. That would help."

"Oh, aye, let me run back to Jerusalem this moment and request my enemy verify for you in writing."

The priest pursed his lips at Ewan's sarcasm. Ewan didn't care. He needed more wine, and the priest wasn't offering another refill.

"I have always been a lawful man. I chose to spare this lass a horrible death, and by that I spared myself the same fate. I choose to continue my commitment to her, for it's the noble thing to do. How am I nay honorable in the eyes of God?"

The priest looked sympathetically at him, but the look was replaced by a stern indifference. "This is not something that God can bargain, I am afraid. Perhaps there is another priest willing to grant your request, but I find it doubtful. I cannot do such a thing in good conscience, and I suspect any man of the cloth would tell you the same."

"You mean this is something you can nay have on your *record*," Ewan fumed, standing up. He had had enough. "Nay conscience."

"You disrespect the House of God by suggesting my motives are personal and without primary concern for your immortal soul, my laird," the priest replied, rising to his feet, too.

"So have me arrested by inquisitors and see me disemboweled, or hung, or drawn and quartered for all I care. Aye, that is the European way to fight, am I wrong in stating this?"

The priest's face turned plum purple with anger. "The Pope beseeches that we fight for Christendom. This war is noble—"

"I faced death many times in this *noble* war that was so holy as to spill nothing but blood. Speaking the obvious now is the least of my problems. It's clear I'll nay find an open mind here. Good day," Ewan growled and slammed the goblet down, splashing the dregs onto the desk as he went.

He arrived outside, feeling the urge to punch something. He held back. An honorable man didn't lose his composure and *dammit, but I'm trying to be honorable!* He was a man of scholarly integrity, not a brawler in a seaside tavern. But one thing was certain. The priest had just lost a substantial annual tithe, being of the parish he was once told his mother came from.

This had been one of many stops on his voyage, having departed Dunwiddie a fortnight earlier. Each church so far had told him the same. The woman needed to be Christian or convert. He was running out of priests to ask and knew that the remaining churches would tell him the same thing. There was no way to legally thwart Malcolm of Fyvie and his ambitious daughter. He just hoped this didn't turn Nasim away from him for good. For even if he had to marry Margaret, he had that one last trick up his sleeve.

"Mi laird!" huffed a messenger boy, running up to him, nearly breathless. "I carry a missive from the office of the King of Scotland!"

Furrowing his brow, he decided it would not have been too difficult to track him to here, considering he had given his itinerary to Colin and Fergus, the captain of his guard.

"Where is this missive?"

"Right here, mi laird," the youth said, pulling free a sealed parchment from a purse hanging at his waist.

"How did you find me, lad?"

"The Laird Malcolm of Fyvie has been looking for you. He's staying at the King's Arms, awaiting you. He said that your steward informed him of your whereabouts."

Ewan frowned further. Colin knew what his mission was. Why on earth would Colin have divulged to Malcolm where to find him? Margaret's father wanted only one thing. Was it not too much to ask that he be limited to one headache at a time?

"Thank you. Run along and tell him I'll seek him at suppertime in the tavern hall."

The boy scampered away into the dirty streets and Ewan stalked into the first tavern he saw for an ale. The first gulp sat in his stomach like a weight. He knew that Fyvie had the law on his side. If the man was insisting on pushing this before the king, Ewan could very well be returning to Dunwiddie with terrible news for Nasim. Being in love with another wasn't reason enough for breaking off a business alliance, such as a betrothal. And he knew it would devastate Nasim. She was already reeling. He worried about her self-imposed isolation, both in body and in mind. He had no idea what she was thinking, but knew she hurt.

He swigged his tankard again and found a secluded table where he pulled forth the parchment and broke the seal.

"Your presence is requested before King William of Scotland in the matter of your betrothal to Lady Margaret of Fyvie..."

Ewan stopped reading shortly after the date specified for his appearance. *So it's to be as expected.* He was being forced into a second marriage. He should just return home now instead and prepare the nuptials. Lady Margaret wanted to be Lady of Dunwiddie at all cost, but those costs would break an alliance between him and her father. Malcolm would never be his friend after this, and he would have to resort to his final efforts to then annul their union after the fact. Yet there was always a small chance the king would rule in his favor. For that reason alone, no matter how much of a lost cause this was, he would attend the summons rather than concede defeat.

"Taverner!" he called to the man near the casks overseeing the barmaids.

The mousy man scurried over to him. "Aye, sir?"

"Have you a parchment and quill?"

The man nodded. "It will cost you a half penny, sir."

Ewan nodded and pulled forth the requested fee. The man soon returned with an inkwell, quill pen stripped of its feathers, and a square of parchment, a pounce dispenser, wax, and a plain seal denoting no heraldry.

He wrote his reply to Fyvie.

"Accept my apologies for canceling supper with you tonight. I will see you on the First of March in the audience of the king."

He didn't bother with an opening salutation or with a signature. Malcolm would know who it was from, and the lack of etiquette would be insult enough. Once dried, he folded it, melted a puddle of wax, stamped the seal into it, and called the taverner to send his messenger. There was no way he would break bread with Malcolm now. But if he had hoped to break bread alone, that was not to happen, either. An older man, stately, with the beginnings of greying hair came through the tavern door.

He perused the room with a lazy gaze as if trying to decide the best bar wench to seduce when his eyes sharpened on Ewan dunking his bread into his stew and taking a bite. He smiled a broad smile and strode forward.

"My laird Buchan! Such an unexpected surprise," the man said. Ewan rose to greet him and they clasped wrists. "I wasn't aware that you had returned from the Holy Land. Word was you were killed and the men at Dunwiddie were in discussions about what to do with your estate since you have no heirs."

"Robert Donald. I'm alive and well. To what do I owe the pleasure of running into you in Glasgow? How are things at Stirling?"

The other man sat without invitation, motioning to a bar maid to bring him a drink.

She came forward, a smile on her face. "What can I do for you, sir?" she asked, leaning a hand on his shoulder in a familiar slouch.

Robert looked up at her, his eyes twinkling as he skimmed over her breasts mere inches from his face. "Hmm, I dare say you already brought what I wanted…though two jugs of ale will also *do me* well."

"As you wish, sir," she smiled.

He slapped her rump playfully. She giggled and returned to the casks to fulfill the request.

"Ah, Stirling is faring well through these winter months.

Stores are full of corn, the buttery is packed with drink, and the king and queen are preparing for a new addition. Finally. A babe."

"That's good news," Ewan replied, thinking of what Nasim might look like with her belly full of child. His child. He had seeded her enough. Sooner or later, he expected her announcement.

"I'm here on the king's business," Robert said. "He has requested the purchase of five new breeding mares and a stud. The stables up the road always have fine horseflesh and are willing to bargain a fair price."

"And the king is in residence at Stirling?"

Robert shook his head. "Not until springtime."

"And you have been well?" Ewan asked.

"Hale as always," Robert replied with a grin. "Nary even a sniffle, even with this grim weather making so many catch their death."

"How is life as their steward?" Ewan continued. The distraction Robert posed didn't ease his mind, but it was a momentary diversion.

"It's been nine years since Colin left. He did a superb job, and I dare say it has taken this long indeed for His Highness to finally accept my way of doing things instead of comparing my work to Colin's."

A red-haired bar maid sashayed by and deposited another ale in front of Ewan, giving him a suggestive smile. He ignored it. He took a swallow, mopping up more stew with his bread.

"Ah, Ewan. There's plenty a woman here for us to both go to bed lucky. What say you? That red-haired lass has been eyeing you and is still doing so now. Take a look at that fetching figure and wanton eyes. I wonder if the rug is as soft and red as the lovely drapery."

Ewan shook his head and laughed. Robert had always been a virile man, and at one point in his not so distant youth, Ewan would have moved on the lass. Such a notion now filled him with...unease? Guilt? The war had forced him to mature. His near death had lay his very life in the hands of a woman. He had never expected to fall in love. He missed what he and Nasim had. *What we used to have,* he corrected himself. For her coldness to him now made him question her love.

"I dare say, Ewan, that she would make a warm and cozy sheath for a stout sword—"

"I admit, man, she's a fine woman, but I'm here for other reasons and will remain faithful to my wife."

"Your wife, eh?" Robert smirked. The other bar maid came back with his ale and helped herself to a seat on his knee. He slid his hand around her waist and tugged her close. "So I'm to assume the lording Lady Margaret is finally your woman to bed? Legally that is? I never heard that the banns had been posted."

Ewan exhaled. "Lady Margaret despairs, I'm afraid, for I returned home three sennights ago with a different wife on my arm, a dark-haired lass from Jerusalem. And I would appreciate it if you refrained from remarking upon her rugs and drapes," Ewan added with an eye of warning as he took a long draw from his tankard.

Robert laughed. "Fine then, I'll play nice. How is that possible? You were already betrothed. I hear Margaret has been in residence at Dunwiddie. No doubt the cat's claws are out if you've usurped your contract and brought Dunwiddie another lady."

"That they are." Ewan sighed, nursing on another long draw, setting it down with a resigning clunk. "Margaret is still in residence, arguing that my marriage be annulled, for the Lady Nasim, my wife, was not married to me in a Christian ceremony and therefore the church sees it as invalid. I've told Margaret I honor my marriage and bid her do the same."

Robert's tone simmered from jesting to serious. "I bet that rankles. Margaret has been determined to flaunt her status as your betrothed since you left for war, and when news arrived of your death, my brother informed me that she intended to stay on as the mistress there. Because of her love for your people, she vowed to offer herself in marriage to the man chosen as your successor so that she could stay true to Clan Buchan."

That bit of news nudged its way under Ewan's skin. She had never lifted a finger for his people that he had seen, so vowing to stay true to them rang false. Margaret wanted him because she wanted his title, not really because of him at all. Of course he had known she chased a title but had not expected it to be bandied about in public. If truth were told, he thought she liked him, too. But if a title was truly what she sought above all else, no wonder she was refusing to concede defeat. Had he been dead, she would have chased the new title holder. Because he was alive, she was chasing him, her sole option. Her father's clan had always been one of Ewan's allies. Ewan had still been given a fortune to start life as his father's heir and had been savvy to grow that wealth through his business, for with the world opening up for trade, skilled cartographers were in demand.

"She hasn't taken it well. I've journeyed to every church along the coast and inland to find a priest who would be willing to see my wife and I wed legally here, or else this matter is to be decided by the king, and I dare say the king might see the need to uphold the contract."

Robert shrugged. "That's not so bad then. You get two women, one as wife, one as mistress. Put them in separate households and take them at your pleasure. Keep Margaret bejeweled and breeding and she'll be no problem at all, and keep your mistress for love when you want comfort and can no longer stand Margaret's forked tongue, and for your love children of course. Women are used to sharing men. She'll get over it." Robert let his hand trail up to tweak the wench's breast and she giggled, leaning over to nibble his ear. The man nuzzled her cleavage. "Or you could act as many a man would and keep them both in such a fashion, and still part that redhead's legs tonight. One look of interest and I bet she would do the rest of the work herself."

"Oh, you mean Christine?" the wench interjected. She sat up straight and called to her friend who turned away from her conversation by the ale casks and scurried to their table.

Ewan huffed an uncomfortable laugh.

"The nobleman here is lonely," the woman upon Robert's knee said to the redhead.

Christine smiled and bit her lip seductively, sliding onto Ewan's lap and running her hand across his chest and down his stomach.

"He *is*," Christine giggled. "Do nay worry, sir. I give very fine service, and for someone with such handsome blue eyes and a…" her hand trailed down his front and slid between his legs, "well-endowed pack of jewels, I'll make sure I'm worth your coin."

Ewan jumped, clamping his knees closed.

"I told you so," Robert smirked with amusement.

Ewan evaded the kiss she tried to plant on his ear and caught her wrist, pulling her hand up, then grabbed her waist and stood her back to her feet.

"Thank you, lass, but I didn't request service."

"But I thought… 'Twould be a pleasure, sir."

He smiled up at her, really looking at her for the first time. Aye. She was bonny, with sparkling eyes and nearly flawless skin. No doubt she was still new to the business. Give her a couple more years and the wear would begin to show.

"All the same. I appreciate the offer. But I'm a married man."

"Then it's my loss and your wife's gain, sir," the woman said, caressing her hand across his shoulder before she left them.

Robert shook his head and clicked his tongue. "Has that woman of yours turned you into a eunuch?" He turned to the woman on his lap. "Tell Christine that I should like two bed partners tonight and will pay well for the service."

"You're truly depraved."

Ewan shook his head and took the final bite of beef in his stew. Yes, Robert Donald was a hale man in every regard, and for some reason, such bawd no longer appealed to Ewan. Even the wench's unsolicited touch had felt like a betrayal to Nasim, much like Margaret's unsolicited kiss had felt. Both embarrassed him. Neither were his fault. He had halted both advances immediately. So why did he still feel guilty?

"Ah, but there's plenty of me to go around." Robert winked. "My sweet friend here can tell *I'm* no eunuch, am I lass?" Robert said.

Ewan stood up to leave and straightened his belt. The wench giggled and continued to nibble at Robert. "No, sir."

"That's right, woman," he murmured, now sliding his hand up her knee and pushing her skirts with it.

Ewan wiped his face and tossed down the napkin. Their display of petting had him missing his wife and their long talks, teasing, and loving. He wished for nothing but solitude, for the troubles of this marriage contract suddenly crashed back over him in a tidal wave of fury.

"Then by all means, man, don't let a married goat like me dampen your lusty mood."

Robert belted laughter at Ewan's jest as the red-head brought more ale and took a seat upon Robert's other knee. Ewan left, shaking his head. Robert might have been a distraction from the current mess he was in, but he was still in his mess.

And he missed Nasim.

He had a few more churches to visit. After that, it would be time to head to Edinburgh and await this meeting with the king, and then, God willing, home to Nasim's arms.

CHAPTER 18

"Ye must be frozen through," Myrtle fussed, rubbing Nasim's hands and throwing her tartan shawl in the Buchan colors around Nasim's shoulders.

The doors to the great hall closed with a whoosh of February air behind her. She shivered and adjusted the basket on her arm, noting the hall was being cleared of its trestle tables while pallets were being assembled. Hamish, the guardsman who had escorted her to the midwife's cottage, took his leave to seek some supper. It had been a fortnight since Ewan had departed, and there was no sign of his return. She shouldn't expect it yet, for it hadn't been a month, but she secretly hoped each day would bring him home early.

"My thanks, Myrtle," she replied.

"'Tis late. You should go and warm yourself in your chamber and tell me all about your lesson at the midwife's today. I'll order a supper trencher to be brought up."

"There's still so much to do. I haven't time to rest yet. How am I to oversee the kitchens, the linens, the maids, when I am still learning what to do?"

As the daughter of Saladin's top commander, other men had handled directing the staff. Food preparation was beneath her status, and though it was beneath her status here, too, she was supposed to understand its complexities. Here, the household staff was female, the kitchens were different, the foods were different, and to say that there was a substantial lack of flavor and spices compared to her native foods was an understatement. She had no idea how much meat a castle the size of Dunwiddie, or any castle for that matter, needed, nor did she know how much flour was used in a month to make enough bread, how long it took to make the bread, how much work it took to mill enough flour, or who ground it for that matter. And that didn't include determining how much grain the castle had in store and how long it would last and thus, how much they needed to harvest, and *thus*, how much to plant... She closed her eyes. Such was an overwhelming thought. As the chatelaine, she needed to ensure that the staff was satisfied and that their requests were met to the best of the laird's abilities. And felt daft not knowing how to answer them.

"Do nay fret yourself yet," Myrtle replied, taking her basket for her. "All in due course. The castle has done without a chatelaine for as long as I have been here and has yet to crumble in a heap of smoke. You've learned so much already, and I dare say taught our midwife a thing or two as well. Your skills as a healer are invaluable. Already the midwife has expressed gratitude that there will finally be someone here to help her for there is always an ailment to treat."

Finding that there were woman healers in Scotland had excited Nasim. And thankfully, the more she helped Ewan's people, the more she was greeted with a smiling face instead of wary whisper. But the clan's gossip and rumors still found their way back to her ears.

"There's gossip that I'm a witch, and that instead of healing, I craft spells," Nasim frowned. "I know not what that is, but the words were spoken unkindly."

"Who said this?" Myrtle demanded.

Nasim shook her head. "I know not their names, just people gathered around the hearth before they knew I was near," she gestured towards the main hearth.

Myrtle looked in that direction but of course, there had not been any congregation there since the nooning meal. The old woman clicked her tongue and shook her head. "Shame they have yet to know you. But when they do, they'll think differently."

"I trained under one of the best physicians in the east. How can they think I might use my skills to cause harm?"

"They're just full of talk, and never you mind," Myrtle said. "But remember, you're different, and we have never met anyone like you before. The church has not spoken kindly of your people in their bids to raise armies for the Crusade. These folk only know what has been taught them and what has been gossiped."

"And that is okay? What is a witch?"

Myrtle tried to lead Nasim towards the stairs to her chamber. "Never you mind—"

"A witch is an evil sorceress who conjures the devil to further her own gains and retaliate against those who get in her way," Lady Margaret drawled, sashaying from around a corner, her handmaidens flanking her.

She smiled down her nose at Nasim as she stood a couple inches taller. Lady Margaret's blonde hair was perfectly coifed, her make-up flawless.

"Tell me, is that how you snagged Ewan? By putting a curse on him so he should stop loving me? Because he did love me," Margaret continued, her smile now becoming conspiratorial as she glanced at her ladies. "And kiss me. Quite thoroughly, I might add. A talented man with his tongue," she said, garnering a round of giggles from her ladies. "But you? I see nothing. How could a man possibly want *that…*" she gave Nasim's body a perusal, "when he could have this?" She lifted her chin, confident in her beauty. "Unless you swayed Ewan's attentions with the evil of a witch. I wonder if there's some truth to the gossip."

"Come, milady," Myrtle urged Nasim. "You've got more important things to do than stand here and listen to this rubbish."

"Has she?" Margaret interjected, stepping in their path to block them.

"I thank you to allow me to pass," Nasim said softly. *Ewan said he never loved her,* she assured herself. *He said he never did.* "I have no quarrel with you."

"But I have a quarrel with you, you little infidel *whore—*"

"Are ye all right, milady?" Hamish's deep voice interrupted them. The guardsman with the chestnut hair was dominating in stature, thickly built, with a proud beard and many a scar on his cheeks.

Blessings upon the man. Nasim sighed with relief. Of all the people here, Hamish had been one of the first to do more than just offer a passing, curious smile. Not only was he one of Ewan's trusted guardsmen, but he was the first man to declare his fealty to her and had conversed with her all day as she walked to and from the midwife, telling her about Scotland's heritage, offering his arm when she needed it to hike over the rocky soil. He had struck her as a witty man who enjoyed banter, liked everyone, and after she tended one of his cuts, of which he insisted was nothing, was impressed with her skill, saying her hands had the gentleness of a dove and the surety of a destrier.

Margaret eyed him now, then swept her skirts aside to clear the walkway, batting her eyes at him. "Oh Hamish, we were simply chatting. Good evening, Lady Nasim. I do hope you sleep well."

Hamish ignored Margaret. "Lady Nasim? You're all right?" he confirmed.

She smiled up at him and nodded. "My thanks, Hamish. I shall be fine."

He nodded, waiting to watch her move onward with Myrtle on her arm.

They arrived at Nasim's chamber in silence. It wasn't until the door was closed that Myrtle released a string of grumbles in Scots, taking out her frustrations on the fire in the hearth with violent jabs. Sparks popped and fizzled, spraying the floor with each thrust. Then she whirled around and pointed the metal prong at Nasim.

"That woman is more trouble than she's worth. Do nay cower to her, lady. Stand firm."

Nasim nodded. "I will."

"But remain ladylike and kind. Do nay sink to her level."

"Indeed," Nasim agreed, eyeing the prong.

With a hand perched on her hip, Myrtle looked at what she

was doing and dropped the tool. "My apologies, milady. I must look barbaric. No one gets my ire up quite like her. Demanding, thoughtless, she came to us in mourning over his lairdship's death, claiming that she wanted to help us, except I have yet to see her help in any way other than helping herself to Dunwiddie's hospitality…" She sighed, replacing the prong to the hearth. "You needn't listen to an old woman's gossip. I'll see to your supper."

She scurried from the chamber and Nasim smiled, doing her best to shake off the confrontation with Margaret as she took her basket to her table. It was the first time she and Margaret had spoken since she had claimed her place at the board, but it wasn't the first contemptuous look Margaret had sent her way in passing. And of course, the thought of Ewan kissing Margaret the way he had kissed her caused a pang of hurt to lurch in her chest. She had thought what they had together was special, but perhaps it had not been as special to him as it was to her.

No. Stop your destructive thoughts. Ewan had kissed Margaret before he had left for war, but he had never made love to her. That was something special only they shared together.

She could understand Margaret's anger, she supposed, for Ewan had been promised to her. In some ways, she felt guilty for coming between them, even though there was nothing she or Ewan could have done. But there was something hateful in the way Margaret said "infidel" much like she had heard men in her land rant about the "filthy infidels of Europe." Now that she had lived in both worlds, she realized how much people were influenced by fear of what they didn't understand.

Pulling off the cloth on her basket, she pulled out several bundles of herbs and laid them out on a wooden pin board upon her table. The midwife had explained the effects of each plant and how to use them. Nasim intended to study them more closely and accompany the woman on calls. Knowing how Myrtle always worried herself over Nasim's routines, she pulled loose the lacings of her gown before Myrtle could return to dote on her and sighed a breath of relief as her bodice stays slackened, stripping it all off and laying it over her chair. She stripped down her hose and wrapped herself in her robe, then went to her toiletries and untied her braids to comb the curls. Her dinner would be here soon, and though she was hungry, she was tired, too, and contemplated retiring for the night. With resting in mind, she went to her bed and fluffed a pillow, then pulled back the blankets.

Nasim screamed.

A snake jerked into a coil and struck. She jumped backward, throwing a hand over her mouth. In the middle of her bed, it began unwinding and slithering further under the covers. After a moment had passed, heavy footfalls thudded in the corridor. Her door banged open and Fergus, Ewan's captain, along with another guard, burst through.

"Lady Nasim!"

She tried to steady her breathing and braced her hand to the wall. Snakes in her homeland could be venomous. How did a snake find its way into her bed?

More people arrived at her door, peering in.

Myrtle pushed through the gathering with the promised trencher.

Nasim pointed. "There is a…" Not knowing the word for snake, she searched her mind. "A serpent beneath the covers."

"A serpent?" Fergus questioned as he strode to the bed.

"Careful!" Nasim cried as Hamish, too, pushed through the people to come stand by her.

Fergus showed no indication of hearing her and ripped off the covers. The snake recoiled again and the room gasped. Nasim gripped his arm.

"'Tis an adder," Hamish exclaimed.

"How on earth did it get in Lady Nasim's bed?" Myrtle demanded.

"They normally avoid people," stated another guard. "I can nay recall ever seeing one come indoors."

"Aye, and I can nay imagine it got in here by itself," Hamish growled protectively.

"Did it strike you?" Fergus asked, not bothered in the least by the creature.

Nasim shuddered and wrapped her arms around her waist,

shaking her head. "I'm not bitten. Someone get rid of it, please."

Hamish nodded stoutly. He stuck out a blade and taunted the beast into striking it, at which point he clamped his other hand around the creature's head.

The crowd gasped. Nasim felt a shiver jolt her body, watching the snake twist and unwind in the air.

"If I hadn't pulled back my covers before getting in, it would have struck my feet."

Fergus looked at her, his brow hardening. "I wager the snake was put there with a design in mind."

The crowd parted for Hamish as the snake writhed around his arm, its head still firmly in his grip. He strode down the hall to dump the creature off the castle walls. Fergus ordered the chattering onlookers out and with a remaining guard, searched the whole of her chamber for more. There were no others. With a nod, the head guardsman bid her goodnight and bowed out.

She let out a shaking breath as Myrtle hustled her to her chair to sit and poured her a cup of wine.

"Here, 'twill calm the jitters. You're lucky that beast didn't bite you, for we have no remedy for the bite of an adder." Myrtle then took a drink of the wine straight from the decanter herself, plopping her hand on her hip, and Nasim realized Myrtle was just as unnerved. Nasim sipped the cup. This drink was an acquired taste. "There now. Eat some supper and relax. Trust that Fergus will investigate and the incident will be reported to the laird upon his return."

She nodded and picked up a piece of venison from her trencher, now cold. Nibbling it, she lost herself in thought as the old woman replaced the wine to the table and wiped the back of her hand across her mouth, bustling from the room. Who would put such a thing in her chamber? In her bed? Where she would feel the least threatened and be the least wary? Margaret hated her, but it seemed unlikely that she would capture and carry a viper into her chamber and tuck it nicely under her covers. And there were many people here still wary and curious about her. Just because Margaret was open about her disdain didn't make her guilty.

Still, Margaret's words trailed through her mind. *"I do hope you sleep well."*

She stifled another shiver. If she shook with discomfort at the mere thought of the woman, then Margaret had control over her. She was the new wife to the castle's laird. She was foreign. She was never supposed to be here. And she had much to learn about this world and its customs. She had her work cut out for her, but she would do her best to win over these people. Therefore, come the morrow, she would put this incident in the past and throw herself into her work. And whoever was responsible for the snake would not have the satisfaction of seeing her fearful again.

***

With renewed spirit, Nasim threw herself into her work, just as she intended. The days breezed by with little issue, and no more threats had been leveled against her. She grabbed the basket the midwife had helped her prepare and walked brusquely from her bedchamber, down the corridor, down the stairs, and through the great hall. Colin was overseeing the cleanup from the morning meal. She moved onward through another archway.

Hamish was injured, she had been told as she finished breaking her fast, and because the man had been so good to her, she hurried all the more to find him and see what ailed him. Her course took her past the buttery and into what had once been a storage room for grain. Having sat unused for years, the space had been transformed by her in a surgery. The guardsman was waiting nonchalantly while gripping a rag over his arm. He glanced up from his stool as Nasim entered, grinning and winking at her.

"It seems I got nicked in the practice yard."

He peeled away the rag.

"Only nicked?" Nasim teased, seeing the filleted skin.

Months ago, she never would have dreamed of looking at a man let alone teasing one. But life here was different. Men and women sometimes flirted. Sometimes the flirting led to more, and she recalled walking in on Hamish bracing the young kitchen maid who had so boldly alluded to his netherparts a month before against the wall of the chandlery, his strong hands holding her rear, her legs wrapped around his waist. So

218

engrossed in their loving, neither Hamish nor the maid had noticed Nasim. She had hastened from the office and flushed with embarrassment. She flushed again now as she looked at the guilty man.

"Aye, Finn and Alan decided to have a go at me at the same time, the bastards," Hamish grumbled with mock anger. "I'll have to teach them a lesson come the morrow."

Nasim shook her head. "Men and their swordplay."

That was one thing that was still the same no matter where someone lived. The men were different, the armor was different, and the swords were strangely fashioned, but the need to fight, strategize, and practice was all the same.

"Shall I burn it shut or stitch it this time?" she said on a sigh. "You've become a familiar patient, but I admit I'm still not quite sure what your favored form of torture is."

Hamish laughed, a deep, jovial sound, his smile hidden in his beard. "I assume you mean I ought to be more careful."

She nodded and quirked her brow. "I think stitches should do nicely. No sense in enduring a hot iron when you're just going to break it open again."

She moved across the room to a table lined with her materials and took to the mortar and pestle, grinding leaves and pouring them into a bowl to blend into a salve.

"You remark upon swordplay is if you've seen much of it," Hamish said.

Nasim nodded. "It doesn't matter where one comes from, the men all practice at it. My family has many men. Training is something they were constantly doing."

"Do you miss your old home?" Hamish asked.

He was only trying to make conversation, but it caused her heart to clench. For all the changes here that had seemed good to her, there were many that were equally bad. What she would give for curried lamb with her mother, or tea, or the soft colorful silks of her clothing and linens, or the hot, sunny wind across her face in their courtyard, or the fruit trees. What she would give to be at home with Fatima, listening to her half-sister gossiping, or with her mother one last time, watching the old woman's fingers embroider patiently.

Life at home had been different, yes, but it had been wonderful in its own right. Her father had seen her educated and well-protected, which was much more than she could say for the noblewomen here. And surprisingly, Solomon was no longer the first person to come to mind when she found herself in her reverie. While she still missed his company and his lessons, she realized she no longer missed the fantasy she had once built up about him. She no longer thought him her *Majnun*.

"If you don't mind my asking, we've been curious about you, but everyone is too shy to approach you to ask…well…"

"What would you like to know?" She smiled. It was her first opportunity to tell others about herself and hopefully quell some of their gossips.

"Just what it was like in the Holy Land."

"What do you mean?" Nasim indulged his curiosity.

"Being a, eh, well, you know…"

"An infidel?"

Hamish had the good sense to look ashamed.

"The customs are different," Nasim replied. "And to us, *you* are the infidels and we, the believers. But I have learned over these months that it's not the religion that determines if people are kind. I start to believe that God reveals himself to us in many ways."

Hamish smiled. "But do the, well what I mean to say is…" He stammered, and took a deep breath, then released a fast stream of words. "But do the men really behead children to offer as sacrifices and burn their daughters at the stake?"

Grinning, Nasim lifted a brow as she ground her leaves.

"Goodness. You forgot eating prisoners and casting evil curses."

Hamish chuckled. "Aye, when ye put it like that, it does sound ridiculous."

"And of course the rack, the gallows, and the disembowelment of prisoners," she continued, slanting a glance at him. "Surely the people of Europe have never committed such atrocities."

Now Hamish laughed. "You have me there, lady. I supposed there are brutal folk everywhere. So what was your home like?"

She grew wistful and paused in her grinding, losing herself in thought. "Fragrant. Colorful. The food had rich flavors. The sun was always bright." She swallowed, and resumed mixing her salve. "Sometimes I miss it very much."

"Do you ever wish you could go home?"

"There's no point in wishing for something that will never happen," she replied.

"How did you and the laird meet?"

Nasim almost laughed. After living here, where Hamish and any willing clanswoman could tryst with impunity, whether they should or not, how on earth could she explain the complexities of her world?

"He was gravely injured, and I helped heal him."

"Do you know Laird Buchan well? We have nay seen either of you together since his homecoming, but he's a good man and a compassionate laird. He'll always treat you well."

She turned back to him, unable to waste any more time grinding her slave as an excuse to regain her composure. "He's been an honorable man and I know him well. I love him deeply."

"We're honored to have such a skilled woman as you here, milady. I know that many have gossiped and don't know what to make of you, but your healing talents are fine and people notice. Despite what happens with Lady Margaret, many of us have sworn our fealty to you and will protect you as the lady of the castle, no matter what. 'Tis what the laird wishes. And when he learns about the adder in your bed a fortnight ago, no doubt he'll be furious."

She smiled and ordered the removal of his shirt, setting to work cleaning his arm. She smeared the salve across the wound. Taking up the needle and catgut, she began stitching. Aside from a few winces, Hamish sat still.

"You tolerate the stitching well," Nasim remarked, changing the subject. But between being labeled a witch and the incident with the snake, she had been uneasy knowing that Fergus' investigations had turned up nothing about the adder. "If I didn't know any better, I would think you couldn't feel it."

Hamish grinned and winked again. "I've had years of practice, lass."

She chuckled, and as soon as she snipped the threading, declared him done.

"I cannot urge you enough to keep it clean and washed. Washing is not a sin of the devil. Festering sets in when bodies are left dirty," she advised. "Too many people in this land turn their nose up at bathing but where I come from, we understand cleanliness to be the first protection against festering."

"What would fools like us do without a fine mistress to heal our follies?"

He stood, towering over her, and lifted her hands in his, kissing each of them. She dismissed him with a laugh and a pat on his arm, when a swish of fabric outside the door caught their ears. They both paused, then Hamish already at the doorway, leaned out. No one was there.

She washed her hands and straightened her medicinals, then ventured into the corridor when a rush of serving staff ran by.

"What's wrong?" she asked a familiar girl.

"Nothing, milady. The laird's vessel is back. He has returned and Colin orders us to prepare a fine dinner to welcome him home."

Nasim's breath caught. *Ewan.* How many nights had she dreamed about her husband, the wonderful bed partner that he was and the tender man he had proven to be? How much she had longed for his protection again. The snake in her bed had left her wary, causing her to have nightmares about the scorpion more than once and the way Ewan, the rugged man she had traveled with who had turned out to be so refined, had quickly saved her from harm. His parting a month ago had felt so bitter. Was he still interested in her? Or had she ruined his affection for her? Had he found other women while he traveled? Women who would tempt a man like the prostitutes in Como? The idea worried her. Ewan might have spoken sweet words to her... *Nay, you must trust him.* He had assured her as they traveled that he'd never returned to the prostitutes, and she believed him. Myrtle declared him honorable, as did Hamish just now.

She remained frozen in the corridor when Myrtle came bustling toward her.

"There you are, Lady Nasim! The laird returns. You must go to greet him, dear."

"But my hair—"

"You look beautiful, milady," Myrtle fussed. "I dare say you will be a sight he has never seen before, the way you used to hide away in your old garments. He will find you stunning."

"But it's freezing out," she protested.

Myrtle huffed with exasperation, producing Nasim's tartan shawl, and tossed it around her shoulders. Without any further delay, Myrtle dragged her outside and down the steps into the bailey. With a push, Myrtle urged her onward. The impossibly cold air of early March assaulted her. She shivered and clenched her shawl more tightly.

With nervous steps, she walked across the yard, reaching the gateway leading down to the sea. From her vantage, she had a clear view of the ocean. She held her breath. She hadn't seen Ewan in so long. He was starting up the stairs cut into the cliff side, flanked by Colin who was busy imparting the castle news and Fergus, who had accompanied him, while the crew from the small ship was unloading a trunk.

Even from afar, she soaked in his beauty. He was a tall, scholarly man. In a way, she had gained everything she had found attractive in Solomon, and was granted her wishes to see the world. She had been given everything she had wanted in a husband, and gained much more than she thought she wanted. Why on earth had she been so daft as to push him away?

***

Ewan looked up, the cold air swaying his kilt and biting into his bare knees. His heart stopped. He stopped. Nasim's dark, luscious tresses were lifting in the wind that plagued the coast. He took in the unexpected sight. His woman was wearing his colors, was draped in a deep red and green tartan pulled tightly around a fine gown and kirtle of dark blue to match the sapphires he had bought her in Brittany. He began walking again, admiring how the colors contrasted against her skin, speeding up his pace, taking the steps two at a time. God, her luscious curves, perfectly enhanced for all the world to see. Now that he saw her dressed as such, he had half a mind to order her back into her old clothing, for surely his men flirted and stared.

Colin's voice receded away. He had to hold Nasim, kiss her, smell the wonderful scent that belonged solely to her, before he shared with her his distressing news. Once she knew, things between them might be ruined forever. Her dark eyes glittered with anticipation, her posture was uncertain yet expectant, and he sped up his pace. He jogged up the steps and crushed her to his chest.

"Ewan," she murmured, her hands gripping his neck with such unabashed fervor, he questioned for a moment if this was truly the same woman who had once shied from public affection.

He held her close, this newly transformed woman he would still have known a mile away.

"Naz, do you turn to me again?" he whispered in her ear as he nuzzled her. "Please say you do. I've bloody-well missed you, lass..."

She squeezed his neck harder.

"Ewan, I'm sorry for the way I behaved. I was childish and selfish—"

He shook his head but instead of finding more words, his mouth crushed hers. He kissed her deeply, completely, lifting her off the ground in his arms. And she was kissing him back. Nay just kissing. Devouring him in return, her tongue stroking against his with certainty. His heart soared. He ripped away from her, planting a storm of kisses along her cheeks, her ear, her jaw. His news was horrid, but he had to have her. Had to lie with her and feel that closeness only she could provide him that he had gone without for over a month now.

"I love you, Nasim. I'm trying my best for you, I swear this. Please say you'll nay leave me," he begged.

"Whatever do you mean?" she asked, pulling back to look into his eyes.

Malcolm of Fyvie walked past them. "Tell your mistress your news, man, and let's get on with the wedding preparations."

Ewan's blood hadn't stopped boiling since his audience with King William.

"I'm sympathetic to your plight, Laird Buchan," King William had said. *"And the court is pleased to see that you live. No successor had been chosen yet, and no assets dispersed. Resumption of your lairdship is noted. Upon receipt of your letter to me, however, I've requested an audience with Commander Murray. It might take some time to summon him, but I've sent correspondence to King Richard of England to alert him. No doubt, the English king will also have questions for him. All of that aside for now, we are faced with this pressing matter of marriage. I see that you wish your infidel woman to be seen as legitimate. But you are under contract to Margaret of Fyvie, and you offer no proof that a legitimate wedding occurred. I'm afraid I can find no good contractual reason for your betrothal to be dissolved. Your marriage was not conducted by the church, nor was it one of Highland hand-fasting. For all we know, a marriage did not even take place and it's just your word you bring to us."*

Ewan had thought right then what a fool he was. He didn't adhere to many of the ancient Highland customs, but hand-fasting would have been the perfect solution and an old tradition all still respected.

"Unless Malcolm should agree to the matter, I'm afraid your wedding must proceed. And Sir Malcolm." The king had then turned to Margaret's father. *"Laird Buchan has professed his immense displeasure, and whilst marriages betwixt nobles are oft meant to secure alliances, it's clear the man has found a love-match in his infidel. You risk losing a strong ally by pressing this matter, and you condemn your daughter to a loveless union. Laird Buchan has requested in good faith to break this contract. I would hope that you would want more for Lady Margaret and I urge you to use your conscience on the matter."*

Court had been dismissed. Malcolm had proven not to have a conscience. An order of marriage was now in place. Fyvie had been resolute that the marriage would proceed and had said no more to him, and though Ewan had royal sympathy, sympathy wasn't enough.

"Nasim," he croaked. "Nasim, please forgive me." He fell to his knee and grasped her hands, pulling them to his lips as Margaret skipped down the steps at the announcement that the laird had returned, having learned her happy news. "The king ruled that I must marry Lady Margaret, and that our union is void."

Nasim's smile faded. And then a look of sympathy washed over her face as well as the unmistakable shadow of hurt. She pulled one of her hands free from his grip but instead of withdrawing from him, to his surprise, she caressed his face.

"It's not your fault, Ewan. I know you've tried. I should have been more agreeable. I shouldn't have been angered at you for something out of your control."

He clutched her hand, kissing her palm and the inside of her wrist. He risked looking desperate, but if he did, it was an accurate reflection of the pain in his heart.

"I'm sorry, woman. I went to priests and asked them if they would bless a marriage betwixt us, but they all said they couldn't unless you became a Christian." He dared a look up into those deep, obsidian eyes of hers. "Naz, please say you'll stay with me. I know it's nay the life you expected, but I have no choice. I can nay defy the king's orders. I marry her on the morrow."

She shouldn't have to stand here among all their people and withstand the humiliation of his confession. After all they had been through together, Nasim deserved a place to truly belong. She had saved his life, withstood exile, and braved a new world. She didn't deserve this dishonor.

"You will do as you must," she whispered in her language, her lips wavering as she tried to smile. "All my life I expected to be one of a man's many wives. This is not so different."

But it *was* different. Here, men married one woman for life until death claimed them. He had told her this. But Margaret now had her title. He would never touch Margaret, not even to administer the expected kiss on the knuckles in greeting. But Nasim's children would never be able to fully claim his lineage. Any children they had would be bastards, just as he had been.

Revulsion roiled. He had never wanted to seed bastards, as he had been raised. He had never wanted the accursed mantle of bastardly shame to be draped upon his heirs, his spares, his daughters, subjected to the spiteful musings of a stepmother who wanted nothing to do with them because their father had bedded another.

He rose and pulled her back to him, nuzzling her. "Please take me into your chambers." *I have missed you so, and have wished only to be home with you.*

She nodded, swallowing a look of pain, and averted her gaze from all the onlookers as he fixed her hand in the bend of his elbow and walked her through the gates, brushing past Margaret without a single look or comment. He would never look at her again unless he had to. And Malcolm could go to hell. Upon their farce of a ceremony on the morrow, if the man didn't vacate his premises on his own accord, Fergus and Hamish would be ordered to drag Fyvie's greedy arse to his borders to dump him there. Fyvie had no doubt relied on Ewan's reputation as being a mannered laird and earl, but his manners had run dry.

Margaret hastened after them as they walked into the great hall where the Laird Fyvie was declaring the celebratory feast for Ewan's homecoming be extra special to commemorate the wedding. The serving staff stood stunned. Ewan's composure snapped.

"There will be no feast to commemorate such underhandedness!" he exploded. "Last I checked, *I* am the Earl of Dunwiddie, nay Malcolm! Supper will be as usual. No feast! And Margaret will not sit upon the dais or anywhere near to me." He pounded his fist upon the board. "That is my order."

"My laird," bowed Fergus. He removed his nasal helm to address Ewan directly, exposing a crooked nose that had been broken before. "Will the banns be posted on the church? Because I would like to object."

From the corner of his eye, Ewan noted that Margaret's face had paled at the first-in-command's clear discontent.

"I would agree," Hamish added as many others filled the hall with similar sentiments. "The Lady Nasim has proven herself indispensable to us. She is a fine healer and has taken on the task of chatelaine with much enthusiasm. Many of your people have already declared their loyalty to her."

Ewan was touched. Their loyalty to his woman during his long absence made his raging pulse ebb a degree. He looked at Nasim, though answered Hamish and Fergus. "The banns will nay be posted." He finally peeled his gaze from her and looked back at his men. "If Laird Fyvie refuses to withdraw his contract, the wedding must proceed, and I'm demanding it happen immediately so it can be over. But Lady Nasim is not going anywhere. She's the Lady of Dunwiddie, and my wife by all accounts. She will remain at my side and continue in her stead."

Fergus and Hamish looked disappointed, but bowed. Malcolm also looked disappointed, though Ewan hardly cared. The man had forced a marriage on him, but he couldn't force him to be happy about it.

"I'll see to it that supper consists of normal fare this eve," Colin replied, and with a bow of his head, he took his leave.

In the hush following Ewan's anger, he turned to Malcolm. "You're my guest here, but do nay overestimate my generosity. Your time as my guest is nearly over, and I shall never hear you ordering my serving staff about again."

Malcolm, scowling, nodded once, and walked away stiffly. "Margaret. I should like to talk to you," he called over his shoulder and Margaret scurried after him.

Ewan nodded to his clansmen. "I thank you for making Lady Nasim feel welcome here. You're good people."

"My laird," Fergus began, having come to his side. "There's some important news to impart of the castle's recent happenings. If I might have a moment of your time—"

"Is it life or death?" Ewan countered.

"No sir, but you should know of it without delay—"

"Later, man. I'm weary. Come to my solar after the meal and we'll discuss your concerns then."

Fergus nodded and stepped away, and Ewan guided Nasim with him. He walked her to her chamber, pulled her inside, and barred the door.

"Lie with me, Naz," he whispered, pulling her close to him. "After what I have to do, I'll understand if you'll no longer share your bed with me, but I've missed you, lass—"

She reached to the laces of her bodice and pulled the strings loose. At her invitation, he took over, pulling at them, causing the gown to slackening. Her chest relaxed. She pulled her arms free, hastening out of the dress as he dragged it over her hips. It fell in a pool of deep blue velvets and satins. In their growing frenzy, he grabbed her, his lips crushing to hers, a hand sliding up to grope and squeeze her glorious breasts through her chemise.

He had fantasized about these breasts while away, sating himself with his hand like an untried lad while he lay in his empty inn chambers traveling from church to church. As his tongue tangled with hers, as his cock throbbed to firmness beneath his kilt, he dragged her chemise down her chest so that her breasts spilled into view.

Aye, his manhood was ready. He had to be one with her. He had missed her so much, and pulled away from her mouth, bending to suckle her instead. He was acting like an animal. His control was about to snap. He couldn't maul her. He'd never taken a woman in such a beastly manner. Yet, he felt her desperate fingers biting into him, her chest arching to him, inviting his rough suckling.

Her head fall back. He tangled his hand at her nape into her long, unbound hair and gripped it. "God, lass, I can nay stop."

"I don't want you to," she sighed. "I'll never deny you. I love you so. I know you did all you could—"

He interrupted her by swooping her into a cradle, leaving her gown in a heap, and carried her to her bed, splaying her on her stomach, climbing on top of her to straddle her rear and drag her chemise sleeves off her arms, ripping the rest of it up over her thighs so the garment was tangled around her waist. He dug a finger beneath the top of her hose.

"Take these off," he nearly demanded, ripping loose his belts and casting them aside.

He yanked his tunic over his head, paying no heed to how his brooch ripped the fabric, and added it to the haphazard collection on the floor. Then he tugged away his kilt as she lifted her rear and shimmied out of the leggings.

"I have to have you," he muttered again. "I have to…" He collapsed upon her, his manhood thickened and heavy, and nearly growled as she reached back to grab his thigh, pulling his groin against her rear. "It's been so bloody long."

His boots were still laced up his calves while the rest of him was stripped. He didn't care. His woman was beneath him, just as desperate for him as he was for her, and he grabbed her wrists, bracing them over her head, and then he thrust himself between her spread thighs in a swift plunge.

They cried out in unison. God, he was mating with her like a barnyard stud. He should be ashamed, be gentler, lay her on her back so they could face one another instead of rutting upon her, her beautiful breasts flattened into the mattress. But Nasim pushed her bonny rear against him. He released her hands and pushed upright, gripped her hips, and thrust with swift determination.

"Ewan!" she cried, her mouth muffled.

He groaned, dropping back his head, rolling his hips roughly. Nothing had ever felt so good. And yet, nothing had ever been a bigger reminder of the pain awaiting him when he woke in the morn. In his efforts to pound away his anger at Margaret and Malcolm, he knew he was only buying a moment's pleasure with the woman he loved, that the misery of what he must do was waiting for him the moment the euphoria of making love ebbed.

Still, he basked in her cries of pleasure. If he couldn't have her in marriage, he would ensure he left his mark upon her every chance he could.

"Aye, love," he encouraged in rough gutturals. "I've missed you, missed this."

She sighed, moaned. Sweat was breaking on his brow as he sped his pace, holding her hips steady against his force. He pulled her against him to match the way he pushed into her. He gazed at her back and her sloping rear with her tumbling dark hair splayed around her in disarray. He felt her hands reach back to grip him and dig into his rear, encouraging his desperate intercourse. "I as well, Husband..."

Husband.

He had to slow down. He was spiraling desperately out of control. It had been over a month since they'd arrived from Brittany that they had last joined. He willed himself to gentle, slowing, easing himself upon her and gritting his teeth to maintain the sweeter pace.

"So beautiful," he said, laying himself flat atop her so he could bury his nose in her curls. He felt the surge rising, held off and held back. His body undulated in long strokes. He was going to spill. He waited, worked, praying Nasim would reach her release before he did, for he couldn't hold off much longer. Her whole body quivered as if on demand and he felt her tense, freeze, and exhale a long sigh into the blankets

"My love," she sighed.

There it was, her warmth, her pleasure. He pulled up from her again, grasped her hips, and tipped his head back as he peaked.

"Ah, Naz, God…" He released within her, held her tightly, sheathed to the jewels, as he drained his pent-up desire for the woman he already felt as though he was betraying.

He collapsed, rolling onto his side and pulling her with him so they might stay joined and so that they could both lie down. He was still in his boots, for Christ's sake. But he reached to the bed curtains and released the tassels so that they fell closed around them. He kissed her head, squeezing her, feeling her reach up to hold his arms encircling her chest and neck as darkness within the curtains concealed them. Nuzzling her neck, he inhaled the sweet perfume of rosewater. Panic threatened to undo him, and he nuzzled her further. He swallowed, trying to tamp down the illness in his gut. How would he ever make it through the morrow?

CHAPTER 19

"Perhaps if we had backed out of the contract when he returned with his infidel we still could have negotiated free passage without taxes. Are you certain this is still what you want?" Malcolm asked.

Margaret fidgeted but did not answer.

"Daughter. I have gone to the highest court to get your wish granted, but pushing this so far was a bad idea. I don't think he'll treat you like the lady of Dunwiddie."

Margaret paced the length of her father's chamber, one hand wrapped across her waist, the other at her mouth. "But I'll still be his wife, and he'll be obligated to see me well-financed, no?"

A fire crackled warmly in the hearth, but the hospitality here had frozen. The look of pain on Ewan's face as he held his mistress had been genuine, and his hatred toward her had been palpable.

Still, marriage wasn't about love, she thought practically. It was about position, trades, and bartering. She would get the status she wanted. Her father would get the tax-free passage to the sea he so badly needed. She didn't need Ewan's love, even if his affection at one time had been a nice boon. *Nay. It wasn't affection. It was lust, plain and simple. And once you're married to him, you'll have the things you really want.* With her status, she would be the envy of many a woman. She would have access to the castle stores to use the fine fabrics whenever she wanted. She would get jewels, as it was expected for a husband of prestige to adorn his wife. And even if Ewan kept Nasim on the side, it didn't matter really, as long as Nasim was installed elsewhere. It would be their children in wedlock that would inherit Dunwiddie and all its wealth, not the infidel's.

Though Ewan was misguided at the moment, eventually his infatuation in the whore had to wane.

"I've wanted Ewan ever since I first met him. I've been waiting years for this moment, *Faither*, and now, that horrible infidel witch hopes to strip it away?"

"Why him?" Malcolm demanded, standing up. "He has made a good name for himself, I'll give him that, and is wealthy beyond measure, and controls access to the sea that I greatly need. But he is bastard born. There are other eligible men, with other trades that could be negotiated. You've been much sought after. We could revisit some of those betrothal offers. Quite frankly, there isn't much of an alliance to be had here anymore. I fear there is little he is willing to do for us now outside of our contract."

"Ewan is the first man to have…to have…" she paused, summoned her tears, and dabbed her eyes. "To have kissed me. He told me he found me beautiful."

"Did he do anything else to you?" Malcolm growled.

She bit back her smile. It wouldn't do her any favors for her father to see through her careful façade.

"No, but he made it no secret that he would enjoy being married to me. Surely he hasn't forgotten."

"That was long ago, Margie, and a man's attentions sway. His have swayed to his mistress."

"Which means he'll sway back to me, *Faither*, I know it. Some day he will." She whirled around to him. "He'll learn to love me once he knows what a pleasing wife I will make. It will be miserable at first, but eventually, he'll come around. This is what I want."

"Margie love," he soothed, rubbing her arms. "Do you even know what love is? It's easy to become attached to that first kiss and the man who gave it to you. But you were not *his* first kiss. It wasn't special to him the way it was to you. And by forcing this, you won't get the wedding you hoped for. There's no time to prepare a gown or for your cousins to travel. He's forbidding a feast. Meanwhile, he all but collapsed at his woman's feet outside the curtain wall and is warming her bed right now. Think about this."

She shook her head and marched to the door, anger breaking her subdued composure. "You think it's a wedding filled with fanfare that I want? Nay. I want the status I was promised. I could care less about flowers and congregations and merriment. Nasim is a dirty infidel. I'll nay allow her to weave her wiles on him and take what I've waited for. For three— long—years, I waited. Only to have my dues stripped away. My chambers should be those of the Lady of Dunwiddie, and tomorrow I will have earned them. Ewan will find he loves me in time...and if he should not remain the laird, I'll marry whoever takes his place."

With that, she exited. Malcolm exhaled and dropped his head in defeat, seemingly puzzled by her cryptic statement. But if he put his foot down on her obstinacy and conceded defeat to Ewan, he would never hear the end of it. From pouting to arguing to flat out anger, Margaret would cause him a headache. As he went to a chair by his hearth and sat down with a decanter of whisky, he sighed. This was one final lesson she would have to learn the hard way because once she learned the lesson, she would be trapped in marriage with no way to escape it.

***

Ewan lay amid Nasim's covers. She was already gone for the day, and early sunlight seeped through the ruffled bed curtains. In a few hours, he would be expected at the chapel.

"Christ, an adder?" he muttered aloud, recalling the words Fergus had spoken to him when he had finally afforded his captain an audience.

His mind was in chaos and despite his long voyage and bed sport, he had slept poorly. Not only had a snake been found in this very bed, but the culprit had never been found. No one had seen anyone or anything suspicious near Nasim's room. Fergus had been thorough, noting what Hamish and Myrtle had described about Margaret's confrontation with Nasim in the hallway that night, but that was where Margaret's association with the incident ended.

He rubbed his eyes, bleary and irritated by all that had happened. Margaret might be pushing his limits of restraint, but she didn't have it in her to put a snake in Nasim's bed, did she? And there had been gossip about Nasim being a witch. He had put an end to that particular rumor at the evening meal prior to Nasim arriving at the board. His reprimand had rung out into the silence as clansmen and women tried to hide their shame for being so foolish and hurtful. After his rant, he had felt a bit of shame himself, for he saw the way his people had greeted Nasim when she did enter the hall. Truth be told, there had been many a bow, warm smile, and words of greeting cast upon his woman, and returned from her as well. And he had just chastened them.

He stood reluctantly and stared back at the empty bed he had just shared with the one he loved, raking his hand through his messy hair. It was profound how hollow he felt, knowing Nasim would never truly be his.

"But what's in a label? For that's all it is, 'husband,' 'wife.' They're only labels, and the ceremony, an act. I can still keep Nasim as mine. I can still legitimize all our children. I can still bring them up in a home with their mother and father united," he muttered aloud. But his attempts to rationalize the situation fell flat. Anger mounted. His stomached still churned at the idea of marrying Lady Margaret, whether or not he planned to nurture the union. Odd, he knew, because until he met Nasim, he had still thought lustfully of her. Oh how someone's true colors could turn others sour toward them. But now that he had Nasim, he realized how much work went into making a happy marriage, or for that matter, that a happy marriage mattered in the first place.

The memory of those thoughts now made him grimace. He hadn't planned on Nasim coming into his life and finding a partner in her. She was intelligent, beautiful, perhaps timid at times, but he had seen a strong woman emerging in her. Margaret wouldn't contemplate the sunset with him like Nasim would or discuss worldly things like Grecian ruins, religions, or the sea. Over these months of travel, they had talked of the Greeks, of map-making, of the world, of the differences in their two homelands, of her medicinal studies, and so much more.

But Margaret's life had revolved around the frivolity of a noble—fine gowns, jewels, and intrigue. Now, he was seeing it for what it really was: an attempt to be more important than she really was. Supposedly Margaret had come to Dunwiddie upon Ewan's death to take over the task of chatelaine, yet instead, she sat in her quarters with her handmaidens, wiling away the time with needlepoint and gossip.

His journey with Nasim had given him time to see how complex a woman truly was. He had found their talks engaging. They had become companions long before they had become lovers. He had been grown and accomplished before going to war. But he had grown-up since meeting Nasim, in ways he hadn't been before. He had begun to love the way she depended on him, the way she looked fondly at the ring and pendant he had given her as if he had gifted her the world instead of a couple objects bearing pretty blue stones. He doubted Margaret would bat much of an eye at a paltry ring. If anything, she would expect them and more.

He looked around Nasim's empty chamber, shaking off the melancholy. Where was she? His heart twisted with betrayal. The priest of the village kirk would be ready to conduct a ceremony midday, and he had not invited his clansmen. If Margaret was bent on marrying him, then a ceremony before God was all she was going to get. And if he played his cards correctly, he might finally earn that annulment from her in the long run. Pray he had the patience to see this last plan through.

He put on his clothing from the day before and opened the door to head down to his chamber, when Myrtle came in with fresh linens and cleaning supplies.

"Good morn, mi laird." She bobbed a curtsey, though her tone was curt.

"Good morn, Myrtle. Where is my wife?"

"Which one?"

"You know who I'm talking about," Ewan growled, biting back a retort for her sarcasm, for this woman was like a mother to him.

"Lady Nasim is tending a woman in the village who is

laboring to deliver a bairn. After that, she agreed to stop by the midwife's cottage to learn more about poultices, then she will look in on Hamish and see how his sword injury is faring." Myrtle bustled past him to straighten the linens. "I assume she will continue to be occupied for the rest of the day checking on the villagers. She has proven herself indispensable to Dunwiddie, Laird, and her industry keeps her busy day in and out. It's a shame, such a shame, for she loves you so…" Myrtle shook her head, and there was an unmistakable thickness to her voice.

Ewan frowned. As if he needed the woman to make him feel worse about matters. Though mayhap it was for the best. He left without another word and arrived in his chamber where a bath and fresh undergarments had been laid out. He prepared himself in silence. Ewan washed, dried, freshened his teeth with a brush Nasim had shown him how to fashion out of horsehair, and chewed a leaf of mint before spitting it in the nearest chamber pot. Once dressed in a plain surcoat, he strode through the corridor and down the spiraling stairs into the great hall. His clan stopped their tasks to watch him pass, though he kept his eyes forward and said not a word. But there would be gossip today about Ewan de Buchan's two brides, and it made his heart hurt for Nasim who would be humiliated by such talks, even if she had been strong thus far and kept her head high.

Walking, rather than riding, he found his way down to the kirk in the village that spread out behind the castle at the base of the mountains. Two horses, those of Lady Margaret and her father, were tethered outside. He paused, took a deep breath, and shoved through the door to the little daubed chapel harder than he had intended. It slammed the wall. Margaret, with a ribbon and flowers woven into her hair, stood expectantly by the door. She jumped at the abrupt entry, but then her face burst into a smile.

"Ewan." She placed a hand of his arm. "I'm so happy today."

"That makes one of us." Ewan laughed with an indignant snort and pulled his arm free. "*Faither*, let us start."

"Em, my laird," the little priest began. "Will there be no

congregation coming?"

"No. I said let us start, so do so."

At Ewan's grim reply, the priest beckoned them to the altar. Ewan walked ahead, sensing, rather than seeing, Margaret join his side. The priest began his lecture in Latin. He let his thoughts trail back to Nasim, working somewhere in his village to help others in a clan she would never fully be able to call her own. She deserved so much more after her father's unfair judgment, and now this harsh judgment against him that affected her far worse. Christ, he felt ill.

"Are you all right, my laird?" asked the priest, interrupting his own ramblings. "You seem pale."

"I object most vehemently to this marriage, *Faither*, but by royal order I must follow through, so continue and let us get this over with," Ewan replied, rubbing at the twinge flaring up deep in his chest at his growing anxiety.

Sakes, but he was so anxious, his long-since healed injury was reminding him of its presence, as it was wont to sometimes do.

The priest looked hesitant. "My lady, my laird, do you wish to postpone these nuptials?"

Malcolm gave Margaret a look as if to say, "last chance to get out of this." Ewan said nothing. He had already objected to everybody that would listen and had still come through it empty-handed.

"My lady?" the priest pressed, watching her exchange looks with her father.

She finally dropped her head. "It was ordered by the king, so it must proceed."

Malcolm released a sigh of disappointment and Ewan's jaw tightened even further.

Reluctantly, the priest continued. Ewan knelt on numb knees, closed his eyes, and went through the motions of vowing to honor and protect Lady Margaret, placing a ring on her finger and accepting the sacrament which tasted nothing like a merciful lord and savior, and everything like dried bread and a life sentence. It was of humor, he thought, that losing his life now to a woman he had come to despise was more gut-wrenching than almost dying in the Holy Land.

What an entire farce this is, he thought, looking to the simple finger of glass rising up behind the altar, embedded in the plastered walls. God would surely bless the union of two pious souls, not two people of like religion. Wouldn't he?

"I now pronounce you man and wife," the priest exclaimed, infusing his words with a smile intended to brighten the mood. "You may claim your bride with a kiss, my laird."

Margaret looked up at him expectantly, her lips soft and ready. He had kissed these lips thoroughly, long ago. Now, he only felt disgusted by her manipulation.

"No," Ewan replied. "We will sign the register and be done."

The priest nodded with resignation and produced the book that kept track of the lawful marriages he officiated, *a useful record to prove all unions, and the only thing now working to my advantage.* The holy man dipped the quill into the inkwell and passed it to Ewan who scrawled his name. He then handed it to Margaret who also signed her name.

And now, in spite of the mess of legalities he had just entered, for some reason he sighed a breath of relief. For the first time, the law was truly on his side. If marrying Margaret was the only way to control her, he supposed it was the only benefit in this bitter affair.

"Good Day, *Faither*," he huffed, and stalked out of the church alone, fists clenched. The overwhelming urge to beat someone, anyone, ate at him.

"Ewan," Margaret ran after him and reached for his arm as he began hiking over the rocky terrain off the road.

He ripped his arm free. "You will address me as *Laird Buchan*, or *my laird.*"

She lowered her head and attempted to look demure, taking a step back. "I'm sorry you're so unhappy. But I will try to make a wonderful wife to you...and a wonderful *mither* to our children..."

Ewan was actually surprised. He didn't think she could surprise him further, but she had. "Children? You expect me to sire children on you after this?"

239

He needed her to leave. She shouldn't be in front of him when he felt like beating the first person to cross his path. He needed time alone, for if he said anything else it would come out in an angry, nonsensical stutter.

"Under the laws of Scotland and Europe, you are now my wife, and you will learn your place. Go back to your chamber."

"But Ewan, I—"

"Go!" be bellowed, pointing his finger in the direction of the castle on the hill.

She cringed backward and to Ewan's appreciation, had the good sense to scurry back to the chapel where her horse awaited her.

"Now see here!" Malcolm protested.

"No! *You* see here!" Ewan stalked to the older man and pointed in the man's face. "Both of you forced this upon me. She wanted me as her husband so she could tout her title and wealth. So now she will obey me or suffer the discipline for it. I suggest you make haste to your chamber, sir, and pack your bags to leave. My hospitality is withdrawn from you, henceforth. You had until this ceremony to order an end to the contract and yet you bent to your daughter like a blade of grass. There's no hospitality here for men who force their will upon me."

"But what of the marriage bedding…" Malcolm's words trickled away at the rage that flickered in Ewan's narrowing eyes.

"You will leave this day, or you will be dragged off my land with naught but the *claes* upon your back," Ewan growled. "That is a promise."

Malcolm nodded, backed away, and went to his horse where he mounted up and began riding ahead. Seeing Margaret struggle, Ewan went to her, lifted her swiftly, and plopped her on her horse, swatting the beast's rear to make it go.

Then he stalked away.

***

It was dark when Nasim returned from the village. She was tired, tired of avoiding the castle, tired of finding reasons to check in on other people's ailments. Nasim entered through the main portcullis and walked up the road to the bailey, making a point to look straight in front of her to avoid the sympathetic stares of the clansmen and women finishing their work for the day.

Hold your head high. This changes nothing. Ewan has professed his devotion to you. In time, this won't seem so bad.

Supper was finishing when she went inside. Normally the room was packed, but tonight the hall was sparsely filled, the mood somber. She glided like a shadow along the walls to the stairs and climbed her way to the corridor leading to her chamber, the torches having not yet been lit. She felt her eyes well with water. Hiding in her chamber was all she wanted to do now, as she had when she had first arrived. She felt so ashamed, so embarrassed, no matter what encouraging words she tried to tell herself. She shouldn't, for this wasn't her shame to bear, but she still carried it heavily—

A hand grabbed her arm and yanked her.

"I am Lady of Dunwiddie now and my first order of business is to order you out," Margaret hissed from the shadows. She held up her hand, light from her open bedchamber door flashing a glint upon the ring adorning her finger. "Your luck has dried up. With you in the way, Ewan will never be willing to accept me as his wife. You are too much of a…" She gave Nasim an appraising look, settling on her show of cleavage peeking through from beneath her cloak. "Distraction. Men are fickle. They lust after beautiful women, but that's all you are, an exotic harlot picked up on the streets of Jerusalem. For all we know, you're a peasant from the gutters who offered good service. And that's where you should return."

Nasim stood stoically, withstanding the barrage of insults. But Lord, the comparison to prostitutes, like those she had seen in Como flashing their wares at Ewan, stung. She had been pure her whole life. She had been educated and trained and well-cared for, until that fateful night in the passageway.

"Go on. Leave. I don't want to see your face again."

Nasim held still, aching inside at having to remain here as a mistress taking orders from this woman. Margaret would be the chatelaine now. She would be expected to sit beside Ewan at the board. And eventually, Ewan would be expected to make children. With Margaret. He was honorable. Would he do his duty on such a matter, even if he disliked Margaret?

Her mind wove images and spun tales of the two of them together. Of course he wouldn't bed Margaret. *Remember his professed devotion.* She scolded herself. *How can you lose faith so easily?* But it was easy to lose faith, when the last several months had thrown her world into tumult. Still. Myrtle had been right. This was the hand she was dealt. She should do what she could to make the best of it.

She took a deep breath and turned away to go to her chambers when Margaret's claw grabbed her and ripped her back by her hair. Nasim stumbled and turned, gripping her head.

"I said leave!"

Nasim gripped her head, smarting from the sting. Still, she turned back to go to her chambers. *Except I wish only to run away from this all!*

Margaret yanked her back again and this time, slapped her. Nasim shoved her back and swept past her as Margaret crumpled to the floor, dashing back downstairs and outside into the blustery cold. She rushed across the yard to the gateway leading to the stairs down to the dock. The gates had not yet been closed for the night. She ran down the hundreds of steps, out onto the dock, stopping helplessly at the end as the churning waves roared in her ears and sprayed her.

She gasped in the freezing air, never having run so far or so hard in her life, and gazed at the watery desolation extending to the nighttime sky. Tears fell. Tears of rage. Anger! Helplessness! All of her efforts to become one of the people here were for naught if Margaret could dash them so easily.

The water crashed against the supports, mimicking the torrent she felt inside. She wanted to go home. She would willingly live in the shadows of dishonor, if only she could be at home in her mother's house. Away from this world.

Turning around, she stared up at the rocky cliff to the looming castle wall extending into the nighttime, unsure of what to do. Climb. She couldn't go back to Dunwiddie and confront Margaret without returning the woman's slap, and no matter her fiercest moments of anger, she had never once lashed out at someone. She had no idea where else to go or what to do. She climbed over the jagged rocks. Tears burned her cheeks even though the icy wind was freezing them. Ewan had been the one good thing in her life after her banishment. He had been kind, had been steady and loyal. But they had hardly spent a few days together since their arrival to Scotland. The ceremony at the church had ended long ago. She had tried to be strong, to work hard, and have faith in Ewan so he would be proud of her. But it seemed Margaret was still winning what she wanted.

Cold wind brought in snow flurries that began collecting between the rocks. She climbed further up the cliff. The rocks were difficult to maneuver. She knew not where she was going, and in her recklessness, her slipper caught between two rocks.

She tumbled forward, crying out, narrowly avoiding a kiss with a jagged rock. A sickening crack popped in her ankle. She cried out in anguish, at first unable to move as pain rippled through her. She looked back. Her foot was wedged. She pulled, struggling to stand back up, but it was firmly caught. She muttered a prayer for strength, wincing as her foot twisted, and reached down to hold her shin. Carefully, she lifted it up. It throbbed. She knew instantly that she had either severely strained it or broken it.

Still, she couldn't go back. She needed to get away. And with an injury, she would only be an easier target for Margaret's displeasure. She dragged her leg as she made her way upward to a natural rock shelter in the cliff. There were no trees and therefore, no wood or sticks to make a splint. Tears of pain raged down her face as she continued to climb but with a final heave, she managed to pull herself into the shelter, scooting backward until she sat against the rock wall.

Her heart raced from the exertion. It was pitch black out now. Dark piles of ash from fires past sat in the middle, barely visible with the storm clouds blocking out the moon. Her lungs filled and emptied in burdened breaths. She left her leg outstretched, curling the other one under her cloak, and pulled the fabric tightly around herself as the cold set in. Nasim closed her eyes and cried. She would never fit in here yet she had nowhere to go.

CHAPTER 20

Walking through the darkness, Ewan returned to the castle, knowing the footpath by heart. He arrived at the gate from the village and the four soldiers who were manning it cranked the chain until it lifted for him. He had drunk his fair share of ale at his village's alehouse, then slept off what he'd consumed in an old byre. Now, the bitter aftertaste lingered in his mouth as did the bitter afterthoughts of what he had done that day. He hoped Nasim would not be repulsed by him, if she would even see him. He entered the keep, climbed the stairs and drifted to the lady's chambers.

All he wanted was to be near her.

He tapped on the door. There was no answer. He knocked harder but still there was no answer. "Fool," he muttered to himself. "She's probably asleep." He opened the door to find her room prepared for the evening, her covers turned down, and a fire waning in her hearth.

"Nasim?" he called.

He walked around her bed to the alcove that overlooked the Minch. There was a chair with plush cushions and a leisure robe draped over it, a small table and a book upon it that with closer inspection proved to be a children's reader intended for teaching the English letters. *She's teaching herself to read my language.* She had never been uneducated in her own land, and he supposed, she wished nay to be uneducated here, either. Next to it was a board with different medicinal plant clippings pinned to it, with their names written in her eastern script. But there was no Nasim.

Surely she was not still tending villagers. If so, he would insist she come in for the night and rest. He tried to ignore the guilt that brought. He was tired of feeling guilty. But she had spent the day helping his people and he, the laird, had spent the day wallowing in self-pity.

He paced out of the room, his jaw hardening, and strode down to the great hall. He stepped over some of the men sleeping on pallets, and down the narrow corridor past the kitchens to the old granary room where he had learned Nasim tended the clans' maladies. He wouldn't behave like such a loafer any longer. This was his lot, but it wasn't the end of the world. If his infidel bride could hold her head high during such a humiliation and be productive, so should he. He had a business to run, for Christ's sake, and yet, he hadn't even begun to get back to work as the matters of marital legalities consumed all his energy.

The door was open. Immediately, he knew she wasn't there. The room was dark and empty except for her table of medicinals, a sick pallet, a chair, and a tiny basket in the corner containing rubbish. He thought where else he might look, but a chatelaine would not be up so late in the kitchens or various offices. Instead, he climbed a narrow set of stairs that also led to the gallery but continued upward toward the smaller rooms of the castle management.

He knocked upon Myrtle's door. A rustling sound ensued and she opened it in her night shift, her grey hair unwound and draped in a braid over her shoulder. Ewan looked around the darkened cell behind her as if Nasim might be lurking there, her candlelight casting a faint glow in the closet-sized apartment big enough for only a pallet, a washbasin, a basket of mending, and a trunk of personal belongings.

"Myrtle, where is Nasim? Is she still tending people in the village?"

"She isn't back yet?" the old woman asked, coming fully alert. "I haven't seen her since she left early this morn. It isn't like her to be out so late and worry us."

Ewan turned tail and jogged back down the corridor, down the narrow stairs, and wound around the gallery to his chamber, in case she had thought to meet him there. One look around his chamber and solar proved it was empty and hardly lived in, for he had idled away his night before in her bed and had been gone for a month before that.

He bolted back out into the corridor and overlooked the great hall from the gallery. Hamish was just barring the main doors for the night while the remaining servant staff prepared pallets.

"Hamish!" Ewan called, causing the hall to stir with snores.

"Aye, mi laird?" he replied, looking upward.

"Have you seen Lady Nasim today?"

"Aye, she checked on my arm this afternoon. Came to my cottage and concocted some herbs to put upon my wound. It's healing well because of her."

"Was that the last time you saw her?"

"Well, come to think of it," Hamish scratched his head. "She did come through the bailey around dusk. I didn't speak to her. I was too far away."

By now, many of the guardsmen had woken up.

"Did anyone else see her?"

"Aye, laird," one of them replied. "She came into the keep around dusk. I opened the door for her on my way out."

"She isn't in her chamber and it's well past time for bed. Has anyone else seen her?" His question was met with shakes of the head and looks of concern. "Gather all available guardsmen in the inner yard, Hamish. I'm ordering a search of the castle."

***

Two hours later, Ewan paced upon the curtain wall, snow accumulating between two bastions. Two hours later, there was no sign of her. He turned to Fergus. His first in command's face was furrowed with concern.

"Fergus, man. How is it none of the guards saw anyone suspicious going in and out of the gates?"

Fergus looked ashamed. "I have no idea, my laird. I always order that two soldiers man each entrance at all times, four at each portcullis."

"Who was put in command of the gates tonight?"

Fergus listed off the names.

"Round them up. I wish to meet with them immediately."

Fergus bowed stoutly and hastened down the steps leading to the outer yard. Ewan followed, waiting until the group had amassed.

"Well? What have you men to say for yourselves? I have seen you better trained than this."

"Colin wished to speak with us on a matter and asked us to congregate with him," a guard replied as snow flurries continued to fall. "It was a last minute request and he insisted it was important. There wasna' time to shut the gates. 'Tis the only time we were nay at our post, sir, and it was only for about ten minutes, but—"

"I care nay how long it was. I care nay if there is a man dying below. *Never* leave the gates open and unattended," Ewan fumed. "Running to the aid of one man whilst leaving the gates open could mean the ruin of us all."

He rubbed the bridge of his nose.

"This is basic training for all of you and I'm disappointed," he continued. "For it seems if Lady Nasim isn't here, she's out there, and we haven't the first clue of where to look because no one was watching. You shall all be on squire duties once the lady is found. You will assist in the kitchens and you will polish swords until they gleams like new. And I shall speak to Colin, but know this: you answer to me above everyone else. You will not take orders from another except for Fergus who has command as my captain."

His men nodded and climbed the ladders and stone steps to return to the battlements. After three years away from home, regaining control of his household was proving difficult without becoming a tyrant. His men had grown accustomed to answering to Colin in his absence, and apparently Malcolm.

"Prepare supplies for search parties," he ordered Fergus. "Food, water, blankets should we find her, weapons and medicinals. I go to gather my arms. We'll meet back here. Make haste. If she's outside these walls, there's no telling what trouble she might have encountered at such an hour in the snow."

Fergus imparted the news to the others. Ewan grabbed the nearest servant boy and jogged back to his chambers to gather his effects.

"My laird," Margaret said, sticking her head out of her door.

Ewan stopped and turned to the lad. "Go and unpack my weapons and my bow and quiver of arrows. I'll be there in a moment." Then he turned back to Margaret. "What do you want?"

His eyes dipped to her revealing nightshift and the seductive way in which her fingernail lingered on her lips. And he felt revulsion.

"'Tis our wedding night, and I have been waiting up for you in case you changed your mind."

Ewan shook his head. "Nasim is missing. I'll not rest until I find her."

Margaret's eyes flashed with awareness.

Ewan caught the gleam and stepped closer. "What do you know, woman?"

She shook her head. "I came straight to my chamber, as you requested, and have been awaiting you ever since. But I did...well, never mind."

"You did what?" Ewan demanded.

"I did nay want to say anything to you about it, for I know of your affection for her, but...well, yesterday as you arrived home, I saw Nasim with Hamish, alone, in a chamber downstairs. You know Hamish's reputation. He has few scruples with women, so of course I was curious. They were laughing and, well, Hamish wasn't wearing a shirt. She had her hands upon his arm, and then he took both of her hands and..." She closed her eyes and shook her head as if remembering something scandalous. "I simply couldn't look anymore. I wonder, though, did she nay go and visit him privately today?"

Margaret let the implication linger in the heavy air between them, then bowed her head when no answer came from Ewan.

"I'll leave you to your business. You're preoccupied and I've been selfish in my want for you. She retreated into her chamber again.

Ewan gathered his weaponry and returned to the bailey outside, wearing his stiff leather jerkin, heavy claymore, his dirk tucked into his belt and his *sgian dubh* in his boot, brushing past Margaret's closed door. She was full of rubbish. Nasim cuckolding him wasn't possible, was it? He refused to believe it. She had been pure. It had taken him months to finally convince her to submit to him. She had grown up in a cloistered world, where being caught alone with a man was cause for forced marriage and banishment. But Hamish was stout, handsome to many women, and charming in his ruggedness. Ewan had been gone for a long time. Nasim was no longer an innocent, and women could grow lonely, too…

What in the hell has gotten into you? You know Margaret never says anything without a ploy up her sleeve. Banish these thoughts, man. Nasim would never do such a thing.

He met his men assembling in the inner yard, torches lit and supplies gathered, and broke them apart into parties, when his sights landed on Hamish. Nasim *had* been in his cottage, alone, cooking at his hearth. Hamish had said earlier that she was making remedies for his wound, but all the same, the picture of their shared domesticity and companionship bothered him and he pushed through the commotion of men organizing their accouterments to pull Hamish into the privacy of a shadow.

The words were out of his mouth before he could stop them.

"Have you taken liberties with my wife?" Ewan growled, pinning the man backwards against the wall.

Though Hamish was built like a curtain wall, Ewan's tall, lean frame was tight with muscle.

"Lady Margaret?" Hamish asked, confused.

"Lady *Nasim*," Ewan corrected. "I have it on account you were seen half-naked with her in private, enjoying her company yesterday."

Hamish's skin paled and his brow furrowed. "Nay, my laird. How could you ever think such dishonor of me? I would never…" Comprehension dawned on his face. "The Lady Nasim was tending the gash on my arm sustained whilst training. I swear it to be true. I had to remove my tunic to allow her access for stitches. I was teasing her and she obliged me by laughing. Mi laird, you must believe me. I hold the utmost respect for her. I have sworn to protect her, and I have sworn my fealty to you."

"Why not do such things in her surgery chamber? Were you in private, holding her hands?"

"Holding her hands?" Hamish looked truly confused and scratched his head.

"Aye, that's what I have on account. And of course, she paid you a private visit today."

"Mi laird, *we were* in the surgery chamber. The door was open, Laird, to protect her reputation. I nay know why anyone would accuse me of such a thing had they been truly watching. They would have seen she offered healing ministrations and I kissed her hands with fondness one has for the mistress of the castle, nay with lust. I swear this. God above, I swear this—"

"You swear this? I've seen you, man, with the womenfolk—"

"Sir, no!" Hamish argued, actually flushing with embarrassment. "There's only one woman right now with whom I share bed sport, a kitchen lass, and I love her. Never would I consider a noblewoman, especially one who has such a claim upon her staked as Lady Nasim does. I'm fond of Lady Nasim, aye, and I could see today she was heartbroken and in need of busying herself. So when she offered to make a poultice for my wound, I didna' argue but let her do her work, for it kept her from thinking about your marriage."

The desperation on his man's face told Ewan he was speaking the truth. Ewan felt a pang of guilt. He sighed. He should have trusted his gut and ignored Margaret's attempts to rile him. Leave it to Margaret to manipulate him once again. He smarted with irritation for falling for her tactic. Ewan nodded once and patted his shoulder. Margaret had succeeded in distracting him, but it wouldn't happen again.

"I'm sorry to accuse you, Hamish."

"Do you believe me, laird? I swear on my oath of fealty to you that I would never lay a hand on your woman unless it was to protect her. Perhaps I did nay realize how deeply you covet her. Perhaps I crossed a line—"

"Nay, man." Ewan cut him off and looked away. "'Tis someone else who has crossed a line. Rejoin the men."

He watched Hamish leave as snow accumulated across the ground, and then stalked back to his men, Fergus jogging up to him.

"A servant who was finishing work for the day near the main portcullis said he thought he might have seen her running out toward the dock, but he couldn't tell for sure since it was dark. She has taken to coming and going so freely to assist the midwife that he thought not much of it, for he considered it to be an important mission."

Ewan nodded. He took a set of two hounds and led his party through the portcullis down toward to the sea.

"Nasim!" he shouted. "Nasim! Answer me!"

Others called her name, their calls muted by the blustery snow. They swept along the path leading out to the dock, the hounds having immediately caught her scent. A new horror lurched in his mind. What if she had fallen into the Minch? What if she had struck one of the many jagged rocks below the wintry water's surface and drowned? His mind concocted a gruesome image of her lifeless body floating ashore, snagging on the rocks.

"Nasim!" he called again, this time with as much force as he could to shove the sickening pictures from his mind.

His call was answered by the wind and the crashing of waves. Torches bobbed in the distance as men trailed up and down the cliffs. The dogs tugged at their leads, barking. Ewan reached to their necks and cut them loose. They bolted out onto the dock and began sniffing, backtracking, and returning to the dock's edge. After a thorough search, one of them caught a scent at the base of the cliff. They began maneuvering around the rocks with renewed purpose, climbing the cliff.

"Dear God," Ewan whispered.

Had she been kidnapped or carried off by a man with mal intent?

This new thought caused a ripple of rage to surge through his veins. He closed his eyes against the imagery he imagined. It would only serve to distract him from his mission. He followed the hounds with torch in hand and his guardsmen spreading out around him. He strained to see his hounds as they disappeared up the cliff, scrambling over the rocks, higher and higher. The healed injury deep in his lung ached at his sudden exertion. *Do nay think on rape or any other such thing.* He took a deep breath and rubbed his chest to make the pain subside. But if Nasim had been violated, he would never cease searching for the bastard who did it, and would see them draw and quartered.

He neared the rock shelter, a shallow indentation in the cliff that served as a point of strategy to the castle's security. He used to come here to sit and think, sometimes draw, before he had gone to war. He had almost come here after his wedding had it not been for the bitter cold. Now he wished he would have, so he could have caught the whoreson with his woman red-handed. Up he climbed, feeling his hand cut on the sharp rocks as he balanced himself with the torch, when he heard the hounds start howling.

"The dogs have found something!" he called to his men.

He charged the rest of the way, leaping over rocks and sliding on the slick snow. Arriving at the rock shelter, he illuminating it with his torch. Nasim was in the shadows, frightened by the dogs, and huddled in on herself.

He called to the dogs. They silenced and sat as he dashed to her side where he collapsed to his knees.

"Nasim, what happened to you?" he demanded, pushing back her hood and examining her face. "Where are you hurt? Who did this to you?"

"My ankle. It's broken," she croaked.

He dragged up her skirts from her outstretched leg and began feeling the bones. Her ankle was swollen and the moment his fingers touched it, she flinched and cried out.

"Naz." He reverted to her language, worry climbing in his voice. He planted a kiss upon her forehead, then her lips. She was freezing. "Who hurt you? How have you come to be here?"

"I don't want to talk about it," she whispered while guardsmen gathered in the entrance, confused by her foreign language.

"I need a blanket and water," he called out to his men.

They stared at him with confusion, and he realized he had ordered them in Nasim's native tongue. After repeating himself, they brought forth the provisions.

"Inform the castle guards that Lady Nasim has been found. Have them light the signal for the others. Demand that the laird wants provisions brought to his chamber. The lady's ankle is broken."

His guard met his command with a nod and dashed away, his sword slapping his thigh with a jingle. Ewan shook out a blanket and wrapped it around her, opening the water skin for her to drink.

"You must tell me. Whoever is responsible will be punished, I'll see to it."

She swallowed and looked away. Ewan examined her. She was hiding something from him.

"Please, Ewan, I…I wanted to rest and…and found this niche here."

"You're lying to me," Ewan said. "I need to know who's responsible for this. Nasim, I'm nay asking, I'm ordering. Disobey me not, lass."

She looked at him, then at his men, then back at him again and replied in her native language. "Your wife stopped me when I came back from the village. She ordered me to leave and struck me. I couldn't bring myself to retaliate, for I've never hit a soul in my life, though I did shove her away." She put her head down again, as if ashamed by it all. Ewan grabbed her chin and lifted it, ordering a torch closer, a slight bruise discolored her nose. "I broke my ankle climbing over the rocks. It was foolish to run off, but…but Ewan I cannot go back!" she pleaded. "Don't make me live here any longer. I miss my family, I miss my half-sisters, I miss not being different. Send me away where I can be free of this, I beg you."

He pulled her to him, cinching his arms around her and resting his cheek on her head. There was no way she could ever return to Jerusalem, and no way he would ever be willing to let her go. Anger blazed through his blood. "You're nay going anywhere. My people love you and I love you. You're never to leave again. I'll take care of this. You'll nay be afraid in your own home."

With the guidance of his men's torches, Ewan carried her carefully down the slippery cliff to the path leading up to the castle. A burst of light shone from atop one of the bastions, signaling to call off the search. The descent from the rock shelter was slow and treacherous in the dark, but finally they reached the path and climbed their way back up the stairs to the gate.

"My lady," Colin bowed to her as Ewan cradled her in his arms, striding across the bailey. "The castle is relieved to know that you're safe."

"Thank you, Colin," she replied, forcing a smile.

Ewan stopped. "Why did you order my guardsmen away from the gates this eve?"

Colin's eyes widened. "I needed to clarify the details of their training schedule for the morn—"

"That's Fergus' job. *He* is the captain of my guard, nay you. I repeat, why did you do it?"

Colin, taken aback by the laird's anger, bowed down.

"My laird, I've gotten into the habit of helping run the castle in your absence. I forget my place. 'Twill nay happen again."

"It had better not," Ewan replied, his face stern. "Because of your negligence, the security of my entire castle was compromised, and Nasim was sent out into the cold to suffer injury. I would hate to think you guilty of a scheme."

Colin turned ashen and froze. "My laird, I beg forgiveness. I would never hurt the Lady Nasim." He dropped to his knee. "Your people are growing to love her. She's made herself indispensable. Sakes, sir, but I made a mistake."

"He has been ever kind to me, Ewan," Nasim whispered.

Ewan looked at her, then glared at him and continued on. He might want to throttle the man for such a blatant oversight, but Nasim's health was more important. He would talk with Colin later when his anger had cooled and his woman was asleep and warm.

The doors to the keep opened and Ewan carried her through, stepping over the empty pallets, up the stairs, and down the corridor where Myrtle stood in the entrance to his personal chambers. Though Nasim was light, his arms and thighs quivered from the lengthy carrying. Myrtle ushered them in, placing pillows at Nasim's back. A hearth fire was stoked to raging. Already the requested supplies were laid out. Ewan unclasped her cloak.

"Goodness, she's blue with cold, sir," Myrtle said.

"Myrtle, warm the bed," Ewan said.

Myrtle bowed to the Ewan's request and dashed to the hearth where she pulled out a stone with large metal tongs, dropping it into a fur wrapping and placing the bundle beneath the covers. Ewan took one of Nasim's hands and began rubbing vigorously.

"I need slats to make a splint, bindings, a bountiful tray of supper and a decanter of whisky. See to it these things are brought up."

"They're already ordered, sir, but I'll hasten their arrival." Myrtle scurried out of the room. One by one, servants returned with supper and drink. Ewan set to work splinting her ankle. At one time, Nasim had tended his wounds and healed him. Now it was his turn to heal her. As the hour grew late, Ewan sat at her side and watched her drift to sleep and rubbed her fingers with his thumb. His anger bloomed again, now that his worry for Nasim had abated, and he felt that damned twinge in his chest.

He finally set her hand down and bowed out of the room, not stopping until he arrived at Margaret's chambers. With whitened knuckles, he pounded his fist on the door, shaking the wood on its iron hinges.

No one answered.

"Open this door!" he demanded.

He banged again and finally the latch was lifted. Margaret shrank from the rage on his face.

"Leave," he commanded her maids.

The women hurried to their adjoining chamber and sealed themselves within. He slammed the door behind him and stalked towards her.

"Damn you."

Margaret began to cry.

"Spare me your false tears, Margaret."

"I'm sorry, my laird!" she exclaimed.

"Sorry will never be good enough for what you've done," he fumed. "You do nay cast orders here. I do."

"I'll do anything to repent," she sobbed. "I'm sorry! But I wanted us to be husband and wife. I used to be your first love interest. I waited and waited to marry into Dunwiddie! Why must I now be second to your infidel whore?"

With a thread of remaining chivalry, Ewan balled his fists and maintained his composure. It was clear, Margaret was a lady only in title, not in behavior, but he would still be a gentleman, even if it killed him.

"And why must you chase a man who says he no longer wants a union? Are you really so petty as to chase my title, no matter the cost to you or your *faither*? You're nay second to my 'infidel.' You're nay anything at all to me. I returned home a married man after three long years. I returned home in love with another, and I would have compensated your *faither* kindly for the inconvenience."

"My laird, please give me a chance to be the lady of Dunwiddie," she beseeched.

Ewan shook his head, his lip curling in disgust.

"You moved into my castle, forced me into marriage, lied to me about Nasim's infidelity, lied about Nasim's whereabouts, and struck her. No doubt you are the one who masterminded placing the snake in her bed."

"That wasn't me—"

"You had best spend the rest of the night packing what things you most desire. For tomorrow, you return to your *faither's* home. You're no longer welcome here, and may live out your days in his walls."

"But you can nay send me away." She squeaked.

"I can, and I am."

"But you have nay consummated our marriage yet. My laird, *I* am your lawful wife, whether you like it or nay!" she pleaded.

Ewan exploded. "Which means you will do as I command or suffer the punishment for it!" His voice lowered into an unfeeling growl. Damn, but he had done a wondrous job of restraining his true anger until now. And his chest injury ached.

Her eyes widened in horror. Genuine tears began pooling down her cheeks. "There's no greater humiliation, than to be refused by a husband."

"What?" he said, folding his arms, knowing he had the upper hand. "Not what you expected? You thought I'd have a change of heart? Thought my honor would extend to bedding you, too, because of some sense of duty and an ideal of right and wrong no matter my feelings? Thought me a man and thus, only an animal excited by the prospect of a rut with a fetching woman? Let me explain something, *wife*. You might have forced me to be your husband under church law, but you failed to think beyond what would happen once the law signed you over to me."

"I thought you would be angry at first. But if you give me a chance, you'll see that I'll make a fine wife," she pleaded, grabbing his arm.

He shook her loose. "You might be beautiful to look at, Margaret, but you're living in an illusion. I've learned a thing or two. I've learned that you came to Dunwiddie in hopes of aligning yourself to whoever inherited my estate. You got my title. But if you thought it would bring you riches, and make you the envy of everyone, you're wrong. You get nothing for your greed. Aye, you're fetching. You could have had any eligible man in Scotland, or beyond. You didn't need me. You almost caused Nasim's death tonight. Your lies and your manipulation have been your ruin. And you've brought it upon yourself."

He stalked back to the door, placed his hand upon the latch, and paused.

"You'll leave at first light. I will personally see to it. Pack tonight what you will take."

The moment the door shut, he heard Margaret cry. A shard of guilt hit him. He didn't like being a hard man. It wasn't his way. And in spite of everything that had happened, the truth was still the truth: he had been betrothed to her. He had been promised to her, as she had been to him before his departure three years before. Coming home with Nasim hadn't been fair to Margaret, even if it hadn't been fair to him or Nasim, either. The forces of the world had dictated he take Nasim to wife. He just never thought he'd grow to love Nasim so. He shook his head. Sadly, with Margaret, reasoning was impossible. Being a hard man was proving to be the only way.

CHAPTER 21

End of March, 1193

Nasim tapped on the midwife's door on the outskirts of the village. No one answered. Despite the hour being early and the weather cold and rainy, the village already bustled.

When she had left the castle, Ewan was tucked away in his solar, pouring over the details of his newest cartography commission, ink smudging his fingers while an untouched tray of food sat beside him. A quick assessment of the castle kitchens, hall, and yards on her way out told her that the morning was carrying on as normal and that Hamish had not injured himself again. Meaning, she had a moment to herself.

She smiled.

"Hello?" Nasim tapped on the door again, cinching her hood beneath her chin as the rain drizzled around her. "Are you home?"

No answer. Still, it wasn't unusual for the old woman to be out calling, for there was often a steady stream of poor humors needing treatment, and another woman further in the village was heavy with child. It was likely she had finally gone into labor and the midwife was preoccupied. Nasim had helped her deliver a babe not long before and it had been one of the most profound experiences of her life, second only to that night so long ago in Lombardy, when she had finally torn down her inhibitions. Now that it was her turn to discuss her symptoms with the old woman, excitement gave her stomach a happy tingle.

She lifted the latch, peeking inside to see that it was dark, the shutters pulled closed. Only a feeble stream of light from the cloudy sky cast its dimness across the hut from the open door. The pungent smell of herbs hanging from the rafter in bunches wafted to meet her. Against the far wall, next to the shuttered window, was the old woman's work table with clay vessels stacked upon it.

"Hello?" she called one more time. Still, no answer.

Instead, she let herself in and closed the door against the chill. The midwife had invited her to do so in the past to await her return when they had lessons planned. She dropped her wet hood and unclasped the cloak. Carrying it to the hearth, she hung it on a hook and turned to see that the fireplace contained a few glowing embers. She rubbed her frozen hands together, set down her basket, and picked up the poker to prod the embers to life.

A basket of chopped kindling sat nearby and she leaned down to pick up a log when a floorboard creaked. She jumped. A hand clamped over her mouth. A scream welled in her throat. She tried to wriggle free. The hand dragged her backward against a strong chest—a man's chest—and she could instantly tell it was not Ewan's. The muffled sound of a blade withdrawing from a leather sheath startled her further. She bit into the hand holding her. A curse escaped the man who released her mouth and gripped her neck instead. She screamed.

"Quiet!" a voice whispered. The knife came to rest beneath her chin

"Help me!" she shrieked. "Help me!"

Her screams were piercing. Someone knocked on the door.

"Is everything all right?" asked a visitor.

"Help me!" Nasim cried again.

Her assailant whipped away the blade and shoved her forward. She stumbled across the room and fell against the midwife's bed. A stream of light shot across the floor as the window shutters were thrown wide, but as she turned over her shoulder, the head of a cloaked figure dropped out of sight. She steadied herself and kicked her feet loose from her tangled skirts, jumping up, and dashed to the window. But when she peered out, there was no one to be found.

Knocking on the door continued. "What's going on in there?"

Nasim scurried across the room, wrenching the door open. A trail of worried villagers from nearby cottages stood beyond the threshold.

"Milady!" exclaimed a young village man who dropped into a surprised bow. "We heard screaming. We thought it was the midwife."

Shaking, Nasim gripped her hands together to keep the tremors from undoing her. She shook her head, unable to find words, and exhaled, dropping against the door frame. She couldn't fill her lungs and fought for breath.

"She's white as a sheet!" said another villager. "Was it another snake?"

"Run for the laird," the man said to a nearby girl, reaching out to steady Nasim. "Ye best sit down until his lairdship arrives."

A woman, followed by her children, pushed into the cottage and guided her to a stool while the fire was stoked and water was boiled to brew a hot drink. Having heard of the incident, the midwife herself came waddling home.

"Milady," she wheezed, out of breath. "What on earth has happened?"

A soothing cup was put into her hands, and as the minutes passed, she felt her breath steady. She shivered, thinking about how that cold blade felt against her skin. She couldn't find her voice. Horse hooves could be heard thundering down the path. A woman nearest the door peeked out.

"The laird is here," the woman whispered. Chattering ensued. Nasim exhaled with relief and saw Ewan dismounting through the open door, soaked from the cold rain. Fergus blazed down the path behind him, the lass who had come for them holding the head guardsman about the waist as they rode together. Ewan dropped the reins of his mount into the hands of a lad.

"Go and tether my horse," he said, patting him on the shoulder, and jogged through the door.

Dropping down to his knee, he nodded his thanks to the

girl sitting with Nasim and drew both of her hands into his own ink-stained ones.

"My thanks," he said to the others, who backed up and stepped outside. The midwife swung the pot out of the fire and ladled more broth into Nasim's cup. She took a shaking sip, still trying to find her voice.

"Nasim, the villagers paint an awful picture. What happened? Why were you screaming?" he asked, searching her eyes with his own.

"I came here to ask the midwife some questions, but no one was here. So I came in to wait."

"I've told her she's welcome to do so if I'm out," the midwife chimed in.

Ewan looked at the midwife, then back at Nasim, nodding for her to continue.

"I bent to get the firewood, and a, a…" A shiver rattled her body.

"Tell me," he urged, rubbing her arm to soothe her. "Another snake?"

She shook her head. "A man came up behind me and put a blade to my…" Again her words trailed off, but her hand migrated to her throat and held it, reassuring that everything was still intact.

Ewan's lips thinned at her statement.

"Who was he, Nasim?"

She shook her head, noticing the grim tick to Ewan's jaw. "I know not. He was behind me. I started screaming and then the villagers began knocking. He must have hoped I'd go silent but it seems I made a scene." She felt his hand squeeze hers her as another shiver racked her shoulders. "He pushed me off balance so that I tumbled over. That's when he made his escape. I fell upon the bed and he jumped out the window. I only saw his head as he dropped, but it was wrapped within a hood. I went to the window to see who might be running away, but by the time I got my skirts untangled, there was no one."

Ewan strode to the window and thrust the shutters wide again. Then he looked back at her.

"I'll return shortly, Naz. Rest easy until then."

***

Footprints were as clear as day in the soggy soil from the drizzle, though other foot traffic had begun to disturb them. Ewan squatted down, pressing his fingers into the ground. They were distinct. There was no question they had come from the midwife's window… *nay…there's a set going to the window, and then another set of the same size running away…* He could tell this from the space between each print and the force at which the mud had been smudged back.

He followed the prints to a neighboring cottage as Fergus came to join him.

"Who lives here?" he asked.

"'Tis empty, mi laird. Old Man Lyall used to live here, but he died a year ago and his daughter has since traveled to another village to live with cousins."

Ewan remembered the old man, a woodcarver who had once made him a set of goblets. The man had been kindly. He had missed much while away at war.

The foot prints halted at the window of the abandoned cottage and the shutters were open. Ewan jogged around to the door, followed by Fergus. The home was empty. An old bed sat in one corner, a bin of tools in another corner that looked as if they had been pilfered through over the months. Cobwebs floated upon the breeze caused by the opening of the door. The hearth sat cold and dusty, the remains of firewood from a year ago sitting in a few charred chunks.

Fresh mud sat beneath the window on the floor, but then nothing else. Either the mysterious man's boots hadn't been muddy, or he'd had a pair of clean shoes waiting for him. Though the cottage was dusty, the floor looked recently swept, explaining the lack of additional footprints. A deliberate perusal told Ewan that there were no more clues to be had. He joined Fergus outside who was examining the ground leading from the front door.

"Nothing, sir. He was careful to walk in the grasses, for there're no more prints to be found."

"He didn't just disappear," Ewan remarked, also looking at the ground, but eventually he had to concede the point.

He returned to the prints from the midwife's window. They were large. "Go fetch the hounds. The rain will have washed away much of the scent already, but any clue we can get, we must seize."

Fergus returned to his horse and mounted up. Ewan returned to Nasim who had mastered her composure now.

"You're coming back to the castle to rest."

"But I need to speak with the midwife. 'Tis important."

Ewan shook his head. "Then she can come to the castle, too. I want you under my protection whilst Fergus and I investigate this matter. Give me no arguments, woman," he scolded, but he put his hand upon hers and pulled her to him, holding her to his chest.

She looked up from his warm embrace. "Do you think it's the same person who put the snake in my bed?"

He kissed the side of her head while the midwife fetched Nasim's cloak. "I have nary an idea. And such frustrates me." Aye, it did. After sending Margaret away a month ago, he had thought that things were returning to a sense of normalcy. But the issue of the adder had never been resolved and, after this, it was obvious a culprit, mayhap more, was still in their midst.

"Come with me now. Your foot has only just healed. You're ordered, my lady Buchan, to lounge idly in your chamber, read, eat, drink, and relax." Upon his teasing upturn of the mouth, Nasim smiled. "You work too hard, wife."

They returned to the castle, the news buzzing around them that the Lady Nasim had been attacked, and a herd of chattering clansmen and women greeted her as they rode beneath the gate into the bailey. Colin jogged down the steps to greet them, flanked by Hamish and a handful of servants.

"What has passed, my laird?" he queried.

"An attack. Someone drew a blade on my woman." He dismounted and lifted Nasim down, swooping her into a cradle and walked up the steps. He turned on the top step and looked out at the gathering of castle workers. "Rest assured, all of you, I will determine who did it, and that person will regret their decisions. Mark my words. There is a blackguard among us. If anyone knows anything, it's best you come forth and speak to me."

He had a killer to find.

***

"Now you're to get plenty of rest and plenty to eat," the midwife concluded, tucking a cloth over her basket to depart.

Nasim nodded. The old woman patted her with a smile, then turned and left. A rush of emotions cascaded through her mind. Excitement for the future mixed with nerves from the attacker in the village that morning, followed by an intense longing for her mother at a time when she would need her most, and then thoughts of Lady Margaret, Ewan's legal wife. Margaret had been gone for almost a month now, yet still, thoughts of her managed to distract her and remind her that she was living a lie.

She drifted to her table, in need of a distraction, and picked up her children's reader, examining the letters one by one and reviewing their sounds. It wasn't until sometime later, however, that she realized she had been staring at the page without any recollection of having read a single word. Were sons as sought after here as they were in her home country? She hoped the news wouldn't worry Ewan further—

"What has you so lost in thought?" Ewan asked from the door where he leaned against the frame, his arms folded and his eyes glancing to her hand resting upon her stomach. He closed the door, unclasped his brooch, and loosened the laces of his tunic.

Nasim, roused from her daydreaming, looked at him and smiled. His face looked weary and grim, but his features always softened when he gazed at her. He pulled the tunic over his head to reveal his naked chest and the fading scar from his surgery incision. Slowly, he was beginning to fill back out from their long trek across Europe, which had thinned him.

He bent and pulled loose his boot lacings that were now caked in drying mud, and pushed them off on her rugs.

"You've been gone all the morn," Nasim said, eyeing the offending items with amusement. For such a learned man, it seemed like a boyish habit to retain.

"And you have been occupied in thought, my lady," he

replied, moving to her bed to lie down and stretch out on his side. "Fergus, Hamish, and I have been investigating what happened this morn. We've just returned."

"Did you learn anything new?" she asked hopefully.

He shook his head, the furrow returning to his brow. "Nay. What had your mind so occupied?" Clearly, he wished not to talk about it.

"I was just wondering what it would have been like if we could have been married here, in this country."

"Naz," Ewan said, looking down with what she thought might be shame. "Do nay dwell on it. I tried everything, but the priests insisted you needed to be a Christian in order for our marriage to be possible. There was nothing I could do."

She nodded, still looking wistful. "Is it possible to become a Christian?"

Ewan gazed back at her. "It is. But I did nay want you to have to make such a decision."

Nasim looked back down at her book. "I would have done it for you."

"Why?"

"I don't want our children to be bastard-born." Ewan's face became serious, and she hastened to amend her statement. "I shouldn't have said such. I know you've done everything you could. I was just wondering about things, 'tis all."

He sat up and swung his legs over the side of the bed, shoving his hand through his dark hair. "I do nay want this for my future children, either. I was born a bastard. I had to work hard to overcome it. Thankfully, as my *faither's* only son, he saw to it I was recognized. I consider you my wife and so does my clan. If our bairns must be bastards in the eyes of the law, they'll at least be recognized as my legitimate and only line and they will grow up knowing their *mither* and *faither* to be faithful."

She smiled at him. "That is good. Because I'm carrying."

Ewan's eyes shot to hers. His face fell to impassivity as he deciphered what she'd said. Then it dropped. When he finally found his voice, it sounded gravelly. "You're with child?"

She nodded, smiling uncertainly at his reaction. "'Tis why I went to see the midwife."

"Nasim, you are a blessing to me!" he exclaimed, jumping up.

She stood and he dashed across the floor, wrenching her into his arms. They embraced for some time, Ewan placing kisses to the side of her head as he buried his face in her hair. Slowly, his kisses became more sensual. Her pulse begin to race, a light flutter warming her blood. He bent to cup her face and kissed her lips, allowing a hand to glide down her front and work open her robe to caress her stomach. His lips pecked their way to her ear, then down her neck, down her chest, over her chemise, until he was kneeling before her.

***

Ewan kissed her flat navel. In the coming months, it would grow rounder. And yet, so overwhelmed and joyous a moment before, his thoughts now turned stormy. The man who had attacked her merely hours before might have killed her, and with her, the bastard would have killed his tiny, unborn bairn. His grip on her tightened protectively and he rested his forehead against her. Renewed determination burgeoned within him to find the culprit, but just as the dark images of what he might do to the man began to take shape, Nasim brought him back to the moment.

"Are you happy with the news?"

"Happy?" he murmured, looking up to see her eyes glittering and her smile beaming down at him. Christ, but she was radiant, and he was killing the moment with his brooding. "I'm overjoyed. You will make a wonderful *mither*."

"And you a wonderful *faither*." Her eyes flit away, then she looked back. He smiled. Hearing such meant much more than she could know. "Do you hope for a boy? I'll do my best to give you one."

His smile gentled. "Lad or lass, this news pleases me beyond words. If it is a lad, he will be my heir, and if a lass, well, may she be as smart as her *mither*. I'm content with either. Did you doubt this?" he frowned.

She shook her head, though unmistakable relief washed over her face. Ewan stood and walked her backward, bumping into the bed, a grin lighting his face as one hand reached down to unclasp his belt. He leaned down to her ear as his kilt loosened and fell down to the floor while he pushed Nasim's robe from her shoulders.

She giggled.

"Suppose I demonstrate just how much your news pleases me—"

A knock at the door interrupted them.

"Mi laird, milady," Myrtle called, her tone anxious.

"Not now, Myrtle," Ewan called back, sharing a grin with Nasim.

"I must insist," Myrtle replied.

Ewan sighed. "What is it?"

"You have a missive."

Ewan looked to Nasim, shaking his head at how absurd the interruption sounded as his hands resumed caressing her shoulders and back. She kept smiling as he winked his eye.

"Is it life or death, Myrtle?"

"It's... Well, aye and nay. It's neither. Colin says it's just...strange."

Ewan's hands slowed to a stop again and he furrowed his brow. "What do you mean?"

"You'd best go see about it," Nasim said, darkness returning to her visage. "In case it has anything to do with this morning."

Ewan sighed with resignation and nodded. "You're right." He pecked her lips. "Do nay get too cozy, Naz. I like to finish what I start."

She grinned. "I would expect nothing less."

"Be out in a moment, Myrtle!"

He collected his rumpled kilt from the floor, laid it out, refolded it, and lay down to wrap himself in the fabric's great folds. With his belts secured, he stood and snatched up his boots and planted one more peck to Nasim's lips and then another to her belly. "Good-bye my wee one," he murmured, and quit the chamber.

Two Brides for Ewan de Buchan

CHAPTER 22

"I do nay understand. Who delivered this?" Ewan pushed aside his measuring tools and ink well on his solar desk, laying the parchment down in the center to examine it. He combed his dark hair back, but the ends flopped back over his forehead.

Colin shook his head. "A servant found it here. Nailed to your solar door. Like a proclamation. She ran to tell me, and I came to investigate. I sent Myrtle to fetch you immediately and have requested Fergus return from his training schedule. He should be here soon."

"The ink is fresh and the parchment unblemished by folds or wrinkles. Indeed, my thumb is smeared from the last line where it wasn't quite dry," Ewan said.

He reread the cryptic words, scrawled in bold letters across the parchment. *"You were supposed to be dead. This was all supposed to be mine. You and your infidel whore had best watch your backs."* Unease filled his gut, superseding his anger.

He was supposed to be killed in the Holy Land. Margaret was supposed to be the lady of Dunwiddie. She had always referred to Nasim in such despicable terms.

But Margaret hadn't wanted him to be dead, had she? She had wanted to marry him, and had succeeded in her pursuit. In fact, she had wanted Dunwiddie so much so, she was willing to force the matter before the king and now had what she wanted, even if it hadn't gained her the riches she had desired. Margaret had never anticipated that his life might be imperiled so many months ago. A horrible thought gripped him, like talons easing

269

into his skin as memories washed across his mind.

"Margaret has been determined to flaunt her status as your betrothed since you left for war... My brother informed me that she intended to stay on as the mistress... Because of her love for your people, she vowed to offer herself in marriage to the man chosen as your successor so that she could stay true to Clan Buchan."

Robert Donald's words had irritated him in that tavern in Glasgow. Did Margaret know something? Was there a larger conspiracy afoot? Was his attempted murder in Jerusalem part of a larger design to see Dunwiddie into the hands of an expectant inheritor and see Margaret to the altar with them? And was this threat intended to warn him that his days were numbered? If so, Margaret would then be a widow, and after some months, she would be free to marry again. To someone who certainly wouldn't relegate her away to her father's house. She had, after all, been waiting a long time to marry, and if she was as anxious as she seemed to be for Dunwiddie's status...

He hadn't once stopped to think that such a convoluted scheme might be possible. He assumed that what Commander Murray did to him, though confusing, was isolated to something between them only, and knowing the king was summoning Murray to investigate had put the issue out of his mind.

Margaret had relished tormenting Nasim. Since her departure a month prior, he had learned of Margaret's threats and taunts. *"I do hope you sleep well..."* spoken just before Nasim found an adder in her bed. *"I would be careful if I were you. Should you sip from the wrong cup one of these days..."* Nothing had happened yet to warrant concern about tainted drink, thankfully, but now that he knew Nasim was with child, his alarm only heightened.

But he had sent Margaret back to her father's house. She wasn't here to level this threatening note nailed to his door. His guardsmen who escorted her confirmed delivering her into her father's care. This new threat was unnerving. And the attack today in the midwife's cottage only added to the concern. If it was indeed Margaret behind the attacks on Nasim, then she must have a henchmen helping do the dirty work. But then how was his murder in the Holy Land related to what was happening to Nasim now? He hadn't even met Nasim when Commander Murray had beaten him from his horse, and certainly hadn't been forced to marry until a month later. How would anyone have known that he would be returning home with a different woman on his arm?

The threat on his desk was clearly directed at him this time, not Nasim. Either there were two separate schemes afoot, or his failed murder and now the threats to Nasim were merging into one.

"No one of suspicion was seen in the halls or out and about?" he asked.

Colin shook his head. "I saw no one. Hopefully Fergus will be able to talk with his men and determine something—"

Knocking on the door interrupted them.

"Enter," Ewan called, standing over the missive and slouching his hands on his hips.

Fergus pushed through the doorway. "Colin summoned me, sir."

"Aye, come in," Ewan said, pushing up his sleeves. "Close the door."

Fergus did so and strode across the rug.

Ewan held out the missive to him. "This was nailed to my solar door. It wasn't here this morn when I was working, nor when I passed by to visit Lady Nasim not long ago. It had to have been put there a matter of minutes ago. Has anything, or anyone, suspicious been reported?"

Fergus' brow furrowed as his eyes skimmed over the words on the parchment. He looked up, frowned, but shook his head. "I do nay understand. Who would want to see you dead? After the threats to Lady Nasim, this is especially disconcerting."

Ewan nodded, agreeing with everything Fergus said as the man turned the page over, then lifted it to his face to inspect the parchment type. Fergus picked up a piece of Ewan's parchment to hold them side by side. The only person he knew of who hated him was Commander Murray, and he was in the Holy Land. He probably hadn't even seen King William's royal summons to explain his conduct yet. Margaret might indeed hate him now, too, considering that he hadn't succumbed to her antics, but again, she wasn't here.

"This is your parchment, sir," Fergus said, setting down the extra leaf, still inspecting the missive and rubbing the corner between his thumb and pointer.

Ewan came around his desk and also looked at it, as did Colin.

"Quite right," Ewan remarked, sliding another sheet off his desk to compare. They were cut to the same size, with the same tackiness, and the same finished gloss. Ewan picked up his straight edge and measured the length and the width of the missive, shaking his head. "Aye. I prepare stacks of my own parchment in batches, so that when I'm working, I do nay have to stop drawing to pounce another sheet and thus, lose my focus. So I have stacks that all look the same because they were prepared together. And I measure the size of the stack before slicing them."

Fergus looked at him and their eyes met. "Then whoever nailed this to your door, took the parchment from this stack. And seeing as you only have about five or so leafs remaining, it's likely they stole into your solar, wrote the missive, and nailed it up, all within the last hour."

Ewan shook his head, drifting to his window and slouching his hands on his hips again. "I wonder if this traitor is the same person harassing my wife."

"I'll investigate, sir," Fergus said. "With all that is remaining unsolved, I feel certain the culprit, or *culprits*, will provide a clue. Sooner or later, even the wisest of criminals makes a misstep or overplays their hand. We'll catch them."

Ewan looked back at his head man, then at Colin who returned his worried look. "Pray we figure it out before something irreversible happens to my wife. For if she is harmed, there will be two lives harmed now, nay just one."

Colin and Fergus glanced at him, when realization dawned in their eyes.

"Lady Nasim is..." Colin's query trailed away as his eyes brightened.

Ewan nodded. "Aye. She's carrying my son or daughter. I plan to announce it tonight, so nay a word from either of you.

'Tis why she went to the midwife's this morn. To confirm. Trust that if anyone harms her and my wee bairn, I will carve them apart."

***

That evening, as the flocks of castle workers and guardsmen herded into the great hall, and as Ewan announced Nasim's tidings to the cheers, well-wishes, and happy exclamations, he took in her beaming face, her bright, dark eyes, and pulled her close to his side. Ewan enveloped her against his heart. This woman, who took care of his people, mended their injuries, and more than sated both his intellectual and carnal needs with her companionship, was carrying his child and bundled in his tartan, was a beautiful sight. But his own heart was restless. People approached to wish them well, to kiss Nasim's hand, and whoops of glee invaded their ears as the clan realized a feast had been ordered to surprise them all. Yet, he had to force a proud smile.

Nasim squirmed.

"Not so tight, Ewan," she admonished with a smile and a pat against his chest.

He realized his grip had grown protective and firm, and he relented.

"I'm sorry, wife. I'm just worried for you."

"I haven't become fragile, simply because I've become pregnant," she teased.

He chuckled. But his eyes were roving the hall for anything suspicious. Or more importantly, any*one* suspicious. He had bid his men keep their investigation hushed, so as not to make the guilty party suspicious. But someone nefarious was lurking in his midst. He could very well be in the great hall, merry-making with the rest of the clan. And Ewan wouldn't rest until they were locked in his dungeon cell.

CHAPTER 23

A shape crept though the corridor, taking care that the torches provided good shadows.

"Who goes there?" called out a night guard walking the halls.

The shape pressed itself into a darkened niche as the guard moved forward with his torch, looking in all directions. Slowly he passed by. As soon as the wavering of light faded around the corner, the shadow continued onward, stopping outside of Nasim's door. A thin, long blade was inserted in between the door and the frame, and with a gentle shimmy, it lifted the latch inside. Quietly, the door was eased open, until just enough room for the intruder had been made. The figure slipped inside and crept around the bed to the table.

A shifting on the bed occurred, affecting the curtains drawn around it. A crack remained in the drapery leaving just enough light from the fire to illuminate Nasim fast asleep, her linens pulled up to her chin. Ewan's broad shoulder rose up behind her. His arm wrapped over her with a hand resting upon her breast.

The cloaked person pulled out a small vial from within their pocket and picked up a goblet of water on the table next to Nasim's plant clippings. With a tip of the vial, a powder sifted into the water. Nasim shifted on the bed and a sleepy moan escaped her. The intruder looked up to see Ewan's lazy hand massaging her, drifting up and down her body in soft caresses. The quiet creaking of the bed ropes took on a synchrony with his steady movements, and soon, it was clear Ewan was coupling with her.

The figure froze and waited for the nighttime tryst to abate until they were finally fully asleep again, at which point the cloaked person made a silent exit.

***

"Call the midwife!" Ewan bolted from Nasim's chamber. "Call the damned midwife!" he thundered, dashing down the hall.

The castle, just rousing for the morn, filled with commotion. Myrtle and some of his guards came running.

"What's wrong, mi laird?" Myrtle cried, grabbing his arms in the corridor.

"Nasim! She's sick! She's—she's vomiting blood!" He held up a rag clutched in his grip, speckled in blood.

Myrtle raced in to see Nasim curled on the floor, holding her stomach, a trickle of blood escaping the corner of her mouth.

"Dear God," Fergus exclaimed, shoving past everyone else before bolting from the room again to fetch the midwife.

Ewan stooped and lifted Nasim into his arms, carrying her back to her bed. She remained in a rigid curl, moaning, before heaving again. Nothing but a shower of red droplets surged forth, splattering Ewan's chest.

"God Almighty!" Myrtle crossed herself, having gone pale. "God Almighty!"

She dashed across the chamber and pulled forth a spare blanket from a chest, returning to drape it over Nasim.

"Ewan," Nasim murmured, her eyes pinched shut. "What is happening to me?"

"I don't know," he replied, caressed her hair back, his lips and hands trembling. "Be still. The midwife will be here soon."

She coughed once, a shaky sound, clenching her stomach harder. "The babe," she whispered. "I'm losing it…"

"No…" Ewan shook his head in disbelief. His voice trailed off into a whisper, and he saw the image of their future, a child frolicking before the hearth or playing in the surrounding countryside begin to drain away. The incision in his chest ached anew, but this time, it felt more like heartache. "Do nay talk like that." He looked to the door. "Where is the bloody midwife?" he demanded.

Nasim drifted into unconsciousness as the chamber filled with guardsmen. The commotion coming through the open door told Ewan the entire castle had been alerted. After fresh water, food, and clean rags came streaming in, the midwife finally arrived, out of breath, and still in her nightshift with a plaid thrown around her shoulders.

"Step aside," she ordered, coming forth to feel Nasim's clammy forehead, "And put on some claes, mi laird."

A quick look downward told Ewan he was only donning *braies*. He felt his eyes moisten, watching the woman set to work stripping back Nasim's covers and gathering the maids about her to begin fulfilling her orders. She noted the blood coming from her mouth and shooed everyone out into the hall except for Ewan and the maids, pushing shut the door. She waddled back to Nasim and peeled open her robe to see her body. There was indeed blood between her legs.

"She was fine one moment, then," Ewan said, scooping up his tunic from the wad he had left it in the night before and dropping it in disarray over his head. God, but he could hardly form a sentence. After everything that had happened to her, she couldn't be losing their bairn. She just couldn't. "Then I do nay know what happened."

"Describe everything that has passed since she went to sleep last night," the old woman asked.

"We came to bed. She and I...as men do with their women, we..."

"Aye, aye, continue," the woman urged. "I'm an old woman. This is nay my first caber toss."

"We slept. At some point I woke up to a draft, but it seemed like nothing. When she got up this morn, she sat to read, like she always does. And all of a sudden she doubled over and complained of a cramp. Then she was curled on the floor expelling blood—"

The midwife scurried to the table and grabbed the goblet of water, sniffing it deliberately, then pouring its contents out onto one of the rags provided. A sludge dripped out of the bottom.

The midwife looked at Ewan. "Did she drink?"

"Aye, water."

"Just the water, you are certain? No tonics or tinctures?"

"Aye, just water," Ewan said.

"Did she drink it last night?"

"Nay, this morn," Ewan paced, running his hand through his hair.

"How much did she drink?"

Ewan shook his head. "I do nay know. Just a swallow mayhap? I was nay fully awake. She did try to drink more when the cramps set in, to ease her discomfort."

The woman frowned at his words, displeased. "She has been poisoned, Laird."

Ewan froze.

The words didn't sound real. *"I would be careful if I were you. Should you sip from the wrong cup one of these days…"* Rage welled up inside him. He would hunt down whoever had poisoned her and murdered their unborn babe, and he would slit their neck. He felt completely helpless. Which only angered him more.

"I've seen this from time to time. Women who do nay wish to carry a bairn have come to me to beg for a powder. I've rarely given it, but one pinch is all a woman needs to expel the unborn. Nasim's goblet contains so much not all of it has dissolved. Either whoever did this does nay know much about medicinals, or they wished her dead for too much powder can be devastating. Given yesterday's occurrence, I believe she's nay safe. But we must think of all possibilities first. Was the lady pleased about this bairn?"

Ewan wanted to shout at her, barely refraining. "Of course she was. Do you suggest she did this to herself?"

"She does have knowledge as a healer," the woman said. "It's possible."

"But she would know it was too much," Ewan retorted. "For you say yourself she has knowledge as a healer. She would know only to use a pinch."

"That is true, but she is also still learning about birthing," the midwife replied, "for she was given no training on the matter in her homeland. If she did this, she might have overestimated."

"Woman, you insult her with such a question. She was pleased with the bairn, I promise you," Ewan ground out.

"Laird, you have every right to fash yourself, but I'm simply trying to figure this out."

Ewan took a deep, angry breath, and nodded. She was right. "What can you do for her?"

"Nay much. Vomiting can be good, for it means less poison goes into her body, but the blood is troubling. It might just be from the violent heaving, or it could be that the powder is hurting her stomach, and only time will tell us if she'll recover. But either way, I fear the damage might be done." She indicated the blood coming from Nasim's womb. "I believe she has probably lost the bairn."

A lump formed in Ewan's throat and he turned away, pinching his eyes with this thumb and finger. Damn the tears. He couldn't stave them off completely. It was no use. No amount of gritting his teeth and pinching his eyes would help him retain his dignity right now. Moisture leaked onto his cheeks. He took a shaking breath and paced to Nasim's window, thrusting the shutters wide and bracing his arm on the sill. He gazed out at the grey, churning waters and grabbed his chest, sucking in at the pain that pinched his old injury. Who would have done this? Margaret was the likeliest suspect. Her words were too coincidental. But how?

"Will she die?"

"Had she drunk it all, as no doubt the blackguard who did this desired her to, then probably."

Ewan's face went cold.

"Mi laird?" He turned back to see that the midwife was covering Nasim back up. "Do nay lose hope. The powder is not always completely effective. There are some women who take it several times before their womb purges itself."

Ewan prayed Myrtle was right, but there was a lot of blood, and her words were of little comfort.

CHAPTER 24

Nasim had been resting for a couple days. There were only signs of improvement in her health, though she remained weak. Which was why Ewan rode high in his saddle for Malcolm Fyvie's estate. With Hamish posted as guard outside Nasim's door, Myrtle taking care of her, and Fergus in the saddle beside him, he was going to get to the bottom of this.

Margaret's remarks to Nasim had been too suspect. Bidding her to sleep well, even if Margaret had said it rudely, hadn't been enough cause to link her to the adder in Nasim's bed, but warning her not to drink from the wrong cup was damning. Whatever part Margaret was playing in this scheme, he wouldn't relent until she confessed all she knew and named her partners in crime. The countryside dipped and lifted, and they wove their way over the landscape, withstanding the continued snow flurries, bundled in fur.

The trek took a sennight by horse drawn caravan, but just the two of them achieved it in a matter of days.

"Laird Ewan de Buchan!" Laird Fyvie's head guard called down from the gatehouse. "What brings you here on such a cold day?"

"I seek Lady Margaret! I've a matter to discuss with her immediately!"

"That's nay possible!" the guardsman replied.

"Make no mistake, she is my wife by all legal means, and has nay the right to refuse me!" he replied, removing his leather gloves and rubbing his hands together.

"Nay, that isn't what I mean!" the guard replied. "She received your missive and returned to Dunwiddie, at your request."

"My what?"

Ewan glanced at Fergus, who returned the look, his own brow furrowed.

"Your summons! Your rider arrived, oh, about a sennight ago, and Margaret prepared a pack and returned with the guardsman by horse." The guard also furrowed his brow. "Why have you come here for her when you summoned her home?"

"I assure you, I never summoned her."

The guard shook his head. "A man came, this I swear, carrying a letter with your seal upon it."

Ewan shook his head, alarmed. Margaret was up to something, and he had another villain in his midst, for someone had delivered a message he had never written. He turned to Fergus. "Who has been unaccounted for recently? Anyone? Any guardsmen?"

Fergus shook his head. "Naybody at all. Everyone has been present for training every day. It couldn't have been one of our men."

Puzzling, so puzzling. He shook his head further. His household staff hadn't suffered any absences. No one recently had claimed an illness where they might be left alone abed for days to sneak off and collect Margaret.

"May we come within?" Ewan finally asked. So far the portcullis hadn't been lifted for him, and he was certain such a rebuff had been ordered by Malcolm on purpose who might still be angered at him. "For I fear if Lady Margaret is nay here, then she is unaccounted for. I never summoned her. And indeed, it is because of some recent happenings that point to her, that I have come to speak to her."

***

After three more days of riding, Ewan, Fergus, and Malcolm began the assent through Dunwiddie land, and by late afternoon, as the last of the glowing sun fell behind the sea, they achieved the village.

"The laird has returned!" called the guard manning the

outer portcullis.

"How fare's Lady Nasim?" he asked, cupping his hand around his mouth, for concern had eaten at him the entirety of his journey.

The chains ground, and the gate was lifted.

"She improves each day! The midwife insists she continue resting, but the word is she is back to herself!"

Ewan exhaled and allowed the blessed words to sink in. She'd lost their babe, but he hadn't lost her. "My thanks for the good news," he finally replied.

"She awaits your return, sir."

Fergus slapped him once upon the shoulders and he lurched flimsily, emotions having drained him. He ignored the sidelong glance Malcolm sent him, unsure if he would still see anger in the man's eyes that the woman he felt so much tenderness for wasn't Malcolm's daughter. They tapped their horses into a trot to pass under the gatehouse.

By the time Ewan reached the inner bailey, Colin was striding down the steps to greet him, his eyes widening to see Malcolm of Fyvie returned, too. The groom was already departing the stables, along with a village lad to help, and as they dismounted, the lad took Malcolm's reins as the groom tended to Ewan's and Fergus' horses. Ewan looked to the lad. He couldn't quite place him. He had been gone a long time during the Crusade, so it was probable that the lad had been a young child when he left, but it bothered him nonetheless.

Nay, man. You're growing paranoid now. Every tiny thing that seems out of alignment is making you suspicious. You have well over a couple hundred villagers including bairns, and you've been gone for three years. There's no way you could remember them all so vividly.

"Colin," Ewan said, shaking off his over-active suspicion. "Is there any sign of Margaret here?"

Colin's eyes widened further. "Nay, sir. Why would she be, after she was sent away in disgrace?"

"One of Dunwiddie's messengers delivered a missive to my daughter, summoning her back here," Malcolm said. "She left with the rider over a sennight ago to return, on horseback."

Colin shook his head, as did several other serving staff who had gathered around him. "Who would have sent such a letter?"

"Mayhap the culprit who left the notice upon my solar door," Ewan replied, loosening the ties to the fur around his shoulders. "Margaret has been missing for more than a sennight—plenty of time for riders to make the trip to Laird Fyvie's lands and back again in time to poison Nasim and leave a note of threat upon my door."

They strode up the steps into the great hall. A guard closed the door upon the March chill, and Ewan passed off his cloak to Colin, who in turn put it into the hands of a maid.

"Let us convene in my solar to discuss anything further."

He wanted to go to Nasim, take her in his arms and feel assured that she was alive. He missed her. But this needed dealing with immediately. Because whatever Margaret was up to, it would never stop until she was found and questioned, and Nasim's safety would remain imperiled.

He pushed into his solar, Fergus and Malcolm following him. "Colin. Is Hamish still holding his guard outside of Lady Nasim's chambers?"

Colin nodded. "He's been ever vigilant, and only switched guard with a man of Fergus' choosing when he needed sleep."

"Good. See to it he joins us, and another guardsman is posted as sentry in his stead."

Colin bowed once and left, returning moments later with his bearded man. They closed the door.

"Lady Nasim is well?"

"Aye, sir," Hamish replied. "And she is most anxious to see you."

Ewan nodded, tamping down his restlessness to check on her. She had lost their babe, and he knew it was probably distressing to her. What if she was regaining her health in body, but wallowing in more sadness herself? As she had done when she lost her family in the not-so-distant past? Christ, but what he would do to have this issue of the murderer behind them, so he could help Nasim move forward and, once healed, attempt to give her another child. He had utterly failed her so far. He had promised himself to her, as she had to him, and the law had forced him into another marriage instead. He had promised her safety in the remainder of her days, as his wife, and now, she had a target upon her, for a reason he simply couldn't figure out. He had looked forward to having a child, to being the father his own sire had never been.

"Let us lay out all we know," Ewan began, seeing that his decanters had been refilled in his absence, and offering a drink to all the men.

He sat and pulled forth a new sheet of parchment, removing a quill from his drawer and dabbing it into his inkwell.

"There are no known persons who dislike Lady Nasim, except for Lady Margaret," Fergus began.

Ewan wrote down the fact as the others pulled up seats.

"Lady Margaret's threat about drinking from the wrong cup," Fergus continued.

Ewan kept scrawling.

"And when I came upon Lady Nasim in the corridors with Myrtle, when Margaret would nay allow her to pass," Hamish said. "Remember, she called Lady Nasim an 'infidel whore,' and then bid that she sleep well."

"Aye, that was the night the snake was reported in her bed, correct?" Ewan asked.

Hamish nodded. He inked his quill again and continued.

"The night of your wedding to Lady Margaret, she slapped Lady Nasim and sent her out into the night, where she broke her ankle," Hamish said.

"Indeed, and I ordered her back to Laird Fyvie that very night," Ewan said, his quill scratching into the parchment.

"Last sennight, Lady Nasim was attacked at the midwife's cottage by an unknown man," Fergus said.

"And later that day, the maid found the threat nailed to your solar door," Colin added. "Of course, that night, Lady Nasim was then poisoned."

"Aye, giving credence to Margaret's threat so long ago about drinking from the wrong cup," Ewan nodded, amending his notes.

"Lady Margaret was summoned to Dunwiddie, by an unknown person representing a Dunwiddie messenger some days before the attack at the midwife's," Fergus said, "as we just found out from our visit to Laird Fyvie."

"My daughter also…" Malcolm began, then, as if thinking better of what he was about to say, fell silent. They all quieted and looked at him. Malcolm had done a superb job, Ewan noted, of keeping his cool as his daughter was discussed in such incriminating terms. Any father might be wont to defend his daughter's honor and throw down with his weapons if they heard such damning things.

"She what?" Ewan urged.

Malcolm rubbed his forehead, exhaling wearily. "The night of our return from the king, the night before your nuptials, I urged my daughter to relent her pursuit of you, and explained that I did nay think you would ever treat her as your wife, nor did I think you would ever work with me in partnership on anything outside of our betrothal contract. I could see your mounting anger, and was saddened her wedding day wouldn't be a beautiful one. But she insisted. We all know this castle and land to be wealthy, and my bargain for free export to the sea without your tariffs was the most ideal contract from a suitor. But I was willing to let it go. When she left that night upon my failed counsel, she said the strangest thing… I do nay know how I failed to see the signs, but her words bothered me. I was blinded to her doting, but what she said didn't sit well with me."

"What did she say, man?" Ewan asked.

"She said a wedding with fanfare was never what she cared about. That she 'wanted the status she was promised.' She said she wouldn't allow your, eh, *woman*, to take what she'd waited so long for. She felt certain that you would eventually come to love her, but if you didn't remain the laird, she would marry whoever took your place."

"Margaret has been determined to flaunt her status as your betrothed since you left for war… My brother informed me that she intended to stay on as the mistress… She vowed to offer herself in marriage to the man chosen as your successor…"

Ewan took a deep breath as the memories of Robert Donald's words once again swirled in his mind, and he looked up at all of the men.

"Has anyone at all that you are aware of left Dunwiddie for

any length of time, since it has been known I was alive and married to another? Think man. Let's think farther back than recent days. Someone wants me dead. And someone has been taunting and threatening Lady Nasim since her arrival. These people might be one and the same, or they could be two separate cases."

"Nay recently, no," Colin said.

"Aside from when Colin left to visit his ailing brother in Stirling," Fergus said, his eyes furrowed as he and the others continued to ponder the facts. "But of course, that was shortly after your homecoming, as you know, and is nothing."

"Your ailing brother?" Ewan asked. "Nay, I didn't know."

"Aye, sir. When you were away, searching for a priest who might marry you and Lady Nasim, I received word of Robert's illness," Colin said. "Lady Nasim granted me permission to go to him, but I wished nay to worry you about it. I know my brother and you are fond of one another, and he began a slow but steady recovery. Word is now that he is quite well."

Ewan sat back, his brow knitted tightly, and leaned onto an arm, propping his temple on his finger. He eyed Colin, an idea striking him. It left him feeling sick to his stomach. The suspicion seemed so far-fetched. He didn't like the direction of his thoughts for Colin had been so devoted a friend.

"I see," Ewan said.

"Master Colin was nay gone for long," Fergus said.

Ewan looked away from Colin Donald, his trusted steward of many years, to Fergus. Fergus, an astute man, seemed to notice a shift in Ewan's thoughts. His head guardsman quirked his brow, as did Hamish, but he didn't indulge their curiosity.

"Then we need to begin a new sweep of the castle and the grounds. Instead of a suspicious man, we ought to be looking for Margaret. Or any clues about her. Malcolm, man. You are invited to remain in the great hall and drink a tankard or two whilst we work."

The men all nodded and stood, and Ewan looked over the list he had written out once more. But Colin's remarks about Robert's illness seemed to twist these facts in a way he didn't want to ponder.

"Colin should help me search the inner yards. Hamish, take a couple trusted men with you to search the outer wards and village, and to Fergus, I allot the castle proper and all of its offices. We'll meet up in the yard as the sand runs twice through the hour glass to discuss our discoveries, if any."

The men all nodded and began to rise. Ewan looked to Colin. "Where do you suggest we start? In the bailey?"

"Aye, that sounds like a good plan."

"Not a single stone left unturned, man, no matter how far-fetched a thought. If Margaret returned here incognito, then she's trying nay to be found. I'll check the guard towers and storage buildings."

"And I will check the smithies and stables," Colin said.

"Good. Go and get started."

Colin bowed and departed, and as the other men began to leave, Ewan eyed Fergus, who lagged back. Ewan moved to the door and looked down the corridor to see Colin's head descending into the stairwell, then closed the door. He drifted to his window and propped his arm on it.

"Something's on your mind," Fergus said. "You have a suspicion."

Ewan nodded, thought a moment longer, then turned.

"I thought nothing of a couple things, but when I see this bigger picture, I wonder..." He picked up the missive with the damming note upon it that Fergus had produced in the course of their discussions. He dropped it again and it floated to the desk surface.

"When I returned home, I found Colin's blade upon my desk here. Probably for opening a missive or something menial. He kept the accounts during the time I was gone, and I knew he would need to work here where I kept all the records."

Fergus furrowed his brow. "Surely you do nay suspect Colin Donald, laird. Do you?"

Ewan looked at him and nodded. "I do. You see, he also spoke to Lady Margaret familiarly, upon my return to Dunwiddie. As I escorted Nasim here, Colin called to her from the steps, by her first name, for all to hear. I thought it just a slip of his tongue, nothing important."

"Aye, it was likely just a lapse in judgment on his part. She had been residing here for a month already, and had taken a fraternal fondness to Colin who ensured her comforts."

Ewan nodded, though now that he knew *that* fact, it only deepened his suspicions. "Colin went to visit his brother's sickbed. What was wrong with him?"

"It sounded as though the man had the sweating sickness, but it passed after a couple days and though weakened afterward, his brother appears to have made a recovery."

Ewan furrowed his brow, then wagged his finger in the air as if having a striking thought, smiling.

"And so now I present you with another detail. Colin only has one brother. Robert."

"Aye, I know of him."

"I knew nay of Robert's supposed illness, but when I left to visit the priests, when Robert supposedly fell ill, I ran into Robert in a tavern hall. Indeed, he was hale as can be. In fact, when I asked him how his health was, he said he'd had nary even a sniffle. He was on the king's business to purchase new horses for the royal stables."

Fergus pondered his words, then ran his hand through his hair. He shook his head. "Then where did he go, if nay to Robert's sick bed?"

"That is the one hundred pound question to answer, I think," Ewan said, casting Fergus a knowing frown. "As far as Colin knows, however, he is unaware of Robert's journey to Glasgow or that the two of us passed a meal together."

"Aye, it would make sense for Robert to go to Glasgow, considering he took over for Colin's old stewardship in Stirling," Fergus pondered.

"It would also make sense for Colin to feel hopeful that he might be able to petition the king for lairdship and earldom of Dunwiddie, as compensation for his years of servitude. He might have been expecting to request the inheritance, for we all know illegitimate royal blood flows in their veins. And then I came back, alive, thwarting his petition."

"He has, after all, always wished King William would recognize him, seeing as he is half-brother to the king himself,"

Fergus noted.

Ewan nodded, then folded his arms across his torso. "I think we're onto something. And what bothers me further, now that I suspect him, is what he knows about Dunwiddie."

Fergus furrowed his brow further.

"What I mean is, he knows everything about this castle. Every in and out. He could easily sneak Margaret in…"

"Through one of the escape passages… Aye."

Ewan nodded at Fergus' understanding. "I admit, right now there is no proof, but Colin certainly has motive. And if it's him, he must have someone else helping him, for he was here in the castle when Nasim was attacked in the village, and he was also here each day whilst Margaret was being summoned by one of my 'messengers.'"

"But if he has a henchman, it does nay necessarily have to be another clansman. He has connections in Stirling, too, from his time in service there," Fergus said.

Ewan nodded. He turned back to the window. "But this henchman, of which we can only speculate whom at this time, is able to get in and out of the castle unseen."

He drummed his fingers on the window frame, gazing out at the Minch but not seeing a single wave as his mind put clues together. "Colin knows of the escape passages, and I'm willing to bet, he has informed his blackguard helper."

Fergus' face dropped, then grew cold. "He keeps the only other set of keys to the tunnels, apart from yours and mine. If Margaret is here, then he probably allowed her secret entry."

Dunwiddie, like many fortified castles, had a series of secret passages that led down beneath the walls, into the cliff side, and out onto the rock shelter where Nasim had taken refuge after she had broken her ankle. The passages were designed to funnel his people to safety in the event of a siege lain upon them.

"Right into Dunwiddie's very walls." Ewan nodded darkly. "I need you to tail Colin. He's searching the smithies and the stables. I go to join him. Lag back, keep an eye out, and report to the bailey in two hours, as we've already agreed. Act as if you've just returned from your search. Do nay say a word of this plan to anyone, nay even Hamish."

Fergus nodded, and at Ewan's gesture, he also quit the solar.

CHAPTER 25

The outbuildings proved to be free of anyone but guardsmen in the battlements, gatehouses, and along the wall. Each storage room, tower, stairwell, and passageway proved to be empty.

"We have only the stables left to check," Ewan noted as Colin came out of the smithies' shops.

Colin nodded but chuckled. "I find it doubtful that she would be sleeping with the animals. She was always so particular about her hygiene. Annoyingly so, for she refused to have the slightest blemish on her skirts."

Ewan shrugged. "We check all the same, man. I found it doubtful that she was capable of such malice, but I now see she is full of many surprises."

"You always knew her to be unrelenting," Colin agreed as they walked side by side to the stable doors.

"Aye, unrelenting," Ewan explained. "But not obsessive."

They moved past the younger lad who had helped the groom, the child he'd had trouble remembering.

"Mi laird, can I help?"

"Relax, lad. Just having a look around," Ewan replied, ruffling his hair as they breezed by.

They moved down the row of stalls beneath the hayloft projecting overhead, a ladder against the far end. The stone foundation wall sat in the shadows, partially obstructed by bales of hay. Ewan prowled up the aisle, peeking into each stall. He went to the foundation wall where a rack stood, and took down a pitch fork to prod the stacks of hay with the handle.

"My laird, I doubt she would hide in a bale of hay," Colin smiled.

Ewan turned an eye on him. He didn't see any mirth in this. The more he thought about it, the more he was beginning to suspect Colin. After all, the servant had ordered his guardsmen off the wall, the very night Nasim ran off and went missing. Which given all their other discoveries, certainly seemed like another part of the design.

"If you have a problem with me looking around my own stable, man, then you may retire for the eve and I'll continue this search alone."

Colin's smile fell and the man shook his head. "I'm sorry, sir. I forget my place."

"Indeed, Colin." Ewan turned to face him squarely, setting his boots in a wide stance and propping the pitchfork on the ground. "It seems ever since my arrival home, you've been forgetting your place. I've had a time regaining command of my house…until now. I am the laird here, no matter how royal of blood runs in your veins. Bastard or no, I will be respected by those I employ, shelter, and pay."

Colin's face flushed and he dropped down to his knee, his head bowed. "My laird. It…it will never happen again. You're right. I'm not recognized by my half-brother the king, and though he acknowledges me as a friend and relation, he has refused to name Robert and me on his family tapestries. Because of that, I should be grateful to work even as a lowly smith. King William gave me a prestigious role as one of his stewards, and you have generously given me the same prestige here. I'm sorry."

Ewan gave him a stout nod. "I will hold you to your remarks."

He strode away to checked the tack room at the back of the stable, then came out, noting Colin in the hayloft.

"What have you up there?" Ewan called.

Colin turned and looked down from the shadows. "I saw movement up here, but it turns out it was only these wee things." He held up three barn kittens. "Their mother has made her nest up here." Colin replaced them and returned back down the ladder. "No luck then, my laird?"

Ewan shook his head. "No. Let's converge with Fergus and Hamish. It's nearly time."

They strode outside to find Fergus already waiting in the yard as Hamish returned from one of the outbuildings.

"A kitchen worker claims she saw the lady, sir," Fergus reported. "She claims someone looking like the Lady Margaret came to the kitchens well after sundown a few days ago, as the kitchen maids finished cleaning for the night so the baker could come in and get to work. The maid ran into her when she went into the buttery for ale, and said she thought she saw Margaret running off into the shadows with a loaf of bread, a wedge of cheese, and a flask."

"Which maid told you this?" Ewan asked.

"A lass named Ruth."

"Ruth?" Hamish said, his brow furrowing.

"Aye, you know her well," Fergus said. "Is she an honest sort?"

Hamish nodded, then turned to Ewan. "She's my lass, the woman I've been carrying on with." Ewan remembered Hamish's admission, given after he had accused his man of taking liberties with Nasim. "I'm fond of her, sir."

"All right. Take me to her, Hamish, so I might discuss what she thinks she saw." He turned to Colin. "Colin, go back to the stable and please double check the tack room and the loft. I was feeling hurried and didn't do as thorough a job as I should have."

"We were quite thorough," Colin said. "We searched through and through."

"Why must you argue? Is there something you know that you're nay saying?" Ewan said, his words firm.

Colin shook his head contritely and bowed it, but when their eyes met again, Ewan sensed irritation. Nay. He sensed frustration and defiance. Everything about Colin's posture emanated displeasure that Ewan wouldn't accept his answers.

His steward nodded and strode back across the bailey to the stables, and Ewan began to walk with Hamish and Fergus toward the keep again. As soon as Ewan spied Colin entering the stable, he nodded to Fergus. Fergus nodded in reply, and said nothing.

Ewan and Hamish climbed the steps to the main doors and disappearing inside. They found Ruth working alone in the kitchens, kneading a fresh lump of dough.

"'Tis late, Ruth. You should be abed by now," Ewan said as he entered.

"The baker was feeling fatigued this eve. She ages, mi laird, so I offered to stay and see the bread baked for her," Ruth replied, dabbing at her brow with her apron.

A young girl, pretty and stoutly built with freckles smattering her nose, Ruth plucked up the massive ball of dough and slapped it over, continuing her kneading.

"Fergus says you spied Lady Margaret here a few days ago. Is this true?"

She nodded, and turned to look at him. "I was nay certain, but it did look like her, though she looked a bit bedraggled. 'Tis her state of dress that had me doubting myself, for Lady Margaret is very particular about her appearance."

"Why did you nay report someone stealing food from the pantry?" he questioned as she returned once again to her labor. The baker always made the next day's bread for the whole castle. Poor Ruth was looking to be up much of the night.

She stopped again, her eyes falling wide and worry lodging on her face. Hamish came around the work table and moved up behind her, bracing his paws upon her shoulders. She looked up at him and he smiled encouragingly, then she glanced back at Ewan.

"But mi laird, I did report it. Right away I reported it. To the head cook, and she then said she would make sure it was brought to your attention."

"She hasn't said a thing to me yet, lass," Ewan replied, folding his arms. "But I have been away at Laird Fyvie's estate."

"She told Colin, since he's the steward, and, well, naturally we've assumed he would pass this information onto you, for that's his duty. I figured since nothing came of it, it must not have been her after all."

Ewan's lips thinned. More evidence against Colin. It was

time to summon his wayward steward and have a discussion. In his solar. Betrayal cut through him. *Colin, my favored man.* Who he thought was a friend. He shook his head.

"My thanks, Ruth. Should you see anything else suspicious, come and speak to me immediately. I will give you audience."

She nodded. "Thank you, sir."

"And get some rest. When the bread is baked, you've permission to remain abed in the morn."

She curtsied. When he and Hamish returned out of doors into the cold nighttime, Fergus was standing behind the vegetable crates. He turned to Ewan, his brow hard, and beckoned him over.

"Colin has nay come out," his head guard stated. "He went in and stayed within."

Ewan shook his head. "He's involved. Ruth reported her sighting of Margaret to the head cook, who in turn reported it to Colin. He never said a word about it to me, and so, Ruth believed she was mistaken."

"Wait a moment… You suspect Colin of being part of this plot?" Hamish said, his brows drawing together.

"Indeed I do," Ewan replied. "Colin is involved. And Margaret is here. Somewhere. Now the question is, who do they have doing their dirty work? Let's go gather him up."

He strode forth and tried the stable door. It was sealed shut. He rapped upon the door but no one answered. He banged harder.

"Open this door, lad!" Ewan ordered, drawing the attention of his sentries upon the curtain walls.

Still there was nothing. Standing back, Ewan kicked the door with his boot, over and over again, until the cracking and groaning finally gave way and the bar on the inside splintered. With a ram of Fergus' shoulder, the door swung open, sending the last remains of the bar flying.

The horses inside started and shifted in protest. The stool by the door where the young groom had sat not too long ago was vacant, as was the bedding of hay near the door where the lad would sleep. He dashed down the center aisle, noting the stalls occupied by horses undisturbed, apart from beasts' ears flipping forward at the intrusion.

"Wait a minute," he muttered, noting two empty stalls at the back of the stable. They had been empty on his previous search, but now, two missing horses seemed suspicious.

"It seems two horses are gone," Fergus remarked upon the same clue, following Ewan's frozen stare.

"Check the hayloft for any clues," Ewan demanded, striding towards the tack room, the door to which stood ajar. "I suspect Colin's search might not have been very thorough up there."

He walked into the tack room, looked around, noting the rows of saddles, stacks of blankets, and the long row of bridles hanging neatly along the wall. But then he walked to a corner where a trap door sat in the shadows. Getting down on his knees, he felt along the seam. The rushes had shifted out of the way as though the door had been lifted open since his previous inspection. It was the only other way out of the stable except for the windows, a secret hatch leading down a ladder into the escape passage that ran out to the cliff side.

"I'm onto you now, Colin…" he whispered to himself. "Fergus!"

He shoved to his feet and strode back into the main stable.

"Mi laird, I think you should see this," the guardsman called down from the hayloft, his face grim.

A few guards peered warily through the broken doors. He walked to the ladder and climbed into the hayloft. Fergus was standing beside a bale. He pointed behind it. Ewan looked down to see Margaret, curled into a ball and fast asleep.

Rage unchecked flamed to life in Ewan's blood.

"Wake up!" He jostled her with his toe.

She sat up, groggy, and looked up at him with bloodshot eyes. A smile spread across her face.

"Ewan, my love!" She threw her arms around his legs to embrace him.

The smell of whisky wafted upward. Ewan curled his nose, stepping out of her hold, as she slumped forward.

Fergus sidestepped her and picked up an empty flask. He tipped it upside down. Only a drop rolled out.

"What are you doing here?" he demanded.

She looked up at Ewan and frowned. "Colin told me"—she hiccoughed, proceeding to fall into a snort of giggles. Then she began to cry and staggered to her feet. "He told me you would be angered to see me. He bid I could stay here until *'things were settled.'*"

Alarm flared in Ewan's mind. When things were settled? What was Colin playing at?

"What did he mean by that?" Ewan demanded.

"He, em..." She seemed to lose her drunken thread of thought and hiccoughed again. "Oh aye. He told me that if all went well, I would be Lady of Dunwiddie after all...that I could marry him if I was patient and waited for him this time. Aye, that's it."

Ewan exchanged a look with Fergus.

"Marry him? How? After you already demanded marriage to me?"

"He said no one would stand in our way." She slurred. "Because, when I couldn't rid us of Nasim, and you sent me away, I knew I needed to be rid of you. I want to be the lady here. If you're going to deny me what I'm owed for waiting three, long, *God-forsaken* years, then..."

She didn't seem to have the presence of mind to keep talking, swaying further from her drunkenness and bracing herself on the roof joist.

Ewan turned to Fergus at her ominous words. "I suspect Colin is the one to have left the note upon my door." Fergus nodded in agreement. "He would have been comfortable scrawling a quick note in my offices, considering he had made his home there for three years. Take Margaret to the kitchens and splash some water on her face. Then put some food into her and confine her to a chamber. I intend to speak with her when she's sober. I need to get to Lady Nasim, for Colin is unaccounted for, and I worry for her."

"*Lady Nasim, Lady Nasim,*" Margaret mocked. "The blasted Lady Nasim!" She flew into an unexpected rage and bolted to her feet, swaying. "I despise the very name! She has ruined everything for me. *Everything!* I wish the whore were dead."

"And I believe you," Ewan bit out. "Fergus, I change my mind. Lock her in the dungeons until I have a mind to see her again."

"You heard him, woman. Away with you now." He picked her up like a feather and tossed her belly down over one shoulder, climbing down the ladder after Ewan who was already jogging toward the castle keep.

Ewan leapt up the stairs, hearing pounding upon a door and running of feet.

"I said, go find the laird!" came a guardsman's call from Nasim's door.

"What's going on… Dear heavens… Screaming…" came anxious murmurs.

Ewan bolted down the corridor. "What's happening?"

"Screaming, mi laird!" the guard replied, Hamish's replacement. "The door is barred! And all has gone silent"—

"Nasim! Come to the door!" Ewan called, beating on it.

Putting his ear to the wood, he heard nothing.

"Nasim!" Still, no one answered.

Alarm exploded in his heart, coupled with guilt. He had left Nasim vulnerable and it gouged him like a lance.

"Myrtle went in with a tray of food," the guard explained. "Next I knew, she cried out, words I couldn't quite make out, and we heard a man. Then I heard your lady, sir! She cried out, as if in pain—"

"Stand watch at this door!" Ewan demanded. "If anyone exits other than the Lady Nasim, apprehend them immediately!"

He bolted back down the corridor until he arrived at his chamber, prying it open and slamming it. If something was happening to Nasim, and the guard had been vigilant the entire time, then it meant someone had used the escape passages to enter her chamber unseen. And the only person to disappear into the passages recently was Colin.

CHAPTER 26

"Colin," Nasim said, her voice shaking as Ewan's steward slowly walked toward her from the door in her wall that had been hidden behind a tapestry. She pulled her blankets around her more tightly. "I don't understand."

Her eyes flickered toward the gleaming dirk he pulled from the sheath behind his back. Her heart began to race.

"Ewan suspects me, and therefore, I need to move along with the plan more quickly than I had intended."

"What plan?"

"My plan to be the laird. I am owed this. I have royal blood in my veins. I have been a servant all my life, instead of having the title I deserve. I have poured myself into Dunwiddie these past three years whilst Ewan was off in the Holy Land. Dunwiddie was going to be mine as my reward. The king was already entertaining my proposal, even if no decision had yet been made as to how to allot Ewan's estate. Rumors from court was that King William was going to approve my petition."

Nasim whispered a prayer in her native tongue, her eyes never straying from the knife.

"Quit babbling," Colin said, now directly in front of her. "And Margaret... Christ, but the lass was going to be mine, too. She was willing to marry me in Ewan's place. Except Ewan didn't die like he was supposed to."

"Tell me what I can do to help you," Nasim said, though she knew she grasped at improbable hopes.

Colin had a light of determination in his eyes, and she

could already tell he didn't want to hear any reason from her. Colin's last words were especially disconcerting. Ewan was supposed to die? That meant, Colin knew about what Ewan's commander had done to him, or perhaps… *Sakes, but what if Colin is part of a scheme with Ewan's commander?* Her stomach still felt cramped and she was fatigued from days upon days with little activity, but now she felt positively ill.

"Do nay try to distract me," he retorted. "Margaret was going to marry me. And then you saved Ewan's life and he brought you back. He was supposed to be dead, not bring back a woman to bear his line and legitimize him further. Do you know how that feels? To love someone, but never be able to have them?" At one point, Nasim had, she realized. Thinking of *Layla* and *Majnun*. Thinking of Solomon. "And now, the laird has sent Margaret away, so not only could I nay marry her, but I couldn't even see her anymore. She only had eyes for him once he returned."

So Colin was a jilted lover, too, Nasim realized. She saw his dirk catch the firelight as he turned it. A memory caused a shiver to roll up her spine. He was holding his blade in the left hand. An odd hand to choose if he was like most and more agile with his right. But the man at the midwife's hut had held his blade in his right hand. The jewels in Colin's handle were decorous, but the blade that her assailant had used, now that she really thought about it, had been plain.

Did Ewan have another enemy in his midst? Someone with a separate design, or someone who was part of this scheme? Panic threatened to overwhelm her but she managed to swallow it, and ignored the sweat collecting at her temples. Her eyes darted back to the dagger, when her chamber door pushed open.

"Milady, how are you feeling?" Myrtle said, nudging the door closed and carrying a steaming tray from the kitchens. "I came to check on you…" She regarded Colin, dirk in hand, and her words trailed off. "What is this about, sir?" the old woman frowned. "Is Lady Nasim in danger?"

"In a matter of speaking," Colin drawled.

Myrtle examined him, then her face dropped. She set down

the tray and hastened for the exit, but Colin bolted across the chamber and pulled her back, jamming the bar across the door. The old woman screamed out, but Colin clamped his hand over her mouth, dragging her back.

The guard in the corridor started pounding, shouting for entry. Gruff demands were made that Laird Buchan be summoned.

"Woman, you come in at an inopportune time," Colin complained. "Not another sound from you."

Nasim jumped up on wobbly legs. "Sir, you must calm down and let Myrtle go! I don't understand your anger."

He dragged Myrtle with him to one of Nasim's chests and pulled out a long chemise, thrust the old servant into a chair, and tore the chemise into strips. Myrtle, stunned, rose to face him. He pushed her back down.

"You're causing me delays," Colin fumed, and began binding her to the chair with the torn garment. She wriggled for freedom, but Colin wrestled her under control. "And now, with the castle being alerted, thanks to your bellyaching, I only have a matter of moments before Ewan arrives on his valiant quest to save his infidel bride."

"What has gotten into you, man?" Myrtle cried.

Nasim ran to them and grabbed Colin's arm, the pounding and shouting outside the door loud. "Sir, please! You frighten us both. You must stop before you hurt her!"

Colin whirled around, whipping his dirk to her nose. Nasim froze. Myrtle froze.

"Step away, woman," he said, so softly, a shiver of fear racked her body.

Nasim stepped back.

"Please don't hurt Myrtle," she whispered.

Colin ignored her and returned to his task, binding Myrtle's body and wrists to the chair and tying a gag in her mouth. Then with no warning, he hit her against the back of her head with the handle of his dirk. The old maid's face slumped forward.

Nasim screamed and ran for the door. Colin bolted after her, snagging her upper arm. The pounding on the door grew furious

"But you see," Colin continued as he dragged her writhing body backward, ignoring the guardsman now ramming the door with his shoulder, "Margaret realized once she married Ewan that she had made a mistake chasing him, because he was never, *ever* going to care for her. He was never even going to honor her status by adorning her with the proper riches the wife of an earl was entitled to. She had trapped him, and in return, he had trapped her in the very house she had tried to escape, exiling her from him forever. And I am a forgiving man, even if she did treat me as second best in spite of my royal blood. I promised her, that we could be rid of you both. As long as she submits to me abed, I'll give her whatever finery I can." He pulled her, in only her chemise with her hair down, toward the hidden door behind the tapestry. "So I sent a messenger to bring her back. Then together we could take care of the *problems* in our midst."

Colin laughed, though there was nothing jovial about the cold tone in which he spoke. Tears of disbelief rolled down her cheeks, and as he forced her into the hidden doorway, into a dank, narrow passage, she screamed one more time, but he pulled shut the door and clamped his hand over her mouth. He took a torch off the wall and began to jog along the corridor, dragging Nasim behind him. The tunnel was claustrophobic, and as they twisted and turned, they periodically passed a door no doubt leading to a different chamber. Stairs brought them downward until they were below the surface of the castle's main floor. She could sense the change in smell and dankness, like they entered a tomb. A shiver passing over her skin.

They came to a door, secured with a heavy lock. Colin let go and pulled forth a ring of keys from his waist pocket. Nasim bolted, her legs carrying her back up the way she had come.

"Christ." She heard Colin's voice bounce off the stone, and footfalls gaining on her.

She pulled the sapphire ring Ewan had bought her in St. Nazaire off her finger, knowing Colin was going to catch up to her despite her best efforts.

He grabbed her arm. She stumbled, falling, and braced her hand outward to catch her fall. He wrenched her back up, and she left her ring upon the floor. If Ewan figured out what was happening and which way she had been taken, this would be a clue to lead him on the right path.

"Nay cause me anymore headaches, woman," Colin said.

Arriving at the door again, Colin braced her to the wall with his body and inserted a key into the lock. It clanked open. Pulling the door closed behind them, he led Nasim down a damp tunnel, singeing spider webs with the torch flame.

A rat scurried past Nasim's feet and she gasped, jumping to one side.

"Now, now. We'll have none of that. Keep moving," Colin said.

She swallowed and allowed him to drag her forward, unable to match his pace. More panic lodged in her chest. What if she was never to come out of this dank tunnel again? Was Ewan looking for her right now? Of course he was. The guard outside her door had made certain to alert him. Surely Ewan, being the learned man that he was, would figure out what was going on.

God above. She felt a wave of anger at Colin and Margaret's betrayal. Ewan was such a good man, and didn't deserve what had befallen him.

They arrived at the end of the tunnel. Waves could be heard crashing on the opposite side of the door. Colin pulled forth his key once again and cranked the iron lock. A door opened. With a shove, he pushed her though it, into the rock shelter overlooking the water where she had sat after running away.

She looked back at the door, having not noticed it before in the darkness of night.

"A secret passage to escape a siege," Colin explained.

Then he pulled her onto the cliff side. The bite of cold air burst upon her skin and the jagged rocks cut into her feet, but she hardly cared. She pulled free her sapphire necklace. She had always worn it since Ewan had bought it. And as the wind whistled, masking all sound and whipping her hair into a wild, dark frenzy of curls, she dropped it among the stones. Another clue for Ewan to follow. She hoped.

CHAPTER 27

Ewan burst through the escape passageway into Nasim's chamber. Her bed lay mused. A muffled sound came from one side of the room. He spied Myrtle.

"Christ, woman, what happened to you?" he exclaimed, dashing to her and untying the gag from around her head. His fingers met with blood.

"Myrtle," he started again, ripping at the bindings around her chest. "Who attacked you?"

"Colin, sir," she croaked, moistening her mouth from the time it had been gagged. "He has gone mad, sir! Mad!"

One arm was now free and she immediately reached up to hold the back of her head.

"*Ooch*, my head…"

"Why?" Ewan asked.

He threw the bindings to the floor and squared the woman's shoulders in front of him.

"I have no idea, mi laird. I came in to bring the lady some food and next thing I know, Colin was grabbing me and throwing me into the chair. Your lady tried to stop him, but he held his dirk to her and warned her not to try it."

"Where is she?" Ewan asked. "Sakes, but I have to know."

His hands shook. He couldn't keep his worry at bay.

Myrtle shook her head. "I…I do nay know. Next thing that happened is I woke up to banging on the door, and now you're here."

"He must have rendered you unconscious. Damn him!" he

cursed and raced to the door, throwing the bar aside, wrenching it open.

Fergus and Hamish, along with several guardsmen were waiting on the other side.

"Is she there?" Fergus asked.

"No," Ewan replied. "Gather the hounds and search the grounds again. Search everywhere. Should you find Colin, apprehend him how you must and discard him in the dungeons. If Nasim is not in the castle compound, then search down to the village and the sea. I want a contingent scouring *every* route of escape around the castle. And send up the midwife to tend to Myrtle. Colin has injured her."

He returned to the passageway. Upon his hasty arrival, he hadn't noticed, but the torch upon the wall was gone. Instead, he retreated to the bed stand and brought back the candle stick.

The walls were blackened from torch smoke. There were two ways to go. The likely route was the escape to the sea. The other route wound about the castle like a serpent, eventually making an exit near the buttery. No, if two horses from the stables were missing, Colin was the likely thief, and he would be heading beyond the castle walls.

He turned to the left and began walking, his eyes roving for any and all clues, until they came to the next chamber. An unlit torch sat in an iron bracket beside it. He held the candle to it until the flame took hold, tossed aside the wax, and continued onward. As he neared the stairs down to tunnel that led out to the sea, he stepped on something hard.

He bent, held the torch low, and saw Nasim's sapphire ring. He snatched it up, clutched it to his chest, then put it in a pocket. She had to have come this way.

With hope renewed, he descended the stairs, reached the tunnel door that led out to the sea, and noted the lock undone. He pulled it open and jogged down the tunnel. With renewed hope came a renewed sense of fear. Pray he could get to them before his steward—nay, *former* steward—did something irreversible.

He spilled out into the rock shelter, seeing no sign of Colin. He looked up and down the shore, though it was dark out.

Damn, what he would do to have his hounds with him, for then he could make swift work of finding her trail, but the dogs had gone with Fergus and Hamish. He looked out over the rocks, trying to determine the best route.

The best route, since there were no boats bobbing on the water, and considering Colin had taken the horses, was to wrap around the cliff toward the slope to the village. Horses couldn't walk on terrain like this, nor could a pair fit safely on a small seafaring vessel, for only small ships could make port here. And as he walked, taking the route his gut told him to take, his foot raked across something. It jingled, like a chain. He stepped aside and lowered the torch. Nasim's pendant. She always wore the pendant, so fond of the gift as she was, as if Ewan had captured her the moon when he bought it for her.

She's leading me on a path.

The realization came out of nowhere. The clasp on the necklace was still fastened, which meant it was removed over her head. The only way it would have come off and remained fastened, was if Nasim had taken it off. Because if Colin had done so, he most certainly wouldn't have discarded it where it might be found.

The relentless wind sweeping up from the water was biting. He climbed over the rough ground until finally he reached the grassy hills. In the distance, he saw Fergus' torches bobbing with the hounds, their noses to the ground in an apparently fruitless search. More snow flurries stung Ewan's face.

Perfect, he scowled. More snow was not what they needed.

"Fergus!" Ewan shouted.

Fergus, on horseback, cantered to meet him as a dusting of white collected between the blades of grass.

"Fergus, lend me the hounds and a horse. I have her trail, but Colin has the advantage of speed, for he and Nasim are likely on horseback."

Fergus ordered one of his men to dismount and they handed over the reins. Ewan took the dogs' leads. He held the necklace to the dogs' noses. It only took a moment for them to find a trail in the grass, leading away from the cliffs. Ewan cut them loose from their tethers and mounted up, tapping the horse into a gallop to chase them.

They shot across a field, noses to the ground, and arrived at a tree. Ewan caught up, watching them sniff and whine with confusion as they circled the trunk, returning to the same stop. They had lost the trail.

Ewan dismounted, swinging the torch around the ground for anything else Nasim might have dropped. Unexpected rustling jostled the branch above him, and both he and the dogs looked up. The faint outline of a person in the barren branches was barely distinguishable.

"Show yourself," Ewan demanded.

No one responded.

"I can see you," Ewan fumed. "You hide on my property, you coward. Show yourself, or I shall come up and drag your arse down."

After another pause, more rustling ensued and the slender legs of a youth slipped into view. Then an old homespun kilt, then a torso, and soon a lad was hanging from the bottom branch and dropping to the ground. He backed up against the tree trunk. Ewan moved the torch close to his face. It was the same, unfamiliar stable boy, his hair dirty and his smudged eyes widening fearfully.

"You…what are you doing here?" Ewan said.

"I…I," the boy stuttered. "I was told to come here."

"Who told you?"

"Colin."

"You aren't from my village, are you? Where did you come from?" Ewan persisted.

The boy, quaking, finally answered. "I come from Stirling, sir."

"Colin sent for you?" Ewan growled.

"I…I didn't know he was going to do anything bad. Colin told me I should accompany him to Dunwiddie. He offered to pay me good."

"When was this?"

"Over a month ago, sir. You were away on a journey."

Ewan's jaw pumped. "What was he doing in Stirling? Nay visiting his brother, Stirling Castle's steward, I take it."

The boy shook his head. "Nay. Master Robert was in Glasgow looking to purchase horses. I know, because he gave me instructions before he left. I've been a stable lad there for two years."

"Colin said his brother was sick," Ewan said. "Was Robert ever sick?"

"No sir, not at all that I could tell."

"Then why did he ask you to return here with him? What was he doing in Stirling?"

The lad shrugged. "He visited the midwife, and he asked me to accompany him back to Dunwiddie as your new groom. I'm nay of high birth, so me *maw* thought it would be good for me. Me *da* died when I was five years, so it helped her to send me off."

"Why the midwife?" Ewan was perplexed. What on earth could he need from a midwife? Yet, as he racked his brain, a thought dawned on him. The powder in Nasim's water. Dunwiddie's midwife had said she on rare occasion gave out such powder to a woman. Had Colin gotten the poison to get rid of Nasim's bairn? Still. His trip to Stirling far preceded any announcement of pregnancy. Had he gotten it to have it on hand in case the announcement finally came? For aye, he couldn't have asked Dunwiddie's midwife without becoming an instant suspect.

"I do nay know, sir. It was his business."

"Why are you here right now, lad? In the snow, hiding in a tree?" Ewan asked.

"Colin asked me to bring two horses down to this tree and tie them here. I did so and hastened back. That's when you came to search the stables."

"You left two of my horses tied to this tree unattended in the cold evening?" Ewan scoffed. "What would possess you to do such?"

"Colin ordered it, but I was worried that two fine animals such as those might get stolen or injure themselves in their tethers, so I came back."

And Colin wouldn't have been able to ask one of Dunwiddie's regular grooms to do such without becoming suspect either. He needed someone who would only take orders from him, with no connection to Dunwiddie, to carry out such an order. Colin had been premeditating his treason for a long, long time.

"Where are my steeds now?" Ewan continued, drilling the boy with his stare.

"Colin and your infidel lady took 'em..." The boy shook his head. "She wasn't willing, but when she tried to run away, Colin captured her. I've been afraid to return to the castle."

Rage, pure and red, lapped like flames through Ewan's blood. He worked with the hounds to catch the new scent of the horses Colin and Nasim rode upon. Once their understanding had dawned, he released them once again, mounting back up to chase after them.

"Return to the stables, lad, and do nay go elsewhere. Do you understand?" The boy nodded. "Go on."

He scampered off through the accumulating snow.

"Mi laird!" Fergus called, galloping his horse with a torch held high. "My man has remounted. We're at your service."

Ewan felt his daggers at his waist and his sword upon his back. There was little else he could do to prepare at the moment.

"We ride," Ewan said, and turned the reins of his mount.

CHAPTER 28

The wind blowing up from the night-blackened firth brought with it an icy lash across Nasim's cheeks. She shivered uncontrollably, her chemise no protection against the March air. She clutched the pommel of her saddle. Her whole body was sore, fatigued, and blue with cold.

Colin stopped. He dismounted. Consciousness waning, she grew alert once more at the change in pace.

Dear God. A cliff. They stood upon a high cliff. The crashing sound told her the sea was just below. Why had they stopped? *Please, Ewan, be looking for me.* She looked around, taking in the barren nighttime. The sky was cloudy, only a handful of stars peeking through. She looked behind her at the path they had traveled and saw no one.

"Get down," Colin ordered.

She hesitated, never having dismounted by herself. The drop was far with no block for mounting without Ewan's assistance, and these horses in Europe were a bigger breed than the sleeker stallions of her homeland. What did Colin have in mind? There was nothing around them. Except for the cliff and the rocky, watery grave below. What if she bolted again, but this time on horseback? Of course he would catch her in a matter of seconds, as he had each other time she had tried to flee. But the thought flitted across her mind.

As if reading her thoughts, Colin waggled a finger at her.

"Do not even think about running off again. You can hardly ride and I will overtake you in moments."

She remained in the saddle, afraid to give up the horse, her last shred of control, and equally afraid of the drop. Even if he did catch her, she couldn't assent to being taken willingly, no matter what the outcome would be. She might have never fought with others, but she couldn't submit to him without the honor of having fought until the bitter end.

"I told you to get down!" he barked.

She did it. She turned her horse and did her best to kick its sides. The animal began to run uncontrollably back across the cliff, down the path they had risen. She clung to the pommel, unable to balance herself. Yet no sooner had she bolted, Colin was beside her on horseback, wrenching her reins free. Her horse tossed its head in protest, prancing aside from Colin's mount.

He led the skittish beast back up the cliff, to the edge, and dismounted, wrenching her from the saddle.

"Why are you doing this?" Nasim cried, landing hard on the ground and feeling her knees buckle.

"You...you ruined everything," he muttered. "Ewan was supposed to die at the hands of warring, thieving, unscrupulous infidels. He wasn't supposed to be saved by a benevolent one. And I was supposed to get Dunwiddie! Imagine! Finally having opportunity bestowed upon you, and then a prodigal laird returns and pulls it all out from beneath you!"

She felt more anger well inside her and rose back to standing. "But he does live, whether you like it or nay, he lives! Whatever your scheme with the commander who tried to kill him, it didn't work! It failed. And your king knows it!" Where on earth her bold shouts were coming from, she knew not. But she was tired of being seen as an inferior infidel, when she was the same as any woman from this cold, frozen land. "His death was secretly murder before, but now that you, your king, and all of Dunwiddie's people know he lives, his death now would *clearly* be murder to all.

"You speak of me, as if my people are lesser because of who we are and where we come from. You complain that you have royal blood, but were never recognized. But I... I was not a peasant from the streets who *serviced* Ewan well. I was the daughter of the emir, Abu Abdullah Habib Abd-al Rachid, Commander of the sultan's army and advisor to Saladin himself, a man who your armies couldn't thwart." She lifted her head taller with pride welling inside of her. "I am a physician, and I trained under Jerusalem's finest healer." She might no longer be Commander Rachid's daughter, but she grew up as such. She was smart, and accomplished. She had performed a life-saving surgery and succeeded. And what had Colin done, besides tally Dunwiddie's accounts for the past three years and expect a royal handout for doing his job? "I have more royalty in my blood than you and Ewan combined. But even my status couldn't save me from Ewan's kiss on the hand, and the scandal that ensued from my dashing off to see him. Being born into a bloodline doesn't mean as much you wish it did, Colin. You are not owed certain riches just because of who sired you. But you sign your death warrant now. Ewan will come for me and you will regret what you have done."

Colin stepped toe to toe with her. She shivered mercilessly, and knew she was turning purple, but she didn't back away, even when the toes of his boots trod upon her bare ones.

"Aye, he might come. But you'll be dead by then. And he walks right into a trap. You see, you can tell me all you like, that you're some sophisticated descendant, but we know the truth of it here. You're people threaten the Holy Land. They infiltrate it with their impurity and lust for power. The priests have told us all the truth of it, which means royalty or nay, you're all cut from the same disgusting, sinful cloth."

"Your lack of understanding matters nay. Kill me, and you will still meet your end. Then what good will your bid for Dunwiddie be? What is the point, when you cannot possibly have it now no matter what you do?"

For some reason, she knew she had to keep him defensive, keep the focus of their exchange on his bid for Dunwiddie, not on his misguided thoughts. Both sides had shed blood in the Crusade. Neither side was pure or righteous. The politics of their world mattered not in this moment in time. They were just Colin's excuses for the things he thought, and his lack of sympathy for her now. He harbored no sanctity for others' lives if they stood in the way of what he hoped to gain for himself.

He pulled his blade from his waistband and grabbed her arm with one hand, holding the blade to her throat with the other as he backed her toward the cliff.

"I promised my lady Margaret that I would get rid of you— a wedding gift for her, even if you do have the wide eyes and lush lips of a wanton. Commander Murray from the field has vowed to get rid of Ewan. A favor for me, and a favor to himself as well, for with Ewan so skilled at his profession, Murray stands to gain quite a bit of commission work without any competition."

She began to quake, feeling her chest rise and fall with every breath. *Keep him talking. Pray that doing so gives you a bit more time.* More time for what, exactly, she wasn't sure. Her mind raced wildly, searching for anything that might delay the inevitable. She thought to the only thing she knew well, better than anything. The body. But how could her knowledge of the body help her while her heels were slowly inching toward a cliff?

You know how to heal people, and Colin has an ailment of the mind that you cannot heal. However, because you know how to heal, you know where people are most vulnerable, too...

An idea struck her.

She knew the human body like the back of her hand. She knew where it was weakest, and where it was sturdiest. And she knew where to aim best to cause him injury.

Her eyes roved the land, seeing no sign of any help. And it was obvious now that Colin intended to murder her and dump her off the cliff into the crashing waves below. With no sign of Ewan coming, she knew her last moments on earth were probably upon her. There was not much to lose by fighting back. She summoned courage, in spite of how sick dying made her heart. She had lived only a little while. She'd had been favored, and then exiled. She had traveled to far off lands and found the love of a man so different from herself. And for only a brief time, she had carried another life within her. All of it was stripped from her now. This entire struggle to overcome was for naught.

Kicking Colin's knees backward would cause him immense

pain, and he likely wouldn't expect it, but barefoot as she was, with her toes frozen through, she risked injuring herself more and then would be unable to run on such an injured foot. His hand gripping her right arm prevented her from making use of her dominant hand. If she had her own blade, she could lodge it between his ribs and pierce his lung, like Ewan's ribs had done to him. But she had no blade. And even in this moment of her fate, she couldn't fathom the idea of killing anyone.

His face.

His face was the most vulnerable place, and she had use of her left hand still. Even if he plunged the knife into her neck right now, she could at least inflict a moment's damage upon him and though the odds were slim, she might be able to get away—

"You'd best step away, Colin Donald, or else you will rue this day. Whilst you live, that is."

Colin whipped around at Ewan's menacing words, dragging Nasim with him. Relief washed over her in such strong surges, she nearly cried, exhaling. He spun her back to his front, standing behind her, and gripped her torso. The knife was still pressed to her neck, but she saw Ewan, flanked by Fergus, and several other guardsmen from Dunwiddie. She exhaled. Even if she died right now, she could see he had come for her. He had figured out what had happened and hadn't abandoned her.

And now that Colin was gripping her chest and putting the blade to her neck, both her hands were free…

She clawed him.

Colin growled in surprise and pain.

She reached up, ripped upon his hand holding the blade, and clawed his face, her fingers gouging his eye, his nose, his cheek. Her heel kicked back into his legs. His grip upon her faltered, and she collapsed down to the ground. Nasim willed her freezing limbs to work so she might scramble away.

He lunged toward her.

"No!" she cried out, twisted in her chemise.

A dagger whirled through the air, sailing over her head, and lodged in Colin's chest. Nasim screamed and shoved herself backward across the ground, watching Colin sink to his knees, the wind ruffling his hair and tangling her tresses further in her eyes. Ewan sprang forth, dove for Colin, and grabbed his tunic. Blood soaked through his coat, and his eyes, stunned, opened wide.

"You weren't supposed to kill me," Colin gurgled as Ewan held him firm, his nose practically touching his former steward.

Ewan withdrew his dagger. "What was supposed to happen, man? You kill me? I faced death many a time in the Crusade, Colin, and fear it nay now from you. Tell me, shall I shove you over this cliff as you wished to do to my lady wife?" Ewan pushed him backward an inch. Colin sputtered, but could form no words. "Well? Should I?" He pushed him back again, closer to the edge.

Nasim found her wits. Ewan had done what he must to protect her, but he was no cold-blooded murderer. And he would hate himself for doing such once the urgency of this situation was over. She rested her hand upon his shoulder. He turned.

"Nay, Ewan. The deed is done and he's no longer a threat against me or you." Ewan's angry blue eyes softened an increment. They gazed at one another. Nasim, wrapping her arms around herself as if they might block the chill that her chemise could not, shook her head, and implored him. "Show mercy."

The anguish in his stormy eyes was vivid, and yet, he finally stepped back and released Colin's coat. Colin crumpled to the earth, groaning. Ewan swept Nasim into his arms, burying his face to her neck and hair. He simply held her, his grip unrelenting. His arms felt so warm, so protecting. She gripped him back.

"I thought I was going to lose you," he finally murmured against her. "I was seeing only anger. I love you, and I'm sorry for all that has happened. When we departed Jerusalem, I vowed to care for you and protect you, and I fear I've failed—"

She lay an icy finger across his lips. "Hush, Ewan."

"Nay. I failed you and I failed our babe. Naz…" His voice shook. And she realized the loss of their child, a child she still grieved herself, was causing him to cry now with unending guilt.

"I can never forgive myself for what happened to our bairn…"

She looked up into his eyes, her own welling with tears for the family she thought they were going to start, the family that had been torn away from them both.

"I would argue that you have done nothing but care for me. Even when I was too childish to realize what you had sacrificed for me. You came for me now, and have done all you can to protect me. Life will always have hardships and the world is hardly safe. You cannot vow to keep harm away, only vow to do what you must for me when harm strikes, just as I must for you. Ewan, I will never doubt your love for me and will never mention your marriage to Margaret ever again. Marriage is simply an arrangement that means nothing without love. This is my home now, and these are my people, whether the laws of your land recognize it or not. I accept this, and will hold my head high."

He rested his forehead to hers, enveloping her. She knew he would always hate that he had failed to legitimize their marriage, but there was nothing to do about it except move onward and leave that tragedy in their past.

"Do nay be so certain that my marriage to Margaret will last. Already, based on what has come to pass, I'm able to file for an annulment."

Nasim's tears intensified and she swiped them away. If Ewan could secure an annulment, then… "Then you and I will be able to marry, legally that is?"

He looked at her, seemingly touched by the hope in her voice. His gentle smile softened his prominent jawline and warmed his eyes. "If you agree to convert, we can marry in the church. Otherwise, we can hand-fast, a common kind of union that Scots have used for centuries. Either way," he murmured, trailing his thumb down her cheek to her lips as tenderness consumed his face, "we'll be legitimized in the eyes of the law. You do nay have to convert, Nasim. I'll nay require such a thing. I'm content with a hand-fast, if you are."

"But do you wish for a chapel wedding?"

He seemed to consider her question, thoughts competing in his mind. "I want you," he finally said. "In whatever way I can have you. That's all I need. The decision is yours, wife, and I'll nay disparage any choice you make."

In spite of her miserable cold, she smiled, and now that the moment of fear was past, he seemed to come to his senses. He hastened to his packs and withdrew his cloak, bringing it back to her and swinging it around her neck to bundle her within. He rubbed her upper arms.

"Then I know exactly what I will do… *husband*."

"You have shown such strength, my lady, nay just today, but since we departed Jerusalem. You lost everything, yet you put your trust in me. It took bravery I rarely see, even in men, to embrace a future of uncertainty. And right now, you're bloody freezing. Let's get you before a fire."

Turning his back on Colin doubled over at his feet, he steered her away from the cliff.

"Fergus, collect Colin. We'll take him back to Dunwiddie whilst he lives, and send his body to his brother for burial when he dies—"

"My lord!" Fergus exclaimed, rushing forward.

Ewan twirled back over his shoulder. Colin was on his feet, his strength waning, and his dagger lifting high to stab him in the back. Nasim felt Ewan thrust her toward Fergus. She stumbled, unable to feel the frozen ground with her blue toes. The hulking guardsman caught her, dragging her behind him, sending her into the arms of another guard.

"Protect the lady!" Fergus ordered.

A scream pierced the air. Nasim shied away from the image of Ewan's dagger once again sinking into Colin. She buried her face in her hands, then buried herself in the guard's chest to blot out the distress. The scream fizzled into a ragged wisp of air, carried away on the wind. She looked up to see Ewan's tall frame stepping away, saw him jerk his arm once more, as he released his hold on Colin who collapsed lifelessly to the ground. Ewan wiped his brow and tried to master his heavy breathing.

It was over. Colin was dead.

Her husband took a step back, then another, pivoting as he walked, and returned to her. He cast aside his soiled dagger for one of his men to collect, and dragged Nasim back to him, scooping her into a cradle. She could feel his chest rising and falling as he came down from the exertion. He lifted her behind his saddle, taking the blanket rolled upon the horse's pack to also drape around her. After she was as concealed as he could make her, he hoisted himself up into the saddle too, urging her to hold him about his waist.

"I need to get you home."

"Ewan." She shivered, hiding her feet within the layers of cloak and blanket. He tightened his hold upon her, pulling the hood up over her head. "Colin said you walked into a trap, that the threat against you isn't yet over."

Ewan's lips drew tight and his jaw muscles jumped. "I know. But you see that man over there?"

He pointed to a man in a saddle, dressed in dark clothing and a black cloak. Something about him was familiar, though she didn't know from where. She didn't recognize him. He had dusty brown hair, unremarkable features, appeared fit. "He was just captured nay far from here. And would you know, that the markings on the bottom of his boot appeared to match the footprints we found in the mud that day at the midwife's cottage. I believe the trap laid for me is no more."

Her eyes widened. "Is he the man who…"

Ewan nodded. "Aye, the cottage, the adder, and the poison—a substance Colin purchased when he had supposedly returned to Stirling to visit his sick brother."

Nasim furrowed her brow, slowly feeling sensation return to her fingertips.

"I had no idea he departed to visit his brother," Ewan explained at her confusion. "No one told me of his outing when I returned home from the priests."

"He had told me not to bother you with the news, because you were friends with his brother and might be distressed by it."

"'Tis of humor, lass, that I ran into his brother in a tavern in Glasgow whilst I traveled. He was in good health and on the king's business. Colin lied to you. Learning such news of Robert Donald's 'illness' made me suspect Colin of foul play, for I knew it to be a lie."

She glanced over at the captured man responsible for terrorizing her. "And this man?"

Ewan followed her gaze. "Some persuasion got him talking. It seems Colin employed my former commander's messenger—or should I say, henchman, right here in my midst. The man has been working here in secret ever since he was sent from the Holy Land to inform the castle of my untimely 'death in battle,' and has done Colin's bidding to ensure that my commander's design for me was fulfilled. Since you saved my life and I didn't die like they thought I had, I have lived to inform the king of the attack against me, something that frightens them, for already, King William is summoning Commander Murray back from the field to question him."

"Indeed he lied to everyone if he said you died in battle," Nasim said. "You were beaten from your horse."

"Aye, but you see, that man over there knew of his commander's attempt to see me killed. I was set up, and nay just by Commander Murray. He tried to kill me after Colin organized a scheme with him."

"Colin wanted to be the laird of Dunwiddie," Nasim said sadly, finally sparing a look at his body now being collected by guardsman. "He felt he deserved a lairdship, considering his lineage. He wanted to marry Lady Margaret, and when you returned and she chose you instead, he felt cheated."

"And my commander wanted me out of the way so he would no longer have to compete with me in business. They all wanted something different, and were willing to work with each other to achieve it: Margaret wanted Dunwiddie's title and in her disillusion, wanted me first as husband; if not me, then anyone else would do. Colin wanted Dunwiddie and Margaret, and Commander Murray wanted my cartography commissions. You just happened to return home with me and further muddle their ill-conceived plans. And because they have false notions about your people, they had few qualms about causing you injury."

Ewan tapped his horse and began taking her home.

"That man worked for my commander, nay the king, and so he harbored no loyalty to anyone but Murray. He's a henchmen, plain and simple. Colin, it seems, knew Commander

Murray from when he used to serve the royal residence in Stirling, and knew Murray hated me, for he has been my stiffest cartography competition. He wished to get me out of the way, as did Colin, so Colin wrote to him and they schemed their plot. 'Tis how I ended up in your *faither's* sick ward."

But the man was now captured. And it was over. And Nasim was so, so cold. She was in Ewan's arms, feeling weariness overcome her.

"Rest against me, Naz, and let's go home."

"Home." She looked up at him and smiled. "My home, and my family…and my people."

Ewan grinned, a welcome image considering the frightening occurrences that had come to pass. "And our people love you."

CHAPTER 29

Spring, 1198

Ewan rolled up his latest map, an intricate detail of Europe extending to Anatolia on a fine piece of vellum, and inserted it into a sheath. His payment was received across his desk and he handed over the map to the English nobleman who had ventured all the way from Berwick for the commission.

"I'm pleased this meets your satisfaction, sir," Ewan said, pushing away from his solar desk and clasping wrists with the man, when knocking thumped upon the door.

Ewan furrowed his brow. Everyone knew not to disturb him when he was in a meeting with a patron. Which meant, it must be something important.

"Enter!"

The door pushed open. "Mi laird," Myrtle said, giving an apologetic curtsy.

"Is everything all right?" he asked.

"Eh, nay, sir. You're receiving visitors of a very unusual nature. They've yet to reach the village, but Hamish tells me your runners report that they're heading toward the barbican, and Hamish hastened to the keep to tell me to tell you—"

"What sort of visitors?" He cut off her worried rambling.

"It's hard to say, sir. There's only nine of them, or so I'm told."

"I'll leave you to your other obligation," said his customer, smiling as he walked to the door.

Ewan nodded his head once. "I apologize for the intrusion

on our meeting. Please, join us this eve for refreshments before you begin your return journey on the morrow."

"My thanks, Laird Buchan," the man from Berwick said, and he departed.

"Who are these visitors?" Ewan asked again, returning his attention to Myrtle.

Myrtle wrung her hands together. "They appear, sir, to be from your lady wife's land, or so Hamish said."

"What?" Ewan paused, thinking. How on God's green earth would anyone from Jerusalem find him here?

"He said, 'They're dressed in the same *claes* as Lady Nasim when she arrived so long ago, and the men have darker skin and dark eyes and strange, curving swords,' whatever that means."

Ewan's mind raced. Indeed, the scimitar was the sword her people had carried, a beautiful instrument, he recalled, even though it had been years. And the only people from Jerusalem who knew generally where he lived were Nasim's family, for he had made a map for Habib, unless, of course, the man passed along his map to someone else and enemies now rode toward his inner gates. Which seemed highly unlikely.

There are only nine people. So certainly not an enemy threat, but mayhap an expedition of sorts? Enemies would never have made it this far, and Habib did say at one point that he had wanted to open up trade… *Could it be him?*

"My thanks. Come, Myrtle, I must find my wife and you must direct the kitchens to increase the nooning meal. Whoever they are, if they pose no threat, then we ought to treat them as we would any guest."

He scooted around her in the doorway. He heard her feet pattering behind him as he jogged down the corridor, down the spiraling stairs, and into the great hall.

"Lady Nasim was in the village this morn, checking on the new bairn born last sennight," Myrtle huffed, doing her best to keep up.

"I'll go find her."

"Aye, sir…"

Myrtle's voice trailed off behind him as he burst out of the keep, noticing his guards jogging to and fro. The general commotion of people going on their errands had paused. Servants laid down their baskets, parked their carts, and gathered toward the inner gates to gossip about who the newcomers might be. Dashing to the stables, he sought out his mount, worked the bit into the stallion's mouth, and secured the bridle, drawing him out of the stable bareback. There was no time to saddle the animal.

He stepped onto a cart and flung his leg over the animal's back, his great kilt billowing around his thighs, and clicked his tongue at the beast. The horse wheeled around and they trotted through the throng and out the inner gates. He took to loping down the path to the outer curtain wall. Nasim was on foot, returning to the castle as he passed beneath the portcullis, which was dotted in wild flowers and summer grasses.

My, she's bonny. Even in his haste, he couldn't help but appreciate her looks, her basket on her arm, surrounded by summer flowers and sunshine. Her long hair hung nearly to her knees now, curling whimsically, the ends lifting on the breeze, *and she still wears the wildflowers I put in her hair this morn.* They had walked down to the dock as the sun rose, and he had picked some Lady's Thimble growing out of the cliff side and woven the blossoms into a ring to place upon her crown. The lavender, contrasting with her black hair, was a fetching sight, as if she was a country maiden from the French *Provence*. She donned a beautiful mauve gown that tied over her shoulders with tufts of chemise bunching through, practical in its design considering her line of work. It laced shut up the front to give her generous breasts a pleasant squeeze while flaring in billows from her elbows.

Even now, he felt that damned pinch in his heart when he realized she belonged to him, and he never would have discovered her if she had not defied her father that fateful night so long ago. He would have departed Jerusalem's gates, returned home, and married Margaret. *Thank the lord I dodged that arrow.* For Margaret now languished in Norway, with a distant cousin. King William had granted him his annulment and ordered her exiled for her crimes. At first, Margaret had protested, but the threat of a dungeon cell prompted her to change her mind and accept.

A forbidden kiss on Nasim's hand, in a darkened alley, had given him the best thing he could have ever asked for: his family.

Connor, their young son, frolicked behind her, his dark hair bobbing up and down in the grasses. In Ewan's moment of admiration of her while he cantered into the field, he had failed to see his oldest offspring jumping through the shafts. And judging by the way Nasim adjusted the pack on her back, he knew their infant daughter was growing like a weed and becoming a heavy burden for her mother.

He had warned her not to exert herself so, that a nursemaid would gladly mind the bairn whilst she attended her daily rounds in the village, but she insisted her daughter would never be cloistered. She insisted young Francine would know the freedom Nasim had come to finally know. *Who would have thought*, she once said, *that being exiled would actually give me freedom?* He knew she still secretly mourned her loss of family after being banished with nothing but a pair of horses, a sack of coin, and a language barrier. He often saw her staring wistfully out their bedchamber window from time to time, contemplating, when she didn't think he was noticing. And yet, she was assertive in her desire that both their children know independence, and fostered their curiosity equally.

Nasim saw him coming, smiled broadly, and waved. The corner of his mouth lifted and he pulled back on the reins, just as he saw the procession Myrtle had announced coming over the crest of the hill behind her.

"Da!" Connor exclaimed with his typical exuberance, and waded to the horse's forelegs.

Ewan swung his leg over the horse's neck, pivoting on his rear, and dropped down to the earth.

"Dada!" came wee Francine's squeal.

Nasim giggled, glancing over her shoulder at the child whose chubby fingers were tangled helplessly into Nasim's tresses.

"Handsome as ever, my husband," Nasim said, "what with your kilt and belts so proud, and your fingers stained black."

He dipped his lips to hers, his grin darkening. "Aye, and I aim to please, woman," he murmured. He rubbed his hand upon her belly, initially brazen, but softening into a tender caress. Her stomach, still so small, hid a tiny bump just beginning to form. "'Tis easy for a man to be so enthusiastic when you're the man's wife."

"Three bairns... I'd say you're ever enthusiastic." Slapping his hand away, she adjusting her basket. "And careful that you don't soil my bodice with your inked fingers."

"I hear no complaints," he chuckled in her ear, causing her to blush, glancing down to see that in fact his fingers were perpetually stained with ink, so much so, he was surprised they weren't permanently discolored.

"If you do nay stop, you'll leave nothing to be anticipated for our wedding night," she teased back, brushing past him to continue walking toward the castle.

His grin didn't dissipate, but rather, softened. In a sennight, they were to be married in the church. Nasim had taken his religion. She had done so for him, and willingly went to the priest to set about the process. The planning had been long. The commission he had just sold this morning was his last before the big day. Nasim's gown, he had heard the maids gossiping, was a thing of marvel. His two older children might always be bastard born in the eyes of the law, but they would be redeemed in a sennight, when they would be legitimized in the annals of royal and church registers as bastards no more. They would never have to carry the stigma that Ewan had carried his whole life, born to a mother he would never know and a father he barely knew any better.

He stepped back, swept his son up, and twisted him onto his back, feeling the lad cinch his legs and arms around him. He swung the reins over the horse's head and led the animal on foot. Nasim looked over her shoulder, her hair and his daughter's dark hair blending together.

"Did you ride all the way out here just to seek me out?" she queried. "For I wish I was done for the day, but you know Hamish. His dagger injury from sennight last was deep, and he is to meet me in the surgery to have it washed and wrapped again."

He sobered. Aye, the party that had just come into view was growing closer. Nasim turned back toward the castle just as a contingent of his men clad in chain mail and helmets, led by Fergus, trotted fully armed through the gatehouse.

"What's happening?" she asked, her brow now furrowing with alarm.

Ewan glanced back at the procession of strangers growing closer. "I came to inform you that we have visitors."

"What for…" She glanced past him.

Her words trailed away. Her face dropped. Color drained from her face. Shock.

Ewan stepped up beside her as Fergus' men converged around them, forming a semi-circle across the path to prevent the strange visitors from progressing. The visitors rode closer. No longer indistinguishable.

There, atop a proud Arabian stallion and flanked by Abdullah and one of Nasim's other brothers, was Abu Abdullah Habib Abd-al Rachid, his robes travel-worn but magnificent, and his headwear banded around his head and flowing down his back. His silver beard was manicured, in spite of the months it had taken them to travel. At the end of the procession was a horse-drawn cart, loaded with supplies and an old woman covered in veiling, softened by age.

"Nasim… Nasim!" The name warbled out of the old woman's throat and she fought to stand in spite of the cart jostling.

She begged to be let down from the cart. Habib, still having not spoken, pulled back on his reins, and dismounted, his eyes riveted to Nasim, and went to help his wife alight from the cart, though she was already trying to climb over the side.

Ewan, too, was stunned to silence. Even though he suspected his visitor was Habib, he still never anticipated seeing the man again, let alone him and the rest of Nasim's immediate family. He glanced sidelong at his wife, pulling her close and wrapping his arm around her and his daughter tightly, feeling her nestled against the incision in his chest, now faded with age. The urge to protect her warred through his mind, as it always had, from the moment he'd clutched her hand in the infirmary so long ago when the menacing official, Faraj, had spoken unkindly of her.

He mentally checked his weapons, just in case. He wore no sword, but he had three daggers on his body. A dirk, a blade in his sleeve, and a *sgian dubh* in his deer-skin boots. Fergus, behind him, was armed to the hilt, and would toss him another weapon if he needed it, though he suspected nothing nefarious from Habib's sons.

He squeezed Nasim, looking down. She was as white as a sheet, as if she saw ghosts. In a way, she truly did.

***

Nasim couldn't breathe. She knew that was her mother struggling to climb out of the cart, but she couldn't move and couldn't speak, secured to Ewan's chest as she was. Tears welled in her eyes as she realized the truth of her vision. Her hand flew to her mouth, stifling a sob that shoved up her throat for escape. Her knees weakened. *This is your mother, and she's no longer ignoring you.* Ghaniyah had traveled across a continent, and was calling her name. Nasim squeezed her mouth tighter, lest that wretched sob should flow forth.

"Da, who is that?" Connor asked.

She felt Ewan adjust their son on his back, lurching with him as he gave the lad a boost, *our miracle*, as Ewan always spoke of him. So long ago, after Colin's treachery, they were certain she had lost the bairn. But Connor was a bright light, and spirited child, and not much ever kept him at heel. He had clung to life in her womb, and right on time, he was born into the world already weighing over a half stone when he took his first, screaming breath, healthy as can be.

"*Wheesht*, son." Ewan quelled him gently.

"Nasim," the old woman said again, her feet now on solid earth.

The woman took a step toward her, then another, and suddenly Nasim tore herself away from Ewan's grip and ran the remaining steps through the grasses to fling herself into her mother's arms. They wept. Long, desperate cries that spoke of grief and long-worn scars. So many questions swirled in her mind. She felt her mother's gnarled grip tightening like clamps upon her, as if her mother couldn't believe she truly held her daughter. Nasim sobbed, heard Francine give an uncertain whimper in her ear, heard her mother's sobs mingle with her own as all the sounds and emotions clawed at her, engulfed her.

"My daughter, my daughter, you're alive…"

"Mother!" Nasim finally managed, pushing the rusty word out of her mouth.

They remained in an embrace, when, knees shaking, she began to collapse. Her mother collapsed with her, and they sat in the grasses upon their knees, holding onto each other. Sakes, but she couldn't breathe. *Is this real?* Her mother, in her patting and grabbing, felt the child upon her back. Ghaniyah pulled away, palming each side of Nasim's dampened face, and peered over her shoulder to the little girl. Then she looked up at Ewan who had walked up behind Nasim, his legs at her back. Rustling behind her told her Ewan was putting Connor down.

"*Two* children?" Ghaniyah asked.

Nasim nodded, wiping futilely at the water upon her face, and placed her palm on her stomach. "And another, due in five more moons."

"Blessed, blessed be," Ghaniyah crooned, also palming her small belly.

Nasim was so confused. She was exiled. These people had forgotten her and vowed that she was dead to them. Happiness, sadness, and every strong emotion in between threatened to prevent her from standing.

"But why are you here, if I'm exiled?" she croaked, gulping to try and master her cries as she held her mother's arms.

Her mother had aged. Her eyes were much wearier, and yet in them, she saw light. A light she most certainly remembered being snuffed the day her father arrived to tell her of her fate. A presence arrived beside her, and Nasim looked up. Habib, so tall and proud, was blocking the sun and casting a shadow on her.

"Daughter."

Daughter. She shook her head, seeing her father's eyes travel over her appearance. Ewan helped her stand again and squeezed her hand like he had so long ago, to give her comfort and perhaps, confidence, then offered a hand to Ghaniyah. It was sweet, but she didn't need that confidence, not anymore. She was comfortable in her clothing, secure in her home, and no longer felt an urge to cover up, but she still knew her display of cleavage, not to mention her entire face and hair revealed, must be shocking.

"What is this word you call me?" she finally whispered.

She looked up into her father's aged face. Jingling, faint in her ears, considering the loudness of her thoughts, indicated that Ewan's men at arms were coming closer, emanating unseen tension. Her father, Abdullah, and all her brothers who had remained in their saddles, were in Ewan's world now, a world he would defend at the slightest provocation.

"I called you, *Daughter.*"

"Your father has begged the tribunals, even going to Saladin himself, for permission to rescind the punishment against you. What happened has never sat well with him…with any of us," her mother spoke, voice shaking. "But no one would listen."

"And so I gave up my position as Saladin's advisor."

Nasim dragged her fingertips over her eyes to push away the blurring tears. "I don't understand."

Abdullah was walking to them, and it was only then that she saw the ceremonial band around his *shemagh* and his prestigious comportment.

"Abdullah was ready," her father said. "And so, Saladin, unable to honor my requests to see your honor and name restored, accepted my retirement and saw Abdullah promoted." Habib now took her other hand, cupping her cheek, and looked into her eyes with his piercing ones. "He spoke few words but what words he spoke held great meaning. He bid I devise my trade route, and travel across Europe and all the way to *Scotland* if I must."

Saladin freed my father from his political obligations and bid he seek out his daughter.

"And Commander Faraj has finally passed on, *sadly,*" Abdullah drawled, though he hardly sounded distraught over the news. In fact, Nasim thought she might see a smile teasing the corner of his mouth. "So, he could no longer voice a complaint about our expedition."

Habib's voice sank low. "I worried about you every day. As did your mother. She never forgave me."

Touched, Nasim wiped her eyes. Ewan's grip tightened.

"There was no cause to worry." Nasim looked up into Ewan's eyes, those damning crystalline-blue depths that had been her ruin from the first moment she had seen them. He returned the fond gaze. "My *Majnun* has always protected me."

"I always will," Ewan said as he lifted her hand to place that kiss upon it that had damned them both so long ago.

E. Elizabeth Watson

ABOUT THE AUTHOR

E. Elizabeth Watson loves to write historical romance and historical fantasy. She is both a coffee and chocolate addict, and loves music, hiking with her yellow lab, baking, gardening, sewing, and all things Scotland. In fact, she's pretty sure she should have been born in Scotland, and visits every chance she gets. Elizabeth is mom to four sons as well as her canine daughter June and feline son Duncan. She lives on a mountainside in West Virginia with her husband and family, but her heart is always traveling. Sign up for her occasional newsletter at:

www.eelizabethwatson.com

Follow Elizabeth on social media!